THE
GUNNER
GIRLS:
EVIE'S STORY

A gripping and emotional wartime saga

SYLVIA BROADY

The Ack-Ack Gunner Girls Book 1

Joffe Books, London
www.joffebooks.com

First published in Great Britain in 2024

Cover art by Jarmila Takač

ISBN: 978-1-83526-278-8

This book is dedicated to the brave women who during World War Two served in the ATS and worked on the Anti-Aircraft guns defending the country against the Luftwaffe attacks. They were widely known as the Ack-Ack gunner girls.

CHAPTER ONE

April 1942
East Yorkshire

It was the best day ever when Evie Sinclair enlisted in the ATS to serve her country in a time of war.

'I've joined up,' Evie told her parents that evening.

'You can just un-join,' commanded her mother, Florence, looking up from her notebook and glaring at her daughter. 'Whatever are you thinking of, girl? You've enough to do here, helping me with running the household and raising money for the war effort. You're a selfish girl,' her mother ranted on.

Her father, Gerald, a distinguished major from the Great War, winked at his daughter and retreated behind his newspaper. He supported Evie, who was just eighteen, and expected her to have a desk job with her excellent education.

Evie let her mother's words float over her head. Nothing was going to stop her. 'I'll come home on leave,' she offered as a pacifier, though truthfully, she wouldn't if she could help it.

Within two days, feeling excited at her venture, Evie was on her way for basic training. She left Island House and rowed across the lake, which was the quickest way she could hitch a lift on an army truck bound for Hull. Otherwise, it would be a longer trip going down the narrow lane from Island House, and then a round hike to the main road. It was not strictly an island though, when the land flooded, it resembled one.

'Good luck!' called the army driver, as Evie jumped from the truck. She waved goodbye, her heart singing with excitement.

She rushed into Paragon Station, mingling with the throngs of people hurrying for their trains and on to their destinations, while loved ones stood forlorn on the platform, weeping a farewell. At last, Evie breathed a sigh of relief. She was on the train steaming up to Durham ATS Training Depot. A strange feeling gripped her, suddenly seeing compartments full of men in uniform with serious faces. It made her wonder, was she out of her depth and had she been too hasty in signing up? Over her shoulder, she looked back. She could always . . . But the train was already moving. She resigned herself to thinking that the country needed her and cast away her doubts. She looked around, hopeful to see a seat, but each one was taken. Then a young woman in the far corner piped up, 'Here, squeeze in next to me.'

'Thanks,' Evie said, as she lowered herself down into the narrow space.

'I'm Lily Grainger,' introduced the petite young woman. Evie admired her blonde curly hair, a complete contrast to her own wavy brown locks.

'I'm Evie, Evie Sinclair. I've just joined up and am on my way to Durham.'

'Fancy that! So am I.' They began chatting. 'I live with me mam and dad and four sisters.'

'Four sisters, you are lucky. I'm an only child.'

'Gosh, I wish I was an only one. I shared a bed with my sisters; top to toe we slept, and I never had an ounce of privacy. I was glad to get away.'

So the girls gelled together via the invisible bond of escaping from their home lives, though both for different reasons.

A man seated next to Evie left their compartment, and Evie was just about to spread out from her cramped position when a tall girl with a beautiful cream complexion and rich auburn hair suddenly rushed into the compartment and dropped into the space. 'Phew, that's lucky. I've been stood in the corridor since Hull.' She looked sideward and smiled at Evie. 'I'm Gloria Russell.'

It was not long before all three girls were chatting, and they discovered that Gloria was also bound for Durham. Evie and Lily told her about their backgrounds. 'Mine's not very exciting,' Lily said. 'What about you?' she addressed Gloria. 'Where's your family?'

Gloria stared down at the floor. She lifted her head and looked into the faces of the two girls. 'I haven't got a family. I grew up in an orphanage.'

The two girls stared open-mouthed. 'An orphanage,' they repeated in unison.

'But why did your mam and dad do that to you?' asked Lily, puzzled. 'Even when all seven of us were squashed into a small cottage, I couldn't imagine my parents ever pushing one of us out.'

Evie thought of her own parents. Her mother was always berating her but she would never put her into an orphanage. 'I'm sorry,' she said to Gloria, 'you don't have to tell us anything if you don't want to.'

'When I was in school, I used to make up imaginary families rather than tell people the truth,' Gloria murmured. 'Well, not anymore. I'll tell you two, but no one else. Promise not to tell?'

'We promise,' they both answered, solemn-faced.

'Joe Russell, an old man who slept rough, found me on the steps of the orphanage when I was a few days old. It was a winter's night, and he hugged me close until the next morning. He saved my life. So why would I want parents who left me on a freezing night and on cold steps to die?'

Both girls were silent, then Evie burst out, 'How terrible for you. We won't say anything to anyone.' And then she hugged Gloria, feeling the girl's trembling body, and Lily hugged her as well. The woman sitting next to Evie tutted and straightened the brim of her hat, which Evie had caught accidentally.

The train slowed down and people began moving. 'This is where we change trains,' Lily said, and they gathered up their belongings.

On the platform, the Women's Voluntary Service had a mobile van and was busy handing out welcoming cups of tea. They drank theirs hastily, then hurried to catch the connecting train up to Durham. They weren't so lucky to grab a seat this time and had to stand in a crowded corridor until they reached their destination.

Arriving at their camp, Evie, Lily and Gloria soon found out that they had to answer to their superiors and no excuses were possible. They quickly learned to obey without question.

'Bloody hell!' Lily muttered. They were shuffling forward in the queue for bedding: itchy blankets, no sheets and blue flannelette pyjamas. 'Have you seen the bloomers? They're like me granny wears.'

'No talking,' a voice boomed out.

Next came the medical inspections. Evie nudged Lily as they watched a girl having her hair cut really short because she had nits. Evie whispered, 'I'm glad I plaited my hair and pinned it up so it would fit under my cap.'

They had their eyes and ears tested and their arms grew sore from the many injections and blunt needles. Gloria inspected her arm, saying, 'It's worse than the school nurse poking me about.' Then they shuffled on to be kitted out with their khaki uniforms.

Bleary-eyed, they were herded towards the canteen. 'Food at last!' Lily exclaimed. Sitting at a table of eight girls, too tired to care, they mechanically shoved the stodgy stew into their mouths and drank the tepid tea.

Next came the allocation of their huts. Evie wondered if they would be together. Luck jumped on their side when they were billeted in the same hut, but once inside, they had to make their beds. Evie hit the mattress with a thump and crawled beneath the rough blankets. She fell asleep within seconds.

* * *

'What's that bloody row!' Gloria yelped.

'Rise and shine, you ugly lot,' bellowed a well-built woman in a corporal's uniform.

There was a lot of moaning. Evie tumbled from her bed and followed her friends from the hut to the ablution block. After a breakfast of tea and toast, they dashed back to the hut to make up their beds for inspection by the corporal. Her name was Hunter and it suited her, for she was forever hunting girls out to give them a dressing down.

There were twelve in the hut. Evie watched as a slip of a girl at the far end was reduced to tears when Hunter pulled her bed to pieces and made her remake it. From that, they soon learned not to shed a tear, for if they did, Hunter made their life hell.

Later, Evie stood to attention, while in a loud voice, Hunter reprimanded her for a button undone on her uniform jacket. Eyes front, she bit on her lip, warding off the tears that threatened to pool.

* * *

'I hate foot-slogging, gives me bloody blisters,' Lily moaned as they were getting ready for bed after a day of marching. Each day, they perfected their drill skills, marching in line with the company.

Evie examined her feet. 'I've got blisters too.' She rummaged in her drawer and produced a tin of Vaseline. 'Here, rub some on.'

'Will they vanish overnight?' Lily asked in a plaintive voice.

Evie laughed. 'Doubt it.'

5

Gloria glanced at her friends. 'Life in the orphanage was regimented like this. I may be used to it, but that doesn't mean I like it.'

They polished their heavy lace-up shoes, ready for the next day. By day three, they had learned to rub the rough inside edges of their shoes with their precious soap to soften the leather. Soon, the coarse uniform and the heavy shoes became like second skin.

'This is such a blessed relief,' Evie said with a contented sigh as she snuggled into her blue flannelette pyjamas and crawled into bed to rest her aching body.

They were studying the choices they could make within the ATS and where they would be posted. 'What do you think of the Anti-Aircraft Defence?' Evie asked, sounding out her friends.

'I'm not firing a gun,' Lily remarked indignantly.

'No, soldiers fire the guns. We would prepare them before the guns are in action.'

After debating and deciding to stay together, the three girls agreed on the Anti-Aircraft Defence.

'When do we start?' Gloria asked the officer in charge.

'Depends if you pass the test,' he replied smugly.

In the canteen while on a break for their midday meal, Lily plonked herself on the chair between Evie and Gloria, saying, 'I thought that was it. Now we have more tests to take. Unbelievable!' Both Evie and Gloria glanced at her but remained silent. 'Aw, God. This rigmarole is never ending. We won't be fit for anything by the time we've finished.'

Evie soon realised that she would have to be alert at all times. They all sat with their hands held out, checking for steadiness, plus precision testing their eyes. There was no time to look at what the other girls were doing. Later, collapsing into bed, her mind in a whirl, she tried to absorb everything they had learned and practised so far. What if she didn't pass her test? Despite being exhausted and wanting to sleep, Evie tossed and turned all night, sleeping fitfully.

She woke up to Lily shaking her. 'Come on, sleepy head. Time to rise and await the judgement of your deeds.'

Evie washed in icy cold water to clear the fuzz in her head. She didn't know about 'deeds'; it felt more like fate. She honestly didn't want to know.

All present and correct, the girls waited to find out their results. 'I've passed,' cried a jubilant Evie, spinning round to Lily, but stopped upon seeing her friend's sombre face. 'Oh, Lily,' she cried. 'I am sorry.'

Then Lily's face changed in an instant, wreathed in smiles, and laughing, she said, 'Fooled you. Of course, I've passed.'

'And so have I,' cried a triumphant Gloria. They did a little jig together.

'Grainger, Sinclair, Russell,' shouted the corporal. 'Control yourselves.'

Meekly, they obeyed, not wanting to jeopardise their future.

Within the week, they were on their way down to Wiltshire to join (M)HAA Battery RA to train as gunners. This training proved to be harder and more demanding. Accuracy was paramount so there was no let-up. Work, eat and bed.

No one moaned about the strict routine. 'For King and Country,' the sergeant drilled into everyone.

Evie found the pace exacting, but her determination to succeed drove her on. 'No flagging,' she counselled Lily and Gloria.

They listened as the sergeant in charge reeled off what being an Ack-Ack gunner girl entailed. 'Now then, pay attention. There are three major procedures. First, a spotter to identify enemy aircraft. Second, the height and range finder. Third, the predictor. Right!' he bellowed, just in case someone wasn't listening. Then he explained what each position entailed.

As she wrote down the instructions, Evie wondered which post she would be suitable for. What became obvious as she listened was that, whichever post she took, a trained gunner girl must only take seconds to perform their procedure.

Later, on a quick tea break, Evie mentioned to Lily and Gloria, 'Do you think they will train us to work all three posts?'

'It makes sense to do that,' offered Gloria. 'But then men think differently from us.'

One night after lights out, Evie whispered to Lily and Gloria, 'I thought our basic training was hard, but this is so intense.' Both responded with gentle snores.

At the end of their gruelling training, they had a week's leave before being posted to Yarmouth. They were in their hut early morning and packing, all eager for a break.

'I didn't think I would be so glad to see my sisters and Mam and Dad,' Lily said. 'What about you, Evie?'

'Like you, I'm going home to Mother and Father. I've missed them.'

Both turned to look at Gloria. 'Me,' she uttered, surprised anyone should care about her. 'I've got a few places I can lay my head. I want to enjoy myself.'

CHAPTER TWO

June 1942

Evie looked at Island House from across the lake. Her home. She hadn't expected to feel this sense of belonging. When she was younger she couldn't wait to leave.

The old rowing boat was still where she'd moored it. She rowed to the middle of the lake and then lay down. The sun warm on her face, she gazed upwards to watch the calming, drifting clouds in the sparkling blue sky. Her eyelids felt heavy and she closed her eyes, letting the boat drift. Its gentle rhythm lulled her into a hazy trance of childhood dreams.

From a distance her name blew on a breeze, lyrical at first, then sharper.

'Evie, what on earth are you doing?'

She sat up with a jerk. Disoriented, her eyes focused on the house. From an upstairs window, her mother leaned out. Gathering her wits about her, Evie rowed towards the house.

'Good,' was Florence's welcome when Evie told her of her week's leave. 'You can help at the village hall dance on Friday night.'

'Bloody hell,' Evie muttered under her breath. Just when she wanted to sleep the clock round.

'What was that?' Florence looked up sharply.

'Of course, I'll help,' Evie sighed, if only to keep the peace. 'I'm going to have a long soak in the bath.'

'Only five inches of water.' Florence wrinkled her nose. 'Yes, you do smell unsavoury.'

Picking up her case, Evie escaped up to her bedroom. Its sanctuary was her haven. In the bath, she soaped her body and felt the pure bliss of not having to rush. She closed her eyes and wallowed in the blessed peace of nothing to do. Far below, she heard her father's voice and stepped from the bath.

Dressing quickly in a skirt and blouse, her hair still damp, she hurried downstairs.

'Dad,' she cried, and with the overwhelming urge to hug him, she threw herself into his arms, feeling the comfort of his warm response. They linked arms and went into the sitting room where Florence presided over afternoon tea.

That night, cocooned in her own bed, she listened to the familiar sounds of the countryside. The barn owl, the rustling of foxes and the clucking of the hens, all safely bedded down for the night. Evie soon drifted off into a dreamy sleep.

When she awoke, she thought, for a few seconds, she was back in camp. Then she relaxed back on to the pillow, glancing at the clock on the bedside table. Eleven-thirty in the morning. She'd slept for a solid fourteen hours. 'Unbelievable,' she gasped, throwing back the counterpane and jumping from the bed. Quickly she washed and dressed and ran downstairs.

The house was empty. Grabbing a quick cup of tea and piece of toast, she headed outside. She found her mother cleaning out the hen-house, which was a great surprise. And to Evie's amazement, she was singing a child's lullaby and looked so content. Evie felt a rush of happiness that her mother loved her, something she'd never truly felt before.

On seeing Evie, Florence's demeanour changed, like the snuffing of a candle. 'So, you are up,' she greeted her daughter.

Evie stared at her mother, feeling confusion mixed with — what? It was as if she had intruded on her mother's private life, which she, Evie, had no part in. She shivered, despite the heat of the day. She'd thought for a fleeting moment that Florence was happy with her, something which had always eluded Evie. So why did she expect it to change now?

Mentally shaking herself, Evie asked her mother, 'Anything you need me to do?'

'The summer dance is on Saturday night, so you can help with the baking,' Florence replied, walking back to the house.

In the kitchen, mother and daughter worked in silence, and Evie was grateful for the wireless tuned into the morale-boosting programme, *Workers' Playtime*. A comedian entertained the factory audience. Evie looked at her mother, who seemed lost in herself.

Evie wondered, did her mother ever think of her? She listened to Anne Shelton and longed to sing along with her, but instead she sang the words to 'I'll be Seeing You' in her head. It made her feel sad because she had no young man to care about.

The days to the dance dragged and Evie busied herself weeding in the kitchen garden, which was rather neglected.

* * *

Saturday night came at last! Evie slipped on her favourite blue dress. It seemed weird to dress up after wearing her khaki uniform for so long. She twirled in front of the full-length mirror in her bedroom. The dress, with its frills and lace, seemed extravagant with the austerity of war. But who knew when she would have another chance to wear it? She wore her long, wavy hair loose, knowing that her mother wouldn't approve.

The church had agreed to host the dance in its hall, it being one of the largest in the small seaside town of Eskthorpe. Quite a few militaries were based in the area, including RAF air bases not far inland. The vicar, well past retirement age but still very active, had announced: 'Young men fighting for their country need to keep their spirits up. We must do our bit for the war effort.'

Evie helped her mother to set up the trestle tables with refreshments and soft drinks. One of the local publicans had organised barrels of beer for the men.

There were plenty of helpers and, feeling bored, Evie went to watch the dancers, tapping her feet to the music.

Suddenly, a voice said, 'May I have this dance, miss?' She turned to see a young man dressed smartly in an RAF uniform with his wings proudly displayed.

She smiled at him and held out her arms. He swung her on to the dance floor as if she was a lightweight, not a sturdy seven and a half stone.

'Matt,' he introduced himself, grinning at her.

'I'm Evie.'

'Not seen you here before.'

'I live locally and I'm home on leave.'

'Land army?'

'No,' she replied indignantly. 'I'm on the guns.'

'Guns! What guns?'

So, she told him all about her training.

'Bloody hell! Is it safe letting women on guns? You might shoot me down by mistake.'

Playfully, she dug him in the ribs. 'I will be fully qualified soon and if you want me to send you in a spin, I will oblige.' His face paled. Mortified by her insensitivity, she murmured, 'Sorry, only joking.'

'Don't. I've only flown two sorties, and believe me, I was shit scared.'

The music ended. 'Come on,' she said, leading him by the arm. 'I'll buy you a drink.'

They sat in a secluded corner and she watched him drink his beer while she sipped on shandy. Evie told Matt about the precision of the guns she would use. 'I'm trained to stop the Luftwaffe, so you have nothing to fear.'

By now, with the help of the drink, Matt's colour had returned to his face. 'That's a relief to know,' he told her, his voice stronger.

Out of the corner of her eye, Evie saw her mother looking for her. The band played a waltz. 'Come on, let's dance and I might just give you a kiss.' The pure joy on his face rewarded her.

She would picture Matt's face in that moment when manning the guns.

Evie felt daring like never before. As they danced the slow waltz, their bodies felt magnetic in the gentle rhythm of the music. She lifted her head to gaze up into his warm brown eyes and he gazed back at her, waiting for her to come good on her promise. His lips were tantalisingly close.

For a few moments, she studied him, watching as his tongue licked his bottom lip. Then slowly she leaned closer to him, feeling the serge material of his jacket against her chin as an electric spark of excitement rushed through her veins and their lips touched. Then it ignited, an unknown passion winding them together as their kiss deepened. As the music ended, they came up for air.

A voice boomed, 'Refreshments are now served.'

Evie knew she was supposed to help her mother serve the buffet, but in a daze, she let Matt steer her to a table. Other young couples joined them, drinking and laughing, asking questions.

'Not seen you before,' a young woman in a WAAF uniform said in a superior manner, her eyes taking in Evie's mode of dress.

Evie wondered if she should have worn her uniform and glanced down at her frock, thinking it was too frivolous. Before she could answer, she heard Matt saying, 'This is Evie. She's in the ATS and mans the Ack-Ack guns, which help to keep the Luftwaffe away from us chaps.' There were many looks of admiration from the group.

'Where are you stationed?' asked another young WAAF.

'I just finished training and I'm on a week's leave before going down to Yarmouth.'

After that, the conversation became light-hearted. Even the first WAAF was now friendly.

Evie and Matt danced together again before they were intercepted, and she danced with his comrades. But she and Matt had the last dance together. Their arms entwined and their lips met so tenderly. Evie wanted the moment to go on forever.

Then someone shouted that the transport for the RAF was waiting. Matt dropped a hasty kiss on her cheek, and then he was gone, though not before she'd seen the adoration in his eyes. She put a hand on her beating heart.

'There you are. I've been looking everywhere for you.'

Evie sighed inwardly, and went to help her mother with the tidying up, but first she slipped into her handbag the scrap of paper Matt had pushed into her hand.

Later, alone in her room, Evie sat on the edge of the bed and took the piece of paper from her handbag. She smoothed it out and read Matt's hasty scribble. 'Evie, can you meet me near the bandstand tomorrow afternoon about two? Matt x'

She sat ramrod still, rereading those words, memorising each one. He wants to see me again. She let the words bubble in her mind, igniting a spark deep in her belly. Dreamily, she prepared for bed, seeing his warm brown eyes, his infectious smile, and remembering the way he held her close, but most of all, the kiss. Her first proper kiss. Not just sloppy lips on hers.

Snuggling down in her bed, she relived every moment she'd spent with Matt. The touch of his hand in hers as he led her on to the dance floor. She shut her eyes tight, recalling the beautiful tingling sensation she had experienced at his touch. She knew, without doubt, that Matt felt special to her. Was she special to him?

After breakfast, Evie went out to the vegetable garden wearing dungarees. She needed to be on her own, away from her mother, who might ask awkward questions. Armed with a hoe, she cleared away the weeds. The physical work did her good, for it stopped her from being in a trance that her mother would certainly have picked up on.

Florence had a committee meeting that afternoon, so she didn't have to know that Evie was going out. Changing into a skirt, blouse, cardigan and sandals, and her hair brushed loose, Evie rowed across the lake to meet Matt.

Approaching the old bandstand, she could see him leaning against one of the stanchions, looking out towards the North Sea. His face in half profile seemed serious. Her heart gave a lurch. Was he regretting their meeting? Her steps faltered and her foot caught on a pebble, which skittered along the ground. At the sound, Matt turned. When he saw her, his eyes lit up and a radiant smile broke out on his face. Evie wasn't sure how it happened, but suddenly they were in each other's arms, his lips warm on hers. There came the sound of a dog barking and a man calling its name.

Breaking away, they held hands and strolled blissfully along the path. It was a carefree moment in time when they forgot about the ravages of war that loomed ahead.

CHAPTER THREE

September 1942

Evie met up with Lily and Gloria on the train and, after a tedious journey, they arrived at the camp near Lowestoft, Norfolk. The night was dark and dreary. 'I just want to sleep,' Evie whispered to her friends, as they listened to the corporal in charge giving out the daily instruction.

'Me, I want a cup of cocoa and the biggest piece of chocolate cake,' Lily said wistfully, and Gloria just shrugged her shoulders.

Evie stifled a giggle and tried to pay attention to the routine introduction, though by now she knew it off by heart. She looked forward to tomorrow's afternoon briefings because new technology was always being discovered and revealed. She enjoyed a challenge. Lily nudged her and she realised that the corporal had dismissed them.

They had a few hours off after they'd settled in. When Evie saw the town for the first time, there was no bomb damage to properties. She stood a moment, eyes closed, trying to sense the sea, but the smell was a pungent one. No taste of the tangy sea touched her lips.

'Come on, slowcoach,' Lily shouted. They made their way to a café on the corner of a street. Evie hurried after them.

Inside, they sat at a square table with a yellow checked tablecloth. Its bright colour lifted Evie's spirits a notch.

'You're in luck,' said the café owner. A woman wearing a flowered overall came from behind the counter to their table. 'I've just made a batch of scones, and my cousin sent me a jar of apple and blackberry jam. You'll be up at the camp?' she said, eyeing their uniform.

'That sounds a lovely treat,' Evie offered, smiling at the woman.

More customers came in, and the three girls were silent as they devoured the delicious scones and jam and drank the weak tea. Soon, the café became full.

Evie rubbed a patch of the misty window with her hand and peeped out, watching people passing by. 'They don't look at all miserable. In fact, they look quite cheerful as they greet one another,' she mused, turning back and accepting a cigarette from Gloria.

'Ah, well, Churchill says we must never give in to the enemy and be positive,' said the café owner, who came to clear their table. Her tone grew wistful as she told them, 'They've evacuated all the schoolchildren down to Devon for safety. My Jimmy's gone there and I miss him like hell.' She sniffled, sweeping imaginary crumbs off the table.

Afterwards, they took a stroll towards the sea. 'Sad, isn't it,' commented Evie. 'On a sunny day, children should be playing on the beach and paddling at the water's edge. Instead . . .' She paused, thinking what to say.

'It is a war zone,' Gloria commented.

'Our freedom is over. It's back to defending the country,' Evie said, linking her arm through both Lily's and Gloria's.

A week later, Evie received a letter from Matt and couldn't believe their luck. His base was the RAF Langham airfield in Norfolk. She skimmed the rest of the letter. 'Hopefully, at some stage, our time off will coincide. I am longing to see your smiling face and to kiss your sweet lips again. I think of you every day.'

At this point there was a small blob of ink on the page. Evie wondered what he had been thinking of at that precise moment.

Later, while having a meal before going on duty, Evie couldn't keep her beaming smile hidden.

'Come on, tell!' her friends chorused. 'Have you got a promotion?'

So Evie told them about Matt being stationed in Norfolk. 'That's swell,' said Lily, mimicking an American accent from a film they'd recently seen.

On site, they worked to a timetable, as every site did. Each shift started after the main changeover, 2 p.m. until 2 a.m., then 2 a.m. to 2 p.m., a 24-hour system. On this evening shift, Evie sat at a small table playing cards in a hut designated for recreation, known to the gunner girls as the waiting game room. They were on the alert and could be ready in seconds, and she marvelled at how quickly she had learned because, during training, it had seemed to take forever. And then, in a click, it happened.

She was just about to play a trump card when the siren sounded shrill and loud in her ears. Now attuned to the deafening summons, she jumped from her seat and, within seconds, was at her command post as a predictor operator wearing battle dress and, in case of falling shrapnel, a tin hat.

The Luftwaffe targets could be the airfields of Norfolk. For a fleeting second, she thought of Matt. Then her mind engaged the planes sighted and she focused on getting her target in line with her predictor. She could see the cross at the end of the telescope, and when all the dials lined up correctly, height, range and bearing, she shouted this information to the men operating the guns. They fired, hopefully hitting the target. Tonight, the droning noise of enemy planes coming over filled the night sky, like birds of prey. Other units nearby would also be on the attack, their guns trained on the target, preventing the enemy from dropping their lethal bombs.

'I'm shattered,' Lily remarked later, as they snatched a cup of tea and a cheese sandwich in the canteen, thankful they had dealt with the Luftwaffe attack.

'It's bed for me,' said Evie, stifling a yawn.

'Come on, you as well,' Gloria yanked Lily to her feet, who had closed her eyes. 'Got to be back on duty at two p.m. sharp for update briefing.'

No sooner were they comfy in their beds than the alarm sounded to rise. 'How can time pass so quickly?' muttered Lily.

A dinner of bangers and mash, with spotted dick and custard for afters, was satisfying. Then it was on to the briefing. 'It's our training,' Evie said, responding to one of Lily's mutterings about how she felt.

The briefing was an update on the detection of new enemy aircraft.

Later, Evie, Gloria and Lily, due a few hours respite, were in the NAAFI, taking advantage of a sing-song around the upright piano. Maureen, a girl from Northumberland, was belting out tunes. Evie watched, fascinated, as Maureen's long fingers seemed to fly across the ivory keys. And the chorus of voices singing, some off-key. 'Bless 'em all, the long and the short and the tall . . .' The evening continued, the atmosphere light and relaxing. Evie felt it lift her spirits as she thought about Matt, and she hoped for a letter from him soon, telling her he'd secured a 12-hour pass. She just wanted to feel his arms around her, holding her close.

Lily nudged her. 'Join in,' she mouthed.

Her daydream broken, Evie quickly took in the line of men and women. Maureen belted out a bawdy tune she'd concocted, and everyone tried the high kicks. A madcap ten minutes followed and, as Evie looked along the line, the one with the highest kicks was Harry, a gunner. Finally, they all collapsed laughing, releasing the good feeling of endorphins.

Evie suddenly fell into the arms of Jack, usually a quiet man. 'Fancy a kiss, darling,' he said. Evie smelled and tasted the beer on his breath and lips but she took it in good humour.

She saw Lily in a clinch with a man, but couldn't see who it was because he had his back to her. And Gloria, seated at the piano, was tinkering with the keys. Silently, Evie left and went to their hut. She'd enjoyed the night, but didn't want to get involved with anyone. They were lucky here, because they had beds, not bunks, which were more comfortable. Though she mused, as she sat on the bed taking off her shoes, that when tired she could sleep anywhere.

A week later, an excited Evie waved her letter at Lily and Gloria. 'Matt's got a day pass.'

'And where is this lover's meeting?' they chorused.

'Yarmouth,' Evie replied, happily.

'No hanky-panky!' They grinned at her.

Lily, with a wicked look on her face, said, 'I would want something more exotic.'

Evie smiled to herself. Being with Matt was exotic for her. She blushed at the thought and, making a quick exit, went to arrange her time off to coincide with Matt's.

CHAPTER FOUR

Autumn 1942

Her first sight of Yarmouth was bleak, but nothing could dull Evie's pleasure at seeing Matt. They met on the seafront, near to where her lift from camp dropped her. She saw him first, leaning against the gable end of a brick wall and was about to call his name when she noticed the stern look on his face. Her heart sank. Had she made a mistake? Did he regret meeting up with her? Swiftly she spun round, but the truck she'd got a lift on was out of sight. A group of young soldiers and young women in uniform were laughing, and Evie envied them. Slowly, she turned back. Matt saw her and his face broke into a smile. The loveliest smile she had ever seen. And needing no other prompt, she ran towards him and into his open arms. He swung her round, then gently he lowered her down and kissed her full on the lips. The sweetest, most tantalising kiss, leaving her lips on fire and wanting more. Someone whistled and they both laughed.

Hand in hand, they strolled along the promenade, avoiding the defence structures in place against enemy invasions. She wanted to ask Matt why he'd looked so stern. But now his mood was so happy that she didn't want anything to destroy it. So they talked about the latest songs of Vera Lynn, who everyone called the 'forces' sweetheart'. The government had realised that music and light entertainment helped to boost everyone's morale.

They rounded a corner and found a deserted area. Matt suddenly wrapped his arms around Evie and hugged her close. Lips hungry with desire, they kissed. It wasn't until they felt the rain lashing against their bodies that they came up for air. And, holding hands, they dashed along the promenade to find shelter in a café.

The bell tingled as Matt pushed open the door and ushered Evie inside. They stood for a moment surveying the bodies crammed on to seats, everyone having had the same idea to get out of the rain.

Someone called from the far corner of the cafe, 'You can sit here.'

They edged through the crowded tables to where a sailor and a young woman were leaving. 'Got a date with her old man,' the sailor said, a mischievous grin on his face. Evie blushed.

Sitting opposite each other, Matt reached for her hands. His touch felt gentle, and yet it sent a tingle of excitement through her whole body. She leaned forward and gazed into his dark, twinkling eyes, and it was as if they were both suspended in time. The noisy hub of the café receded, and it was just the two of them, alone. He caressed her hands and she watched his fingers tracing up and down her own, sending waves of pure pleasure, making her heart beat faster. She wanted to keep this experience close to her and never let it go. And she saw he felt the same.

'Are you ready to order?' A bored voice broke the spell.

When they had given their order of tea and a bun, they both giggled.

Later, after leaving the café, the rain had stopped. Matt slipped his arm around Evie's waist and she snuggled closer to him. Both happy in their pleasure in each other, they strolled along the promenade. She longed to be kissed again by Matt, but everywhere seemed crowded. Most people were in uniform, joyful to be spending time together or in a group out for some light relief. Then she spied a cinema. 'Look, shall we go inside?'

'What's showing?'

'Let's look at the poster. *Holiday Inn*. I like Bing Crosby and Fred Astaire.'

Matt looked at the poster too. 'I like Marjorie Reynolds.'

Inside the cinema, it felt warm and cosy, and they were in luck. On the back row, known as lovers' row, were two empty seats. They shuffled along, murmuring apologies for their disturbance, until they reached the seats. Feeling the heat — or was it the anticipation of what was, hopefully, to follow? — Evie unbuttoned her jacket with trembling fingers. She glanced at the screen. The film had already started. She stole a glance at Matt and saw he was watching her. Her heart gave a somersault, and she put her hand there to steady it. Matt leaned into her and covered her hand with his, and her heart gave another somersault. His fingers caressed hers, and she felt the heat of her body intensify. She turned to look into his eyes, seeing the longing there that mirrored hers. His hand slipped under her jacket and drew her to him, their lips touching. Softly at first, then with a yearning desire, their kiss deepened.

Unbuttoning his jacket, her fingers explored his body, loving the touch of his hard, muscular chest and the heat of him. Then his fingers explored her body, caressing her breasts. She wanted more, as she knew he did. Suddenly, the lights came on for the interval.

Drawing apart, they both sat up, adjusting their clothes. Evie ran trembling fingers through her hair to smooth out the ruffles. Matt lit two cigarettes and passed one to Evie, their fingers touching, their eyes meeting.

Then he leaned closer and whispered, 'I think you are lovely, Evie Sinclair.'

She gazed at him, her flushed face blushing brighter, if that was possible. 'You are not so bad yourself.' She wanted to say more, but he might think her too forward. She lowered her eyes, so he couldn't see the desire glistening. He had awakened a yearning within her she never knew she had. Now she wanted to experience more. But here in the cinema wasn't the place. For the rest of the showing of a light-hearted comedy, they held hands and laughed.

After a short walk along the promenade, it was time to go back to camp. As Evie sat in the transport lorry, she still felt the lingering last kiss tingling on her lips. As she went over in her mind everything that had happened between her and Matt, she realised she was in love with him. A warm, delicious feeling enveloped her, and she knew without a doubt that Matt was special to her.

* * *

A few days later, Evie sat in the canteen, grabbing an early breakfast after being on night duty. She daydreamed, reliving every second spent with Matt. If she closed her eyes, she could still feel his powerful arms holding her close, his tender lips hot and passionate on hers, and—

Somebody banged a tray down on the table, shaking her from her reverie. She opened her eyes to see Lily smiling at her.

'You've got it bad. Now tell me all,' Lily commanded, sitting at the table.

Evie told her of the walk along the promenade and the café, when Lily cut in. 'Not the boring bits. The juicy bits.'

Evie blushed as Gloria sat down at the table. 'I can't tell you that.' Feeling embarrassed, she pushed back her chair, lifted her tray and made a swift departure.

As she hurried away she heard Gloria ask Lily, 'What's up with Evie?'

'She's in love.'

For a few days her friends ragged Evie, pretending to swoon every time they saw her. 'Stop it, you two. We've a war to fight,' Evie admonished them. No sooner were the words out of her mouth than the alarm sounded. She grabbed her tin helmet and was at her post in seconds.

Beams from the nearby searchlights were already criss-crossing the sky. Men and women manned the heavy anti-aircraft battery guns, though the women never fired the guns. Evie, Lily and Gloria were in a team of six women who operated the predictor. But the first key role was the team of girls who sighted the enemy planes. When the targets were spotted, they passed on the information to the second team. This team, on the height and range finder, calculated the distance a shell would take to find its target. When ready, the girl on the dial called out the information to the third team working on the predictor, and they calculated the length of fuse required and shouted this information to the men on the guns, who fired. This procedure took a matter of seconds, so precise was their ongoing training, which incorporated new equipment as technology advanced.

Lectures on aircraft recognition were also an important part of their ongoing training, especially the introduction of new aircraft and the ability to recognise their own aircraft.

Tonight was a heavy raid and many enemy aircraft crowded the sky, coming from across the North Sea. Evie lost count of how many times they performed each task, and she didn't have time to consider that they were also a target for the Luftwaffe. A piece of falling debris hit her tin hat, and she felt thankful she was wearing it, though at first she had hated it.

Evie was with A-Team crew on the 2 p.m. to 2 a.m. shift. The B-Team prepared to take over. Although it was relatively quiet now, the enemy could regroup and send in a fresh batch of aircraft.

After the handover, they made their way to the canteen. 'I'm ready for a hot drink,' Evie murmured. The adrenaline she'd been working on had suddenly deserted her.

After a quick debriefing (it had seemingly been a successful night, though that never registered when they were working) and a welcome meal of corned beef hash, they were back in their hut.

In her bed, Evie's thoughts always turned to Matt. A bomber pilot, so young for such an incredible task, it seemed to her. She felt so proud of him for serving his country in such a dangerous occupation. She wondered when they would next be able to meet. Later, she would pen a letter to him. With those thoughts, she drifted into slumber.

* * *

'Guess what?' Lily came bouncing into the hut a few days later, where Evie and Gloria were on cleaning duties. Gloria swiped at her with a brush, which Lily dodged. 'There's a dance in the NAAFI to boost our morale. Yep!' she called, doing a jig. 'Now, which dress shall I wear?'

'We can wear a dress?' exclaimed a girl. 'How super. I must ask Mummy to send me one.' Penelope — 'Posh Penny' behind her back — put down her duster.

The three girls stared at each other. Lily and Gloria giggled, so Evie said to Penelope, 'She is joking. It's uniform, no dresses.'

Penelope laughed, seeing the funny side.

They looked surprised. 'She's turning out to be a good sport,' Evie whispered.

Evie wrote to Matt immediately to tell him of the NAAFI dance, hoping he could come. Then later, passing the noticeboard outside of the NAAFI, she spied written details of the dance. They'd sent invitations to other gun sites in the area, and also to different serving forces, including RAF camps. As she read the details, she noticed people behind her and soon the camp was abuzz with excitement. Apparently, so the rumour went, they all needed a morale boost to give them more fighting power against the enemy.

'I'll drink to that,' came the chirpy voice of a gunner.

'What, you're not contented with us beautiful girls?' one of the Ack-Ack girls exclaimed.

'Could do with a bit more spice,' he ventured, dodging a playful punch.

'Haven't you anything better to do?' bellowed the drill sergeant.

Everyone stood to attention and then quickly dispersed.

By return of post the next day, Evie received her reply from Matt. She read it as Lily and Gloria looked on in the hut.

An impatient note in her voice, Lily asked, 'Is he coming?' Then she saw Evie's sombre face. 'Sorry.'

Unable to hold back any longer, Evie broke out into a beautiful, rapturous smile. 'Yes, Matt is coming.'

* * *

The next time Evie saw Matt was at the NAAFI dance. A dance to keep your spirits up, was the mantra. And to a certain degree it did, releasing endorphins throughout the body. Evie stood on the edge of the dance floor, watching the main door for Matt, when a gunner, Clive, came and asked her for a dance. She couldn't refuse him. He was a swinging dancer, quite good fun, but she wanted to be in Matt's arms. When the dance ended, she excused herself and went to the ladies' cloakroom. On leaving, she stood away from the dance floor. She saw other RAF crew members, but not Matt.

'What are you doing hiding?' Lily wanted to know.

'I'm waiting for Matt.'

'He's dancing.'

Moving towards the dancers, Evie saw Matt dancing and chatting with Maureen. Her heart gave a lurch of pure jealousy. She wanted to rush and pull them apart. Instead, she controlled this terrible urge and waited for the dance to end. Then, smiling her brightest smile, she went up to them, saying, 'Thank you, Maureen, for taking care of Matt for me. Darling,' she purred, kissing Matt full on the lips.

'Sorry,' he said, as they waltzed away. 'She asked me to dance. Apparently, ladies desire the foxtrot.'

'We're together now,' she murmured, feeling her whole body tremble with relief. She didn't want to share Matt with anyone.

As they danced, Evie felt as though they were the only two in the room. At the interval, refreshments were served at the buffet table. Collecting plates of sandwiches and savouries, they joined Lily and Gloria and a couple of pilots at a table, soon to be joined by quite a crowd. All jolly, but Evie noticed the dark signs of fatigue in the RAF men's eyes. She could see the strain of hitting the target and watching out for enemy aircraft, always having your wits about you. What she did, as a predictor operator, required precision and alertness, but she couldn't imagine doing what they did. For the first time, she realised how easily their lives could be destroyed. She shuddered and reached for Matt's hand and held it secure in hers.

The evening continued. They danced the Gay Gordons, then the barn dance where everyone changed partners. There was so much hilarity, all good humour, and much clowning from the men showing off their sporting antics and singing ability. Evie laughed until her sides ached.

As they danced, Evie and Matt became locked in each other's arms as one. 'Let's go outside,' Matt whispered in her ear and they glided towards the exit door.

The night air felt cool, and Evie shivered. Matt wrapped his arms around her until she felt the heat from his body flow into hers. Their lips met, gentle at first, touching, savouring the sweetness. And then an urgency filled them as their passion rose to a crescendo, their lips desiring more. 'I wish we were back in the cinema,' she whispered.

'One day, my darling Evie, we will have our own place to be together forever.' Matt sealed the promise with a kiss.

The music for the last waltz drifted on the night air, and they went back inside. Matt held her close in his arms and she buried her face in his chest, feeling the beating of his heart. Then she lifted her face to meet his eyes, gazing down on her, their lips meeting.

Evie watched as Matt's transport prepared to leave. She blew him a kiss, calling, 'Until we meet again.'

CHAPTER FIVE

December 1942

Evie looked up at the night sky, seeing bombers flying low as they came into land. She and Matt hadn't seen each other since the dance in the NAAFI, though they wrote a few words to each other almost daily. She smiled, blushing at some of the things she'd written.

Coming off her shift, Evie went straight to their hut, knowing it would be quiet. She sat on her bed to pen a letter to her parents. 'Damn,' she said, screwing up a precious piece of paper. She rubbed her forehead in concentration. She just couldn't find the right words to tell her parents that she was bringing Matt. She thought about saying she was just bringing a friend, but Matt was the love of her life and more than a friend.

'I am bringing a very special person with me who I want you both to meet. He is an RAF pilot, Matthew Goodwin, and he is looking forward to meeting you both.'

Of course, her mother wrote back, wanting details of this man, his life history . . .

Evie penned a brief reply: 'Tell all when I see you. Must dash, duty calls.' Which was true.

For the next couple of weeks, Evie didn't have time to think about her and Matt spending Christmas with her parents. There was a lot happening at the base: daily domestic duties, marching, attending briefings, where they kept up with ever-changing technology and, most importantly, maintained the heavy gun equipment. This had to be kept in immaculate condition, leaving no chance for errors. Evie took pride in this necessary labour of love because lives depended upon it. They were there to help defend the country. She stood back from the equipment and eyed it critically to make sure everything was perfect.

That evening, Evie, Gloria and Lily were at their posts ready for the forecasted raid. The clear night sky gave them a good view of the enemy. In turn, the enemy had a clear view of their objectives. Evie slipped on her sheepskin mittens, specially adapted with short topless fingers and a nifty flap that covered the finger tops or could be fastened back when needed.

The Luftwaffe came, bombers high in the sky. In the dugout, the plotters monitored and traced each aircraft. Every member of the crew was on alert, communicating loud and clear. The guns fired, the sound deafening, but Evie had become quite used to the noise. She concentrated on following the planes to get them in her sight and relay their precise information so that the guns could hit their targets. Though tonight, the enemy planes zig-zagged about the sky, a game they played to fool the guns. But for the Luftwaffe to hit their target, they had to fly straight. This is when the guns would fire, hitting the enemy planes. One of the bombers was hit slightly and Evie saw it go off course and drop its bomb. Mercifully, it exploded in a field, though the farmer wouldn't be pleased at the damage. Better than losing lives. The enemy pilot banked quickly, heading back over the North Sea.

After a few rough days and nights, Evie lay on her bed, and so did Lily and Gloria. 'Only two more days,' said Evie, stifling a yawn.

Lily chuckled. 'We'll think of you when we're living it up in the NAAFI. We are going to have a party. I don't reckon the Bosh will turn out on Christmas Day.'

Evie sat up and smiled at her friends. At that moment, she envied their uncomplicated lives. And then she thought of Matt.

* * *

Matt came to the camp to meet Evie. 'Thanks,' he called to the driver of the van he'd hitched a lift with. He hauled his bag on his shoulder and turned, his face flooding with sheer joy as he saw Evie waiting for him.

'Matt,' she called. She ran to fling herself at him when she noticed army personnel all around. Instead, she kissed him on the cheek, and looking deep into his eyes, his love filled her with its warmth. She reached for his free hand, squeezed it, and they walked off to the station.

The train rattled on, and there was standing room only in the corridor. People continually passed up and down, so there was no chance of a proper conversation, just a few whispered words of love. They changed trains at Doncaster, waiting on a draughty platform. They clung together, their bodies oozing warmth. This time, they were lucky and secured seats on the train. Sitting side by side, their bodies touching, she felt safe with Matt. Snuggling closer, she rested her head on his shoulder, loving the feel of his breath blowing through her hair, which had come unpinned from its neat roll.

'Tell me about your parents,' Matt asked.

'My dad is a fine man. He fought in the Great War, and now he is something to do with the home guard. You'll get on famously with him. He's lovely and easy to talk to.' She fell silent.

Matt prompted her. 'And your mother?'

'My mother . . .' Evie faltered. She wanted to say — my mother is rather a distant person. She'd never been asked about her mother before, so she gabbled on. 'She's involved in good works, the women's group who knit for victory. She raises money for the church and organises dances in the village hall. She's always busy.' She could have added, 'But she's no time for me', but that sounded too bitter.

'What about your parents?' she asked. No answer. She lifted her head to look at him. His eyes were closed and, by the gentle rhythm of his breathing, she could tell he was asleep.

When they reached Hull Station, Evie gently shook Matt. He opened his eyes and, for fleeting seconds, she saw he didn't know where he was. She kissed him lightly on the lips, not caring who saw. 'Time to move,' she said, rising to her feet. He was up and by her side, reaching for their bags.

Stepping on to the platform, steam billowed from the train engine. 'It always reminds me of when I was a young lad and would go trainspotting,' he said.

She linked her arm through his and they moved along with the crowd to the exit. Outside the station, people were busy going about their business. No one loitered. There was no train for the next part of the journey, so they caught a bus. Finally, they could see the city, Matt's first visit. 'Bloody hell!' he exclaimed. 'Hull has suffered a right battering from the Luftwaffe. More than any town I've seen, apart from London.'

Sitting in front of them, the old man turned to look at Matt. 'Aye, bloody Jerry. If I could get me hands on Hitler, I would throttle him. He wiped out all my family and neighbours in one go.' Tears filled the man's eyes and ran down the stubble of growth on his cheeks.

'Sorry, mate. We are doing our best to eliminate the enemy and stop the war.'

It was then the man noticed Matt's pilot uniform. 'Sorry, lad, to go on. You're doing a grand job.' He sniffed, rubbing away his tears with the back of his hand.

Matt pulled a packet of cigarettes from his pocket, offering one to the man. Evie shook her head when Matt offered her one. The man turned back in his seat, inhaling deeply, becoming lost in his sad thoughts.

For the rest of the journey, neither Matt nor Evie spoke, both deep in their own thoughts. She had never considered that one of them could be killed. The ravages of war were happening all around them, so neither of them was immune. Maybe when this war was over, she and Matt could settle down. The thought pleased her, and she reached for Matt's hand and gave it a gentle squeeze. Their eyes met. Was he thinking the same thoughts as her?

They alighted from the bus and walked down the narrow lane to Island House. Night was already drawing a veil across the sky.

'I'm disappointed,' said Matt, as they walked side by side.

'Disappointed,' she echoed, about to question him, when she noticed his beaming smile.

'Yes, I thought you would have rowed me across the lake.'

Laughing, she replied, 'My darling Matt, you have that pleasure to come.'

Her laughter must have carried, for as they approached the front door, her father flung it open and came down the steps to greet them. 'Daddy,' she cried, hugging him. Then she stepped back, saying, 'I want you to meet Pilot Officer Matthew Goodwin. Matt, to friends.'

Gerald welcomed Matt and shook hands with him.

Through the open door, Evie could see her mother hovering in the hall, watching.

They all went inside and, after kissing her mother on the cheek, she introduced Matt, but didn't add 'Matt, to friends'. No, she knew Florence preferred to be formal, so Matthew it was.

'Dinner will be in one hour, but drinks in half an hour. That will give you both time to freshen up. Matthew is in the guest room, with a view of the lake,' Florence announced.

Matt carried their bags up the curved staircase, and Evie led the way to his room. It was at the other end of the corridor from hers. She went inside his room and drew down the blackout blind. Turning straight into Matt's arms, their lips met, hungry for love. They began to peel off their clothes when a voice sounded. Her mother's.

'Evie, show Matthew where the bathroom is.'

Going out into the corridor, Evie leaned over the balustrade, peering down at her mother below. 'I have, Mother,' she said with forced brightness. Her mother watched until Evie went to her own room.

After freshening up and tidying her hair, Evie left her bedroom to find Matt waiting in the corridor for her. Peeping over the balustrade, 'All clear,' she whispered. And immediately they were in each other's arms again, their lips touching with a fierce passion.

Then, hearing movement down below, they parted and descended the stairs.

They joined Gerald and Florence in the drawing room. 'We've not used this room much, so we could save the fuel for Christmas,' Gerald volunteered.

'It's nice and cosy, Dad.'

Florence said, 'We're having a few people over after the service.'

'Service?' Evie queried.

'It is Christmas Eve, and war or not, I like to keep my standards,' said Florence.

After the formal drink of dry sherry, the men went into the dining room and Evie helped her mother carry in the dishes.

Gerald kept up the chatter, knowing not to ask them too much about the practical manoeuvres.

They tucked into ham and roast potatoes, with apple pie for afters. Both Evie and Matt listened attentively as Florence told them about happenings in the town.

'We have evacuees, staying from Hull. Surprisingly, they are polite children, though a couple of the lads are a bit rough, so I've placed them on farms. And there is a dreadful rumour—'

Gerald cut in, stopping Florence from continuing. 'We won't talk about that now, dear.'

Evie looked to her parents, and could see whatever it was, it upset her mother. Upset! Usually, nothing upset Florence; annoyed her, yes, but never upset.

Florence gave her husband a frosty stare, refusing to be silenced, and announced, 'We are being forced to have officers billeted with us. So inconvenient.'

By the look on her father's face, Evie guessed he would welcome the officers.

Dutifully, Evie and Matt accompanied her parents to the church. Evie smelled the fresh, tangy scent of pine branches placed around the church, and the smell of wax from the flickering candles. She reached for Matt's hand as they walked down the aisle towards the pew where her parents sat.

Standing side by side, they sang the first hymn, 'O Little Town of Bethlehem'. Matt sang in a beautiful baritone voice, and Evie's heart sang with joy. When they sat down, she noticed in front of the lectern was a nativity scene. Instantly she felt transported back to when she was a young child, attending the magical nativity service. Tears wet her lashes. With the advent of war, she had completely forgotten what the meaning of Christmas was.

CHAPTER SIX

Christmas 1942

Christmas Day was all hustle and bustle. After the late night, Evie would have loved a lie-in to catch up on her sleep, but her mother needed her help in the kitchen. After a quick breakfast of tea and toast, Evie set to preparing the vegetables: potatoes, sprouts and carrots, surprised to learn that they were from Gerald's vegetable plot, so her hoeing in the summer had not been in vain. Apparently, some vegetables had been traded for the chicken now roasting in the oven. That's one advantage of living in a small town as opposed to the big city, Evie thought, as she scrubbed the mud off the potatoes. She looked across the table at Florence, who was making the stuffing. A concoction of, sage, onion, breadcrumbs and grated carrot, which she bound with water.

'It's not the same without sausage meat,' Florence grumbled, as she patted the mixture into balls and placed them on a baking tray.

'You do your best with the rationing,' Evie offered. As usual, she was finding conversation stilted with her mother and wanted again to avoid Florence's probing subject of what Matt's intentions were towards Evie. She and Matt hadn't talked about it. They just enjoyed each other's company, especially the loving part. She heard voices and glanced out of the window to see Matt and Gerald heading towards the vegetable plot. To her father's getaway shed, she guessed, where he was bound to have a bottle of whisky hidden away.

When she and Matt got married, he would have to help with the cooking, she thought. No sneaking off. A condition of marriage, she would tell him, if the occasion arose. She laughed and her mother glared at her.

As they worked in silence, Evie wondered what kind of Christmas Lily and the other girls on duty would be having. They would be sure to fit in some merrymaking with plenty of laughter, and Maureen would belt out the tunes on the piano. Harry and Jimmy would do a fine rendition of the well-loved music hall entertainers, Flanagan and Allen, with songs such as 'We're Gonna Hang Out the Washing on the Siegfried Line' and 'Underneath the Arches'. Passing the men's billets one night, she had heard them practising, and stopped to listen awhile, though she quickly moved off when she heard footsteps behind her. It wasn't the done thing to loiter in the area, neither for the men to loiter near the women's sleeping quarters.

'Have you finished yet?'

Her mother sharp retort pulled her away from her reverie. 'All done,' she replied brightly. Glancing out of the kitchen window, she longed to walk around her beloved lake. She looked back at her mother and noticed how tired she looked. Before the war, Florence had a daily housekeeper, so that she could play her role as lady of the house and entertain acquaintances and guests. A woman in the village helped her out. She tried to maintain her standards, but with each day that passed it was proving more impossible.

Evie suggested to Florence that she rested for a while and she would check on the chicken and vegetables. To her surprise, her mother agreed.

'I will bring you up a cup of tea,' Evie said.

'Thank you, dear,' her mother said wearily as she left the kitchen.

Tapping on the bedroom door, Evie entered, putting the tea down on the bedside table. Florence lay on her bed, snoring gently. Evie covered her mother with the counterpane and slipped quietly from the room.

Downstairs, she poured herself a cup of tea, first checking on the chicken and the potatoes roasting in the oven. She went to stand by the window, her eyes towards the corner of the house, hoping Matt and her father would soon appear and come indoors. But there was no sign of them.

As she busied herself tidying up in the kitchen, she heard a faint meow. Opening the kitchen door, she saw a smoky-grey cat, looking pitifully at her. She poured out a saucer of precious milk and put it on the back step, watching as it lapped it up, then purred contentedly at her. 'You are welcome,' she said, laughing to herself as she went back indoors, thinking how mad it was that being at home reduced her to talking to a cat. She missed the camaraderie and buzz of the site. Her heart was Matt's, but she would not be a housewife like her mother. That thought surprised her, but her mind was her own. Her role in this war was fighting the Luftwaffe and keeping Britain safe.

Just in time, she rescued the chicken from the oven and laid it to rest on the big oval plate. She placed the vegetables in the warming dishes on top of the stove. There was a fire in the dining room grate where the table was laid. The fir tree stood splendidly in front of one of the two long windows, which looked away from the lake. She gazed in wonderment at the tree decoration that she had made years ago, the fir cones she'd painted in different colours, though some of them were fading now. The paper-chains in various colours, with different-sized baubles hanging at precarious angles. The angel took pride of place at the top of the tree, her wings glittering. Evie felt a lump in her throat. She'd made the angel at school when she was nine. There were parcels tied with string at the foot of the tree.

Suddenly, she heard voices. Matt and Gerald were back.

She went into the kitchen to greet them. She kissed Matt on his cold cheek, smelling the whisky on his breath. He grinned boyishly at her, saying, 'I'm starving, and something smells good.'

Florence came down, looking refreshed and taking charge of the meal while Gerald poured the drinks. Suddenly, normality was restored and, for a short period, the war was forgotten.

After the delicious meal and once the table was cleared, Gerald did the honours and gave out the Christmas presents. To her mother, Evie gave four embroidered handkerchiefs made by one of the gunner girls, and to her father, from the NAAFI, a packet of pipe tobacco, which she knew he loved to smoke in his hut. From her mother, she received a hand-knitted pair of socks, and so did Matt. Her father provided the bottle of wine with their meal. So frugal when she thought of the extravagant gifts of Christmases past. Matt had brought a small basket of tasty snacks from the NAAFI shop. She had given him a precious bar of chocolate, and he had given her a small wooden carving in the shape of two hearts entwined. The act of giving was what mattered.

She held the tiny carving in her hand, seeing the marks of hours he'd spent whittling away at the wood, and tears sparkled in her eyes.

Her parents retired to the sitting room to relax, but Evie yearned for fresh air and to feel Matt's lips on hers. 'Matt, take a stroll around the lake with me.' He nodded, his eyes watching her as he followed her through to the back porch. There he came up behind her, slipped his arms round her waist and nuzzled her neck. She felt his warm breath on her face as he turned her towards him, pulling her into an embrace, his lips seeking hers. A kiss promising more to come.

Dressed warmly, Matt wore his uniform and greatcoat, while Evie was in civvies, glad to abandon her own uniform for a short time. Her pre-war dress was made of silk, and over it she buttoned a warm woollen cardigan and her long mackintosh, donning a wool hat with a pom-pom, which nodded as she pulled on her sensible boots. Laughing, they both set off, relishing the relaxed freedom together. The azure blue sky, bright with winter sunshine, shone through the filigree branches of the trees, sparkling with magic to capture them strolling hand-in-hand. The grassy bank of the lake gave way to rougher ground and they walked carefully along it.

'Does the lake freeze?' asked Matt, as they stopped to admire the view towards the house.

'Yes, when I was younger we ice-skated a few times, but Mother didn't approve.' She shrugged. Matt drew her to him and kissed her on the tip of her nose. Laughing, they continued.

They stopped to wish an old man, walking his dog, a Merry Christmas. 'House is too full of children,' he grumbled. 'And me and Floss wanted some quiet time.' They watched the man and his dog amble away.

Evie was curious to learn about Matt's family, whom he hadn't mentioned much, except to say they lived near to the village of Grassington, in West Yorkshire. 'My dad's a farmer, though I'm not sure how he manages with just a couple of land army girls. I've one brother in the army and one on submarines, and a sister married with two children. My mother and younger sister run the dairy.' He paused.

Glancing up at him, Evie remarked, 'I couldn't imagine you as a farmer's boy.'

'Err, no! I went to a technical college. Aviation has always been my ambition.' He paused, looking into the distance, then said quietly, 'I never expected it to come so soon.

'What about you?' he enthused, swinging Evie's arm in a beat with his own.

'When I left school, Mother wanted me to help her. Father had the family agricultural seed firm and said they didn't need me to earn a living.'

'Did you enjoy it, being at home?'

'No, it was boring. I was glad to join the forces for the war effort.'

Matt stopped walking, pulling her to his side to face him. 'I always thought that girls who are married like to stay home.'

She took a deep breath and met his gaze. 'Are you proposing, Matthew Goodwin?'

His face broke out in a beaming smile, and he lifted her up high and swung her round. Then, breathlessly, he set her down and kissed her, tenderly. His arms wrapped around her, holding her so close she felt his breath on her face. She watched his lips moving as he said, 'Yes, I love you, and I am asking you to marry me, Evie Sinclair.'

She gazed at him in wonderment, her heart racing, matching his. 'I love you, Matt, and want to spend the rest of my life with you. But . . .' He was about to speak, so she put her finger on his lips. 'While the war is on, I want to stay on as an Ack-Ack gunner girl. Then, when the war is over, we can be married.' She looked earnestly into his eyes. 'If you still want to marry me.'

He didn't speak. The sunny sky had turned to a dull grey. Evie shivered, not sure if it was the chilly wind now blowing off the lake, or the coldness emitting from Matt that whipped at her heart.

In silence, they walked towards the house, then parted to their respective rooms to freshen up before the guests were due early evening. Evie half expected Matt to come and knock on her door, but he didn't. She knew she had upset him, but she didn't want to marry while the war raged on. She knew some girls were happy to marry and escape from the forces when they became pregnant. But she didn't want that. She loved being an Ack-Ack gunner girl. This had opened a whole new way of thinking for her, an independence she wasn't willing to give up. If they married so soon, she would become pregnant, and she would then be like her mother, the dutiful wife. She loved Matt, but he would still be a pilot, serving his country and fighting against the enemy.

She sat at her dressing table, staring at her reflection in the mirror, and for the first time, she noticed the difference. She no longer felt like the naive girl who had joined up. She dabbed a touch of rouge on her pale cheeks and applied deep pink lipstick.

Downstairs, Matt was already there, talking with her father. She smiled at him and he replied with a polite smile.

Her heart sank. She went into the kitchen to help her mother. And for once, she was glad of the silence.

The evening dragged on. Florence and Gerald's friends were jolly, and pleased for Evie to wait upon them. 'More cake?' she asked Matt brightly.

He eyed her with suspicion, as if she was going to pounce on him. 'Thank you,' he murmured. When everyone was happily eating or drinking, she poured herself a glass of her mother's sherry, took a big gulp and sat down next to Matt on the sofa. She didn't like this coldness between them. She took another gulp of the drink, feeling its warmth run through her body, which ached to touch Matt's. She glanced sideward at him, surprised to see him watching her. On impulse, she reached for his hand and he rewarded her with the strength of his fingers, clasping hers. She moved closer to him, her thighs touching his, his heat transcending to her. She closed her eyes.

'Are you all right, dear?' It was the vicar's wife, standing before her.

'Yes, of course.' Noticing she was holding an empty glass, Evie offered, 'Another sherry, Mrs Watson?'

'Splendid, my dear.' And she thrust the glass into Evie's hand. When she came back with the refill, Mrs Watson was chatting with Matt.

After that, Florence played the piano, and Gerald sang Bing Crosby songs popular before the war.

When everyone had departed, her mother went to bed and her father said to Matt, 'Join me in a nightcap.' So Matt did.

Evie went to bed. She couldn't sleep, but listened for Matt coming up the stairs. And when she heard him, she held her breath, wondering, would he would tap on her door? But his footsteps never faltered as he passed by. It was a long time before she fell into a fitful sleep.

CHAPTER SEVEN

Late December 1942–April 1943

Evie and Matt, a subdued couple, travelled across the country by train to his parents' farm. Matt hadn't made any attempt to come to her room at her parents' home, and had only shared a fleeting kiss. Evie wrestled with her conscience. She felt guilty for not wanting to marry Matt before the war ended. It shocked her to think that he assumed she would leave the Ack-Ack gunner girls if they married and she became pregnant. She wasn't turning him down, she was just not ready for such a commitment. She had escaped the life her mother had mapped out for her, and the truth was, she wasn't prepared to give up her freedom.

Matt's family was the opposite to hers. For the last leg of the journey, they had hitched a lift on a waggon to the farm, and as soon as they set foot in the yard, the dogs came bounding over to greet them and the farmhouse door was flung open. A man in army uniform — Tom, Matt's brother — appeared, as well as his mother, Mary, and older sister Beth with her two young girls. There also appeared a shy-looking girl, Amy, his younger sister. Evie felt herself being hugged and one of the little girls held her hand. This warm and loving family made her feel even more guilty, because this was what Matt wanted. His own family.

They showed her up to her room, sharing with Amy, while Matt was in with Tom. She thought of the time they had spent together in Yarmouth and wondered if they would share precious moments like that again. She looked out of the window at the hills beyond and her heart felt heavy at the thought that Matt might meet someone else. Why did their relationship have to be so serious? Romance and fun was what she wanted, to give light relief to the consequences of war. Was that so wrong of her?

The time with Matt's family passed in a whirl of make believe. Of happy families. Amy was a treasure to speak to, reminding Evie of herself when she was that young. 'I want to travel,' Amy told Evie, her big brown eyes shining.

'When the war's over, I'm sure you will.' They were sitting at the dressing table, and Evie was brushing Amy's long, dark hair.

'You've not to tell our Matt or anyone, because it's a secret. Mam and Dad want me to stay and work on the farm.' She looked at Evie's reflection in the mirror.

Evie smiled. 'Your secret is safe with me.'

Time passed quickly, and soon they were saying their goodbyes to the family. Tom was travelling with them on the train and the brothers chatted about football and fell races. Evie tuned out and closed her eyes, feeling utterly miserable.

When Tom departed, Evie turned to Matt. 'Are you still angry with me?'

He didn't answer immediately, but stared ahead. Then he turned to her. 'I was at first. But I've had time to think and you are right. After the war, we will have the rest of our lives to spend together. Yes, I still want to marry you, Evie.' He leaned into her, kissing her lightly on the lips. 'You're still my girl.' He slipped his arm around her shoulders.

She snuggled up to him. 'You are a lovely man, Matt Goodwin,' she whispered. Her insides were warm and glowing with relief.

* * *

Evie arrived back at the gun site just as the rumour spread that they were moving. The gunner girls were in their hut, and speculation cast them wide: France, Belgium, down south, up north to Scotland. Then Lily contributed, in a dreamy voice, 'Hollywood.' Everyone laughed, and Evie, dressed only in her regulation underwear, danced, imitating Rita Hayworth. The girls clapped, loving the light relief, as she performed between the narrow bed spaces and up and down the central aisle.

Suddenly, a whoosh of cold air hit the room and a hush fell. Turning, Evie swayed and lost her balance, to be saved by the powerful arm of Corporal McDonald, a huge Scots woman. Evie groaned inwardly, trying to stand to attention, avoiding the stern-faced corporal.

The corporal marched into the room. The laughter and good humour of the girls vanished without a trace. 'Disgraceful behaviour,' she boomed, her spittle spraying the faces of those nearest to her. 'I have a good mind to put you terrible lot on jankers. However, we have a war to fight. Haven't we?'

'Yes, Corporal,' they all responded in unison.

After the corporal departed, everyone was subdued. 'She's an old misery guts,' Gloria whispered to Evie.

Next morning, Evie and Gloria were given the task of cleaning the dining room floor and the floor in the Officers' Mess as well. Just as they thought they were finished, they were given another chore, fetching a bucket of coke for their fire and cleaning out the stove. By the time they got back to their hut, changed out of work overalls, freshened up and grabbed a bite of dinner, it was time to attend the briefing meeting. They squeezed in at the back of the room.

Evie listened intently. They were being moved to East Yorkshire, where a great number of permanent gun sites were operational. All she could think was that she was moving further away from Matt. It had been a bonus, with them both being near Yarmouth.

Lily, next to her, nudged her and whispered, 'Isn't that your neck of the woods?'

Evie nodded.

They were on a crowded train again within two days. Evie, Lily, Gloria, Maureen and Penelope were assigned to Station H31, Walkington. It was close to Hull, which was relentlessly targeted by the Luftwaffe and suffered many bombing raids, with a heavy loss of life and countless homes and workplaces destroyed. The enemy came across the North Sea, attacking the east coast, using the River Humber as a map to target docks, railways, shipbuilding, the aircraft factory, and many operational airfields in the area. Passing through the city and surrounding villages, Evie could see the fresh scars of devastation since she was last in the area. People were salvaging belongings from their bomb-damaged homes, and some houses were flattened to the ground, their ruins still steaming from the raid. Oblivious to the destruction that surrounded them, she spied a group of small girls playing hopscotch on a cracked pavement.

Once on site, Evie didn't have time to think about Matt, though she had penned him a quick letter telling of her move. They soon settled into the new site, and after collecting bedding and sorting out her corner of the hut, which was quite spacious compared to other sites she'd been on, Evie glanced out of the window to see, a field away, a farmhouse and outbuildings, and the hope of fresh milk slipped into her mind. Next, she made sure her uniform was perfect, the buttons polished and her shoes shined to perfection. What she enjoyed most was familiarising herself with the layout of the camp and the equipment, which changed as technology advanced.

'The food's not bad,' said Lily as they sat in the dining room, devouring a tasty plateful of cottage pie and carrots.

Evie glanced over her shoulder at the next table, her nostrils twitching as she smelled the milky aroma of hot rice pudding. 'I'm going to like it here,' she said to Lily, 'if only for the food.'

'Look over there.' Lily nudged Evie.

She saw a man eyeing up Lily. 'He's a bit old for you.'

'Maybe. But all I want is a bit of fun. Nothing serious.'

The next day, Evie was surprised to receive a letter from Matt, as she hadn't expected to hear so soon. Opening the envelope, she drew out the single sheet of paper, written on both sides. First, she scanned it quickly. He was in sick bay with an injured shoulder. It was nothing serious, but would take time to heal. He mentioned food, jokes and life on the base. Then he wrote:

'I won't be flying for a couple weeks when I leave sick bay. They could transfer me to another base, which could be anywhere. As you know, things are always happening.

'Love you forever and always, Matt.'

Evie was sitting in an empty corner of the dining room when she read the letter. She pondered his words. If he transferred to another base, he could be down south and then there would be no chance of them meeting up.

Campaigns and strategies were always being advanced, and nothing ever stood still. In war, anything could happen. Their important training combated the enemy in the sky and, as the Luftwaffe brought in new types of aircraft, they had to keep abreast of their own defence plans. Tonight, Evie felt something in the air; she could almost taste it.

Her senses proved right. The Luftwaffe came over in droves via the North Sea. Some targeted the docks of the city of Hull and the important transport structure of the railway system. Others swept overhead, to the industrial cities and towns of West Yorkshire, though not all got through. The Ack-Ack guns were in action and some aircraft came spinning down. Plus, the RAF fighter planes were in action, too. The ability to identify enemy aircraft and your own aircraft was crucial in warfare.

The night proved endless and winter daylight was slow in making an appearance.

'I can never get used to wearing a helmet, it plays havoc with my hair,' Lily moaned as they made their way to the canteen and a welcome hot drink.

Evie laughed, 'It's only because lover boy likes your golden locks.'

Lily had been on a few dates with the soldier who had made eyes at her. Fred Jackson, otherwise known as Jacko, was married. But Lily insisted, 'It's only a bit of harmless fun. I'm not gonna run off with him.'

Evie envied her, wishing that Matt was stationed nearer so they could at least have some precious time together.

Then it happened. A few weeks days later, a letter from Matt telling her he'd been transferred down south. Evie burst into tears.

'Bloody hell, what's the matter?' Lily asked, startled, looking up from the old magazine she was reading. She had never seen her friend cry before.

In between sobs, Evie told Lily, 'When will I see him again?'

'Won't he get leave?'

Evie shook her head. 'He doesn't say.'

Just then, the siren sounded. Instantly, Evie became a professional, all her concentration on the task before her, the defence of the country against the Luftwaffe, the enemy.

Despite all the padding of her clothes, Evie felt the cold of the night air penetrate her body. 'There's a frost about,' she whispered to Gloria, who was standing next to her. Then she heard the drone of the Luftwaffe planes.

* * *

Evie and Matt only met once more before he went south. She sat on a train heading towards Doncaster, hunched in a corner, and throughout the journey, she kept her head down, not wanting to speak to anyone. At last, the train juddered to a stop and she hurried off, not wanting to waste precious minutes. Once through the barrier, she stood surrounded by a babble of noise and people rushing past her as she scanned the platform for signs of Matt. Panic gripped her. She couldn't see him. She stood on tip-toe. Someone knocked into her and her bag plunged to the floor. She bent down to retrieve it, but a man's hand reached down to grab it. In horror, she made to snatch it back, angry tears welling in her eyes. She was about to land the man a kick on the shin when he spoke.

'Evie.' Matt enfolded her in his arms.

She felt the steady beating of his heart through his jacket and this comforted her. She was safe.

He picked up his kitbag, which he had dropped at his feet, and drew her away from the other passengers and towards the station buffet. On reaching the door, he turned, touching Evie's face tenderly, and kissed her. She sighed with happiness, wanting another kiss.

'Are you going in, then?' boomed a voice. A burly man in an army uniform stood behind them.

'Sorry, mate,' Matt said, pushing open the door as they went inside.

They found an empty table away from the door and next to a window that was covered in condensation, giving them a certain amount of privacy from people passing by outside. Matt went to the counter. While he was gone, Evie glanced around the room. Most occupants were in uniform, like her and Matt. There were couples in conversation and holding hands, some on their own, smoking and gazing into space, with suitcases or kitbags at their feet. People in transit. Matt appeared with a tray of two steaming mugs of tea and a plate of corned beef sandwiches. Sitting down, he passed her a mug, their hands touching.

'If only we had more time,' he said, looking longingly into her eyes.

She gulped back her unhappiness and gently stroked his hand and smiled. 'We'll pretend we have.' She turned his hand over, tracing her fingers up and down his strong ones until his tension abated. She felt him relax and watched as he curled his fingers around hers. She felt his strength and, looking up into his eyes, she saw his pure love. Her heart overflowed with adoration for this darling man. And then guilt tormented her, for she had denied him, her true love, of being together as man and wife. A wave of emotion and regret swamped her.

'Evie, why are you crying?'

With the back of her hand, she brushed the tears away. She whispered, 'I'm so happy to see you.'

He lifted her hand to his lips and kissed it. 'Drink your tea while it's hot,' he said gently.

After devouring the sandwiches, they left the buffet. Glancing round, Evie spied a newspaper stand, and next to it a niche tucked away between the stand and the corner of a stone building. Slipping her arm through his, dodging people scurrying about, they edged forward.

Out of sight and safely ensconced, with their arms free, they held each other close. Then Matt tilted up her face and Evie smiled at him and kissed him. The first of many. Their bodies becoming almost as one. Until it was time for Matt to board his train south.

Evie stood on the platform, watching Matt's train gathering speed until it went from sight. Slowly, she turned to catch her train back to camp, not knowing when she would see him again.

CHAPTER EIGHT

May–December 1943

Evie didn't take leave for the rest of the year, saving it up for meeting Matt. She had been hopeful they could meet up in London and spend time together, but their off-duty times hadn't coincided. Although his letters were always loving, she wondered if he had met someone else and only wrote to her out of a sense of duty. Should she let her hair down and go out with different men? Lily and Gloria enjoyed doing so. Yes, I will, she told herself, on the next night off. Then the enemy interfered with her plan.

The searchlights criss-crossed the sky. Evie blinked her eyes against the lights, as they raced to their positions on the predictor, the adrenaline surging through her body. Within seconds, the spotters had identified the Luftwaffe aircrafts, and the Range-Finders team calculated the distance the shell would travel to hit the target. The information was relayed to the predictor team, who worked out the measurement of the fuse to make sure the shell exploded on target. Immediately, this information travelled to the soldiers on the guns.

Evie stood firm, as around them the ground shuddered from the mighty force of the powerful guns. When first on operations, she had thought the ground would open up and swallow her. She'd often dreamed about it, but not now. The procedure allowed no time for such thoughts. Her powers of concentration and endurance were paramount. Targets were hit, preventing destruction, but tonight the Luftwaffe were relentless, as if they were taking a last stand. The countryside and Hull were lit up by fire.

Evie looked up at the now eerily silent night sky, seeing the searchlights criss-crossing for any more enemy aircraft. But all remained quiet. They stayed at their posts until the clearance order came.

'A cup of hot tea is what I need,' Evie murmured to the others. They hurried to the canteen where a large metal teapot was waiting in readiness. Sitting at the table, sipping the hot liquid from big white mugs, Evie let out a sigh of relief, saying, 'We are lucky. Remember when we were training, tea was often in a big bucket and tasted foul.' An arm reached over and placed a plate piled high with toast on the table. And just as quickly, everyone at the table devoured it.

After a quick trip to the ablution block, Evie tumbled into bed for a few hours of sleep. Later she was on parade, then lectured. This routine continued for a few nights. And every night before sleep, her last thoughts were of Matt. In his last letter, he said he had good news for her. Wondering what it could be, she drifted into a restless slumber.

She dreamed someone called her name, then awoke with a start. 'Sinclair.' The face of the corporal glared down at her.

Instantly alert, Evie sprang from her bed, thinking the enemy was attacking. 'Telegram.' The corporal pushed it into Evie's startled hands and departed.

Evie sank back on to her bed and, with shaking hands, opened the telegram, thinking it was about Matt. But it read 'Father has had a heart attack. Come home immediately. Mother.'

'What's up?' asked a sleepy Gloria. Evie showed her the telegram.

'I've to go home,' she said in a trance. Turning to her locker, she hastily pulled out her dress uniform. When dressed, she said, 'I'll sort it out with staff for compassionate leave and transport.'

Lily was now wide awake and gave her a hug. 'Take care,' she whispered.

Leave granted, she arranged a lift to Beverley Station to catch a train to Hull and then changed to the coastal train to Inversea. From there she legged it until she reached the lake and her boat and rowed over to the house.

On opening the door, she was met by her tearful and overdramatic mother. 'You took your time. You must take me to see Gerald immediately.'

Evie went to open the garage where her father's Austin Seven Ruby waited, its dark green bodywork polished to perfection. With the shortage of petrol, Gerald had only used it on war work and emergencies, conserving his petrol. She cranked up the car and slid into the driving seat, her impatient mother already in the passenger seat. 'Come on, come on,' Florence wailed.

Evie felt a moment of panic, her body trembling, for she'd only driven the car in the grounds, never on the open road. Then her Ack-Ack gun training kicked in. The car sputtered into action and they were off, hoping the tank held enough petrol. Slowly, they made it to the Cottage Hospital, five miles away. Evie thought she could have walked it in less time.

On the ward, Gerald was in bed, propped up with pillows. Evie gasped inwardly at the sight of her father's grey, drawn face. On seeing them, he attempted a smile, which was more of a wince.

Florence fussed, 'Why aren't you in a private room?' Swinging round to Evie, she said, 'See to it.' Gerald gestured his hand and signalled no.

'Mother, you have a word with the doctor,' Evie suggested, watching thankfully as she went.

Tiredness overcame him and Gerald sank back on his pillow. Evie reached for his hand and gave it a gentle squeeze. She didn't speak, waiting until her father summoned up enough energy to do so. Her mind a dull blank, she listened to the quiet hum of the ward as the nurses went about their duties of caring for patients. She guessed her father would welcome others in the ward rather than be left in a silent room on his own.

Suddenly Gerald spoke. Evie glanced up at him. 'I just need to rest more. Been overdoing it. In a couple of days I shall be able to come home. How long are you here for?'

'Five days. I will see you settled in.' Mentally she made notes, to arrange for someone to help with household tasks, and to ask Gerald's friends to pop by to chat.

Florence came back, excited. 'Such a lovely doctor, he said you will be home soon. Now isn't that good news, Gerald?' she said, sitting on the chair Evie had vacated for her.

After the visit, Evie took her mother home and garaged the car. Then she walked to the post-office-cum-grocery shop. Mrs Little, who ran the shop, knew everyone and their business. When Evie mentioned her needs, she quickly replied, 'Maggie Hilton has just left school.'

Armed with the address, Evie went to see Maggie's mother. 'Will yer be paying her?' she stated bluntly.

Evie hadn't thought about payment, but quickly calculated. 'Yes, three shillings a week and a midday meal. I will draw up a timetable for her for each day, starting tomorrow.' Mrs Hilton called fourteen-year-old Maggie in from the garden.

Maggie stood looking down at the floor, her eyes not meeting Evie's as she outlined the duties expected of her. 'If you aren't happy with the arrangement of work, you must say.' Mrs Hilton was about to answer for her daughter, but Evie raised her hand to stop her.

Slowly, Maggie lifted her head of light brown hair. 'Yes, miss, I'll do it.' She went back into the garden to hang the washing on the line.

'I shall miss her help,' Mrs Hilton lamented, Maggie being the eldest of her six children.

The next morning, Maggie arrived at ten prompt. Last night, when Evie had explained to her mother about Maggie, Florence's only reaction was, 'Is she wearing a uniform?'

'No, an apron will suffice,' Evie answered. So, she'd raked through the kitchen drawers until she found a suitable apron for Maggie to wear.

The two officers billeted in the house were helpful. They brought a bed downstairs for Gerald until he was well enough to manage the stairs. Gerald had chosen to sleep in his study, as this looked down the lane so he could see who was coming to the house.

When dinner time approached, Evie hadn't given any thought to food, having been too busy showing Maggie around the house. Then a voice called, 'Cooee.'

Evie opened the front door to a woman who lived further down the lane. 'Hello,' she offered, unable to remember the woman's name.

'I am so sorry to hear of Mr Sinclair's illness. I've brought you this.' She was holding something covered by a tea-towel.

Evie's nostrils twitched at the delicious aroma coming from the cottage pie, and her stomach rumbled ungraciously.

'Come through to the kitchen, Mrs . . .'

'Mrs Tudor,' the woman said, following Evie.

Maggie was washing cups and saucers at the sink when they entered the kitchen. Evie asked, 'Maggie, can you find Mrs Sinclair and say we have a visitor, please?' And off she scurried.

Leaving the two women to chat, Evie and Maggie walked down the garden path to take stock of the vegetable situation. Evie surveyed the neglected plot, saying, 'There's potatoes, a few carrots and onions.'

By the time Gerald returned home, the routine of the house had become established.

'Now, are you sure you are comfortable, Gerald?' Florence fussed after shedding a few tears at his homecoming.

'I feel tired and need to rest,' he answered, his voice weak. And then, seeing Florence's bottom lip quiver, he said, 'I will feel better and be able to have a chat with you.' He was rewarded with her face brightening up.

Evie witnessed this touching scene and felt it pull at her heart. And then a wave of guilt swamped her. While away at camp, she never gave her parents much thought and didn't visit them as often as she could have. Now, with her father's heart attack and seeing how vulnerable her mother was, she realised that the war was taking its toll on them as well. They had both lived through the Great War, so to live through another . . . Evie couldn't imagine how that was affecting them both.

'I'm returning to camp tomorrow, Dad. Will you be all right?' Evie asked anxiously. She was sitting with Gerald, having persuaded Florence to attend her committee meeting.

He reached for her hand and squeezed it gently, saying, 'I am feeling much stronger now and the tablets the doctor prescribed are doing their trick. Your mother is much calmer too, thank goodness.' He paused, getting his breath, then added, 'Willy Talbot promises to keep me up to date with happenings, and spend time on the vegetable plot, and that delightful young girl, Maggie, is a breath of sunshine. I listen to her singing while she works about the house. And I think we can afford to pay her an extra shilling, which will be a help for her family.'

'Dad, you are kind.' She kissed him on the forehead. 'Have a rest and I will bring you a cup of tea later.'

In the kitchen, she took stock of the cupboards to see what ingredients she could use to bake with, so that when she went tomorrow, at least there would be food to last a few days. Maggie was quite a good cook for her age too. 'I help Mam a lot,' she told Evie proudly.

Soon, it was time to say farewell. Evie felt peace of mind that she was leaving her parents well catered for in the immediate future. She vowed to write more often, and would try to come home on a 24-hour pass when possible.

On the train back to camp, she thought of Matt and missed him so much. With the worry of her parents, she hadn't given him much thought, but now he took over her innermost feelings. As soon as possible, she would write to him. It seemed ages since he'd held her close in his arms, and right now she longed to feel his arms around her, the touch of his warm skin and his hot lips on her. She sighed with pleasure as a feeling of desire raced through her. The woman sitting opposite lowered her book and glanced across at Evie. She hoped the woman couldn't read her thoughts. Closing her eyes, Evie leaned back in the seat and began again to relive the tender moments she and Matt had shared.

When she arrived back on site, a letter was waiting for her.

CHAPTER NINE

March 1944

Matt arrived at 158 Squadron, Lissett, East Yorkshire on a bitterly cold day. The airfield was reputed to be the closest one to Germany. Placing his gear in his locker, it raced through his mind what he had heard about the squadron; that they'd had a run of bad luck losing men and aircraft. He straightened up and dismissed those facts from his mind. His only goal now was to win the war against the enemy.

Later, he joined the crew he would fly with. The new crew were replacing men who had died in battle. 'One decent thing,' the welcoming officer said, 'the food here is very good.' There were murmurs of pleasure. Matt felt thankful. Good food was a great asset to morale, reflected on the cheerful faces of his crew.

After the welcome briefing, the dining hall was the next step. The meal was a hearty beef pie with a succulent crust, cabbage and a mound of mashed potatoes and tasty gravy. Food that filled every satisfying corner. Afterwards, in the NAAFI, he had a drink of beer with another pilot, Richard Marsden, from the south, nicknamed Rich. 'I wish I was,' he said, taking a long draught of his beer.

That evening, Matt sat on his bunk to pen a letter to Evie. He glanced at her smiling face in the photo on his locker. He loved her twinkling eyes, which seemed to watch him, giving him an inner warmth and strength.

'A good-looker. Your girl?' Rich asked from his bunk across the aisle, pointing to Evie's photo.

Matt looked up, forgetting that he wasn't alone, and smiled. 'Yes, Evie, she's with the ATS on a gun site near Beverley. Do you have a girl back home?'

'Nope, she ditched me for a guy with money.'

'Sorry!'

'She's not worth it. I might just find myself a nice Yorkshire girl.' They both laughed.

'Berlin!' It was the next day in the briefing room and Matt was listening intently. Berlin was still their target, having been targeted since November 1943. Their route was across the North Sea towards Denmark and then south to Germany, and then Berlin.

On the runway, they prepared for take-off. The routine of the crew was to concentrate on their individual tasks while working as a team. The pilot, Matt, was in overall control of the flight engineer, bomb aimer, navigator, wireless operator, mid gunner and rear gunner. Cloud persisted over the North Sea, only clearing when they flew over Denmark. On reaching Germany, they flew through the ring of anti-aircraft guns and used manoeuvre tactics to avoid the powerful searchlights and the guns. When the mission was complete, they returned to base safely.

They repeated this mission many times until the last raid on Berlin that month. No one mentioned the lives and aircraft lost.

'Bloody good show,' Matt told his crew. 'Drinks are on me.'

'We'll hold you to that, skipper,' said Bill, the rear gunner.

Back at camp, Matt remarked to Rich, 'I didn't realise how shattered I was. Surely, we must be due a 24-hour pass.'

When he had the date, Matt sat on his bunk writing to Evie, asking her to take the time off too.

Rich, sitting opposite, asked, 'Your girl got a friend I can tag on with?' And so they arranged that Lily would make up the foursome.

* * *

'What's he like, this pilot? Hope he's as handsome as Clark Gable,' Lily fantasised.

'You might have to pretend,' Evie laughed.

They were making sure that their uniform was spotless, otherwise they might get pulled up by the corporal. Evie rubbed away at her brass buttons until they shone and twinkled in the dimly lit hut. Holding her jacket up, she gave it a final check then replaced it on its coat hanger.

She propped a piece of mirror on her locker top, careful to avoid her fingers catching the jagged edge. Glancing in the mirror, her dark smudged eyes stared back at her. She gave a hiccup of a laugh and sighed.

Looking up from her half of the jagged mirror, Lily asked, 'What's up with you?'

'With all the strain of concentrating, my eyes are so dark.'

'You will have to practise a sultry smile, just like the Hollywood stars. Like this.' Lily pouted her lips and flicked back her curly hair. She leaned too far back and nearly toppled over.

'You look more like a comedian,' Evie said, her body shaking as she erupted into a fit of laughter. Then, turning back to powder her face and apply her precious red lipstick, she noticed that her eyes now had a sparkle. Laughter was a marvellous medicine.

All present and correct with their 24-hour passes, the two young women strode out towards Beverley, carrying their overnight bags for sleeping over at the ATS lodging house. They were meeting Matt and Rich in the pub down

Hengate for a drink. Afterwards, they would go to the dance venue. Evie pushed open the bar door and entered.

'Gosh, gaslights!' exclaimed a surprised Lily. 'How quaint.'

A whiff of cigarette smoke and beer hit Evie. The atmosphere was reminiscent of days gone by, dark and mysterious, full of people with hidden faces. Then a cheerful voice called out, 'Evie, over here.'

Through the gloom, she saw the smiling face of Matt at the bar. And she suddenly felt shy because she hadn't seen him for such a long time. Taking a deep breath, she said. 'Come on, Lily,' and took hold of her friend's arm to guide her through the crowd.

Matt leaned forward to kiss Evie lightly on the lips and she felt a lovely tingle of pleasure fill her body at his touch. It felt as if they had never been separated.

'This is Rich,' he said.

She hadn't noticed the tall, blond-haired man with his piercing grey eyes. He held her gaze, as if staring into her soul. She felt . . . what? She wasn't sure. Hastily, she said, 'This is my friend, Lily.'

'Hello, Lily.' He reached for her hand, raised it to his lips and kissed it.

Lily, not one to hold back, said, 'Well, hello there, Rich.' And she moved closer to him. Matt handed both girls a glass of shandy.

After laughing and joking for an hour, Matt asked if they were ready to dance. So off they trooped. In fact, quite a crowd of people moved with them. Evie noticed the other RAF men and WAAF as well, as they went out into the moonlit street.

On reaching the hall, Evie and Lily left their overnight bags with the cloakroom attendant, a middle-aged woman who sat knitting, her needles clicking in rhythm to the music coming from the bands. Evie imitated a Fred Astaire tap dance as they went into the dancehall. A soldier tried to claim a dance with her. 'Sorry, I'm spoken for.'

Matt had seen what happened and quickly whisked her on to the dance floor. After a quickstep round the floor, he pulled her into a corner, away from the dancers. She melted into his arms, feeling his strength and smelling the freshness of soap. His lips were as hot and passionate as hers and all her pent-up emotions of longing for him overflowed. Then, breathlessly, they came up for air. 'I've missed you so much,' he whispered in her ear. She felt his breath hot on her neck.

'I've missed you too. When can we spend some time together?' The words were out before she could stop them.

'I wish, my darling, I wish. The damned war seems to last forever.'

The tempo changed to a waltz, and Matt led Evie on to the floor. Instinctively, she went into his arms, their bodies touching, and she felt the heat from his body wrap around hers. The next dance was a jive, a dance imported by the Americans. They sat at a table and it was too noisy to talk, so they held hands and watched the dancers, their arms and legs going in all directions.

'Rich is enjoying dancing with Lily,' Matt remarked. 'I'm not sure where his energy is coming from.'

Evie followed his gaze and watched her friend enjoying herself with the pilot. 'I'm pleased for Lily to meet an unattached man.' Matt glanced at her, but she didn't enlighten him on Lily's dalliance with a married man.

The dance ended and Lily and Rich came to join them at the table. 'Drinks, ladies?' asked Rich. They nodded, and the two men went to the soft drinks bar.

'What do you think of Rich?' Lily enthused, not really wanting an answer. 'He's a smasher and just my type.'

Evie listened as Lily babbled on, pleased for her friend. The foursome met up three more times, twice at the cinema and at another dance. Matt and Rich always seemed to manage a transport lift, whereas Evie and Lily often used pedal power. When they had to be back on site, they acquired the bikes from the nearby farm, where a young lad did them up and charged a small fee for their use and maintenance, which suited the two women. They also ventured into Hull, now that the nights were getting lighter, plus the double summertime was a bonus.

They enjoyed their bicycle ride into Hull, with the wind behind them, and found a café, a welcome change from NAAFI food. The café was in the old town area, hidden down a narrow street, which catered mainly for the forces. Twin sisters Muriel and Myrtle ran it; both had lost their fiancés in the Great War.

'Everything is homemade,' they chorused in unison. 'You can leave your bikes in the backyard. They will be safe there.'

Evie and Lily settled down at a table, which had a brightly coloured red-checked cloth. 'Gosh,' said Lily, 'I ain't seen a tablecloth since I left home.'

'Mentioning home,' Evie said, 'I really should see how my parents are. In her letters, Mother only mentions the charitable work she is involved in.'

'Lucky you,' replied Lily. 'My mother doesn't bother to write. Unless she wants more money.'

'Now then girls,' Myrtle bustled up to their table. 'Today, we've nice Hull pasties with a drop of gravy, and jam roly-poly for afters.'

'Hull pasties, don't you mean Cornish pasties?' ventured Evie.

'I do not. These pasties have secret ingredients passed down from our mam, and her mam before her,' retorted Myrtle, with a twinkle in her grey eyes.

They served the pasties on blue Old Willow plates. Both girls were speechless. 'Only the best for our forces,' Myrtle said with pride, looking at their astonished faces. 'Got to keep your strength up to keep Jerry away.'

They both inhaled the delicious aroma and tucked in, not talking until their plates were empty. 'That was the best ever,' Evie declared. 'The meat and vegetables were so tasty, and the pastry melted in my mouth, but the secret ingredient makes it magic. Must be some kind of herb.'

'Are you ready for afters?' Myrtle asked as she cleared the table. Both girls nodded.

Muriel brought over the roly-poly pudding. 'Our own special jam,' she said. Lily was about to ask what fruit, but Muriel intercepted. 'Our secret jam.'

It was hard for the girls to keep a straight face.

Later, as they sat drinking a cup of weak tea, Evie said, 'Don't you agree, Lily? This is a magical café.'

Lily lay back in her chair. 'I do, and I could just fall asleep.'

* * *

In May, Evie received a letter from Matt. She sighed as she put it down on her locker. 'No leave for Matt. He doesn't say why. Something is in the air. I can sense it.'

Dropping her magazine to the floor, Lily asked, 'Anything about Rich?' He had told her he wasn't a letter writer.

'No, but I guess it goes for all on base.'

They both got ready for the morning parade and for a briefing lecture. Listening, Evie detected that the briefing was reminiscent of their early days, as if it was all new to them. She studied the officer's face as he spoke; it didn't reveal anything, but his body language was taut.

That evening, the sky proved busy with aircraft from the surrounding bases on the move.

They were on alert that night and at their post, for couldn't the Luftwaffe also be out in force?

CHAPTER TEN

May–June 1944

Evie and Lily were on their bikes pedalling into Hull. 'No fear,' Gloria had said when they'd asked her to come, 'I've seen enough of that place.'

Pedalling fast against the headwind, Evie said, 'Gloria must have had a sad life, brought up in an orphanage with no mother or father. She doesn't talk much about it, except for saying it was very strict and there were no hugs, or goodnight kisses at bedtime. Every night they knelt by their beds and said prayers, and often, when she was naughty, she had to kneel all through the night and repeat her prayer for forgiveness.'

'No wonder she joined up to escape,' Lily said, wobbling as she hit a stone on the road.

'Careful, we'd best dismount.'

In the centre of Hull, a gang of men were busy cleaning up bombed buildings and loading rubble on to handcarts. One of them wolf whistled and shouted, 'Need any help, darling?'

The girls giggled, waving as they passed by.

Passing the railway station, they saw hordes of uniformed men making their way through the entrance. Both girls looked at each other, but neither spoke. They'd had the perils of careless talk drilled into them. They remounted their bikes and soon reached the sanctuary of the café, where they enjoyed a piece of homemade cake and the banter of the two sisters.

Putting her cup down on the saucer, Lily blurted out, 'I thought Rich might have been in touch with me. Has Matt mentioned him in his letters?'

Evie shook her head and offered, 'If he does, I'll tell you.'

'Umph! Seems he's not as keen as me, so I'll have to find someone new.'

They didn't care about the rain on their way back to camp. Sitting on her bed to take off her wet shoes, Evie said to Lily, 'I'll write to Matt first chance tomorrow and ask if he and Rich can meet up with us soon.' Joy filled her as she saw Lily's face brighten. Then she wondered why Matt hadn't already been in touch with her.

Evie hurried to the ablution block to freshen up and prepare for duty at 2 p.m. She glanced in the mirror over the sink, and two half-closed dark eyes stared back at her. Heavens, she mused, I look a sight. Quickly, she splashed cold water over her face and fumbled for her towel. 'Damn!' She hadn't brought it with her.

'Here.' Lily pushed the towel into her hands. 'You'd forget your head if it was loose.'

Evie dried her face and saw Lily grinning at her. Instinctively, she gave her friend a hug.

'Oh aye. Didn't know you two were like that. How much to keep quiet?' came Maureen's dulcet tones.

'You want a hug as well?' asked Lily.

'Only if you're one of them good-looking Yanks.'

'Yanks!' Lily was alert. 'Where are they?'

Maureen tapped the side of her nose.

Going back to the hut, Lily said dreamily, 'I fancy a Yank for a bar of chocolate — and I'd give anything for a pair of nylons.'

Evie laughed. 'I thought you were keen on Rich.'

Lily shrugged, adding with a gleam in her eyes, 'It's all fair in love and war.'

There was no letter from Matt, only one from her mother. A few days later, Evie sat in the mess, reading the letter and hearing Florence's complaining voice in her head, saying how busy she was and how she needed Evie to come home and help. She sighed heavily.

'What's up?' asked Lily.

Evie pushed the letter across the table for her friend to read. A quick perusal and Lily pushed it back to Evie, saying, 'Doesn't she know there's a war on?'

* * *

Matt read Evie's letter. He lay on his bunk, trying to catch a couple of hours' sleep before he was off on another mission. Tomorrow, he would reply and tell her how much he desired to hold his darling girl in his arms and kiss her tender lips, and tell her how much he loved her. Hopefully soon, when their days off coincided, they could spend precious time together. He wanted to spend a night making love to her. In his dreams — though dreams could come true.

His attention returned to his next mission, to stop the enemy causing more destruction and pave the way for the biggest advance of the Allied forces. A step closer to victory. He tried to ignore the fact that the squadron had recently lost several men. They didn't want to lose more because of this big operation. He felt his heavy eyelids droop, his fingers slackened and Evie's letter drifted to the floor, lodging under his bunk, forgotten.

He heard the call loud and clear and automatically sprang from his bed, feeling as though he had only just closed his eyes, though two hours had passed. Lighting two ciga-rettes, he passed one to Rich, who ran by his side as the crew raced across the airstrip to their respective Halifax aircrafts, ready for action. Their mission — flying to northern France to continue bombing bridges, railway junctions, dumps of supplies and ammunitions, battery guns and radar stations, to stop the advance of the enemy.

* * *

On duty, Evie heard the roar of the RAF bombers in the night sky on their way to battle. She offered a silent prayer for Matt and his crew and for all those flying tonight to be successful and return safely to base. She wanted to scream at the futility of war. Instead, she took a few deep breaths and focused on her duties.

The next day, off duty, Evie sat in the NAAFI, enjoying a welcome cup of tea while composing a letter to her mother, when Lily came rushing in, waving a newspaper. The date, Wednesday 7 June 1944.

'They've done it. They've got the Germans on the run,' yelled an excited Lily.

Evie's pen jolted in her hand, leaving a blob of ink on the letter to her mother. Not caring, she jumped up, joining in the excitement created by Lily as the NAAFI became alive with joyous exhilaration.

Standing on a chair, Lily read the longed-for news. 'Churchill announces successful massed air landings behind the enemy lines in France.'

Evie listened as Lily read on, and then her mind drifted to Matt. She'd sensed something was being planned, though Matt would not have been at liberty to mention anything to her. Obviously, this had been a closely guarded secret. There were plenty of posters around saying 'Careless talk cost lives'. She prayed for his safe return, and his crew, though whether they were in Lissett or in France, she had no way of knowing. He wouldn't be thinking about letter writing right now. Though she could write to him. Someone gave a big 'Whoopee!', breaking her mixed-up reverie.

Lily jumped down from the table, having passed the newspaper on. 'A cup of tea?' Evie asked her as she sat down on the chair next to her.

'I could do with something stronger. Fancy going into Beverley, testing out the pubs?'

Evie was about to say no when she saw the hope on Lily's face. 'Sure.'

'What's this?' Gloria asked, pulling up a chair. 'Did you mention pubs?' she said with a big grin on her face.

An hour later, Maureen joined them, the Ack-Ack gunner girls, looking smart in their uniforms, strolled towards Beverley town centre and the pubs. They were all eager to celebrate the success of the Normandy landings, and Hitler's unwanted surprise. After drinking in two pubs, they eventually landed in one with a piano, and the pianist began belting out tunes. Hopefully, Evie looked around for the RAF uniforms, but there were only home guard soldiers coming in for a quick drink before going on duty. A few shifty-looking men working the pub seemed to be selling goods on the black-market. She wondered how they avoided being called up for military service.

'It's me back, see?' one of the men explained to her.

'Come on, Gloria, give us your rendition of "I'll be Seeing You".'

Before she could give an answer, they hoisted Gloria up to sit on top of the piano. Clearly glad she'd downed a few drinks, she sang the song made famous by Anne Shelton, who entertained the forces. Towards the end it became sad, and the pub grew quiet and a few wiped away tears. Gloria jumped down from the piano and pulled Lily and Evie to her, then whispered to Maureen, who took the pianist's place and played 'Boogie Woogie Bugle Boy', made famous by The Andrews Sisters. The girls got into the singing, swinging mood, and held the audience in the palms of their hands. The crowd called for an encore, and the girls obliged, with everyone joining in.

'A smashing evening,' Lily sang out. They all made their way back to camp, still in a jolly mood, and sang as they marched along, the night still light.

'British-double-summertime,' Evie shouted, and they all laughed. Advancing the clocks two hours forward was an ingenious idea, and she remembered learning about it at school. William Willett had campaigned for it way back at the beginning of the century.

'Shush,' Evie said, putting a finger across her lips as they neared the camp. But Lily started walking on her tip-toes, swaying her hips, causing the girls to have a fit of laughing.

'Attention,' boomed a voice. It was the corporal. 'What is the meaning of this outrageous behaviour?'

Evie felt Lily, wobbling on her tip-toes, fall against her back. It took all their strength to keep Lily upright, and to hold their faces in a neutral position.

'Sorry, Corporal,' they said in unison, their voices bland.

'You will be up at six for extra parade duties. Understand?'

'Yes, Corporal.'

'Miserable bugger,' muttered Gloria as they entered their hut and prepared for bed.

'I feel sorry for her,' said Lily.

'You what!'

'Because she's no idea how to have fun. And I've never seen her with a bloke.'

'Who the hell would want her?'

And so the banter continued. Evie went to the ablution block, wanting a few moments of quiet. Here she allowed her thoughts to turn to Matt, picturing his handsome face and longing to feel the strength of his arms around her body.

A few days later, much to her joy, she received a letter from him. She left the noise of the NAAFI and sat in the sunshine on a grassy bank beyond one of the gun sites. It looked across the farmland and felt quite tranquil, with the calling of birds as they flew overhead.

My darling Evie,

I am sorry it has taken me so long to reply to your letter. Busy. Busy. I have missed seeing your beautiful face and kissing your sweet lips.

Tears welled in her eyes, and for a few moments his words blurred on the page. Dashing away her tears, she read on.

70

I have a 24-hour pass for this coming weekend. Can you get away? I have the promise of a caravan on land near to the sea.

Evie had time off due. Hoping it would be granted, especially as they were so busy, she stood before the commanding officer, her eyes fixed on the portrait of King George secured on the wall above his head. She held her breath, her stomach tight, and bit her lip. The silence stretched on.

'Approved. Do not be late returning to duties,' he barked.

For a moment, she stared at him. Then quickly said, 'Thank you, sir.' She saluted and left the office. Once outside the building, she breathed in the warm summer air, glancing up at the fleeting puffs of white clouds, and the tension drained from her face. She hurried back to the hut to pen a letter to her darling Matt.

CHAPTER ELEVEN

July–August 1944

The smell of the salty sea assailed her nostrils as Evie stepped out of the blue two-seater car. An Austin 7 Swallow on loan from a fellow officer, Matt had told her. Shading her eyes, she glanced towards the North Sea, its waters calm. The incoming tide rode gently up the sandy beach, the waves breaking into white foam. A tranquil scene. Then she looked down over the cliff top to the monstrosity below and shuddered. Matt came to her side, slipped an arm around her waist, and she leaned into him.

'If it wasn't for the wall of barbed wire on the beach, you wouldn't know there was a war raging beyond the quiet sea.'

Matt steered her towards the caravan, his voice soft. 'These hours are ours, so no talk of war. Agreed?' She stretched her arms around his neck and pulled his face towards hers and kissed him full on the lips.

Inside the caravan, it surprised Evie how cosy it appeared. A wide fitted sofa, which doubled as a bed, a small table on a spring lever that let down to provide more space, and two stools. She glanced at the shelf, holding a two-ring gas hob complete with a tin kettle. Wedged in a corner was a tiny washroom with a concertina door.

Matt entered, bringing in their overnight bags and a box of picnic food. She noticed his tired-looking face and the dark rings around his eyes. 'Here, let me help.' She took the box off him and placed it on the table, stowing their bags under the sofa. Then she sat down and patted the cushion next to her, saying, 'Come and sit down, Matt.'

He did, but he didn't speak. Just stared ahead. Evie looked sideward at him, guessing he felt like her — strange, because it had been so long since they had been this close together. Ignoring her own jangling nerves, she reached out to him, slipping her arm around him, her fingers playing with his tendrils of dark curls. As she did so, she felt the tension leave his body. Suddenly she felt shy, not sure what Matt expected of her, or she of him. But the thought of losing him stirred up her insides, making her heart beat faster, and in that split second, she knew what she wanted.

He turned to look at her. 'Oh, my darling, I have missed you so much.'

'I've missed you too.'

She saw tears in his eyes and brushed them away with a finger, letting it slip down to his lips. In the next instant, she was in his arms and his lips were hot on hers. His pent-up emotions flared into passion, and she felt his eagerness. He unbuttoned her blouse, his hands tender as he caressed her body. She murmured with pleasure, her body arching to his. Suddenly, they were undressing each other. His fingers pulled at her clothing, and hers at his, until they were naked.

Their desire to be as one was fast and furious. Evie lay back on the sofa, her heart racing, her body aflame. She could feel Matt's body as he lay close to her. The touch of his skin on hers sent her into ecstasies of pure delight, and she forgot the world of war outside their cosy nest.

They must have slept for a short time, as she awoke to feel the touch of Matt's tender lips on hers. This time their love shone brightly and Evie felt rapturous as they took time to caress each other's bodies and reach their fulfilment. Enriched, they slept again, their bodies entwined.

Evie woke first and raised herself on her elbow to gaze at Matt as he slept. She could see that the dark circles around his eyes had faded. Being a bomber pilot must involve a lot of concentration, more than being an Ack-Ack gunner. She banished any thoughts of war.

Carefully, she eased from the bed, pulling on her clothes. Setting the kettle to boil for a cup of tea, she glanced out of the small window, surprised that daylight still shone. She foraged in the picnic box, suddenly starving. The cook back at camp had been generous: cheese and corned beef sandwiches, cold sausages, two big wedges of a Victorian sponge cake, and two bottles of beer, plus a small bag of fine tea-leaves.

When the kettle hissed and came to the boil, Matt woke up. Yawning, he stretched up his arms and Evie saw the flexing of his muscles. He grinned at her, saying, 'I could get used to this cosy life.' A thoughtful look on his face, he said, 'This war will soon be over, and you, my darling Evie, will be my wife.'

Evie passed him a cup of tea, saying, 'Mrs Evie Goodwin, I like the sound of the name.' They both laughed joyously.

After eating their fill, they dressed and, determined to take advantage of the pleasant weather, they strolled, hand in hand, as lovers do, only stopping to gaze into each other's eyes and kiss. With not a care in the world, it was as if they were on holiday. As they walked along the cliff top, they talked about their plans to build a home together. 'I want a garden to grow our own vegetables,' Evie enthused.

'I shall have a workshop to build furniture and make toys for our children,' Matt sang out.

They laughed and talked, swinging their arms. The sea air was fresh and barmy, just a gentle breeze blew, ruffling Evie's hair. They stopped walking and Matt drew her to him, his fingers warm on her skin as he tenderly brushed her hair off her face and back into place. Then his fingers traced her lips.

It sent shivers of desire running through her body, and her knees weakened as she felt his lips on hers. Then, unsure how it happened, Evie found herself lying down on the tufts of wild grasses, their garments scattered. With wild abandonment, they made love. The warmth of the soft breeze fanned their naked bodies, adding to their sheer joy and exhilaration, and with only the seagulls as their witnesses.

Afterwards, they lay looking up at the sky until they heard distant voices. Quickly, they gathered up their clothes and, laughing, raced naked back to the caravan. He drew her inside and Evie felt the strength of Matt's love as he held her close. She gazed adoringly at him, and they kissed, the anticipation of further love-making mirrored in their eyes.

Neither noticed the disappearance of the sun and the dark clouds appearing on the horizon.

* * *

Back at camp, Evie slipped into daydreaming of the time she and Matt had spent together whenever she had a spare moment. She wanted to make the wondrous feeling they had shared last forever.

'You've got it bad,' Lily remarked to Evie as she sat on her bed, staring into space.

'I was thinking of when the war ends. Matt and I are going to marry and have children, and I want a garden, and he wants a workshop,' she finished in an excited rush.

Lily hugged her, saying, 'He's the man for you, but why do you want to have kids and spoil it all? Me mam always says, you don't get medals for having kids, and she should know.'

Undaunted by Lily's remark, Evie said dreamily, 'You can be my chief bridesmaid,' then added, 'Matt's got the caravan for next month, so I've got to be on my best behaviour and butter up Corporal.'

'Lucky you. I'm going into Hull. Some Yanks are there. They know how to entertain a girl.'

At one of the staff briefings, the officer mentioned Hitler was sending over V1 Rockets, often referred to as doodle-bugs or flying bombs. 'Mainly targeting London and causing much damage, though some are landing further north. Whether this is intentional or off target, we must not become complacent.' His stern look swept the room. He continued, 'And at all times, be alert. Dismissed.' There was a buzz of voices as everyone began talking at once.

A week passed and there were no sightings of any V1 Rockets bombs in the area. One night, Evie, Lily and Gloria were on duty and the sky appeared calm. Suddenly, Evie angled her ear. She heard it. The whooshing sound and then the stillness, followed by an almighty explosion.

'Bloody hell! That doodlebug was too close for comfort,' Lily yelled over the noise.

'I think it's targeted the nearby Victoria Barracks or one of the air bases,' Evie gasped, feeling the trembling of the earth beneath her booted feet.

Later, someone pushed along a handcart loaded with a huge pan of hot tea and metal mugs, handing them round to the Ack-Ack girls and men on the guns. There was no leaving their post for a quick break tonight. The next rocket could be aimed at their base.

Evie's shift finished without another incident, and after a quick breakfast of porridge, they were in their bunks, hoping to sleep for a few hours. Evie fell on to her bed and closed her eyes, but sleep refused to come. The noise of the rocket still filled her head. She tried reciting a poem by Anne Brontë. 'Because the road is rough and long . . .' But she got no further than the first line, which she kept repeating over and over, until she drifted into an uneasy sleep.

The next week, Lily went on a 24-hour pass to Hull to see a Yank she had met, and Gloria was very quiet, nowhere to be seen. Evie sat alone in a corner of the NAAFI, penning a letter to Matt. Some girls were practising for a sketch to be performed in a concert next month. This was the way officers in charge boosted morale among the Ack-Ack gunners. Their mantra: a happy mind is an alert mind. Evie paused a moment, pen in mid-air, listening to their laughter. She smiled to herself and then continued writing to Matt. She wrote about the flowers she would like in their garden when they married, and in his reply, he would write about his workshop and what he would make for her and their children. Since their last time together, they now wrote about their future life together after the war. For surely it would end soon, by Christmas at the latest. Never did they write about their involvement in the war.

Her heart sang when she received his reply a few days later. 'We can spend time at the caravan now I've secured a 24-hour pass. I've no transport, so will have to hitch a lift. Are you able to do the same?'

As soon as she had secured her pass, she wrote back to him to confirm she was going. When in uniform, hitching a lift was guaranteed, though some farm tractors could be rather smelly. If she was in luck, maybe Lily's Yank would give her another bottle of perfume and she would pass on the dredges of her last one to Evie.

Whenever she had a spare moment, Evie would embroider delicate stitches on her underwear. After seeing American films and the pretty underclothes the stars wore, hers looked drab, and she wanted to add colour and tantalise Matt with her glamorous underwear.

She laughed out loud.

'Boo!' Lily crept up on Evie, making her jump as she sat outside the hut on the grassy bank. 'What were you laughing at?' Evie held up the underskirt she was embroidering. 'Sexy,' Lily replied. 'Why do you want such underwear when you have a job keeping it on?' Evie swished it at her friend, and they both giggled.

Evie continued stitching, thinking how wonderful it was to have Lily and Gloria as friends to confide in.

'What about your Yank? Are you serious or is he just a bit of fun?' She watched as Lily, her head bent, pulled on the tufts of grass, and wondered if it was all over.

Lily flicked away the blades of grass. Then looked up, saying, 'I'm not sure.' She pulled at more grass. Evie waited, wondering. Then Lily spoke again. 'He's amazing to be with. He makes me laugh, and he's a great kisser, but I get these funny fluttering feelings inside of me.' She paused and then blurted out, 'I'm not sure what they mean.'

Evie wanted to laugh, but held herself in check for her friend was serious, and she didn't want to hurt her by being insensitive. Quietly, she said, 'Lily, I think you are in love.'

Relief flooded Lily's face and her eyes shone. 'Is that what it is, love?'

Evie folded her garment and put it in her bag. She rested it on the grass and gave Lily a hug. 'Shall we celebrate with a cup of NAAFI tea and a bun?'

Arm in arm, the two friends walked down the path.

'What are you two so happy about?' Gloria had just come up behind them.

A joyous Lily replied, 'Be careful, it's catching.'

'Wait until I tell you my good news,' teased Gloria.

CHAPTER TWELVE

September 1944

Gloria's news had come as a shock. 'You're moving to London? But it's dangerous there,' Evie and Lily cried in unison.

Gloria laughed, saying, 'I shall miss you both, but London is where the nightlife and the music is. When this war is over, I shall make my home there.'

'But what about your home in Hull?'

Gloria shrugged at the question, then replied, 'I never felt as if I belonged to Hull — or anyone.'

Evie felt sorry that Gloria was moving on. Brought up in an orphanage, Gloria never talked about her life there, except when she'd told them how she was abandoned as a baby with no knowledge of her parents. They wished her luck and gave her a good send-off, a night of fun in the NAAFI, plenty of singing around the piano. She hoped Gloria would find what she was looking for in life.

Now, as Evie jumped down from the tractor, her only thoughts were of Matt. As she hurried along the coastal path, waves crashed on the incoming tide as mist swept in from the North Sea. Despite the inclement weather, nothing could dampen her spirits at the thought of seeing Matt. She quickened her steps, eager to be in his arms and to feel his soft, luscious lips on hers. As she neared the caravan, she expected the door to fly open as he rushed to meet her, but the only sounds were the crashing waves and the plaintive cries of seagulls. Perhaps he was tired and had fallen asleep. She reached out for the door handle and tugged. Locked. Her heart sank. He must have been delayed. She found the key under a stone and opened the door.

Closing the door, the smell of damp and stale smoke hit her and she opened a window to freshen the air. She checked the bed. At least the sheets were clean. Unpacking her bag, she held up her nightgown, admiring the tiny delicate flowers she'd lovingly stitched, then laid it on the bed for Matt to see. She put the picnic food in the cupboard. Matt had said he would bring a couple of bottles of beer and a flask of real coffee. She sat at the window, looking towards the coastal path, watching eagerly for him. As soon as he was in sight, she would jump down the steps and race to greet him. She pictured him swinging her up in his arms and kissing her. Then they would gaze longingly into each other's eyes.

Time passed slowly. She watched the sun travel across the sky to the west. As though she was on duty, trained to observe the smallest movement on land and in the sky, she didn't move. Until the cramp pulled at her leg muscles and she rose stiffly to ease them, never taking her eyes off the target of the path beyond. Like a sentry, she stayed on guard. The sun set and the light faded, and an inky blackness wrapped around the caravan. She strained her eyes, but the path now merged into the darkness.

She opened the door, softly calling his name into the night. 'Matt, Matt, are you out there?' She listened for his answer, which never came. Many scenarios filtered through her mind. Then she berated herself, calling out loud, 'There must be a good reason he hasn't come, and I've no way of communicating with him.'

Then she listened, as if someone would answer this demented woman. But no stars twinkled, and no moon shone, and then, looking in the direction of the sea, she sniffed the tangy air. 'A sea roake,' she muttered, feeling the isolation all around her.

Back inside, she took up her sentry position. After a couple of hours of just staring at blackness, shivering, she stretched and yawned. Undressing, she slipped on her night-gown and climbed into the lonely bed. When Matt comes, he will welcome the warmth of my body, she comforted herself. She lay awake, listening to the night sounds outside, the sea, now receding, becoming fainter, but something stirred, a rus-tling of wind circled the caravan, rattling it, until it gradually became a gentle rocking, like a baby's cradle, lulling her into a fitful sleep.

Suddenly, she woke with a start. She sat up, listening, hearing the wind and rain pelting on the caravan roof. And then she heard a vehicle driving along the pot-holed road. Her heart lifted with joy. It came to a halt outside, and she expected to hear a car door slam and a rush of footsteps to the caravan. But only silence filled the air. She knelt on the bed and lifted the corner of the blackout curtain. Rubbing away the condensation, she peered out to the stationary car. With the rain on the window obscuring her view, she squinted, trying to view the dark figure hunched in the car. Focusing, she could see his RAF uniform, but he faced in the direction of the sea. She watched his still figure and wondered what he was thinking out there in the darkness alone. Maybe he was late because he'd been on a mission. All that mattered to her was that he was here. Impatiently, she was about to throw her jacket on and shove her feet into her shoes, when the vehicle door opened and, head down, the man stepped out.

Her heart sang with joy and happiness as his tall figure dashed for the caravan door and wrenched it open. She was waiting, and the moment he entered, she threw her arms around his neck and snuggled up to him, not caring that he was wet and the dampness clung to her nightgown. They were together in each other's arms. Eager for a kiss, she stood on tiptoe, her lips seeking his.

They were stiff lips, unyielding at first, and then, with a hungry, guttural sound, he let out a sob as his lips crushed hers, his hands clamped to her body, pulling her so close, she felt the buttons on his uniform jacket.

At last, they came up for air. He spoke just one word — 'Sorry' — the word stilted.

She stepped back, wondering what he was upset about. Something must have happened. She turned away to light a candle, saying, 'You need to get out of your wet clothes.' She held up the candle so she could see him.

Shock ran through her body, the candle holder wobbling in her hand as she gasped, 'Richard!'

Quickly, he took the candle from her and placed it on the table. 'Sorry,' he said again.

She stared at him in bewilderment. She tried to form words, but she was finding it difficult to articulate them.

He reached out, took hold of her trembling hands, his face full of sorrow, his eyes wet with tears.

'Oh, no!' she cried, breaking away from him. 'Not Matt. Not Matt.' She screamed, launching herself at Richard, pummelling his chest with her fists.

He stood there and let her, wanting relief for them both.

When she slumped against him, exhausted, her tears dried up and he put an arm around her floppy body. Tenderly, he guided her to the bed and tucked her in. As she curled up on the bed, he sat on a chair and watched her. Eyes drooping shut with tiredness, she was half-aware of Richard kicking off his boots and taking out a small bottle of whisky from his jacket pocket. He drank from the neck of the bottle and lit a cigarette, inhaling deeply.

The last thing she heard before she fell asleep were his muttered words, 'This is a hell of a war.'

Then darkness overtook her.

* * *

Evie woke with a start, feeling for Matt, but he wasn't there. Then she remembered. She lay, reliving what Richard had told her.

'Matt,' she sobbed, burying her face in the pillow. 'No, not my Matt.' She cried until her insides were hollow and the pillow wet with her tears.

She heard a groan and raised herself up on her elbow, saw the slumped body of Richard on the chair that was about to topple over. He and Matt were best buddies, and she guessed he was suffering as well as her.

Quietly, she crept from the bed and went to him, intending to steady his body on the chair, but he fell side-ward into her arms. She looked round, eyes wide, desperate to know what to do with the dead weight of his body. Pulling his arm up round her shoulder, she dragged him over to the bed and dropped him on it. It had taken all her strength and she just flopped on him. After a few seconds, she rolled over to the other side of the bed, thinking she would stay until her breathing became steady. Oddly, she found the warmth from his body comforting and, gradually, she sank into sleep.

Turning on the bed, she felt the heat of him. She slid her arm over his body, relaxing into its warmth. In her drowsy state, she thought she was in bed with Matt, and she must have had a terrible nightmare. She snuggled closer to him, arousing him, and he turned to her, their lips seeking one another's and kissing, their love-making a frenzy. Feeling an ecstasy of joy she hadn't felt before, Evie turned to him, wanting more. Eventually, naked, they fell asleep in each other's arms, their bodies entwined in pleasure.

When she awoke and stretched out her arms to feel Matt near her, he wasn't there. Eyes still full of sleep, she eased herself up on her elbow, the blanket dropping away from her breasts, to see a figure sitting on a chair, watching her. 'Matt.' He didn't speak. She rubbed her eyes with her hand, then gasped. 'Richard!' She stared at him in amazement, and said, 'What are you doing here? Where is Matt?' She reached up to look out of the window, forgetting she was naked, the blanket sliding down her body.

The sky was untarnished by the day to come. And then she saw the RAF vehicle. She gasped, as the terrible realisation that Matt wasn't coming back to her struck her, and she screamed, an awful haunting noise of an animal in pain.

She felt strong arms wrap a blanket around her and enfold her close while she sobbed her heart out.

After an eternity, she sniffled and Richard handed her his handkerchief, saying, 'You get dressed and I will take you back to your camp.'

He went outside to wait. She watched him through the window, smelling his tobacco as he drew on a cigarette, then he walked to the cliff top and stared out at the sea.

Now dressed and in the van and on the road, she sat next to him in the passenger seat, neither of them talking; nor did they mention what had happened between them. In her delusion, she'd thought he was Matt. Matt! She bit back a choking sob and turned to look out of the van window, seeing nothing. If she closed her eyes, it brought back the scenario of the night before. Making love with Richard when it should have been Matt. How could she have done it? She would never forgive herself, never.

Richard lit a cigarette and passed her one, their eyes not meeting and neither one speaking.

On reaching the sentry on guard at the camp entrance, Richard was about to seek permission to take her right in, but she laid her hand on his arm, saying, 'Thank you, this is fine.' She looked into his eyes and saw his sorrow. But she had no words to comfort him. Silently, she climbed from the van, hauled out her bag, and without a backward glance, she walked away, conscious of his eyes following her.

Thankfully, she didn't meet anyone who would ask her questions about her leave. In the hut, she unpacked and went along to the ablution block, washing her whole body down in cold water, trying to erase the memory of the night of passion spent with Richard, but it kept invading her mind.

Why had she allowed it? Surely, she should have known it wasn't Matt. 'Matt,' she sobbed his name out loud. They were going to marry and share the rest of their lives together. Have children, be a family. Now all their hopes for the future had been so cruelly snatched away. Devastated, she called out, 'Matt, oh Matt,' falling to a heap on the cold stone floor.

CHAPTER THIRTEEN

September 1944

From a distance, Evie heard her name being called and felt someone shaking her, but she couldn't summon the strength to rouse herself. Then a sensation of being bodily lifted filled her, and then nothing.

She opened her eyes and a feeling of confusion swamped her as she stared up at the dark ceiling. Inching her head round slightly, she saw a table and a night light giving off a faint glow. She didn't recognise where she was. Panic gripped her, and she struggled to sit up. A shadow flitted across her vision, and a hand eased her back down on to the bed.

A kind voice said, 'You are awake.'

Evie focused her eyes and saw a nursing orderly. 'Where am I?'

'Hospital ward. They found you in the ablution block, where you had fainted,' the orderly explained as she checked Evie's blood pressure. 'Do you know what happened and why?'

For a fleeting moment, her mind went blank, and then the pain of grief gripped her heart. 'Matt, Matt,' she cried, trying to get out of the bed. 'I must find Matt.' Great gulps of sobs escaped her lips. 'He can't be dead. Not Matt.' She struggled as strong arms held her close. Then her body went into freefall.

After what seemed an eternity, Evie stopped sobbing, drained of all feelings.

'Drink this.' The orderly held a glass of water to Evie's lips. 'When did you last eat?'

Evie thought, but couldn't remember when, and whispered, 'Not for some time.'

The nurse signalled to another staff member and, five minutes later, an orderly placed a tray with hot buttered toast and tea on the bedside locker. 'You will feel better when you've eaten.'

She felt a little better when she'd finished eating and drinking, and she lay back on the pillow and slept.

A few hours later, she opened her eyes to see the corporal sitting by her bedside. Evie wanted to slide down into the bed and cover her face. Was she in for a rollicking? She waited for the corporal's brash voice to ring in her ears.

'How are you feeling, Sinclair?' The corporal's voice was low and modulated. Surprise must have registered on Evie's face, for the corporal smiled. 'I can be nice when the situation warrants it. It worried me when I found you in a heap, out cold on the ablution block floor.'

Evie's eyes widened. 'You found me.'

She nodded and said, 'Apparently, the RAF officer who brought you back to camp told the sentry on duty, who reported to his superior, that your fiancé was killed on a mission, and he was concerned about you.'

At the mention of Matt's death, Evie's eyes filled with tears.

The corporal continued speaking. 'I have arranged for you to have two weeks' compassionate leave, transport to take you home, and we have informed your parents.' She rose to her feet, saying, 'Take care, Sinclair. We need you here.'

Evie stared after the departing figure of the corporal, thankful for her kindness and care.

Later, Lily came to visit her, carrying Evie's suitcase. By now, Evie was up and dressed and sitting by her bed. Lily hugged her friend, saying, 'I'm so sorry, Evie.' She hugged her again. 'Do you want to talk about it?'

Evie shook her head, not able to find any words.

So Lily prattled on with tales of gossip. 'And fancy old McDonald turning up trumps. I've packed all your belongings in the case and the photo of Matt.' After half an hour, running out of chatter, Lily left. Evie sat with her eyes closed, trying not to think that she would never see Matt again.

Seated in the rear of the car, Evie kept her eyes closed, not wanting to talk. Arriving at her parents' house, she alighted from the car and thanked the ATS driver. For a few moments she stood forlorn, staring up at the house. Then, on an impulse, she left her case on the step and walked around the house to the lake. She stood, breathing in the tranquil air and watched a water hen move silently among the reeds. Weariness engulfed her, and she sat down on the tufty grass, looking towards where her old rowing boat was moored. At the first opportunity, she would row out on the lake. She closed her eyes, and a shiver ran through her. Rising to her feet and brushing grass off her skirt, she turned to the house. She noticed the peeling paint of the window frames and a few loose tiles on the roof. An air of neglect surrounded the house. She wondered if her parents were coping, running this big house and gardens. Mentally shaking herself, she returned to the front of the house and went indoors.

In the hall, she could hear the wireless coming from the kitchen. Leaving her case at the foot of the stairs, she took a deep breath and opened the door. Her mother was seated at the table preparing vegetables and, on seeing Evie, tears welled in her eyes. Thinking her mother was upset because of Matt's death, she felt touched and tears filled her own eyes. Going to Florence's side, she kissed her mother on the cheek, saying, 'It's a devastating shock for me. I miss him so much.'

Florence's body shot away from Evie, her voice odd. 'What do you mean, you'll miss him? He's asleep in the sitting room.'

Evie stared at her mother, thinking she had gone mad, and then she understood. 'I was talking about Matt,' she said, trying, unsuccessfully, to keep the hurt out of her voice.

Ignoring her daughter's sorrow, Florence carried on. 'You father hasn't been himself lately. How will I cope if anything happens to him?' She dabbed her eyes with her pretty lace handkerchief.

Evie turned away, wanting to scream. Instead, she filled the kettle to make a pot of tea.

She carried the tea tray into the sitting room, where her mother was already with Gerald. On seeing Evie, his face broke out in a smile. 'My darling girl, how are you? Matthew was such a fine young man.' His face crumpled with weariness as he muttered, 'War has taken far too many lives.'

She set the tray on the small table and instinctively went to her father to hug him, wanting to feel the security of his arms around her. He rose to his feet and she snuggled against him, comforted by his love and warmth, the familiar smell of his pipe tobacco and old tweed jacket mixed with her tears.

Florence poured the tea, sniffing her disapproval as she did so.

Thankfully, Evie sank down on the comfortable sofa, wanting to close her eyes and forget the terrible nightmare of losing Matt. She only half listened to her mother prattling on about something that happened at one of her meetings.

'Tomorrow, Evie, you can come and help.' Evie stared at her mother, not having any idea what she was talking about. 'When—' Her mother was about to speak when Gerald's voice cut in.

'Florence! Let the girl be. She is here to rest. To recuperate from her loss.'

'Well!' Florence blundered.

Evie jumped up, saying, 'Please excuse me, I need to rest.' And she fled from the room.

Once in her room, she fell on to her bed and sobbed until her body ached with the pain. 'Matt, Matt,' she whispered. 'Why did you have to die when we had so much to look forward to? A whole life together.' Now only a life of emptiness, she thought bitterly.

She slept fitfully, vaguely aware of someone covering her weary body with a blanket and kissing her forehead.

When she awoke, it was to a dawn chorus of birds in the tree outside her window. For a while she listened, wishing she was a bird so she could fly free from the carnage of war.

She crept along the corridor to the ancient bathroom, thankful that the water was hot, and filled the bathtub with the five-inch regulation. She didn't linger, not wanting to see her mother. Hastily dressing in a skirt, blouse and cardigan, she went downstairs to the back porch and pulled on a pair of wellington boots. Outside, the air was fresh and invigorating and she strode towards the path around the lake.

Trying not to think sad thoughts, she took in the glimmering lake in the early morning sunshine. The bulrushes were tall and splendid as they guarded the lake, and the aromatic scent of the frothy meadowsweet filled her nostrils. Walking on, she came to overgrown bushes and trees, which formed an ethereal overhead canopy, reminding her of a cathedral she had once visited.

As she circled the lake, she stopped in front of the gap in the bushes and viewed the house. The house which didn't feel like home anymore. Her mind was in a whirl, unsure what to do next. She stared down at the lake, as the early morning sunlight caught it and the tiny ripples of water looked like fairies dancing. Mesmerised, she watched the graceful movements and gradually the whirling in her head diminished and cleared.

Slowly, her feet moved forward, her footsteps lighter, and she knew what she was going to do. She strode on.

In the kitchen sink were the dirty dishes from last night, so she set to and washed them. And glancing round, she noticed how unkempt the kitchen looked since young Maggie had left. Her mother wasn't used to housework and needed help. Having tidied the kitchen, Evie made breakfast, first taking a tray of tea and toast up to her parents' bedroom.

Florence was sitting up in bed and glanced in surprise as Evie set the tray on the bedside table, first moving the book. Evie glanced at the title, *Jane Eyre*.

Seeing her daughter looking, Florence said, 'I borrowed it from your room. Reading helps me sleep at night.'

At the sound of voices, Gerald stirred and sat up. On seeing the breakfast tray, he said, 'This is a lovely surprise.'

Back in the kitchen, Evie ate a solitary breakfast. She knew neither of them would leave the large house, though Gerald liked the company of military personnel who stayed for temporary spells of time. She tidied the kitchen, listening to music on the wireless, finding it therapeutic.

When her mother came downstairs and into the kitchen, Evie suggested, 'Mother, you go to your meeting and I will cook a meal for later.'

'Oh, well. If you say so.' And off she went, much to Evie's relief.

Gerald was involved with the home guard and the wardens. Evie was never sure what he did, but she suspected his meetings and activities kept him from being at Florence's beck and call.

Evie wandered from room to room with her brush, pan and duster. She was suddenly caught off guard as she remembered something Matt had said to her. She dissolved into tears, and was so glad no one was around. For a few moments, she stared out of the window until she felt able to carry on.

She found a tin of steak, flour and a lump of lard in the pantry. In the vegetable rack were only a few potatoes and an onion. Outside in the vegetable plot, she lifted carrots and a cabbage.

Evie sieved the flour and fat through her fingers, finding the movements calming, and she felt able to think of Matt without bursting into tears. She relived their cherished time together, the way he touched her cheek and stroked her hair, letting it run through his fingers. Holding hands, running along the cliff top without a care in the world. And making love beneath the blue sky, with the sun warm on their bodies.

Suddenly, she stopped what she was doing. Another memory intruded into her mind. Richard. She wanted to banish it. Erase it from her memory, but it continued to linger.

'Something smells good,' Gerald announced as he entered the kitchen. Evie was just lifting the huge steak and potato pie from the oven. 'Are we expecting guests?'

Placing the pie on the countertop, Evie said, 'No, it's for this evening's meal, and the rest for you and Mother for another day.'

'And you?' he asked enquiringly. She sat down at the table and Gerald sat opposite her. 'Tell me, love, what's on your mind?'

Evie gathered her thoughts and then spoke. 'I'm going to see Matt's parents in a couple of days. I've written to them.' She pointed to the letter on the dresser. 'I need to catch the post.'

They heard the front door opening, and Florence call out.

'You slip out the back door. I'll tell Florence your plans.'

'Thanks, Dad.' She kissed him quickly on the cheek, picked up the letter and was gone.

Two days later, she was sitting on a crowded train on her way to Matt's parents' home, with their letter of welcome in her bag.

CHAPTER FOURTEEN

October 1944

Matt's mother hugged Evie warmly. 'Welcome, my love,' she whispered.

Overwhelmed by the greeting of this lovely, warm-hearted woman, compared to her mother's lack of compassion, it took all of Evie's resolve not to dissolve into tears.

'Sit down, Evie.' Mrs Goodwin ushered her to a chair by the window, which overlooked the dale beyond. 'Would you like tea, or something stronger?'

Evie pulled her handkerchief from the pocket of her dress and blew her nose. 'Tea would be fine,' she sniffed. Mrs Goodwin went through to the kitchen. Feeling restless, Evie stood up and gazed out of the window. The farm stood in an elevated position overlooking the village, and behind it the Wharfedale rose skywards, and beyond a vast ravine from the Ice Age. She thought of Matt, who would never walk the dale again, his boyhood joy. Now, his manhood had been so cruelly snatched away, denying him that joy. A lump rose in her throat and she wanted to scream, but she covered her mouth with her hands, trying to breathe slowly to ward off the panic within her.

The door handle rattled and, on auto-pilot, she opened the door for Mrs Goodwin to enter carrying a tea tray. Neither woman spoke. It wasn't the time for niceties.

Evie felt comforted by the warm liquid and held the cup. Her stomach gurgled ungraciously, and she remembered she hadn't eaten today. She watched Mrs Goodwin cut a slice of the bread, still warm from the oven. Its delicious aroma made her stomach gurgle again.

Mrs Goodwin spread farm butter on the bread, placed it on a plate and handed it to Evie, saying, 'My dear, you need sustenance. You still have a war to win. And I need to discuss a matter with you.'

Evie glanced at the older woman and saw the sorrow etched on her face.

Mrs Goodwin fetched a fresh pot of tea. 'Tea helps me,' she said simply. Then, after a few minutes, she cleared her throat. She sat facing Evie, but directed her gaze to the window and the dale beyond, speaking in a soft voice. 'Our Matt's death was devastating news, though deep down, I expected it. This meaningless war has killed so many pilots, young men with their lives before them.' She paused, and Evie saw the tears welling in her eyes. Composed, she continued, 'What I didn't expect . . .' Her voice faltered again, and she lowered her eyes to stare at her hands in her lap.

Evie's heart missed a beat, and instinctively she went to Mrs Goodwin and knelt by the side of her chair. Her voice gentle, she asked, 'What is it?'

Mrs Goodwin lifted her head, looked into Evie's concerned face and said, her voice quivering, 'We don't have his body to bury.'

'Where is it?'

Mrs Goodwin looked up towards the window and the sky beyond.

Evie gasped, her hands covering her mouth, her eyes wild with the realisation. She placed her head on Mrs Goodwin's lap and sobbed, letting her grief and bewilderment take over. She felt Mrs Goodwin's fingers twist through her hair. Just like Matt used to do. Tears swamped her, and she felt as though she was drowning.

'Let me help you up,' said the quiet voice of Beth, Matt's sister, who guided Evie to the settee. Once sitting down, Beth said, 'Now drink this.' And Evie felt brandy run hot down her throat. Beth lit two cigarettes and passed one to her. The brandy and the nicotine slowed Evie's fast heartbeat down.

Evie glanced round the room. 'Where's your mother?'

'Gone to lie down. It's hard for her, for us all. It's the not having Matt's body to bury that has hit her hard. We are having a memorial service for him, and I am glad you are here.'

'When is it?'

'The day after tomorrow.' Evie nodded in response, not trusting herself to speak.

'Come, I'll show you up to your room. You can have a rest before the evening meal.'

'I'll help.'

'No, Amy will help.'

Up in her room, Evie unpacked her clothes, putting her underwear in the dressing-table drawer and hanging up her clean blouses and spare skirt in the wardrobe. In the bathroom, she freshened up, washing her tear-stained face and combing her tangle of hair, leaving it loose.

The evening meal was a quiet affair and everyone retired to bed early. For that, Evie felt grateful.

She slept until seven in the morning. Not wanting to linger and start thinking, she slipped from the bed. She opened the curtains to see the dale beckoning to her. Hastily, she dressed, and quietly, not to disturb anyone, went down the stairs and pulled on a pair of wellington boots from the many in the back porch. She went outside and stood for a moment, letting the gentle morning breeze play on her face. Then she set off, away from the farm to climb the hill. The healing power of solitude accompanied her as she breathed in the unpolluted air. No smell or noise from the Ack-Ack guns, the war a distant part of the universe. War, she believed, served no purpose other than aiding those that wanted power, but in the end, they didn't win. She felt sure Hitler would suffer defeat.

Up on the hillside, she found a smooth boulder to sit on. Here, she could see for miles and enjoy the beauty of nature. She tried to empty her mind of sadness but she couldn't completely.

Soon her thoughts drifted back to the last time she and Matt had been together at the caravan on the cliff top. A memory to treasure of that idyllic time they'd spent together. She closed her eyes, her thoughts drifting back. She could hear his voice clearly as they made plans for their future together after the war. A surge of guilt gripped her. How she wished she had agreed to marry Matt when he'd asked her instead of saying she wanted to wait until after the war.

'Why did I do that?' she shouted out to a bird flying overhead. 'Matt, forgive me. I was such a fool.' An unknown voice in her head said, 'You would have been a widow.' Quickly, she glanced round, expecting to see someone standing close by, speaking those words. Her only companion was the breeze rustling by, blowing her hair. She shaded her eyes against the sun, looking down the dale to the farm below, seeing dots of movement. She found solace in the dale's solitude and was content to stay here, to grieve alone for Matt, but that wouldn't be fair to his family. They had lost a son, a brother and an uncle.

She climbed down from the rock and made her way to the farm below.

In the farmyard, she came face to face with Mr Goodwin. She looked into his eyes, so like Matt's, and gulped back her tears, trying to stay strong.

'How do, lass.' He set down the pail he was carrying, lifted his cap, and scratched his thinning grey hair. 'Our Matthew was a brave man. All he wanted to do was fly, ever since he was a youngster.' He paused, trying to keep his emotions hidden, before continuing. 'Aye, last time he came home on leave, we had a beer together in the pub, and he told me then that so many of his comrades had died.' He stopped talking and Evie saw the raw emotion in his eyes.

Just then, Mrs Goodwin called, 'Breakfast is ready.'

They were all subdued as they sat round the table. The atmosphere hung sombre, and Evie kept her eyes on her plate. After the meal, Evie offered, 'I'll do the dishes and tidy the kitchen.'

Mrs Goodwin began, 'I couldn't possibly let you. You're a—'

Evie cut in, 'I'd rather be busy.' Or alone up the dale, she thought.

'I'll feed the hens,' said Mrs Goodwin.

Beth and Amy had gone into the village for groceries, to prepare for Matt's wake.

Evie felt humble as she cleared the table and wiped down the oil tablecloth and the work surfaces. Then she washed the dishes in the stone sink and left them on the draining board while she scoured the pans thoroughly. She recalled one of the Ack-Ack girls telling her that, at the beginning of the war, the government had asked for pans to help build war machines. Her mother hadn't surrendered her pans, but they had taken the iron gates leading to the house.

That afternoon, Evie helped Beth and Amy with the preparation for the wake while Mrs Goodwin had a lie down. They made savoury pies of rabbit, vegetables, and sausage meat with sage. Apple pies, curd cheese cakes and a pile of freshly cooked ham sandwiches were covered with damp tea-cloths and put into the cool pantry along with cheese and biscuits. 'Dad's got a keg of beer and we have Mam's home-made wine,' said Beth.

Amy, who had been quiet, blurted, 'We're giving our Matt a good send-off.' Then she burst into tears and ran from the kitchen.

Beth put a restraining hand on Evie's arm as she made to follow Amy. 'No, let her cry. She needs to cry. She has been bottling it up.'

Evie stood helplessly, not sure what to do.

Taking command of the situation, Beth said, 'We'll go in the sitting room and take a look at old photos of Matt when he was a young lad.'

Once in the sitting room, full of comfy chairs and sofas, Beth opened a sideboard cupboard, took out a shoebox and a pile of photo albums and placed them on the low table in front of the sofa where they sat.

Evie held the black-and-white photo of Matt as a young boy, about two, sitting on his dad's shoulders. Then a photo of Matt sitting on a tractor age seven, his thin legs dangling from the seat, his arms outstretched, touching the steering wheel. Tears sprang to Evie's eyes when she picked up a photo of Matt standing next to a glider, seeing the shining joy on his face, and guessed that was when he first discovered his love of flying. 'At least he did what he loved best, flying,' she whispered. She looked at the marvellous array of photographs portraying Matt's life and an idea sprang into her mind. 'Beth, can we make a collage of the photos?'

'Yes, what a lovely idea. It will please Mam.'

And so the two women, who both loved Matt in their own ways, set about pinning his photos on to a large piece of cork board salvaged from the barn. They worked tirelessly until they'd filled every space with Matt.

Later, when Mrs Goodwin came downstairs after her rest, and Amy too, both looked much perkier when they saw the collage of their beloved Matthew. It held pride of place on the sideboard.

'It can come with us to church,' declared Mr Goodwin, who had entered the room.

Beth went home to be with her own family. Tomorrow, Mr Goodwin would drive himself and his wife to church and take the collage with them. Everyone else would meet up in the village and walk to the church in Linton.

Supper was a quiet affair, the wireless on, and they listened to the nine o'clock news. 'Them Nazis are still holding on,' commented Mr Goodwin, then reached to turn it off.

Evie rose, about to clear the table, when Mrs Goodwin said, 'You have an early night, love. We'll tidy up.'

'If you're sure.' She looked at their faces, and guessed they had things to talk about.

She lay awake a long time before sleep came.

Waking up early in the morning, she thought about going up to the top of the dale, but it didn't seem the right thing to do. She brushed her uniform and polished her shoes, and sat on the bed for a while, hearing voices below. She glanced in the mirror. 'My face looks pale,' she whispered to herself, wishing she had some of Lily's rouge. For a moment, she wondered how they were faring back at camp.

Tom, Matt's brother, had arrived home late last night and was downstairs. Evie nodded to him because she was unsure what to say. When they were ready to leave the house, Tom fell into step with her.

Villagers streamed from their homes to pay their respects to the bereaved family. Men doffed their caps and women and children stood silent, heads bowed. Down the lane, the mourners trod across the old stone pack bridge and turned left to walk the path leading to the church.

They entered the full church and walked down the aisle to the front pews.

Evie sat in the second pew next to a man in RAF uniform. As they rose to sing, Evie's body shook and the hymn book fell from her hands. The RAF man bent down to retrieve it and handed it to her. She turned to thank him and looked into the face of Richard.

CHAPTER FIFTEEN

October 1944

Evie felt shock ripple through her body, her hands trembling as she held the hymn book. Richard was the last person she'd expected to see. Yet why would she think that when he was Matt's best friend? The words of the hymn sounded hollow in her head, and she forced herself to concentrate. She was here for Matt and only he deserved her thoughts. She sang for him, picturing his loving face in her mind.

Tom delivered his eulogy eloquently, about Matt as a boy growing up and loving life, and his ambitions to fly. Tears filled Evie's eyes and she bit on her lip to stop the sobs escaping. They stood to sing another hymn. When it ended, she was about to sit down when Richard said to her, 'Excuse me.' She watched him walk to the front and stand tall.

'Matt was my best friend, like the brother I never had. I miss him terribly. We began training together at the very beginning of the war. Both pilots, we shared our difficulties, enjoyed a glass of ale together, and laughter. On that fateful day, because of a shoulder injury, they grounded me.' His voice broke, and Evie could see tears sparkling in his eyes. Then he lifted his gaze upwards and continued. 'That is my biggest regret.' He stood, silent for a moment, and then said, 'What can I tell you? Matt's greatest joy, after flying, was his girlfriend Evie, who he adored and talked about constantly.'

When Richard returned to his seat, Evie felt the tremble in his body as he brushed past her. As he sat down, she instinctively reached for his hand and held it, to comfort him, and herself.

After the service, Richard caught up with Evie. Silently, they strolled side by side. And then he said, 'I wasn't sure if you could make it.'

She glanced at him, seeing the raw sadness in his face, and whispered, 'Your eulogy for Matt was beautiful, thank you.' Her foot slipped on a cobblestone and he took hold of her arm to steady her. 'I miss him so much it hurts,' she whispered.

'He's left a great void in my heart, too.' Gently, he squeezed her arm, and it felt comforting.

When they arrived back at the farmhouse, Evie went into the kitchen to help Beth. She glanced at Evie and said, 'I've told Mam to stay and talk to our guests. We can manage.'

Evie made a big pot of tea to distract her from her grief. She handed round endless cups of tea and plates of ham sandwiches. People were very compassionate and told her about Matt in his younger days.

'Yer a bonny lass, I'll say that for yer. Matt always had good taste,' said a neighbouring farmer.

Evie looked into his grey, rheumy eyes and saw deep sadness. Not just for Matt, she guessed. 'That's kind of you,' she said, sitting by his side on the vacant chair. 'Matt loved flying, the freedom of being up in the sky.'

'Aye, damned war does no good. My Henry, he loved the sea and served on minesweepers until . . .' His eyes filled with tears and he fiddled in the top pocket of his jacket, bringing out his pipe. Evie watched his deft fingers fill the pipe and then light it.

'Glass of ale, Bert.' It was Matt's father with two glasses in his hands.

Quickly, Evie sprang to her feet and offered him her seat. She wandered back to the kitchen with a full tray of dirty crockery to wash and keep her busy. Richard was near the window, lighting a cigarette.

He turned when she entered and took the heavy tray from her, offering her a cigarette. She felt the tremble in his hand as he lit it for her. 'Shall we sit on the bench outside?' she said.

Both looked up the dale to the hill, absorbed in their thoughts.

Suddenly Richard said, 'Would you walk with me up the hill? I want to see where Matt roamed as a young boy. He often spoke about the wild countryside here.'

As they began their climb up the hill, Evie felt the sensation of Matt walking with them.

When they reached the top, they sat on the same boulder Evie had sat on yesterday. She closed her eyes, letting the peacefulness of the dale filter into her very being, glad that Richard didn't talk. For a while, her mind was empty, and then the inevitable thought, never far away, came. The night she'd thought and wanted Richard to be Matt. The sense of guilt filled her. What must Richard think of her?

She opened her eyes, gazing down the dale to where she could see the rooftops of cottages. Smoke curled upwards from the chimney pots and she pictured cosy family scenes, something she and Matt would never have. Her eyes brimmed with tears. If only she had married Matt. They could have been together, sitting by their own fireside.

Suddenly, Richard moved, and she turned to see him looking at his watch. He jumped down from the boulder, saying, 'I have a train to catch.'

'You're not staying over?'

'No, have to be back at base.'

Not talking, they began their descent. Before they reached the farmhouse, Richard said, 'Evie, I have some personal things that Matt left for you. They are in my bag.'

He went to retrieve his bag and Evie sat down on the bench, shivering as the sun disappeared and the temperature dropped. In a few minutes, Richard returned. He handed her a small brown paper parcel. She looked up into his sad eyes. 'Thank you,' she whispered, her heart leaden with pain.

Suddenly he took hold of her free hand and said, 'You take care, Evie.'

And the words slipped out, 'I'll see you again?' she asked.

He looked away from her as he answered. 'No, I am being transferred down south.'

And then he was gone.

'That those I care about slip away' flashed in her mind. She went into the kitchen and busied herself with washing the dishes and tidying up.

Later, when the guests had departed, Evie went into the sitting room. Beth and her family were ready to go home. Mr Goodwin was out seeing to the livestock. She looked round for Mrs Goodwin.

'Gone for a lie down,' Amy said. 'I'll see if she wants a cup of tea.'

Up in her room, Evie sat on the bed, holding the small brown paper parcel in her hands, wondering what was inside. She stared at it for a long time until she found the courage to open it. Carefully undoing the string which held it together, she unwrapped the paper and saw a small blue velvet box and a letter addressed to her in Matt's handwriting. With trembling fingers, she opened the envelope to reveal one sheet of writing paper. Her eyes filled with tears as she read.

My darling Evie,

You are reading this letter because I have gone to that great place in the sky. Next to you, I lived to fly. I loved you with all my heart and now our future together is not to be. To have known and loved you was the best joy in my life. You brought me great happiness. Think of me often and remember those cherished moments of the time we shared.

Goodbye, my adorable Evie. Matt xx

Tears streamed from her eyes, falling on the letter as she read it repeatedly. Sitting still, she thought of Matt and those cherished moments they'd spent together, now forever locked in her heart.

She sat for a long time before opening the blue velvet box. Slowly, she lifted the lid and gasped in surprise, for nestled on a bed of satin lay a gold ring with an opal stone.

'Oh, God, Matt!' she cried. She'd never known about this ring. He must have bought it when he asked her to marry him. And she'd wanted to wait until the war finished. 'Oh, Matt, I was such a fool.' She didn't cry anymore because she felt all dried up and consumed with guilt.

The next morning, Evie said goodbye to the Goodwin family. They didn't mention staying in touch at all, and neither did she, because of the guilt she felt deep within her soul. For them, she guessed, it was because she would always remind them of the son they'd lost.

She got a lift back to the station. Work would give some meaning to her life. Fill the empty void, ease the ache in her heart, and lessen the guilt. Though, truthfully, none of it really would. But then, what option did she have? On the train journey, Evie huddled on a seat in a corner, wrapping herself in misery and guilt.

Arriving at Beverley Station, she walked back to camp, needing the quiet time to process her thoughts in preparation for the questions and sympathy sure to come from her fellow Ack-Ack gunner girls. Walking along Highgate, she passed a group of young lads on the lookout for a bit of fun. They followed her, mimicking her marching step.

Suddenly, she turned on them, and in her most professional voice, she barked at them, 'You are out of step! Attention!' To her amazement, they stopped and stood perfectly still. She walked round them and said, 'Stand in one straight line.' The lads shuffled about until they formed a line. 'Now, put your left foot forward.' As they did so, two of the lads giggled. 'Quiet!' she called out. She walked around them again. 'Now, right foot.' One of them slipped on the cobblestones, but one look from her and no one laughed. They did this exercise a few times, gathering quite an audience. 'Now!' she barked, a twinkle in her eyes. They stood at attention. 'Eyes front,' she ordered. Satisfied they were all correct, she said, 'You can follow me as far as the Minster. Then I must report to camp.' Dutifully, they followed her, marching in step. When they reached their endpoint, they stopped. She turned and saluted them, surprised to see the look of achievement glowing on the boys' faces.

Walking down Keldgate, her steps felt a little lighter, and so did she.

After reporting to the officer in charge, she went to her hut, thankful to find it empty. She unpacked her case and sat on the bed to gaze at the beautiful ring, Matt's last gift to her. She slipped it on to her wedding finger, but it didn't seem right without the gold band of a wedding ring. Back home, she had a gold chain, and she would wear the ring on it, round her neck, as a loving keepsake in memory of Matt. Tears flowed unheeded and her heart ached with the loss of him and of their shared plans for the future. Suddenly she heard distant voices, and quickly put the velvet blue box, holding the precious ring, in her locker. She picked up her wash bag and hurried to the ablution block before anyone could see her.

'Evie, you're back!' Lily greeted her with a hug when she returned to the hut. 'How were things?' she asked quietly. The other girls discreetly kept their distance.

Evie told her friend about the lovely memorial service for Matt, attended by family, friends and a lot of the villagers. 'Tom, his brother, read a eulogy, and so did Richard.'

'Rich, how is he?' Lily asked.

'Upset, as you can imagine. He was Matt's best friend and misses him. And he feels bad because they grounded him on that mission so he didn't fly.'

'I'll cheer him up,' Lily said, bouncing off the bed.

'He's being transferred down south.'

'Well, goodbye to that romance.'

Evie turned away from her friend, feeling guilty for having slept with Richard. Truthfully, until that moment, she hadn't given Lily's feelings a thought.

Then Lily jabbered on, 'Just as well I've got my GI.'

Evie glanced at her friend. 'Your heart's not broken, then?'

'No fear. Love 'em and leave 'em, is my motto. Though Georgio is hot.' She giggled.

And Evie sighed with relief.

CHAPTER SIXTEEN

November–December 1944

The war raged on, and Evie, along with her comrades, was busy at her post. She wrote dutiful letters to her parents, and it was her mother who wrote back. She complained about how much she had to do, although in her last letter she mentioned, 'Your father isn't any help. He's always falling asleep, it's so annoying . . .'

Worried about her father's health, Evie contacted the family doctor, who agreed to see Gerald. The doctor wrote back to Evie. Her father had suffered another heart attack. Shocked by this news, she felt queasy. Her dear father was ill again. She shuddered and hoped it was a mild attack. She must see him.

Standing before the officer, Evie felt relief when he granted her four days' compassionate leave to check on her father. Not wanting to waste time, she hitched a couple of lifts, something she didn't normally do. On arriving home, she dashed upstairs to see her father, who was resting in bed.

His ashen-coloured face lit up when he saw her.

'Dad,' she cried, and kissed him gently on the cheek. 'How are you feeling now?' she asked, taking hold of his hand.

His voice trembled as he replied, 'The medication the doctor prescribed me seems to do the trick.' He tried to inject a lighter note into his voice, but failed as he continued, 'I'm relieved of my war duties, but I hope to go back.'

'Oh, Dad. The war's nearly over,' she said too brightly. 'You've done your lot.'

He smiled weakly at her, and said, 'It's your mother I'm worried about. I don't think she's coping.'

After making her father comfortable to settle down to sleep, she went in search of her mother.

She found Florence in the sitting room, sat staring into space. On seeing Evie, she greeted her with the words, 'You have to come home for good. This is too much for me.'

Wasting no time, Evie donned her outdoor coat and headed down to the post office to place an advertisement for a housekeeper. Then she headed off to Jim's house to ask him to round up pals of her father's and put a rota in place to visit him.

'I reckon he needs to be downstairs again,' said Jim. Then, on seeing Evie's face drop, he continued. 'Don't you worry about that, lass, I'll see to it. We'll make Gerald comfortable.'

Evie dashed back to Island House. By now dusk was approaching and, when she arrived, the house was in darkness. Switching on the staircase light, she ran up the stairs to her father. She stood in the open doorway and could see he still slept. She tiptoed over to the bedside and listened to his erratic breathing, thankful that the doctor was coming in the morning. Downstairs, she peeped into the sitting room where her mother was still sitting, omitting gentle snores.

Feeling weary, she went to the kitchen to make a cup of tea. She poked life into the fire and put on a log, settling down on the rocking chair. Only then did she let her thoughts dwell upon herself. She had noticed herself feeling queasy over the last month or two and she couldn't ignore it for much longer. She would see the doctor here because she didn't feel comfortable seeing the medic on camp.

The next morning, Evie was in the kitchen preparing breakfast. A knock sounded on the back door. Opening the door, Evie saw a middle-aged woman with a pleasant round face and grey hair showing from beneath her hat.

The woman spoke. 'I'm Mrs Mabel Jenkins. I've come about the advert for a housekeeper.'

Evie opened the door wider, saying, 'Come in, please.' Mrs Jenkins glanced around the kitchen. Evie hadn't noticed how untidy it was, with crockery and utensils not put away and a couple of dirty teacloths on the backs of chairs.

Seated opposite each other at the kitchen table, Mrs Jenkins explained, 'I'm a widow and my family are all leading their own lives now so I'm free to lead mine. And the job you advertised will suit me fine, if you like me.'

Although she did like Mabel on sight, Evie needed a little more time to process her thoughts. 'I will make a pot of tea and we can talk.'

Glancing out of the kitchen window at the lake beyond, it seemed to beckon her and she yearned to be out there walking by it. Bringing the fresh pot of tea to the table, it surprised her to find that Mabel was studying her.

Evie poured the tea and Mabel asked, 'What do you want me to do besides cooking and cleaning? You have a laundry room that is handy for drying clothes indoors.'

A capable woman, was Evie's immediate thought. 'Would you like to see the house first?'

'Aye, lass. Sorry — Miss Sinclair.'

Evie laughed. 'Call me Evie, please.'

Florence was in Gerald's room, reading to him. 'My father's room,' Evie said, not opening the door to disturb them. Along the corridor, she said, 'This is the sitting room.' She opened a door to a room with comfy sofas, a bookcase, an occasional table and, by the fireside chair, her mother's knitting basket. The heavy curtained windows looked to the front of the house and down the lane. The dining room was next to the kitchen and looked across the lake. 'We rarely use this room, though occasionally the billeted officers use it for meetings, and they also have two rooms upstairs.' After a tour of the bedrooms, they went downstairs.

In the kitchen, Evie asked the silent Mabel, 'Could you manage the house?' She wondered if the size of it had put her off. Just then, Florence shouted Evie's name with a request for tea. 'We will talk more after I see to this.'

Evie made tea in the china pot and set out the matching cups and a plate of biscuits, then whisked it away to her parents.

Her father looked tired, but he seemed happy that Florence was giving him her attention. Evie stayed for a few minutes, chatting about the book her mother was reading. *John Halifax, Gentleman* by Mrs Craik, one of her father's favourites. Then she hurried back to the kitchen.

A joyful surprise awaited her, for the kitchen was now tidy. 'Mabel, how kind of you.'

Mabel smiled, enjoying her moment. 'I would like to take the job, miss, if you approve.'

Evie could have hugged her, but restrained herself. 'Excellent, that's a weight off my mind.' She knew she could return to camp and not worry about her parents.

The next morning, Evie felt queasy, but by the time Mabel arrived at 8 a.m. to prepare breakfast, she felt much better. Afterwards, she and Evie made a list of groceries to be purchased. Florence was relieved that she didn't have to worry about managing the house. 'I have my voluntary work and committees to attend,' she stated with an air of grandeur.

Evie sat with her father for an hour until one of his friends arrived.

After a quick lunch, she donned her outdoor clothes and said to Mabel, 'I'm just popping out for an hour. Dad's friend is still here, so they may need a cuppa later.'

'I'll see to it. You get off, miss.'

She was the last patient to see the doctor. 'It's nothing really, doctor, just sometimes I feel nausea and I wanted it cleared up before I go back to camp.'

Doctor Jones looked at her over the top of his spectacles. He had known her since a child and she always felt at ease with him.

'Hop on to the couch and I'll examine you,' he said, as he washed his hands at the small basin in the room's corner.

Leaving the doctor's surgery, Evie felt light-headed and unable to process the doctor's verdict about her health check. Not able to face anyone just yet, she went to the lake. There she sat in the rowing boat, hidden from view of the house. The trees all around her had shed their leaves. She laid in the bottom of the boat and looked up to view their winter beauty, but the filigree outline of their branches didn't lift her spirts. A chilly wind blew and she sat up, watching as the sun began its descent behind the clouds. Then she picked up the oars and rowed mechanically across the lake.

'You took your time,' was her mother's greeting as Evie entered the kitchen.

Ignoring her mother, she went to see her father. He was alone in bed with his treasured books around him. Gerald looked much brighter and relaxed. She kissed him on the cheek, saying, 'You look comfortable. How are you?'

'You've done wonders for me. The chaps are coming every day. We're going to set up a chess school. And the gracious lady, Mabel, is a superb cook, so I'm doing fine.'

Evie thought back to her childhood, when her father had attempted to teach her the game of chess, but she had been a lost cause. 'That's wonderful,' she replied softly, and added, 'I'd better see what help Mother needs.' She turned around to look back at her father, desperately wanting to confide in someone, but she couldn't inflict her devastating news on him. Maybe when he was stronger. Could she tell her mother?

When she walked into the kitchen, her mother was busy preparing her notes for the Women's War Effort meeting the next day.

'What time are you leaving tomorrow?' Florence asked bluntly.

'The late afternoon train.'

'Good, then you can give your father his lunch.' She glanced up at her daughter, her face set in a tight line. 'I don't know why you must go back when you are so obviously needed here.'

Evie replied, keeping her voice even, 'Because there is a war on.' She turned, feeling weepy. In the laundry room, she tackled a pile of ironing which Mabel had washed.

That night, in her room, she opened her jewellery box, a fancy name for her trinkets, and found a fine gold chain. Retrieving it from the box, she threaded the beautiful opal ring from Matt on to the chain and hung it around her neck. Tears misted her eyes as she looked in the dressing-table mirror. Then the most extraordinarily beautiful thing happened. She felt a soft touch on her neck, as if unseen hands were caressing her skin. 'Matt,' she whispered, sensing his presence watching over her.

The next morning, when Mabel arrived, Evie was in the kitchen. Her father had a visitor and her mother had gone to her meeting. They chatted about the weather and the fact that Gerald was looking much better. 'Though if you don't mind me saying, miss, you are looking peaky.'

Evie glanced at Mabel as she bustled about the kitchen and she felt tears prick her eyes. This woman, a stranger, took more notice of Evie than her own mother did. 'My fiancé, a pilot, was killed in action,' she replied.

'I am sorry, dearie. Sit down and have a rest.'

Evie did so, wishing Florence was the motherly type. She so wanted to confide in her, to ask for her advice.

Evie and Mabel sat opposite each other at the kitchen table, chatting about food rationing. 'God only knows how those poor people in Hull survive on such poor rations. When I go to visit my sister, I always try to take her something, be it a couple of eggs or fresh vegetables.'

Evie only half listened, feeling the queasiness of her stomach and a sudden need to retch. She dashed from the table to the back porch lavatory. She kneeled for a long time on the cold, hard floor, resting her head on the wooden lavatory seat. Then, slowly, she levered up her body and leaned against the stone sink, washing her hands and face in cold water.

112

Gradually, feeling better, she went back into the kitchen, where Mabel was preparing a big pot of stew. Evie forced out a cheerful voice, saying, 'I must have eaten something that didn't agree with me.'

'You know what it is, don't you, love? I've had six of my own.'

Evie slumped on to a kitchen chair and nodded. 'Please don't mention it to Mother or Father. They have enough to contend with.' She looked straight into Mabel's concerned face.

'Bless you, love, you do that in your own time. But you will need help. What with you losing your young man and not being married. I was lucky, my Bill married me.'

Evie looked into the middle distance, saying, 'I haven't thought that far ahead.'

'Best to have a cup of tea and a biscuit before you get up in the morning, to help stop morning sickness.'

Evie wondered how she could explain her situation to the others at camp. Lily, yes, but no one else. She gave a heavy sigh.

'I could mix you one of my tinctures to help stop the morning sickness.' Mabel glanced at Evie.

'Would you, Mabel? Anything to stop this.'

'You see to the rest of the dinner. I'll dash home on my bike and mix it for you. I'll be back in no time.'

* * *

Evie arrived back at camp in the evening, feeling absolutely worn out. So, when the others came into the hut, she was fast asleep. Up early in the morning, she took a few sips of the tincture, which tasted of tree bark, ginger and herbs she couldn't identify. Although she felt queasy, she wasn't sick, which was a relief, for she knew that if the commanding officer heard of her situation, she would have to leave the services. But she wanted to confide in Lily, needing an ally. How else would she survive?

A couple of evenings later, both Evie and Lily were off duty until the morning, but on standby in case of emergency.

In the NAAFI, some gunners were having an impromptu singalong. As Lily was about to make her way over to join them, Evie grabbed her arm, saying, 'I need to talk to you.'

'Oh, something nice,' Lily quipped, and began laughing until she saw Evie's serious face. 'What's up?'

Evie manoeuvred Lily into a quiet corner of the canteen. She had been rehearsing in her head what she would say. But as soon as they sat down, she blurted, 'I'm pregnant.'

Lily stared, open-mouthed, then gasped, 'Bloody hell, how did you do that?'

If it wasn't so serious, Evie would have laughed at Lily's response. 'The usual way.'

'Didn't you take precautions?'

Evie shrugged. 'Yes, but . . .' And then it hit her, like a gun blasting too close to her head. She felt the colour drain from her face. Lily scraped back her chair, moving away, and Evie felt her uncertainty. Closing her eyes, she tried to recall her last night with Matt, not certain now if they had taken precautions. And then there was the night Richard had brought the news of Matt's death, the night she wanted to forget. She opened her eyes. Had Richard taken any precautions? She had been too full of sorrow to take notice. But surely he would have done?

Just then, Lily placed a steaming hot mug of tea in front of her. Thankful, Evie clasped her hands around it and lifted it to her lips, sipping it. She didn't want to voice her mixed-up emotions, the shocking realisation that she wasn't sure if Matt or Richard was the father of her unborn child.

CHAPTER SEVENTEEN

Christmas 1944–January 1945

During the run-up to Christmas, everyone in the camp talked about the concert they were putting on. 'Evie, are you and Lily up for doing the Andrews Sisters again? I can take Gloria's part,' Maureen enthused to the other girls sat round the table in the NAAFI. They were discussing ideas for the forthcoming show.

Before Evie could answer, Lily chimed in, 'I think, Maureen, we should let the newer girls do that. It will make them feel more welcome. Besides, you're our best pianist.'

Maureen rose to the bait and puffed out her chest, replying, 'You're right.'

With relief, Evie let out the breath she didn't realise she was holding, and gave Lily a grateful nod. Though she had no interest in the concert, she didn't want to arouse suspicions about her pregnancy. 'I'm happy to help organise and sew any costumes that might be required,' she offered.

'That's smashing. I always get landed with that job,' piped up a voice.

Evie leaned back in her chair. Thankful for her reprieve, she let the excited voices float over her head as they chatted about the programme. She suddenly sat up straighter, aware that her skirt pulled across the gentle swell of her stomach. Since joining the Ack-Ack gunner girls, she had initially lost weight, so her clothes were quite roomy, but now she was filling out, and soon the extra weight would show. Under the guise of wardrobe mistress for the concert, she could let out the seams of her skirt, though she was not sure if she was skilled enough to do the same for her jacket. Luck was with her because the style of the battle dress she wore on duty was quite roomy.

Days for Evie seemed to pass in a haze, and a few nights later Lily called gaily to her, 'I'm off.'

Sitting by the stove in the hut, Evie looked up from her sewing and smiled at her friend. 'Enjoy yourself, Lily. And give Georgio a kiss from me.' Whenever she could, Lily went to meet her GI. Evie missed her company, but was happy for her, and glad Lily never mentioned her pregnancy.

Evie paused. Laying down her sewing, she poked at the stove with a fire-iron, coaxing more warmth from it on this cold winter's night. Without warning, her thoughts drifted to Richard. She wondered where he was now stationed. He would no doubt would be back on missions now. The newspapers were full of the story of the Allied troops advancing and driving the enemy into a tight corner. It was the bombers' mission to blow up selected bridges, ammunition dumps and other strategic areas to halt the Nazis. She stared into the fire, watching the flames jump higher. Why did thoughts of Richard invade her mind? She wasn't sure, but she hoped he might write to her. What if he did? Would she tell him about the baby? And if she did, would he feel trapped, thinking that the baby might be his? He might offer to marry her out of pity. She couldn't bear that, to lose Matt and marry another man who would pity her. But who was she fooling? Only herself. As the saying goes, he would probably run a mile.

She picked up her sewing, and to drown out her unwanted thoughts, she began singing the popular tunes that Vera Lynn sang to the troops and which were often broadcast on the wireless.

The concert was a tremendous success and lightened the restless mood on the camp. Evie loved the two gunners, Jack and Jimmy, who performed a singing routine like Flanagan and Allen. They got a resounding round of applause. And three of the newer Ack-Ack gunner girls did themselves proud by singing popular songs by The Andrews Sisters. The concert finished with a sing-song, Maureen belting out rousing tunes on the piano and one officer playing saxophone.

Christmas came and went. Lily went home with Georgio to see her family, while Evie was going home for New Year. Her parents, according to her mother's letter, had quite a few invitations over the Christmas period, and Florence wrote: 'We are entertaining on New Year's Eve so could you come home then and help me.'

As she travelled homewards, Evie wondered if any clothes in her wardrobe would fit her, although the problem of telling her parents about her pregnancy was uppermost in her mind. Would they welcome a grandchild? Her father would, but her mother? From Florence's letter, Gerald's health, with medication and plenty of rest, had improved.

When she arrived at Island House, the day before New Year's Eve, Florence was in a flap, and Gerald had retreated to his bed. The preparation for the next day was under control, thanks to Mabel. After changing out of her uniform into a skirt and jumper, and ensconced in one of Mabel's big wrap-around aprons, Evie set to making pastry. She found the motion of rubbing the flour and lard through her fingers therapeutic, giving her mind and body a steady, relaxing rhythm.

Not until Florence was safely up in her room, resting to ease her headache, did Mabel ask Evie, 'How are you feeling, love?'

Evie smiled at her and replied, 'Your tincture worked well, and the routine at camp has sort of kept me on balance.' She didn't mention her uncertainty about who the father was.

'And your parents, will you tell them?'

Evie bit her lip. 'I'm not sure yet. It depends how things go here.'

'Don't leave it too long, love. You'll need lots of help and support, especially when your time is near.'

Later, as she lay in bed, Evie thought of Mabel's words and knew she was right. She must tell her parents. Suddenly, surprisingly, the baby within her kicked, as if to say, 'You better sort it out before I come.' A warm glow filled her whole being, and she gently rested her hands on the swell of her belly. Her baby settled and for the first time Evie felt a surge of love for this little one growing within her, for whom she, and she alone, was responsible.

On the day she intended to tell her parents of her pregnancy, her father had a coughing fit and the doctor came.

Evie and Florence both watched anxiously as the doctor examined Gerald. Evie felt a knife-edge panic fill her as they waited until the doctor packed away his instruments with careful precision. The examination seemed to take forever, but when she checked the clock on her father's bedside table, it was only a matter of ten minutes. Florence fussed with Gerald's pillows, and Evie noticed how her hands shook.

Finally, the doctor spoke. 'Mr Sinclair's had too much excitement.' He directed his gaze at Florence before continuing. 'I recommend rest for a further two weeks, carry on with his medication, and light nourishing meals. On fine days, have the windows open for short periods for the patient to have fresh air.' He picked up his bag and strode to the door, gave a curt nod and went.

'That's New Year's cancelled,' said a disappointed Florence.

Evie hastened after the doctor, to show him out and to thank him. She watched him climb into his pony and trap, every inch of him an old-fashioned country doctor who had served in the Great War. She stared down the empty drive and gave a deep sigh. Now wasn't the time to tell her parents of her baby. Instinctively, she rested a hand on the gentle swell of her stomach. 'Sorry, little one. Not this time.' She took in deep breaths of the frosty air to steady her mind.

Indoors, she went to her father's room to see Florence sitting by his bedside, holding his hand. As Evie watched, she saw her father's eyelids droop, flicker and close as he drifted into sleep, his breathing gradually becoming more even and gentle. Quietly, she closed the door.

Down in the kitchen, she kept herself busy. She filled the kettle to make a pot of tea and turned to look out of the window towards the lake. The urge to run to the edge of the lake and jump into the boat gripped her. She walked to the porch and was about to don her outside gear when a voice called, 'Good, you are making a pot of tea. I'm going up to my room to rest. Bring it up to me, please.' Florence swept from the room.

Evie stared after the retreating figure of her mother. Unbelievable, she thought, and shrugged.

Her trip on the lake thwarted, Evie concentrated on checking what chores needed to be done around the house. After finding their evening meal of fish pie, left in the warming oven by Mabel, she went to sit with her father. Kissing him lightly on the forehead, he murmured a sigh of pleasure. She watched over him for a few moments and then tiptoed to the door, her heart heavy with love for her dear father.

As she lay in bed, wrestling with her conscience, she wondered if her parents would welcome a grandchild. Yes, no doubt they would. But a child born out of wedlock? She pictured her father's kindly face. He would, but he wasn't strong enough to bear the burden. Her mother, no! With the disgrace of an illegitimate grandchild, she wouldn't be able to keep her position as a model of righteousness in the village. Evie tossed and turned, arguing with her principles until the early hours of the morning. When she awoke, she was no nearer a solution.

That day, she kept up a cheerful persona. From time to time, Mabel gave her a knowing look, but mentioned nothing, for which Evie was grateful. She spent time with her father, reading to him, and even helped her mother to unravel an old jumper for re-knitting. In the kitchen, she helped Mabel with baking meat pies, though she wasn't sure what the meat was, some kind of game she suspected, mixed in with potatoes to bulk up the pies and give quality.

On her way back to camp, Evie was ensconced in a corner on the train to Beverley. She closed her eyes and listened to the rhythm.

She felt relieved to be back on site; the familiar routine of work, and listening to the other girls' jovial chatter, made her feel normal again.

The Luftwaffe raids were not so frequent, but they remained at their post, doing morning drills and attending lectures in the afternoon. Some of the Ack-Ack girls moaned but Evie welcomed it, as the drills stopped her from thinking too much about her and her baby's future. She liked to keep up to speed, especially with the advance of technology. There were often new procedures to learn and training to stay up to date with, keeping her mind alert. The news they heard was that Hitler and his troops were on the retreat.

Lily caught Evie's eye and rolled hers as they listened to the lecture that afternoon. Having a short time to spare, Lily said, 'Come and have a ciggy with me.' Wrapped up in their greatcoats, they sheltered against the lea of the canteen wall.

They lit up and Evie glanced at Lily and, knowing her friend, asked, 'What's on your mind?'

Suddenly, Lily's eyes shone like bright stars. 'Georgio asked me to marry
him.'

Evie was speechless at first but then her face lit up. 'You said yes?'

'Yes,' Lily whooped with joy and Evie hugged her dear friend. Lily prattled on, 'Mam and Dad like him, and me sisters want to be bridesmaids, and you as well, Evie.'

Instantly, Evie put her hand on the gentle swell of her stomach, feeling her child kick. 'Sorry, I think I will have to forgo that pleasure.' Then, on seeing Lily's disappointed look, said, 'But I will be there to cheer you on.'

'And guess what? I am going to live with him in America. Me, a GI bride.' Her face shone with pride and pleasure.

Evie hugged Lily again, trying to ignore the lonely, sinking feeling in the pit of her stomach.

CHAPTER EIGHTEEN

April 1945

Lily's wedding was a glorious affair. Evie travelled to the venue and met up with Gloria. They were both staying overnight in the village inn, because Lily's family home was only a small cottage and bursting with family members. After dumping their bags in their room at the inn, which was near the church where Lily and Georgio were to be married the next day, they strolled down the main street to the lane leading to Lily's cottage. It was in the middle of a row of quaint cottages and Evie was surprised to see how small it was. A square sitting room, which was filled with Lily's four sisters and Lily. She rushed to Evie and Gloria and flung her arms around them both, tears of joy sparkling in her eyes.

'You've come, thank you!' Lily's voice was jittery with nerves.

The four sisters, ages ranging from ten to seventeen, hung back shyly on seeing the two Ack-Ack girls in their dress uniform, looking authoritarian. Then Evie smiled and asked the girls, 'Are you excited at being Lily's bridesmaids? What's the colour of your dresses?' She already knew, because Lily had told her, but that didn't matter. The two older girls were dark-haired and pretty, and the two younger girls were fair-haired with freckly faces. At first, the girls didn't speak, but then they started talking. The younger girls' dresses were in pink and the older girls' dresses in blue.

Suddenly, Mrs Grainger came bustling in from the kitchen. 'Sorry, I was in the lavvy.' Everyone in the row of cottages shared the lavatories. Evie had to visit one later and there were two, side by side, one for adults and one for children. She had never come across this arrangement before and was glad they didn't have to share at camp, or at her home. She hoped the inn had better facilities.

After a cup of tea, Lily linked arms with Evie and Gloria and they walked down to the inn to spend an evening together. They sat in the quiet snug, away from the noisy men in the bar.

They was a lot of laughter, and Evie and Gloria kept the conversation light. 'Go on, Lily,' they chorused. 'Tell us where you are going for your honeymoon?'

'Down south, somewhere near the coast. Georgio has arranged it, near to where he's transferred to. I'll be living in digs until the war's over and then we'll sail for his home in America.'

'What will you do with yourself?' asked Gloria, as she produced a packet of cigarettes and handed them round.

'I fancy working in a dress shop. You know, one of them high-class ones where I will have to model the dresses for the rich women.'

'Go on, pull the other one,' laughed Gloria.

They tried to get Lily to talk about her wedding dress, but she wouldn't budge. 'Top secret, and Mam said it's unlucky to talk about it.'

Gloria went to order more drinks at the bar, and Lily whispered to Evie, 'I'm feeling scared. Not about marrying Georgio, but going to live with his family. I won't know anybody.'

Hoping her voice sounded positive, Evie replied, 'There are bound to be other GI brides, and you could be in touch with them. Start up a club.'

'I never thought of that.' Gloria came back with their drinks and they began chatting about the time they'd all joined up together.

A lull came in the conversation as Lily talked to one of the local women, and Gloria was chatting with a soldier. Relaxing in her seat, Evie thought how lucky Lily was to be marrying the man she loved. And she . . . She thought of Matt, gone forever, and the child she was carrying. But who was the father? Matt or Richard? A sob caught in her throat, and to hide it, she coughed, then picked up her drink to take a long gulp. Her future was so uncertain.

'What do you think, Evie? Shall we give it to her now?' Gloria asked, sitting down next to her. They had bought Lily a wedding gift. Gloria had found it in a second-hand market in London, and both girls contributed half of the cost. Evie nodded, and Gloria bounded up the stairs to their room and came racing down again, holding a deep blue velvet case. She thrust it into Lily's hand, saying, 'Open it now.'

Her fingers trembling, Lily undid the catch of the case and it sprung open. Wide-eyed, she stared at the beautiful delicate gold locket on a fine gold chain. 'Wow!' she exclaimed, her face broadening into a smile, her eyes bright. 'For me?'

'Yes,' both Evie and Gloria chorused. 'Open it,' Evie instructed, watching as Lily fiddled with the tiny clasp and then opened the locket to reveal two miniature photographs of Evie and Gloria. 'So you don't forget us,' Evie said, tears welling up in her eyes.

'As if I would. My two best friends.' Lily jumped up from her seat and flung her arms around Evie and Gloria, hugging them close.

After another shandy, they walked Lily home, linking arms and singing at the top of their voices. A few curtains twitched, and some cheeky lads joined in the singing as well.

As they returned to the inn, the soldier who Gloria had spoken to earlier called to her, and Evie went up to their room alone. She was glad of this because she hadn't told Gloria of her pregnancy. She was relieved to take off the corset she wore, trying to maintain her figure. 'That's better,' she said out loud, and on cue, the little one inside her kicked.

When Gloria came up to the room, Evie was in bed, leafing through the pages of a book from the bookcase in the room.

Gloria yawned and was quickly in bed. She switched off the overhead light, and soon she snored gently.

Evie, restless, could not get comfortable in this strange bed. She thought about her baby, and could only guess how many months gone she was, because there was a month between her love-making with Matt and Richard. Could she really call it love-making with Richard? They were comforting each other, she concluded. She wondered if they had feelings for each other. Pondering on this, she thought not. Richard had never been in touch with her since his transfer. And was she just looking for a father for her unborn child? With that thought lodged in her mind, she drifted into sleep.

* * *

Evie and Gloria took their seats in the pews on the bride's side, as was the custom. Both were smart in their immaculate dress uniforms. Gloria had talked about them wearing a dress, and Evie had frozen at the idea because her baby bump would show. Glancing around the church, someone had gathered wild flowers and greenery and made posies at the end of each pew. Evie inhaled the summer fragrance, light and breezy, her fingers straying to touch the feathery fern leaves.

Suddenly the organ struck a loud chord and Mendelssohn's 'Wedding March' began. There was a shuffling as everyone got to their feet and Evie glanced behind her. She glimpsed a radiant Lily in a shimmering dress of silk, as the sun shone on her through the open doorway and the gold locket glinted with pride around Lily's slender neck. She glided down the aisle on the arm of her proud father, a portly man, with a beaming smile. Her four sisters followed behind, their faces matching their father's. On reaching the groom, Georgio turned to gaze with wonderment at his beautiful bride, and Evie felt her heart fill with joy for them both.

After the ceremony, they were outside the church, and one of Georgio's GI friends produced a smart-looking camera and began snapping pictures of the happy couple and the family. 'Evie, Gloria, come and have a photo with me,' Lily called. Gloria dashed forward, eagerly, but Evie was slower. As they stood by Lily's side, Evie touched the skirt of her wedding dress. 'It's parachute silk! You are a dark horse.' Lily laughed and Evie, still holding the skirt, edged it gently across her bump, as she felt the child within her kick.

The wedding reception was informal and held on the village green. They erected two big tents, one for the food, and one with seats for those who wanted to sit down away from the sunshine. Evie looked longingly at the seats, but the older guests mostly gathered there, and she felt obliged to be with Gloria and the other younger people. Looking around, most of the villagers were at the wedding. So, she talked and laughed, and helped the junior bridesmaid carry their food to sit on the grass in picnic style. Gloria stood talking to a couple of Americans, so Evie wandered into the seating tent, saw a vacant seat next to Mrs Grainger and sat down. Two young village girls came round with cups of tea and sandwiches, and she enjoyed the refreshments, listening to how Mrs Grainger grew up in the village as a child.

Out on the green, a man played an accordion, and she heard a woman say, 'Old Jenkin's 'as got his squeezebox going.'

Evie went outside to sit on the grass under the shade of the oak tree. Soon, the four bridesmaids, tiring of running around, came and snuggled up to her. Gloria and some other young women, and young men, were dancing on a makeshift wooden dance floor.

Lily came across to talk to Evie. 'What did you think of my wedding?'

'Like one of those Hollywood films, but classier,' Evie replied, honestly.

'Come and help me change into my going-away outfit,' Lily said, reaching out to pull Evie to her feet. The bridesmaids, now refreshed, ran off to dance.

Back in Lily's home and upstairs in the bedroom, Evie helped her to take off her wedding dress and placed it on a padded coat hanger in the wardrobe. Then she helped Lily into her powder-blue two-piece suit and frilly blouse. 'Gosh, Lily, you look radiant. Blue suits you. I'm going to miss you.' Tears filled their eyes, and Lily quickly picked up a handkerchief and dabbed them.

Downstairs, Lily poured them both a glass of port. 'Need a bit of Dutch courage.'

Together, arms linked, they walked back to the reception on the village green. Lily went to say goodbye to her parents and siblings, her mother shedding a few tears. 'I'll be back to see you before I go to America, Mam. So don't fret.'

Everyone wanted to talk to Lily before she went on her honeymoon with Georgio. He sat with his comrades, smoking, laughing and drinking. Evie went to him to say goodbye. Gloria came from around a corner with a GI, their arms around each other, and grinning. She winked at Evie and smiled.

Georgio and friends went to get their transport, two jeeps on special secondment to them for the wedding. While they were busy loading Lily's suitcase and their belongings, Lily was saying her goodbyes. As she watched Mrs Grainger fuss over her daughter and hug her, Evie noticed the marked difference with her own mother, who was always cold towards her.

Somebody started singing, and Georgio helped his bride up into the jeep. Before sitting down, Lily threw her bouquet of spring flowers over her shoulder. Amazed by her dash forward, Evie caught the bouquet, feeling stunned, as all around her people cheered.

'Another bride to be,' someone called.

Tears flooded Evie's eyes, for that would never be. Who would want an unmarried woman, pregnant with another's man's child? To hide her tears, she buried her face in the sweet-scented bouquet.

CHAPTER NINETEEN

May 1945

The cheering was deafening when the end of the war in Europe was announced. Evie wasn't sure how she felt, as one gunner grabbed her hand and swung her around, narrowly missing banging her bump against the edge of the dining table. 'Hear, let me have a go.' It was Maureen, and she grabbed hold of the gunner, nudging Evie away.

Throwing Maureen a thankful glance, Evie left the NAAFI and went outside. She sat on the grassy bank near to the guns. They stood silent and oddly peaceful, and she lay back, her fingers trailing through the blades of grass. Suddenly, she felt a kick that was stronger than usual, causing her to sit up with a jerk. Tenderly, she placed her hands on her stomach, feeling the lively movement. 'I know,' she whispered to her child. 'It's time to go home. You'll be wanting to come out and play soon.' She wasn't sure how long the demob process took, but if it came to it she would take sick leave. Lying back on the soft grass, she closed her eyes for a few moments to relish the peace.

She must have nodded off, for she awoke to the potent smell of tobacco smoke. Sitting up, bleary-eyed, she saw a figure standing in the lea of one of the gun ops rooms, smoking. Rubbing her eyes, she saw to her dismay that it was the corporal, looking at her. Hastily scrambling to her feet, Evie brushed bits of grass from her work dungarees. She saluted and turned hurriedly to make a quick getaway.

'Stay, Sinclair,' the corporal said, her voice unusually low.

Slowly Evie turned, conscious of her child kicking within. She breathed in and stood to attention, waiting for what? A reprimand? Whatever it was, she could take it.

The corporal came and stood nearer to Evie and said, 'Isn't it time you made your condition known?'

The words knocked Evie. Did she know? But how could she? Evie had kept her pregnancy well hidden. Only Lily had known. Shock must have registered on Evie's face.

'I am one of ten children, and my mother was always pregnant, so I know the signs.'

Amazed, Evie said, 'You never reported me.'

'You were a damned good predictor operator, so I thought I would test your strength. By the look of you, the nipper will soon make an appearance. I will write the report for your early release on medical grounds. How you deliver that to the Medical Office is down to you.'

Evie felt her mouth dry, like she had eaten cardboard, and tried to speak, but all that came out was a strangled guttural sound.

'Dismissed,' the corporal bellowed.

A quick salute and Evie fled to the barrack room, hoping it was empty. Quietly, she inched opened the door and peered inside, seeing only dust motes flying around. She fell on to her bed and sobbed, all her pent-up emotions and fears overwhelming her. She cried for Matt, the man she loved, who would never return to her. The man, her lover, lost to her, wishing she knew for sure that he was the father of her unborn child. Without warning, the face of Richard flashed before her, an unhappy face filled with pain over losing his comrade. Her mind rolled on like a film, recalling his sad pearl-grey eyes. She'd never noticed the colour of his eyes before, or had she? Turning over on the bunk, for a fleeting moment she wished they had not transferred Richard from the area. What if the unborn child was his? Maybe he'd wanted to distance himself from her, but she could have talked to him. Sitting up, a sigh of self-pity escaped her. Then she shook herself and swung her feet to the floor, patting her swollen belly. Mimicking a line from an American film, she whispered, 'It's just me and you, babe.'

* * *

It happened so quickly: the goodbyes, the hugs, the handshakes, the promises to keep in touch. 'Let us know if it's a boy or girl,' two Ack-Ack girls called out. Evie felt a little shocked that her pregnancy had become common knowledge. But what did it matter now? She had written to her parents, telling them of her homecoming, but not about the forthcoming baby. Alighting from the train at Inversea Station, she had the mad idea to row across the lake. Then, on reflection, she realised she wouldn't have the strength, so walking the last stretch was her only option. Picking up her suitcase, she strode forward. After ten minutes, she stopped to catch her breath and ease the heavy pain in her belly. Wiping the sweat trickling down her face, she wished now she had rowed across the lake. She heard the coughing and spluttering of a motorcar engine as it came to a halt by her side.

A jovial voice called out, 'I'm going up to the house. Can I give you a lift?' Evie looked up into the weather-beaten face of one of her father's friends.

With relief, she answered, 'Yes, please, Mr Smith.' Her case stored in the car's boot, she eased herself into the passenger seat.

She half listened as he rambled on. 'Well, we gave the Hun a run for its money. I knew they wouldn't win. Never thought they would when I fought in the Great War either.' He glanced across at her. 'You've finished your little job?'

Evie nodded in response, ignoring his patronising manner. 'Now you can help your mother run the home.'

The car came to a halt on the drive and Mr Smith carried her case indoors. She thanked him and he went into her father's room. In the kitchen, Mabel was singing along to a tune while ironing a pile of clothes.

'Well, I'll be blessed, didn't know you were coming home, Evie.'

'Didn't my mother tell you?'

'No, her head is full of organising the Victory in Europe party.' She rested the iron on the stove. 'You look done in. Sit down and I'll make a pot of tea.' She bustled about, fetching a plate of her homemade scones, and jam to spread on them. 'That'll perk you up.'

The tea and scones helped Evie to feel better, though it was Mabel's homely chatter and good humour that really helped to restore her spirits and build up her strength to tell her parents.

As if reading her thoughts, Mabel asked, 'When are you telling your parents about the little one?'

'Tonight. I cannot put it off any longer.'

'Best now to see the midwife and make arrangements.'

Leaving Mabel to her chores, Evie went upstairs to sort out something decent to wear. The blouse she was wearing pulled across her bust and her skirt wouldn't fasten. Hunting through her wardrobe, she found a pre-war dress with a full skirt, and she unpicked the dart seams to make the upper part fit across her bust. In the bathroom she filled the bath with water, well past the five-inch regulation and found a handful of bath crystals. She lowered herself into the warm water, which felt heavenly and peaceful, if she ignored the gurgling water-pipes. She closed her eyes, relaxing for the first time in ages.

From a distance, she heard her mother's voice and quickly emerged from the bath. She wrapped a big towel around her body and went to her room. Drying her body and her hair, she dressed as swiftly as her cumbersome movements would allow. Glancing in the full-length mirror of the wardrobe, she could see that the dress didn't hide her pregnancy. Gently putting her hands on her bump, she whispered softly, 'Soon, my darling one, I will be nursing you.' With these words focused in her mind, she went downstairs.

The kitchen was empty. Mabel had gone home and Evie heard her mother's voice coming from her father's room. With a purposeful step, she went in that direction. The door was ajar, and she pushed it open and went inside. 'Hello, Mother, Father. How are you both?'

Her mother turned to glance at her and said, 'Good, you are home. I need your help with the Victory in Europe party. You can organise the decorations in the village hall.' And then, as if seeing her daughter for the first time, she remarked, 'Why are you wearing that old dress? Change into a smarter one.' Then she turned her back on her daughter.

Evie went round to the other side of her father's bed and kissed him on the cheek. 'How are you, Daddy?' she whispered, thinking how frail he looked since the last time she had seen him.

'All the better for seeing you, my darling girl.' His thin hand grasped hers.

'Would you like me to make a pot of tea?' She directed this question at her mother.

'Yes, that would be fine.'

In the kitchen, Evie knew she was only putting off the inevitable. Waiting for the kettle to boil, she looked out of the window, seeing a break in the dull sky, where a dash of blue peeped through. She hoped it was a promising omen. But when she next looked, the sky was grey and dull.

Carrying the laden tray, she let it rest gently on the top of her bump, and somehow, her child nourished the positive strength of her mind. Evie felt a strong yearning to hold her child in her arms and, by the way the unborn baby moved about inside her, she knew her time was near. After telling her parents she would consult the local midwife and Mabel would advise her.

She set the tray on Gerald's bedside table, poured the tea, and proffered the delicious scones made by Mabel.

Sitting by the bedside, Evie could only nibble on her scone, her normally healthy appetite deserting her. She poured out a second cup of tea and cleared her throat.

'I've some news to tell you both.' Florence looked up, and Gerald glanced at her. She had prepared a pretty speech about the joys of being grandparents, but the words disappeared from her mind, and instead she blurted out, 'I'm pregnant.' Instinctively, her hands clasped her swollen belly, desperate to feel her baby, but all was still and Evie's heart plummeted. Then she felt a slight stirring within her and a gentle kick revived her. She sat up straight in her chair and waited for her parents' reaction to becoming grandparents.

'Repeat what you have just said.' Florence put down her teacup on her saucer with a clatter. Her hostile gaze fixed on her daughter.

Evie stood up and smoothed her hands over the child within, emphasising the swell of her belly, leaving no doubt of her condition.

'You're a slut!' Florence shouted. 'Bringing disgrace to our family name. You can't stay here.'

Gerald, so far quiet, said mildly, 'Be quiet, Florence, let's hear what our daughter has to say.'

'Hmm!' Florence picked up her cup and drank the tepid liquid, her eyes blazing over the rim of the cup.

Gerald turned to Evie. 'Sit down, my dear, and tell us your plans.'

Evie stared at her father. Plans? 'Why, to stay here at home, Father.'

'What does the father of your forthcoming child have to say?'

She bit on her lip. What could she say? She was unsure who the father was. 'The father is not involved.'

'What do you mean, not involved?' Florence asked, sharply.

'Just that. I have no contact with him.' Inside she cried out, because the father of my child is either dead or his best friend I hardly know.

Silence spun around the room. No one spoke. Her mother seemed to sink into herself, and her father looked gaunt and tired. Momentarily, Evie closed her eyes, her mind racing. She needed to stay at Island House, her home. There was plenty of room, but now she had a sinking feeling. Opening her eyes, she glanced at her father and he looked terrible. Then his breathing rasped.

'Move.' Florence was by her husband's side, administering his medication. 'You need to rest now, Gerald,' she soothed, straightening his pillows and tucking the blankets in around him. She motioned to Evie to pick up the tea tray and follow her through to the kitchen.

Once in the kitchen, Florence rounded on Evie. 'You cannot stay here. I will not have your father upset by the disgrace you have brought to our respectable home. What would our friends say? They would shun us. No, you've got yourself into this mess, so you must take the consequences. You are a disappointment to me and your father,' she said, her voice becoming hysterical.

Evie's mind raced. This wasn't the plan. Everything was happening too quickly. 'Where will I go?' she uttered.

Florence left the room, returning with her address book, and leafed through the pages. 'There!' she exclaimed. 'In Hull there is a mother and baby home, run by a charity. The committee makes donations from time to time. I, personally, will donate enough for your keep while you are there. When you are relieved of the baby and have had it adopted, only then will I allow you home.' Her face was hard, and devoid of any pity for her daughter.

Evie stared in disbelief at her mother and whispered, 'My baby adopted? Your grandchild?'

'You foolish girl. How can you, an unmarried mother, possibly keep a child?' Florence stood up, saying, 'You'd better pack and leave.'

As she went upstairs, Evie whispered to her child, 'I will never give you up for adoption. I am your mother and I love you with all my heart. We are alone now, little one.' The baby within responded with a dance of hope.

CHAPTER TWENTY

May–June 1945

Evie stood looking down the drive of the cold stone house and decided she wasn't going into the home until absolutely necessary. She shivered, turned away and walked along Holderness Road. Stopping to look in a shop window full of advertisements for things for sale and rooms to let, Evie rested her case by her feet. She pulled a pencil and note-book from her handbag to jot down the details of those who would take in lodgers. Then she began tramping the streets, knocking on doors, but when the occupants realised she was pregnant, they quickly shut the door in her face.

On Burleigh Street, she stood at the top of a row of terraced houses, resting her aching body against the broken brick wall that was all that remained of someone's home bombed to smithereens. She glanced at her crumpled note-book, realising she had exhausted all the addresses. With a heavy sigh, the only option now was the Mother and Baby Home.

Just then she heard a cry and saw an old woman lying on the pavement. Hurrying over to her, she put her arm round the woman's thin body and eased her up. 'Would you like me to get someone for you?' Evie asked, smelling beer on the woman's breath and the reek of her unwashed body.

'Just help me home.'

Evie retrieved her suitcase and, holding tight to the woman's body, helped her along until they reached one of the terraced houses tucked in the far corner. The door was locked. 'Do you have a key?' Evie asked. The woman pointed to the letterbox. Evie lifted the flap and pulled on the string to reveal a key on the end. Once inside the small house, Evie eased the woman into an old fireside chair. The woman had a bruise on her face and her leg was cut. 'Is there anyone I can call for you?'

'All gone. Jerry took them all.'

Evie glanced round the sparsely furnished room of a table, a wooden chair and the wing-backed chair the old woman was sitting on. 'I'll clean your wound for you.' The woman nodded to the other door. It led to a tiny kitchen with a small window. Once her eyes became accustomed to the gloom, Evie spied a cast-iron kettle resting on a solitary gas ring, and lit it with a match from the box by its side. She found a pot basin on a ledge containing other kitchen utensils, but couldn't find any cotton wool or a clean rag. She withdrew her handkerchief from her coat pocket. Taking the bowl over to the woman, she knelt on the cold lino and dabbed at the cut on the woman's bare leg, noticing she wore a pair of old woollen socks. Her mother always wore stockings.

The wound cleaned and the dressing applied from Evie's attaché case, she rose to her feet and sat on the other chair, needing to rest her body.

'Thank you, dearie, for being kind to me. Not much of it around these days.'

'No problem.' Then an idea sprang into her mind, and before she could stop herself, Evie blurted, 'Would you consider taking me in as a lodger?'

The woman stared at her, not speaking. Evie was about to leave when she spoke. 'Do you mean you would pay me rent?'

'Of course.' She quickly calculated her savings.

'What about the bairn you're having?'

Evie winced inwardly. 'I'll be going into the Mother and Baby Home for the birth. I can pay you five shillings a week in advance.' The old woman, who she learned was named Mrs Hodgson, smiled, showing her missing front teeth.

That settled, Evie asked, 'Can you show me to my room, please?'

Mrs Hodgson pointed upwards. 'You'll have ter tek yerself. I can't get upstairs. Me knees are bad.'

'Where do you sleep?' Evie asked, looking around to see if there was a bed.

'Me chair,' she said, patting the arm of the chair she was sitting on.

Evie picked up her attaché case and climbed the steep staircase leading from the kitchen to the two bedrooms above. As she opened the door of the front bedroom, a musty smell twitched her nostrils and she sneezed. Crossing the lino floor to the sash window, she eased it open from the bottom, to let in some fresh air. She was surprised to see the furniture looked better than that in the living room downstairs. The double bed had a fancy mahogany headboard and there was a small table by the bed, as well as a rug on the wooden floor. On the opposite wall stood a wardrobe with a mirror in the centre, and a two-tier set of drawers beneath. In a corner stood a chair, a Hepplewhite, similar to the one in her mother's bedroom. Wearily, Evie sank on to the chair, casting her gaze to the bed covered with a colourful patchwork quilt. She would have to rest before she tackled the state of the bedding.

After twenty minutes of relaxation, her strength was restored. There were clean sheets and pillow cases in one drawer. Taking the blankets and the quilt off the bed to air, she put on the sheets. Just like the bed-making days in the camp, her corners perfectly matched. Feeling suddenly bereft, she longed for the camaraderie of the Ack-Ack gunner girls, and her best friends, Lily and Gloria. Lily, who was now enjoying married life. Evie felt envious, and wished she had married Matt when he'd asked her. The child within her kicked, as if to say, stop wallowing in self-pity.

'I know, little one. I have you to look forward to.'

She stared out of the window as a sudden downpour lashed against the windowpanes, distorting the outside view, just like her mind. What would she do when her baby was born? Where would she live? Fleetingly, she wondered if her mother would change her mind, though she doubted it. A rasping cough sounded from downstairs, and she wondered if Mrs Hodgson would let her return here with the baby, though the accommodation was far from ideal.

Her stomach rumbled. She hadn't eaten all day, so she would have to see what her landlady had for dinner. Easing herself up from the chair, she made her way down the steep stairs.

The room downstairs was full of cigarette smoke, making Evie cough. Clearing her throat, she asked, 'I have my ration book. Where is the best grocery shop?' Seeing that the rain was still pouring down and not wanting to get wet, she asked, 'Is it possible for me to share with you today, Mrs Hodgson?'

'Of course it is, dearie.' She pointed to the kitchen. 'Pantry's in there.'

Tucked in a corner of the kitchen, Evie tugged open the door and surveyed the shelves, all empty except one. A half loaf of bread, a small portion of butter, a tin of corned beef, an onion, two potatoes, a tin of peas, Oxo cubes, half a jug of milk and a caddy of tea. She thought about how she would use the ingredients. Soon, sliced onion was simmering in a pan on the hob. Evie added gravy made with an Oxo cube mixed with water and thickly sliced corned beef. Next went in finely sliced potatoes, seasoned with salt and pepper, and she put the lid on the pan for the corned beef hash to simmer and absorb the juices. She emptied the tin of peas into a small pan, ready to cook, and put two dinner plates to warm near the stove. In the sitting room, she said to Mrs Hodgson, 'Ready in half an hour.'

'Smells good. I never bother to cook much for myself since they killed my husband. He was an air raid warden and was helping to rescue a family trapped in a bombed house when it collapsed, killing him.' She sniffed and rubbed away her tears with the sleeve of her cardigan.

Silence filled the room, and Evie thought about the futility of war. War achieved nothing. All that fighting and killing. For what? A man crazy about power.

After the meal, Evie filled the copper with water to boil for a bath. It was a tin bath, which hung on a hook in the yard. After her bath in front of the fire, she persuaded Mrs Hodgson to have one. 'Oh, I don't know, dearie. I don't have 'em.'

Evie assisted the old woman into the bath. With tender movements, she washed her back and her matted grey hair. While Mrs Hodgson finished bathing, Evie found clean clothes for her in the sideboard drawers. When they were both sitting in front of the fire, Evie combed the tangles from the woman's long hair. 'You have beautiful hair. You've shades of chestnut colour among your grey,' she said.

Mrs Hodgson's voice sounded dreamy as she replied, 'As a young girl, I had ringlets.'

Evie looked at the old woman's face, seeing a faraway look. She's reliving her girlhood, she thought.

On another evening, Evie made her baby's layette while listening to the wireless, usually *Henry Hall's Guest Night* for variety, music from the movies, or George Formby, who was a favourite of Mrs Hodgson. She sourced the materials from second-hand shops, making nightgowns from old winceyette sheets, trimming them with odd bits of lace. One wonderful find was knitting wool in white, which she tucked under a shelf. 'Must have been there since before the war,' the shop-keeper muttered.

Evie looked up as Mrs Hodgson laughed at something the comedian said. She smiled, feeling an inner glow of happiness, something she hadn't expected in this tiny house, living with a woman who was so unlike anyone she knew. She was the very opposite of her mother in looks and dress, but Mrs Hodgson proved to be a kindly soul, something Florence Sinclair lacked, at least towards her daughter.

Her thoughts drifted to her father, and she wondered how he was faring. If he hadn't been ill, he wouldn't have turned her away from the house. As the beloved face of Matt came into her mind, she coughed and bit her lip. And then the inevitable happened. As Matt's face faded, Richard's took his place. She still didn't know if he was the father of her child. And then, on cue, she experienced a powerful movement of her child within.

Her time was near and she could no longer put off the inevitable. Willington House, she understood, was established and part funded by a Quaker family of the same name, and they adhered to a strict code of conduct. What that was, Evie wasn't sure. 'No doubt I will soon find out,' she said aloud.

'What's that, dearie?' Mrs Hodgson asked.

'Cocoa time, I think.' Evie rose stiffly and slowly made her way into the kitchen. This had become their nightly ritual. A cup of hot cocoa before bedtime that Mrs Hodgson said helped her sleep. How she did so in her chair, Evie wasn't sure, though the footstool she'd bought for her from the second-hand shop proved beneficial for her swollen feet.

Eventually the time came for Evie to leave. She hugged Mrs Hodgson goodbye, promising to bring her baby to show her, but the dear lady didn't mention Evie and the baby coming to stay. Evie guessed that was because the neighbours gossiped about her. An unmarried woman lowering the tone of the neighbourhood. To avoid contact with them, whenever Evie left the house to shop or for fresh air she always used the back door leading to a passageway that ran between the terraced houses. Today was no exception.

On Holderness Road, she took a bus, because she didn't have the strength to walk and carry her bag. Alighting near Laburnum Avenue, she slowly made her way to Willington House.

Surrounded by trees, the view of the cold stone house was visible as she walked down the long drive. On reaching the impressive front door, Evie rang the bell. Suddenly her insides trembled, and she felt more terror than when she'd faced the Luftwaffe. She didn't want to be here. But where could she run to? Nowhere.

'Are you going to stand there dallying all day?' a crisp, authoritarian voice snapped. For a fleeting moment, Evie was back at the barracks. But as she stepped over the threshold into a square hall smelling of disinfectant, she knew she wasn't. Then the door slammed behind her, shutting her off from the outside world.

CHAPTER TWENTY-ONE

June 1945

Evie walked as if in a trance as she followed the woman in a blue uniform who introduced herself as Miss Watkins, one of the two midwives. The other was Miss Davis. She led her along a narrow corridor to a solid wooden door. 'Wait here. Matron may be free to see you.'

Evie felt an overwhelming desire to run. She didn't want to be here. Her baby kicked, and she put both hands on the swell of her belly and caressed it gently. 'I know, little one,' she whispered. 'You want to come out and play. When you do, we can focus on our lives together.'

'First sign of madness is talking to yourself,' said a chirpy voice.

Evie looked up in surprise to see a young pregnant girl waddling towards her, carrying a pile of clean sheets, and she couldn't help but smile at her welcoming manner. 'Hello, I'm Evie,' she offered.

'Betty, maid of all works at the moment. You will be fine once you've left the lion's den.' She nodded in the direction of the office door, which suddenly opened. Betty trotted off down the corridor.

Miss Watkins ushered Evie into the bleak, white-walled office and she stood awkwardly before a grey-haired woman seated behind an enormous mahogany desk. Miss Watkins introduced her to Matron, a tall, angular woman who wore a navy dress with a white starched collar and cuffs. Somewhere in the distance, Evie heard the twinkling of a bell. Excusing herself, Miss Watkins left the room. Evie felt her legs wobbling.

'Sit down, girl.' Thankfully, Evie sat down on a high-backed chair. 'Now let me see.' Matron opened a big ledger, extracted a loose sheet of paper and read it. 'Most irregular. You should have come last month. Why didn't you?'

Evie wasn't expecting this question and, thinking quickly, her fingers crossed in her lap, answered, 'I had to care for a sick friend.'

'We cannot reimburse Mrs Sinclair. After the birth, you will remain at the home for two months. Here is our book-let about rules, regulations and your duties. You will receive more information when the baby is born,' she said, handing Evie the booklet. She pressed a buzzer on her desk and a knock came at the door. 'Enter.' A dark-haired woman in a print overall opened the door and waited. 'Take Miss Sinclair up to the dormitory.'

The woman bobbed a curtsey and turned. Evie followed her past a wide staircase and on to a narrow set of stairs at the back of the house; for the servants, she surmised. The dormitory was situated to the east side of the house. On the brown door was a small plaque with the words 'Ante-natal'. It took Evie a few seconds to grasp its meaning. The woman, Masie, in her mid-thirties and a general helper in the kitchen and the house, pushed open the door. Evie stood on the threshold and surveyed the room, seeing eight metal bed-steads with pale green bedspreads standing out against the starkness of the white walls. She shuddered and, breathing deeply, stepped forward.

'This is your bed, miss,' said Masie, standing by a bed next to the window. 'And this is your chest of drawers. I can help you unpack.'

Evie stood in the middle of the room, feeling like a lost child, not like a woman who had had responsibilities as an Ack-Ack gunner girl. This world was alien to her. She thought of her cosy room at Island House and vowed that if she ever had a daughter in the same predicament, she would never turn her away. No matter what people said.

Masie took the case from her hand and opened the drawers, and she began chatting. 'I'll put baby's clothes in the bottom drawer, your clothes in the second drawer, and,' she turned to look at Evie, then continued, 'top drawer for your personal things.'

Evie made her legs move forward and placed her two books, writing material, pen and ink, and a photograph of Matt in his pilot uniform, smiling at her.

'Now for a cup of tea and a tour of the house.'

Soon, Evie was sitting in the small dining room, with the same white walls, wooden tables and chairs. She could hear Masie talking to someone in the kitchen. Then she appeared, carrying a tray with a cup of tea and a plate with two gingerbread biscuits and placed it on the table in front of Evie, saying, 'I'm going to help cook, but when you've finished, I'll show you round.'

After drinking her tea and nibbling her biscuits, Evie stood up and Masie appeared, drying her hands on her apron. She led Evie into an adjoining room. 'This is the sitting room,' she said. Evie looked at the mismatched assortment of easy chairs, upright chairs, two rather battered low tables, a bookcase with a bible and a few old books (of which Evie didn't recognise any of the authors or titles) and dog-eared magazines. Next was the laundry room.

'This is where you wash and iron your clothes, bedding and baby's clothes.' There was a brick-built copper, a scrubbing board, a deep chipped porcelain sink and an overhead pulley full of clothes airing. A side door led into a yard where rows of washing lines hung, and Betty and three other young girls, in various stages of pregnancy, were unpegging the dry clothes in readiness for ironing. They paused in their task to stare at Evie, but didn't speak, though Betty smiled. 'We do all washing early morning, hang it out to dry, and iron in the afternoon after dinner. You have a booklet on jobs to do and, if you are lucky, you might get a rest in the afternoons. That's it, miss, and if I was you, I'd get a rest now and be down for dinner sharp at twelve o'clock.'

'Thank you, Masie, for your help and for showing me around. It's so silent here. Where are the babies and their mothers?'

'Yon side of the house. Mothers and babies have their own dormitory and nursery. You're not allowed to venture there. And mothers in-waiting will be out in the garden, working.'

'Working?'

'Yes, they have to work on the vegetable plots and fruit bushes. Keeps 'em fit, so the midwives say.'

Slowly, Evie went upstairs to the dormitory to rest and to study the booklet of jobs to do, but, exhausted, she fell asleep.

Someone shook her shoulders and immediately she was alert.

'Do you want supper?' a voice asked.

She jerked up to stare into the round face of a girl of about sixteen years of age. For a fleeting moment, Evie thought she was in her bunk at camp. Rubbing sleep from her eyes, she roused her cumbersome body and sat up, remembering where she was. She had slept through dinner, and if she hadn't been woken, she would have slept until the morning. 'Thank you, yes,' she said, going to the bathroom to splash cold water on her face.

The young girl, Milly, waited for her. 'I'll show you the way.' Entering the dining room, everyone turned to stare at Evie, who appeared much older than the other moth-ers-in-waiting. Two women towards the end of the table looked more her age. She noticed how thin one of the young girls looked, like a stray kitten, and her eyes were red-rimmed. She'd been crying. Evie hoped her baby was all right.

Noticing Evie's observation of the girl, Milly said, 'They're taking her baby away.'

Evie sat down at the table and looked in horror at Milly. 'What do you mean?'

'Adoption. Her baby is having a new mother. Some of us ain't got a choice.' Milly's eyes brimmed with tears.

Just about to take a bite of a jam sandwich, Evie asked, 'What about your baby?'

'They bombed us out of our house so we all live with granny. She said there's no room for my baby. Betty's the same, she ain't got nowhere to live.'

Evie looked around the table at the other mothers-in-waiting. She would not give her baby up for adoption. There must be some kind of help for mothers on their own. By the time she came to drink her mug of cocoa, it was cold.

Later, as she lay in bed, tuning out the noises and snoring from the other girls, she thought about the girls having to give their babies up for adoption. She was certain she would never give her baby up for adoption. She had money saved, although some of it she'd used while lodging at Mrs Hodgson's. To survive, she would have to work. That was no problem. She placed her hands on her big bump, caressing it gently, whispering, 'Wherever I go, you will too. I will always care for you, so I will need a live-in job. What do you think?'

'I don't know, but I need to sleep, so shut up talking to yerself,' a voice yawned.

Evie smiled to herself and closed her eyes.

The next morning, the clanging of a bell woke her. She was out of bed in a jiffy, then stopped, her back aching. Her mind had automatically gone into war zone mode. A quick cup of tea, then everyone began their chores before breakfast.

'What've you got?' Betty asked Evie.

'Sweep and polish the sitting room.' According to the booklet Evie had read, they had one hour before they had to head upstairs to wash before breakfast. Afterwards, you either washed clothes or tidied up in the garden and swept the path around the house. Then dinner, followed by washing dishes and cleaning down the wooden table tops, sweeping the floors and cleaning all indoor windows. Evie tidied up in the garden. She didn't mind the routine, having grown used to it in camp during the war. She didn't wish for the war to be back, but how she missed the friendship of the Ack-Ack gunner girls, and the work she'd carried out where she'd had to use her brain.

One evening, a week later, a new girl entered the recreation room. Evie was knitting a pair of bootees for her baby, while four of the other girls were playing dominos, two were reading, and Betty was dozing, her magazine having slipped to the floor. The girl, about eighteen, was dressed rather smartly in a matching two-piece maternity outfit, with blonde wavy hair and lips painted as red as poppies. She walked rather regally and, as everyone stared at her, she sat in the chair next to Evie. 'Hello,' Evie said, smiling.

The young woman pouted her lips, her reply a sneer. 'I am Miss Camilla Bentley. I will not live with such common people.'

'Where will you go?' Evie asked, her voice smooth but with an undercurrent of authority.

'My fiancé, Henry, is coming to marry me and we will have a grand house.'

'That's nice,' Evie said. 'And when is Henry coming?'

'He's away on business so as soon as he comes back.' She tossed back her hair, assessing Evie. 'What about you? Are you to be married?'

Evie felt the colour drain from her face and she closed her eyes. A picture of Matt flashed before her. An unwritten law in the home was not to ask about the father. Abruptly, she stood up, her knitting dropping to the floor and her body swaying. Then she felt a firm, steadying hand on her arm, and Betty led her from the room and upstairs to her bed.

CHAPTER TWENTY-TWO

June 1945

Evie avoided Camilla Bentley, not wanting to answer her probing questions. Though wicked, she smiled to herself when she heard that Camilla's duties were to clean the bathroom and toilet. 'I will not demean myself. That is a servant's job,' she pouted, and stamped her feet, reminding Evie of a naughty child who wants her own way. Everyone stood around, witnessing the show, for they soon recognised that Camilla liked a captive audience.

Then Matron appeared, stern-faced, saying in a voice of authority, 'What is the meaning of this disgraceful behaviour?' The girls melted away but were still within earshot.

Camilla began her spiel, but Matron put up her hand. 'While you are under my roof, you abide by the rules.'

'I refuse to do such menial tasks,' Camilla replied, with a flamboyant toss of her head.

'As you wish,' Matron said in a mild voice. A look of triumph filled Camilla's face.

But then Matron said, 'Pack your bags and leave this instant.' The girls crept nearer, keeping out of Matron's line of vision.

Camilla's face dropped, her mouth gaping open, giving her a comical look. 'But where will I go?' she stuttered.

'Wherever you wish.'

Camilla's eyes filled with tears, and she sniffed, 'I've nowhere to go.'

'You may stay here, but only if you obey the rules. Is that clear?'

Dejected, she muttered, 'Yes, Matron.'

Then Matron turned swiftly, before anyone could move, and said, 'Betty, show Camilla what to do. And you lot,' she pointed a finger, 'get back to work. We've had enough nonsense for one day.'

One girl went into labour while they were in the recreation room. Her waters broke, gushing over the immaculately polished floor. Evie groaned inwardly, for it had been her job that morning to polish the floor. She got a mop and bucket, while another girl comforted the one in labour. Someone went for the midwife. When Evie returned with the mop, Camilla was sitting on a chair, a scared look on her face. 'It happens to us all,' Evie said. 'It's normal.'

'I don't want this,' Camilla said, putting her hands on her belly. 'I want it to go away.' She began to cry, and Evie gave her a look of sympathy, knowing that she had experienced a similar stage of non-acceptance. Some girls were in denial right up to the birth of their baby.

Later, in bed, Evie couldn't get comfortable and she lay awake. Her little one was making a lot of movements and she sensed they were preparing to come out. To keep her mind occupied, she went through the items of clothing she had made for her baby that were ready in her drawer. Three of every garment: embroidered nightgowns, matinee coats, pairs of bootees, bonnets and outdoor coats. She'd spent endless hours cutting up old sheets into squares and hemming the edges to use as nappies.

She sighed and moved her body, trying to get comfortable, but still sleep wouldn't come. So she tried working out if her baby was overdue or early, but everything became hazy and jumbled up in her mind. A thought about the letter she'd received from Lily slithered into her head. It had been a jolly letter and she'd sounded so happy, having made friends with the other GI brides who all met up regularly, forming a friendship group. For a few moments, she envied Lily, then admonished herself for being fickle. She was pleased with Lily's happiness, and would always value her friendship. Though would an ocean between them halt their friendship? Then her thoughts drifted to Gloria, living in London, with the promise of singing with a band. Gloria didn't want to get married. 'I value my freedom too much,' she had once stated. Evie gave a little laugh, remembering the tone of her voice.

Evie turned again on the bed. The night seemed endless. She squeezed her eyes tight shut, willing sleep to come, when Matt's handsome face flashed before her and tears wet her lashes. Why, oh why did he have to die? She buried her face in the pillow so no one could hear her sobs. Eventually, she blew her nose on her handkerchief and settled back when the little one inside her began moving about again. She closed her eyes, willing sleep to come, but it didn't because Richard's face, looking so serious, came into view and her mind began working. What if he was the father of her baby? How would she know? Sleep caught her up in its arms and rescued her from these tortured thoughts.

The next morning, Evie had difficulties in getting out of bed. She waddled to the bathroom, then struggled to dress. She put her hands on her aching back, hoping for some relief. Slowly descending the stairs, she arrived last in the dining room for a cup of tea. Masie came in and said, 'I think you should sit tight. I reckon you are due soon.'

After a second cup of tea, Evie went to the lavatory and experienced a big gushing as her waters broke. She sat there for ages, not daring to move, then a sharp pain ripped through her lower body and she screamed.

Footsteps came hurrying down the corridor towards her. Masie reached her first, followed by the midwife, Miss Davis. Between them, they took her to the labour ward bathroom and made ready for the birth. Laying her down on the bed, Miss Davis examined Evie, muttering, 'Not quite ready yet.' Then she left Evie on her own.

She drifted in and out of sleep, Miss Davis coming to check on her periodically, and the day dragged on.

An almighty feeling of a fight going on in her belly woke her with a start. The room was in total darkness. The frightening sensation within her intensified and she screamed. A scream of fear and agony.

Suddenly, light flooded the room, and Evie looked up to see Miss Davis, who examined her.

'Almost here.'

Evie felt a contraction so fierce and she pushed it away.

'Don't push until I say,' commanded the midwife.

Covered in sweat, and only wanting to release the pressure, Evie screamed again.

'Now you can push.'

Evie felt the warmth of something slivering from between her thighs, and with relief, she let out the breath she'd held back. The cry of her baby filled the room. She tried to sit up, to see her baby, but the midwife bade her lay still for a few minutes while she cleaned the baby.

'Is it a boy or girl?' The midwife didn't answer and Evie became agitated, thinking something was wrong. I'll shout if she doesn't tell me, she told herself.

Then the midwife came to her side and said, 'You have a beautiful baby boy, my dear.'

Evie experienced the most wonderful sensation, the warmth of her baby's body next to hers as the midwife placed him in her arms. The midwife beamed down upon mother and child.

Evie's tiredness fell away from her body as she cradled her baby in her arms. 'My darling son,' she whispered, kissing the top of his forehead. She studied his tiny red face and marvelled at how perfectly formed he was. He did the most amazing thing and opened his eyes and looked up into hers in a precious moment she would never forget. Her heart melted with pure love for this wondrous creation of a beautiful bond between her and her baby son. A bond never to be broken. She vowed vehemently that she had no intentions of giving him up.

Suddenly, the midwife moved to take the baby from her arms. 'No,' Evie said fiercely. 'He's mine.'

'Baby needs to be weighed and measured, and you needed to be cleaned up and checked if you need stitches.'

Reluctantly, Evie let go of her precious baby.

'No stitches,' the midwife declared, and she swabbed down the birthing area with a solution. Its sting couldn't dilute Evie's pleasure at the birth of her son.

'He weighs seven pounds two ounces and his feet are a size one. A healthy baby,' Miss Davis commented as she wrote the details on his chart.

After a rest, they transferred Evie and her baby to the dormitory for the mothers with babies. She saw that by each bedside was a canvas cot for the baby. She laid her son gently on his cot, and the midwife helped her into bed. Suddenly feeling very weary, she settled into a position so she could see her son.

Masie came in with a cup of tea and a plain biscuit. Peeping into the cot, she cooed at baby and said, 'I never tire of seeing newborn babies. That's why I work here.' Then her voice became a whisper. 'I don't agree with them taking the baby away from its mother. It's cruel.'

By now, Evie felt sleepy, and she didn't fully absorb the meaning of Masie's words.

While she lay in bed during the expected ten days after the birth, Evie composed, in her head, a letter to her parents to inform them of the birth of their grandson, James Sinclair, born on Saturday 30 June. Finally, she wrote the letter in the hope they would allow her and James to live at Island House. After debating with herself, she finally gave the letter to Masie to post.

Once her laying period was over, Evie was soon up and about, and her baby was in the nursery with the other babies.

She could no longer ignore the tight, itchy binders around her breasts that were supposed to stop the flow of natural milk but didn't. Preparing a bottle for his 6 a.m. feed, Evie hummed to herself to distract from the cries of babies shut away in the nursery since 10 p.m. last night.

'Poor little mite,' she said as her baby guzzled down his milk. Afterwards, she bathed her son, dressed him in clean garments and put him back into his cot. Next were the chores. They were different for mothers with babies, such as going into the sluice room to clean their little one's nappies. It was an unpleasant task, but Evie didn't mind. 'Whatever I do for my baby son is a pleasure,' she crooned to herself. In the afternoon, she settled James in an old pram which she'd cleaned until it shone. With the other mothers, they were permitted to promenade around the green for one hour if accompanied by a member of staff, with instructions not to talk to anyone. People crossed the road when they saw mothers from the home.

Today, as Evie proudly pushed James in his pram, she couldn't take her eyes off him. His little face was no longer red and wrinkly, but shone with a healthy pink glow, and appeared a contented baby. She marvelled at his strength when she laid him across her knee when changing his nappy, stretching out his body, trying to grasp a stray strand of her hair. 'You are a proper Leo the Lion,' she told him. And he smiled as if he understood her, which he probably did, she surmised.

There were six mothers, all younger than her. The youngest, she learned was only sixteen. They all listened to Mary crying every night.

'I want to keep my baby,' she sobbed one day. They were in the recreation room, having quiet time before giving their babies the last feed of the day. The other girls ignored her, but Evie gave her a hug and asked her about her family.

'All gone,' Mary sniffed. 'Killed when a bomb exploded in our shelter. I was late coming home. I saw it happen. They want to take my baby away. The only living family I have.'

Evie held Mary as she sobbed, raging in her head at the cruelty of the authorities. They should support this young, traumatised girl instead of taking away her precious baby, the child she'd given life to.

One of the other mothers voiced her feelings loud and clear. 'They can take the bastard now,' she said. 'I just want to get out of here and live my life.'

One mother whispered to Evie, 'She was raped by her uncle.'

Evie saw the determination on the girl's face and the fear in her eyes. She was also traumatised. Thoughts raced round Evie's head. She wanted to do something for these girls. But what? Her own life was up in the air and might come crashing down. But come what may, she would never give up her son.

One afternoon, about a week later, Evie was in the garden with James nearby in his pram while she hoed weeds from a row of cabbages, when Masie called to her. She was waving a letter which had come in the afternoon post. Other mothers were in the garden and Evie wanted to read it in peace, so she placed it in her skirt pocket for later.

Tasks finally done, Evie washed her hands under the outside tap and pushed James in his pram to the bench at the far side of the garden. As she pushed the pram along, the rhythm of the movement lulled James into sleep. The day was hot and, on reaching the bench, she sat down, welcoming the shade of an oak tree as she pulled the letter from her skirt pocket. She looked at her mother's neat handwriting on the envelope. Florence had taken her time in answering the letter. Was it because she had been busy planning to accommodate a baby and mother at Island House? Evie wondered if a downstairs room could become a nursery.

Carefully, she opened the envelope, her fingers trembling. James murmured in his sleep, and she rose to check on him, looking lovingly into his sweet face. Sitting back down on the bench, she carefully opened the envelope and extracted the single sheet of paper. Just then, a breeze blew, rustling the oak leaves, causing a shaft of sunlight to catch her eyes, and the words on the page danced about, becoming blurred. Moving to the shade of the tree, she straightened out the paper and focused on the words. One word stood out boldly: 'No. How could you ask such a thing when your father is so ill? Have you no shame.'

The letter fluttered from Evie's hand and she watched as the breeze picked it up and whisked it away.

Rising to her feet, she looked down at her beautiful son, sleeping so peacefully, and her heart ached with unconditional love for him. 'Well, my little one. It is just me and you, together.'

CHAPTER TWENTY-THREE

September 1945

Evie waited until Masie was on her own. It was the afternoon, and James was in his pram in the garden, sleeping and taking in the late summer fresh air.

'Masie,' Evie called softly, as the woman came into the garden to shake a tablecloth from the staff table. Masie looked in her direction, and Evie hurried over to her. 'I need to ask you a favour. Could you look after James while I go out for an hour?'

Masie pondered, folding the tablecloth, then, looking into Evie's serious face, replied, 'Of course I can, love. Anything special?'

'Can I explain when I come back?'

Evie pulled her coat and beret from the bottom of the pram. Glancing over her shoulder to check no one was in view, she hurried out of the side gate. She kept to the shadow of the hedge until clear of the house. She walked fast with her head lowered until she reached Holderness Road. Then she mingled with the shoppers, avoiding a queue of women, some with restless children, hoping to buy meat from the butcher. Rationing was still in force. At last she reached

Burleigh Street, and Mrs Hodgson's house. It was a rash plan, but she couldn't think of anything else. She needed a place for her and James to live. She would never give up her precious son for adoption.

She knocked on the door and waited. Hearing no movement within, she knocked again, louder. Still no reply. She tried peeping through the window but the curtains were drawn. She was about to knock on a neighbour's door when it opened. A woman with her hair in a turban stepped out.

'What do you want?' she asked. A cigarette dangled from the corner of her mouth.

'Is Mrs Hodgson at home?'

The woman stepped closer, eyeing Evie up and down, saying, 'You be the woman carrying a bastard child. Got rid of it, have yer?'

Ignoring the woman's insensitive remarks, Evie asked again, 'Mrs Hodgson, is she home?'

The woman cackled. 'No, poor old sod has gone to her grave. And before you ask, the house is spoken for, gone to a respectable family.' With those parting words, the woman went inside, shutting the door firmly behind her.

Evie stood and stared at the house where Mrs Hodgson had given her sanctuary when she needed it. Turning away, she made her way back to Willington House, needing to feel the comfort of her son in her arms.

Back in the home, outwardly Evie appeared normal, but inside she felt downhearted, and despair was in danger of invading her body and mind. She shook herself vigorously. There was no time for self-pity. She needed to come up with another plan, fast, to keep her son James safe. The thought of him snatched from her and placed into the arms of another woman filled her with dread.

The next day, Evie sat next to Mary as they fed their babies. Mary's baby girl was two months old and she'd named her Celia, after Saint Celia. 'She will protect me and my baby girl,' Mary said in her sweet, lilting voice. She would sit crooning lullabies to Celia, and Evie loved to listen to her soothing voice.

Annie, the girl raped by her uncle, found her baby had gone up for adoption the next day. Annie sat in a corner crying as the parents left with her daughter. The next day they sent her home. Evie wondered what kind of life was waiting for her.

Then a few days later, Mary, the loving mother of Celia, had her baby girl dragged from her and placed in another woman's arms. They did it in an underhand manner. The day was quite mild, and Matron came along with a brown paper parcel containing a beautiful set of knitted leggings, matinee coat and bonnet, in matching delicate pink. 'A donation,' Matron said. 'And Mary, they will fit your baby perfectly.'

They all gathered round. 'You're a lucky blighter,' one mother remarked as they watched Mary tenderly dressing her baby in the beautiful clothes. She cooed with delight, enjoying all the attention from the admiring faces. When dressed, her baby looked a treat, and Mary held her up high for everyone to see her gurgling and laughing. Then she hugged her close, kissing the top of her downy head of hair. 'I'll take her out for a walk.'

Miss Davis came in and said, 'What a bonny girl. Let me hold her while you get the pram ready.' Mary went, and Miss Davis snapped, 'Return to your jobs.'

No one spoke, but they felt the unease.

Then they heard it, the car driving away and the screams of Mary running after it down the drive, crying, 'Celia, my daughter! Bring my baby back. Please bring her back to me. Bring her back, please . . .' From an upstairs window, Evie watched the terrible scene and heard the cries of Mary, sounding like a wounded animal, trapped in pain, which she was. As she lay face down on the gravel road, her body wracked in agony, two midwives ran out and went to her, hauling her to her feet, but Mary refused to walk and so they dragged her. Mary's cries, so pitifully raw, echoed in Evie's head for a long time.

They put Mary to bed in the vacant labour room and gave her a sedative to make her sleep. The next day, they took her to a homeless women's hostel.

Evie couldn't believe the insensitivity of the people in authority. They ignored the needs of a young woman who had lost all her family by sanctioning her baby to be cruelly taken from her. It was barbaric! All the mothers were subdued for the rest of the day, and the injustice lingered on in Evie's heart.

Where was the support for young mothers? She hurried to Matron's office and knocked on the door. Not waiting to be asked to enter, she opened the door and burst in.

Matron looked shocked but only for a moment. She said in her official voice, 'What is the meaning of this?'

Evie had no time for niceties and stood firm. 'Why haven't the authorities arranged for provisions to help young girls and women when they need it?'

'What on earth are you talking about?'

'Why isn't there a home, a halfway house for young mothers to allow them to come to terms with their lives, where they are not forced to give up their babies?'

'You and they are fortunate to have a home to have your babies in. And may I remind you, this home is all from voluntary subscriptions? Otherwise, you would have your illegitimate child on the streets. You have only yourself to blame, giving your favours too readily,' Matron scorned, a look of contempt on her face.

Evie was about to reply, but Matron held up her hand, saying, 'Dismissed!'

Anger still seething through her body, Evie marched from the office. Outside in the corridor, she saw Masie standing nearby.

'You heard it all?' Masie nodded. 'I need a live-in job so I can have my son with me.'

'I can look out for you, see what's advertised in shop windows.'

Evie felt a ray of optimism catch her. 'Would you?'

'Yes. But don't get your hopes up.'

By the end of September, Evie was feeling desperate and started planning a haphazard escape in her mind. Each day she gathered supplies, which she stored in the bottom of

James's pram: nappies and clothes, a tin of formula food and a bottle, as well as food and clothes for herself. She would sneak away with James during the night. The only person she could think of to help her was Mabel, at Island House. Would she take them in or know of someone who might? Walking to the village would take time, two days at least. If the weather stayed fine, they could sleep out under the stars, and she would knock on the doors of strangers who would make up the bottle of feed for James. Or some kind soul might offer them a lift.

As she lay wide awake in bed, mulling over her sketchy plan, the sound of rain drummed heavy on the windowpanes. Her heart sank to its lowest depth. But if she had to walk through the rain, what did it matter if she got wet as long as James was snug and warm in his pram?

The next day, the rain persisted, but it didn't deter Evie. She made everything ready to leave that night. This was her last hope. Masie was off duty and hadn't come up with anything.

Up in the dormitory alone, Evie stared out of the window as the rain still lashed against the windowpanes and the laden branches on the trees swayed downwards. She had to go this evening because every day that she stayed meant a day nearer to . . . 'No!' she shouted out loud.

'Talking to yourself,' a voice called out.

Startled, Evie spun round to see Masie standing in the doorway, wearing her outdoor clothes and wellington boots. Rain dripped from her, pooling on the floor. 'What are you doing here?'

'Shush, I'm not supposed to be here.' She stepped into the room and quietly closed the door behind her. From the inside pocket of her coat, she took out a scrap of paper and handed it to Evie. 'I saw this on my way home. I couldn't come any earlier as I had a meal to prepare for my family.'

Evie squinted at the tiny words in the half light, which read: 'Live-in position to cook and clean, apply Joshua Backbencher, pawnshop, Craven Street.'

'Masie, you treasure.' Evie hugged her.

'You best go first thing in the morning before it's taken. I'll keep an eye on the little one. Now, I must go before I'm seen. Tat-tar.' And she disappeared into the night.

Evie read the job description again before slipping it safely into her skirt pocket. She went down for supper and to give James his last feed. All the time, she felt as if something was going to explode within her.

Someone accidentally knocked against her, and she startled backward. 'Bloody hell, you're jumpy,' jeered one of the new girls.

Evie couldn't trust herself to speak and hurried away to feed her son. The times when she sat nursing James and held him close were her most precious moments. She'd bathed him and dressed him in a clean nightgown, hugging his tiny body smelling of sweet-scented talcum power. She nuzzled her lips on his soft, downy hair, loving the feel of it and smiling as it tickled her nose. She whispered to him, 'When you grow up, I will tell you all about your baby years and growing into childhood.'

Suddenly, he reached out his tiny hand and wrapped it around her little finger. A powerful feeling of protective love for her son filled her. She vowed that she, his mother, would keep him safe from any harm.

On tenterhooks, she climbed into her narrow bed, sure she wouldn't sleep. But she did, waking up feeling refreshed. As soon as she had fed James, finished breakfast, tidied away the dishes and swept the floors, Evie was ready to slip out to see Joshua Backbencher. She sighed with relief when she saw Masie, then her heart thumped and she took a few deep breaths. Masie gave her the thumbs up sign.

Opening the laundry door, Evie looked out. All clear. Stealthily, she inched round the side of the house and, keeping to the hedgerow and with her head down, she dashed to open the side gate and hurried through. Out on the tree-lined avenue, she quickened her pace, wanting to be the first to apply for the live-in job.

CHAPTER TWENTY-FOUR

October 1945

Evie arrived at the pawnbroker's shop before 9 a.m. She grabbed hold of the door handle only to find it was stuck, so she pushed and pushed to no avail. The door remained tightly shut and locked. Looking through the grimy window, she saw haphazard piles of goods. Then she stepped back with a start. A man's face peered at her over the screen that separated the window from the shop. Recovering, she quickly gestured for him to open the door and waited. Inside, she could hear shuffling footsteps. Her nerves jangled as she willed the man to hurry and open the door. The sound of iron bolts being drawn back screeched and grated on her nerves, and she bit on her lip at the noise coming from the riddling of a key in the lock. She took deep breaths, stopping herself from exploding with frustration.

At last! The door opened, but only a crack. 'What do you want?' growled the disembodied voice.

Evie stared at the face glaring at her. Its two coal-black eyes were bloodshot, its mouth lost within the entangled beard. 'I've come about the live-in job,' she blurted out.

'Have yer now.'

'Yes, can I come in?' Without a word, he opened the door wider and she stepped over the threshold. Immediately, the revolting, stale smell hit her in the face. 'I can see why you need someone to clean for you,' she offered, peering around the gloomy shop.

'I'll have no cheek,' he growled at her.

'Sorry, it was just my observation.' Then she looked him full in those troubled eyes and continued. 'During the war, I was an Ack-Ack gunner girl. I'm trained to observe and deal with situations promptly.'

He didn't reply at first, just raised his thick greying eyebrows, then spat out, 'Why do you want a downtrodden job if you are that experienced?'

Her voice was quiet and measured. 'I have a son.' And with her fingers crossed behind her back, she added, 'His daddy, an RAF pilot, was killed in action.' A lump rose in her throat and she held back the tears which threatened to break free. If this obnoxious man said anything derogatory about Matt, she would give him a piece of her mind. So there!

He looked away, and his voice was low when he spoke. 'I lost my daughter in action, too.' He turned to her, and she saw tears glinting in his eyes.

Daft as it might seem, she wanted to hug this crusty old man. Instead, she said, 'War is so cruel and senseless.'

He sighed deeply and uttered, 'Aye, lass, it is.' Then he straightened up his bent body and looked her in the eye. 'You'll do. When can you start?'

Evie realised she had been holding her face stiffly, as when his words filtered into her brain, she smiled and answered, 'Thank you, Mr Backbencher. As soon as I can make the arrangements. Would tomorrow be convenient?'

'Yes. And I'm known as Bencher.' She stared in surprise. 'Everyone knows me by that name,' he grunted.

Returning to the home, Evie realised that Bencher hadn't mentioned her wages or where her accommodation would be. It didn't matter, she mused, as long as she had a place to go to with her beloved son.

She opened the door and found Masie waiting in the laundry room.

'Thank goodness you're back. Matron came looking for you, and I had to play dumb. She wants to see you in her office.'

'I got the job,' Evie whispered to Masie. 'I'll take a peep at James first.' When she went into the nursery where he lay in his crib and bent over to look at him, he sensed her there and opened his eyes wide. She kissed him gently on his forehead and said, 'I'll be back soon, my darling.'

Her heart sang as she made her way to Matron's office. She smoothed her hair and put her shoulders back as she reached the door.

'Enter,' called the voice from within.

Evie's feet made no noise as she crossed the thickly carpeted floor to stand before Matron's desk. As usual, she was writing in a ledger, a ploy to make the girls feel uneasy. Today, Evie felt ebullient. In her mind she was already going through the clothes she had assembled for James. She didn't have her own pram. She could ask Matron if she could borrow one.

'Ah, Miss Sinclair, are you going home to your parents' house, as you stated earlier? Otherwise, I must put plans in place regarding James.' She gave a tight-lipped smile.

'No, Matron, I am not going home to my parents.'

'Ah, just as I thought.'

'I have secured a live-in position as housekeeper and my son is welcome.'

Matron stared, stony faced. 'I have not heard of your arrangement.'

'Sorry, Matron. I have only just confirmed the details.'

'I shall need a forwarding address.'

'Yes, Matron. I leave tomorrow.'

'Tomorrow,' she spluttered. 'This is most irregular.'

'My employer wishes for me to begin immediately. I couldn't refuse, Matron.' She crossed her fingers behind her back and continued. 'I am so grateful to you for taking me in when I needed help the most. I am sure Mother's committee will make a donation to such a worthy cause,' Evie finished sweetly.

Matron fixed a glare on her face, lowered her head, and wrote in the ledger. Dismissed, Evie slipped out of the office.

Outside in the corridor, she leaned against the cool wall to give her hot, trembling body some relief. She couldn't remember feeling like this when she faced an officer as a gunner girl. She sighed deeply. Back then she hadn't had a son to care for. Walking on shaky legs, she hurried to see James, needing to feel his tender body in her arms.

She picked him up from his crib and he uttered a cry. 'Yes, my darling,' she crooned. 'You are hungry. And I have wonderful news to tell you.'

'Oh, aye. What's this news then?' Evie spun round and saw a mother feeding her baby.

'I'm leaving tomorrow, and I am taking James with me.'

'Are you running away?' the young mother asked. Evie guessed she was about fifteen.

'No, I have a live-in job and I can take James with me.' She hugged him close, kissing his soft cheek.

The young girl sighed wistfully, and said, 'Mam said I'm too young to care for a baby, and she's got too many kids to take on another. I can go, but I've not to get myself in the family way again or she'll kick me out.'

The girl's tone was matter of fact about her future, but the hard bit was to come: when you gave your baby up into another woman's arms, a woman who would become your baby's mother, not you. Evie didn't voice her thoughts, knowing it would be a painful parting.

Evie soon had James's feeding bottle and tin of feed, his clothes and her few belongings packed, ready to leave tomorrow. She wrote to her mother, giving her the address in Craven Street, but she didn't say that it was a pawnbroker's shop. She mentioned the good work of the home and that a donation would be welcome.

Next morning, in Matron's office, Evie asked, 'May I borrow a pram, Matron?'

'Certainly not,' she replied in her cold, authoritarian voice. 'I understand you have made your arrangements.'

The door firmly shut behind her, Evie found herself outside, holding James in one arm and their bag of belongings in the other. But nothing could dampen her spirits, and her heart sang as she strode away to freedom. By the time she reached Holderness Road, both James and the bag seemed heavier and she stopped to rest on a chair outside a shop. It felt heavenly to rest her aching limbs. James became fractious, and she kissed his forehead and crooned to him, hoping he would go back to sleep, but then he let out a loud wail for one so young. Just then, the shopkeeper came bustling from the shop and stared disapprovingly at her.

'Madam,' he declared in a sonorous voice. 'This chair is for my customers.'

Reluctantly struggling to her feet, Evie muttered, 'Sorry.' She heaved James up into her arms and picked up the bag. As she stepped forward, a young lad on a homemade bogey cart bumped into her.

'Sorry, missus,' he called cheekily.

He was about to continue on his way when Evie shouted, 'Stop! Would you like to earn a shilling?'

At the mention of money, the boy, about ten years old, stopped and said, 'Do you mean it?'

'If you can give my baby and the bag a ride, I will.'

Gently, she laid James on his blanket with the bag supporting his head. Wide-eyed, he looked around. The lad fixed a rope handle, and he carefully pulled the cart along, with Evie trotting by the side, watching over James.

Within twenty minutes, they arrived safely at their destination. Evie handed over the shilling and the lad went off, whistling a merry tune.

Bencher must have been looking out for them, because the door jangled open and he came out to Evie and reached for her bag to carry indoors. As Evie stepped over the threshold with James in her arms, the mustiness greeted her, but strangely, after the disinfected smell of the home, it felt

165

comforting. The same couldn't be said for James, who started crying.

'I hope he doesn't wail a lot,' Bencher said, as he looked at the bundle in her arms.

'Only when he's hungry,' she answered cheerfully. And on cue, from the tiny alcove kitchen, the kettle on the small gas burner whistled. 'I'll mix his feed.' She looked round to see where she could safely lay James down, but every surface appeared cluttered. Without hesitation, she thrust her son into the arms of the startled Bencher.

'Whoa, I'm not a baby minder,' he said, when James reached out a tiny hand to grasp at the man's beard.

Evie watched with relief as a smile filled Bencher's rough face and he seemed mesmerised by the baby. She set to make his feed.

When her son was fed and changed, his soiled nappy in a bucket of cold water out in the yard, Evie asked Bencher, 'Do you know where I can buy a pram from?'

He scratched his head and looked round the shop, as if there was one lurking in a corner. 'Mrs Potter is yer best bet. She's a big brood of kids, so might have one spare.'

'Where does she live?' Evie asked, as she held James on her shoulder, patting his back to bring up his wind.

'She'll be in later. I'll show you your quarters.'

She followed him up a flight of rickety wooden stairs to a room at the top of the house overlooking the yard below and the rooftops of other buildings. Looking out of the grimy, uncurtained window, she could see the top of a tree in the distance, its leaves turning golden and bronze. Turning back to survey the room, she was surprised to see a big brass bedstead, a tallboy, a nursing chair and an enormous wardrobe. Someone, a woman, must have decorated the room by the look of the faded rose pattern wallpaper, and the door and skirting-boards which were painted a delicate green. She wondered if the room had been his daughter's.

Bencher led the way along the landing to a bathroom, which at one time must have been a bedroom as the off-white stained bath and lavatory looked lost in the big room. Further along the landing was a linen cupboard, and another two rooms with the doors closed. He didn't mention them, so she assumed they must be his private rooms.

Going back to her and James's room, she laid him on the bed, watching the gentle rhythm of his breathing as he slumbered. She put a hand on her heart and felt it overflowing with love for her precious son. She thought of mothers who were forced to give up their babies for adoption. Unwed mothers, blamed for getting pregnant, who had no support, while the men faced no blame or accountability.

Bending over to kiss her sleeping son on his cheek, she thought of the injustice against unmarried mothers, and the sad figure of Mary came to mind. No organisations existed to support unwed mothers and their babies. 'I'm one of the lucky ones,' she whispered to James. In response, he gave a contented sigh.

CHAPTER TWENTY-FIVE

October 1945

Evie glanced at the outside world through the grimy window, seeing the dull, murky October morning. Keeping herself busy, she boiled a kettle of water and poured it into a bucket, added soda, and was searching for a piece of cloth when the shop bell jangled and the door swung open. A large woman came bustling in, wearing a big floral apron patched with various bits of material, her dark hair partly hidden by a colourful woollen shawl which covered her shoulders. Evie wondered why she was carrying a man's suit. A demob suit, by the look of it, in navy-blue with pinstripes.

The woman glared at Evie and spoke in a sharp tone. 'Where is he?' She dumped the suit on the counter. 'I ain't got time to hang around.'

Evie stared at the woman, who reminded her of one of the corporals on the gun site. Just then, Bencher came from behind a curtained partition, rubbing his hands. 'Ah, Mrs Potter. Pleased to see you.' He lifted the suit off the counter and examined it. 'Getting a bit worse for wear.'

'Don't give me that coddle talk. It's only a bit of dust.' She held out her hand while he wrote out the docket.

Then, from under the counter he brought up a metal tin, lifted a bunch of keys fastened to a chain around his girth, selected one and unlocked the box. He opened it and slowly counted out five shillings into the woman's hand. She snatched it and put it in a deep pocket of her apron. She turned to hurry off when Bencher said, 'You got a pram to sell this young woman?' He pointed a finger at Evie.

At the mention of the word 'sell', Mrs Potter turned to look at Evie, taking in her smart appearance.

Her years in the ATS had taught Evie to be neat and tidy at all times. Well, mostly.

'Aye, I have. You can come and look.'

Evie fetched her coat and purse and lifted a sleeping James from where he slumbered in the corner of an enormous chair, following Mrs Potter out into the street. The woman hurried across the road. Evie had to pause while a horse and rulley trundled by. She saw Mrs Potter turning into a side street but by the time she got there, the woman had vanished. The street was empty except for a small group of boys playing marbles on the road.

'She went down there,' one boy pointed to a side passage between two houses.

Evie smiled her thanks and hurried down the narrow passage, side-stepping a broken sink. She noticed the bomb-damaged walls of the backyards as she heard a voice shout from one of them. 'In here.' Evie followed the sound of the voice into a backyard, careful not to stumble, and holding tight to a restless James. Under a makeshift lean-to, she spied a battered old pram. Mrs Potter was busy chucking out the junk that filled it. Evie's heart sank at its filthy state, and her idea of popping James straight into it evaporated.

Mrs Potter must have seen the horror on Evie's face because she said, 'Don't you worry, love. I'll have it shiny in no time.' Evie would have liked to believe her. 'You, Ginny, put kettle on and mash a pot of tea,' Mrs Potter shouted.

A skinny girl with auburn hair poked her head out of the kitchen door. 'Are you sure, Mam? It ain't afternoon.'

'Less of your cheek, my lass, and do as you're told.' Turning to Evie, Mrs Potter said, 'You go inside, love, and have a cuppa. I'll soon have pram shining like new.'

Evie, bemused by this exchange between mother and daughter, went into the kitchen, wanting to make the fractious James more comfortable. She was surprised to be welcomed into a large, clean and shining kitchen. The black leaded stove gleamed, and the kettle came to the boil on the open fire.

'Best use the good china,' Ginny said, giving a lop-sided smile. Evie noticed the scars on her cheek. 'Old Hitler chucked a bomb at me and hit me face as I ran to safety. Lads make fun of me so Mam says I don't have to go to school.'

'I'm sorry,' Evie murmured as she sat down in a rocking chair. The gently rhythmic movement soon lulled James to sleep. She watched Ginny fetch a flower-patterned cup and saucer from a magnificent, highly polished mahogany dresser full of delicate crockery.

'It's Mam's pride and joy so I'm glad old Hitler didn't get it or life wouldn't be worth living,' Ginny spoke as she poured the hot water into a china teapot.

'I am honoured,' Evie remarked.

'It's part of the deal when Mam sells anything.'

Evie nodded her thanks as she accepted the cup of tea. 'A business- woman, your mam?'

'Aye, she has to be with our dad. He'd spend all the money down the pub if he had a chance. He said Mam's worse than his bloody sergeant major. And she tells him he won't get any of the other.'

Evie nearly choked on her mouthful of tea at this innocent, matter-of-fact explanation by Ginny.

Just then, Mrs Potter's voice bellowed from the yard. 'Ginny, tell Harry to get himself down, now!' Ginny relayed the message.

Evie heard someone jumping down the stairs and a gangly lad with the same tight auburn curls as Ginny came tearing through the kitchen and out into the yard.

'He's me twin,' she said with pride. The sound of childish voices squabbling came from upstairs and Ginny rushed out into the narrow corridor that led up the stairs to the bedrooms and the attic beyond. 'Shut your bleeding row or I'll come up and whack yer.' Breezing back into the kitchen, she said to Evie, 'Four little ones under five. They like Harry to play with 'em.'

With all the commotion going on, James stirred in her arms. He would soon be due for his next feed. Rising from her chair, she laid him on it and wedged him in with a cushion, then went to the kitchen door to see how the cleaning of the pram was going. Harry was kneeling on the cold concrete yard, polishing the spokes of the pram wheels. They sparkled in contrast to the grey daylight. Despite the bitter day, Mrs Potter had rivulets of sweat on her face. Amazed, Evie looked at the pram. The inside material was now a lovely shade of cream, and the cover and hood were both a deep burgundy. The outside body of the pram was in swirls of cream and burgundy.

Evie felt a warmth of gratitude rise within her and gave a cry of pleasure. Both Mrs Potter and Harry looked at her. Stepping into the yard, she said, 'It's perfect and you've both worked so hard to make it so.'

Mrs Potter beamed and Harry said, 'Can I go now, Mam?'

'Aye, go on.'

'Thank you, Harry,' Evie smiled at the lad. He blushed and quickly made his getaway.

'I'll get my purse and baby.'

Ginny was nursing a wide-awake James, whose tiny hand tried to pull one of her curls.

'Thank you, Ginny,' she said, reaching for her son.

'I like babies,' Ginny said shyly.

In the yard, Evie asked Mrs Potter, 'How much?'

'Four shillings,' she said, placing one hand on her hip, the other itching for the money.

Opening her purse, Evie counted out five shillings into Mrs Potter's hand, whose eyes widened. 'I think that is a fairer price. I am satisfied.'

Overjoyed, Mrs Potter said, 'Thank you kindly, love. Though I'm sorry, I've only got a scrap of linen for the pram.'

'I've not far and baby is warm tucked up in his blanket.'

Carefully, Evie wheeled the pram down the rutted passageway and on to the street. Proudly she strolled along, so pleased with her purchase and feeling a sense of freedom, something she had not felt since leaving the ATS. Now, she and James had a future to look forward to.

She wrangled the pram through the shop doorway and parked it in a far corner away from the goods on sale. She did not want Bencher selling James's pram. From the back of the shop, he came to view her purchase, and muttered about it. He reached out to take James while Evie made his feed.

They had their own room, but she liked to sit on the rocking chair behind the counter. During the daytime, she liked the company of the people who came into the shop. She was amazed by the number of children who came in with goods to pawn, often snotty-nosed ones who looked in need of a good meal. 'It's a ploy,' Bencher told her. 'They send those bairns who might pull at yer heartstrings, but I'm hardened to it. Otherwise, I'd never make a living.'

'It puzzles me why men's suits are brought in at the beginning of a week and redeemed at the end of the week.'

Bencher laughed. 'So that they can get the housekeeping money off their husbands on payday. He needs his suit to go to the pub on a Saturday night, so he has to give his wife the money, otherwise he will be in the shit with his mates. It's a matter of pride and his perceived standing in the community.'

Evie gently rubbed James's back to release his wind after his feed. As she did so, she thought of her parents and, although they lived in a different environment, the principle of pride was loosely similar. They did not want her and her fatherless baby. Changing James's nappy, she made him comfortable and kissed her son. He was her life now. She laid him to rest in his pram with the new covers she had bought for it. It pulled at her heartstrings to see him looking so cosy, warm and safe. Rocking the pram gently, he soon slumbered. This gave her time to concentrate on her cleaning duties.

Armed with a bucket of hot water suds and a wash-leather and duster, she set about cleaning the window display. Some objects had been there for a while, judging by the state of them. When finished with her task, she sat back on her heels to survey her labours. All the items were clean and polished to perfection, displayed to their best advantage. The large painting of a pair of young lovers took centre stage. The outside of the window needed cleaning now. In the street, she stood on a wobbly stool to reach the top, then stepped down to admire her efforts.

From behind her, a cheerful voice said, 'You could get a window cleaner's job.'

Evie spun round to a familiar face. 'Oh, Masie. How wonderful to see you. I've missed you.' She hugged her friend. 'I get along with Bencher fine, but I miss talking to another woman.'

'Come round to mine next Saturday afternoon. My sister and family will be out. We'll have a really good gossip.' She gave her address down Westcott Street, further up Holderness Road.

'I'll look forward to that.' Evie gave Masie another hug and went indoors.

Bencher admired the window display and Evie felt a sense of satisfaction, something she had not known since her demob from the gunner crew. James murmured in his pram and, smiling, she whispered, 'You, my darling, are my greatest achievement.'

That night, snuggled down in her bed, with James in his cot by her side, her thoughts turned to Richard. Her heart gave a tiny flutter, and she wondered if he had returned home to London. She gave a deep sigh. Would she ever see him again?

CHAPTER TWENTY-SIX

December 1945

The settled way of life with Bencher added structure to their daily lives. James thrived on it, and so did Evie. On Saturday afternoons she looked forward to visiting her friend Masie when she wasn't on duty at the home. Masie, a widow with no children, whose husband died when his battleship was torpedoed, lived with her brother and family in a striking Edwardian house with four bedrooms. Evie admired the extensive garden with plenty of room for children to play and an area for vegetables and flowers. She missed having a garden. As a child, she'd loved to go out in the garden to feed the birds and, when it snowed, to have snowball fights with friends. She pictured James when he was older, running about on sturdy legs and free-falling on the lawn or playing with a bat and ball.

'He's certainly coming on. Yes, you are, little fellow,' Masie crooned, as she bounced James on her knee. He gurgled with mirth, enjoying the lively action.

Evie sat back in her chair, loving this interplay, and thought of her mother. Aloud, she said, 'I wonder if Mother ever thinks of her grandson and regrets not having us home.'

Masie slowed her play with James and said, 'Why don't you have a photograph taken and send it to your parents? They might invite you both for Christmas.'

'Why didn't I think of that? Who's the best photographer?'

'Mr Merton, further down Holderness Road on the way to town.'

'Ah, I know. He has pictures in his studio window.'

'Best make an appointment; I know he has weddings on Saturdays.'

The following Monday afternoon, on a bright December day, Evie left the shop dressed in a warm dark green coat with fur trimming and matching hat, a bargain from a second-hand shop. She pushed the pram with James sleeping peacefully down Holderness Road to Mr Merton's photograph studio. She parked the pram outside. At first, she felt reluctant to leave James outside a shop in his pram, but other mothers did. 'Who'd pinch a bairn and have another mouth to feed?' retorted a mother with a brood of six. Gradually, Evie felt she could safely do so too.

She gazed lovingly at her son and then entered the studio. In the reception area, behind a counter, stood a middle-aged woman with a welcoming smile.

'Good afternoon, madam.'

Evie was glad she wore gloves so that the woman could not see her ringless wedding finger. Evie explained that she wanted a photograph of her son to send to her parents.

'We have a special bargain price for a Christmas family photograph. Would you be interested in that offer?'

Evie felt herself growing hot, and then decided she did not need to feel embarrassed. Standing tall, she smiled. 'Just a photograph of my son is fine, thank you.'

The receptionist studied the appointment book, then looked up, saying, 'Two p.m. on Wednesday suit, madam?'

'Yes, thank you,' she smiled, and left the studio.

She hurried back to the shop to finish her chores and check the meal in the oven. Bencher preferred his main meal in the evening. When cleaning the room at the back of the shop, she had discovered a gas stove and persuaded Bencher to have it serviced. It was now in working order. Knowing she would be out this afternoon, she had prepared a casserole of minced beef, onions, carrots and potatoes, which was simmering in the oven on a low heat, so she just had the dumplings to make. She would pop them on top of the casserole to cook for twenty minutes before eating. She had learned that from Bencher's late wife's cookery book; an invaluable help, Evie mused, for her cooking skills were limited to a few basics.

When she arrived at the shop, one of Bencher's cronies was sitting on the customer chair, chatting. 'Mouth-watering smell,' he said to Evie, showing his missing front teeth. 'I wish my missus could cook like you.'

Evie glanced at Bencher to see if he was happy for them to share the meal, and he nodded, saying, 'Just a basinful.'

Taking off her outdoor clothes and settling James, she fastened on her apron. She checked the casserole, its savoury aroma filling the kitchen. She found a white basin in the dresser cupboard and spooned casserole into it, filling the basin and covering it with a clean cloth.

'By heck, my missus will be pleased,' the man said, when she placed it on the counter in front of him.

'Aye, and bring the basin back,' grunted Bencher. Evie left the two men to their rumination.

The following day, sorting through a job lot from someone's home, Evie carefully unpacked a dinner service with different-sized tureens and washed it all in a bowl of soap suds before displaying it in the window. In a wooden box were family photographs in silver frames, all from a bygone age, she mused. Pulling a duster from her apron pocket, she began rubbing at one frame until the silver shone.

Other frames were more tarnished, but she remembered Mabel making up a concoction to clean silver, a thick paste with baking soda and lukewarm water. She applied the mixture with care and gently rubbed the frames, leaving the mixture on for a few minutes, before removing it with a damp cloth and buffing them with a soft dry cloth. They sparkled. She set them on an old gate-legged table for Bencher to evaluate their worth. However, she kept two frames aside, hoping they were not beyond her own pocket to buy.

When she had bathed James and given him a feed at 6 p.m., he was happy to sleep in his cot until his night feed. At first, she would sit in her bedroom during these hours, but one night, Bencher said, 'You can sit with me on an evening, if you want, lass.'

'I'd love to,' she said. So now she sat with him in the comfortable room next to the kitchen and listened to the wireless. However, most Saturday evenings, he went out to the pub to drink with his cronies, and on these solitary evenings she wondered what it would be like to be married and sitting with her husband. She pictured Matt and his charming smile, but then he would fade and be replaced by a dreamy image of Richard by her side. She would berate herself for fantasising. 'Get a grip, woman,' she murmured out loud.

Wednesday afternoon approached. Evie dressed James in a beautiful blue outfit of coatee, leggings and hat, all of which she had knitted in an evening. They arrived at the studio promptly. James, her darling son, gurgled and cooed as she lifted him from his pram and kissed his chubby cheeks. 'You know this is special,' she whispered to him. Over the past month, she had noticed how he picked up on her moods, and this amazed her. If she felt sombre, James would look at her with his big, expressive eyes. Then she would tickle his tummy and make him laugh, and they would both feel much better. 'A kind of therapy,' Masie had said, when Evie told her.

'Hello, madam. You have arrived in good time. Come through into the studio.' The receptionist greeted Evie. 'And baby looks happy. A good sign.'

The studio was windowless, and Evie presumed this stopped light entering and spoiling the photographs. James felt restless in her arms and the receptionist gave him a tiny fluffy toy dog to hold his attention. Glancing round the room, Evie saw a wicker chair with a white satin cushion and a small imitation of a chaise longue in a beige colour.

'Would madam prefer your son to sit or lie down? Shall we see which he is happiest with?' smiled the receptionist.

First, Evie laid James on the chaise longue, but he wriggled about. Picking him up, she whispered to him, 'You have to look your best for Grandma and Grandad.' She sat him on the chair and he gurgled and cooed, then slipped sideward. The receptionist fetched another cushion, and James fitted happily between the two.

Mr Merton entered the room, a man with a beaming smile and a soft, intimate voice. Acknowledging Evie, he turned his attention to James, who appeared mesmerised by the photographer's facial expressions and laughed, his eyes wide, watching. The fluffy toy fell from James's hands.

Evie watched, enthralled by the photographer's way of interacting with the sitter. It is an art, she acknowledged.

Evie did not realise, but they were in the studio for about thirty minutes. By the end, she had two photographs of James, one to send to her parents and the other one for herself. She would negotiate a price for the two silver photograph frames with Bencher. It would take most of her savings, but it was worth it.

She thanked Mr Merton and the receptionist, who was Mrs Merton, who gave James a small bottle of orange juice as Evie settled him in his pram. 'See you on Friday to collect the photographs,' Mrs Merton called.

Outside, the daylight had gone, but street lamps and shop windows illuminated the way, so different from the war years when it was a total blackout.

Bencher had generously given her money to buy fish and chips and mushy peas from the fried fish shop. It was a rare treat and saved Evie from cooking.

By the time they'd finished the meal and James had been fed, bathed and settled, Evie felt tired but happy. She flopped down on a chair to listen to the wireless with Bencher. He smoked his pipe and laughed at the comedy programme, while she sat quietly contented, staring into the fire-grate at the dancing flames. Dancing . . . A distant memory of when she went dancing with the Ack-Ack gunner girls came to her. She wondered when Lily would sail to America, and about Gloria down in London, setting out on her singing career. She must write to them, because she never wanted to lose touch with them. Their lives sounded more exciting than hers, though she wouldn't swap with them.

Later, going upstairs to give James his night feed, she tiptoed into the bedroom to gaze lovingly upon her son, and a feeling of pure contentment filled her. 'He's my reason for living,' she murmured, gently touching his cheek. 'I am blessed, my darling son, to have you in my life. Nothing can equal that.'

James stirred, opening his eyes at the sound of his mother's voice.

* * *

'He's a fine-looking chap,' Bencher said, as Evie proudly showed him the photograph of James. She sat at the small table, carefully wrapping the image in the silver frame that Bencher had gifted to her, along with the second one, which stood proudly on her bedside cabinet. 'Call it an early Christmas gift,' Bencher had said to her when she asked about the price of the frames. She'd knitted him a pair of fingerless gloves for when he served in the shop on a winter's day. Their relationship was quite informal, and they seemed to rub along well, a quiet companionship. Evie thought of her father. She missed his gentle and understanding ways. Though she did not miss her mother's coldness, and the feeling that Florence only tolerated her. Evie shuddered.

After Evie posted her small parcel, she called to see Masie on Saturday afternoon, to give her a Christmas gift, knowing Masie was working on Christmas Day on the Tuesday. She had knitted her friend a scarf and matching mittens in a cheery red. The wool she used for knitting came from old pullovers and cardigans that she unravelled, washed, dried and rewound. She found this quite therapeutic, as she sat by the fireside on a winter's evening, listening to the wireless with Bencher. He appreciated the work she did in the shop, shopping and housekeeping. But she didn't enjoy queuing for food, which was still on rations, even though the war was over. She would often see Ginny, Mrs Potter's daughter, who was quite adept at securing a bargain. 'Sausages at butcher's,' she would whisper in Evie's ear.

'Can I open the parcel now?' asked Masie, eagerness aglow on her face.

'Yes,' laughed Evie, and James gurgled, his tiny hands trying to clutch the wrapping paper. They spent a lovely afternoon together, and Evie kept hers and James's gifts to open on Christmas Day.

As they were leaving, Masie said, her face sombre, 'It's not the same at the home with the new matron. The other one was strict, but this one is cruel. It's unsettling.'

On her way home, Evie thought about what Masie had said.

Having a baby out of wedlock was a traumatic experience, and it was a tragedy when your baby was snatched from your arms. She was one of the fortunate ones, and her heart sang with love and pride for her son. But now there was a new matron, whose cruel ways could only add more distress to the mothers and their babies. What could be done?

Pushing the pram along the darkening street, Evie wished she had an answer.

CHAPTER TWENTY-SEVEN

April 1946

James was now ten months old and thriving. 'Yes, you are, my darling son,' Evie cooed to him as she dressed him on a fine spring morning in early April. She loved watching his animated facial expressions as he took in his surroundings and reached for his toes. His face became an expression of puzzlement as he was unsure of who they belonged to. 'But now you know.' She tickled him under the chin, lifted him into her arms and went downstairs and into the shop. 'Morning, Bencher.'

'Hmm,' he grunted, not lifting his head as he studied a row of figures in a ledger. James gurgled his good morning, and Bencher's head shot up, his face wreathed in smiles as he feasted his eyes on James. 'He's growing. Soon have him serving behind the counter.'

She sat James in his pram, where he watched the comings and goings of the customers, who always had a few kind words to say to him, keeping him happy, while Evie did her morning chores. Taking advantage of the warmer weather, most afternoons she would take James for a stroll in his pram, shopping or further down Holderness Road to East Park, where he loved to see the ducks on the pond.

As she swept the floor and washed the windows, Evie's thoughts dwelled on Bencher's earlier remark about James helping him in the shop. A throwaway remark, maybe. However, she could not imagine her and James living here forever. She only considered their stay as short term. The amount of her weekly savings was small, and it would take her years to have enough money to invest in a home of their own. She would need employment, which would have to fit in with James's needs. Her head spun like a Catherine wheel as she thought of ideas for their future. Maybe more knitting? She would not ask her parents for money. At Christmas time she had received a card, but there was no mention of James's photograph in the silver frame.

One afternoon, after James's feed, Evie set off to look in the second-hand shops or any church jumble sale to buy an old knitted garment for a few pence, so she could reuse the wool. She planned to ask Bencher if she could display and sell it in his shop.

'A business deal?' he asked, his rheumy eyes narrowing.

'Not exactly. Maybe I could do extra work in exchange for selling garments in the shop?'

He smiled and said, 'You have the makings of a businesswoman.'

She laughed, and he held out his hand for her to shake.

She worked diligently, selling her knitted garments, but money was slow to mount up. There did not seem enough hours in the day or night. Her chief priority was to look after James, then housekeeping, shopping, and her knitting and book-keeping for selling her knitted garments. Often, in her lonely bed, she thought that she would have loved a night at the cinema with friends. She missed Lily and Gloria, both down south and too far for her to travel with James. She thought of their nights in the NAAFI, when Gloria would sing and drag her and Lily up as her backing singers. What fun they'd had. Lily seemed contented with her life, judging by her letters. She was working in a NAAFI shop and had made friends with the other GI brides. Gloria's letters were infrequent, being too busy establishing her singing career. Gloria didn't reply when Evie asked if she'd be on the wireless. Evie wondered if life in London was tougher than Gloria had thought.

She crawled into bed each night and was asleep in a moment, but all too soon, James would wake her for his early morning feed. However, now he was eating solids, which she mashed up for him, soaking his breakfast rusk in milk. She wished she had his energy and his strength as he kicked his legs while she changed his nappy. 'You will grow up to be a fine boy, just like your daddy.' The words flowed from her before she could stop them. James looked up into her face so trustingly. One day, he was going to ask that question. And what could she say?

A few days later, coming in from her afternoon walk, Bencher greeted her. 'There's a telegram come for you.' He pointed to the dresser.

Evie's body stiffened as she went over to where it was propped up against the candlestick. Her legs felt rubbery, as if they did not belong to her, and her fingers trembled as she reached for it. James whimpered, as if he sensed something was wrong. Then he laughed as Bencher tickled him under the chin. Clutching the telegram in her hand, she sank down on to the nearest chair, an old armchair with a sagging bottom. She made herself read the words. It was from the family solicitor informing her of her father's death and the date of the funeral.

Stunned, not able to speak or move, she stared ahead, seeing nothing through the blurring of her wet eyes. The clock kept on ticking away as life went on around her. She heard the voices of Bencher and Ginny, talking to James and making him laugh. Bencher touched her shoulder and said in a quiet voice, 'Drink this brandy for shock.' He held the glass to her lips, forcing them open. She drank, spluttering as the liquid rushed down her throat, warming her insides and dulling the pain.

She felt the light touch of someone tucking a blanket round her and she floated off. She dreamed she was back on the gun site and couldn't get the instruments in place while an enemy aircraft was diving towards them. She ducked, and it missed her, but she fell sideward. Then a firm hand lifted her to her feet and walked her up some stairs, and they did not let go of her until she sank on to something soft. 'James,' she whispered. 'Safe,' replied the voice. Then oblivion overtook her.

The sound of James crying woke her, and she struggled to raise her throbbing head. Then she heard Ginny's voice saying, 'Hush, James, I'll give you your milk.'

Lying on her side and facing James's cot, Evie saw Ginny sitting on a blanket on the floor, cradling James and holding his bottle of milk as he sucked contentedly. She put her head back on the pillow, closed her eyes and slept.

'Evie,' a voice called softly.

Evie opened her eyes to see Ginny holding a tray with a mug of tea and a plate of toast. She raised herself on her elbow and looked at James's cot. 'He's downstairs with Bencher. You have your breakfast and get up when you're ready. Mam's said I can look after James for you.'

Tears filled Evie's eyes and, in a daze, she ate her breakfast and dressed. She needed to send a reply telegram to the solicitor and attend her father's funeral. Sitting on her bed, she sobbed. Eventually, giving an enormous sigh, she rose and went to the bathroom and washed her face again in cold water. She must try to remain strong, and she wondered how her mother was coping. Florence never showed her emotions, or at least Evie had witnessed none.

She hurried to the post office and sent off the telegram to the solicitor. On leaving the post office, she stopped and wondered. Should she send her mother a telegram?

'Make up your mind, missus,' a man's voice grumbled at her elbow.

Turning, she saw a man with a barrow loaded with paint pots and ladders. She had not realised she had stopped still in the middle of the pavement. 'Sorry,' she muttered, side-stepping. As he moved off, she began walking slowly back home. She decided not to contact her mother because she might stop her from attending her father's funeral. Evie gave another deep sigh, guessing she might be an embarrassment to her mother.

Later, she was at Mrs Potter's house, where Ginny had taken James. They never asked about James's father. In fact, no one did. There were a few whispers in the shop, but they died away eventually. The delicious waft of hot bread cakes baking in the oven filled her nostrils as she entered the kitchen. It reminded her of Mabel back at Island House when she made hot cakes. Her stomach rumbled, and she felt a shock that she could feel hungry when her father had just died.

Mrs Potter and Ginny looked at her; they had heard the noise of her stomach as well. 'You look like a wilting daisy,' Mrs Potter remarked. 'If you don't build your strength, you'll be no good to man or beast. Sit yerself down.'

Looking round, Evie asked, 'Where's James?'

'In the passage, sleeping soundly,' she said, putting a mug of tea before her along with a hot cake sliced in two with lashings of golden syrup spread on it.

After she had eaten, licking the syrup off her fingers, Evie felt much better and sipped her tea. She glanced at mother and daughter as they busied themselves, Mrs Potter putting another batch of bread cakes in the oven, and Ginny washing the dishes in the scullery sink, both contented. Tears filled her eyes and ran down her cheeks. She had never been that close to her mother. Theirs was a distant, formal relationship. How she envied Mrs Potter and Ginny, two very ordinary people, whom her mother would look down upon, but who held a very special bond of love between them. She thought of James and her special bond with him, a loving, protective bond between mother and son. James cried, as if on cue. Evie jumped to her feet and was by his side.

On seeing his mother, he held out his arms to her. She lifted him from the pram and held him close, smelling his baby scent and talcum powder. He rammed his tiny fist into his mouth. 'You, my darling boy, are teething.'

She sat in a cosy chair near the fireside and fed James his rusk and milk, then changed his nappy.

'Poo, that's a pong.' The children were home from school and crowded into the kitchen, hungry for their tea.

'Wash your hands,' Mrs Potter called over the excited voices of the children. Soon all five of them sat around the table, tucking into their hot cakes and golden syrup.

'Have you got a black coat for the funeral?' asked Mrs Potter.

Evie looked up from wiping dribble from James's chin. 'No, only my dark green coat.' Panic filled her as she realised she had forgotten that you wore black for a funeral.

'Not to worry, love. Give it here and I'll sew a black diamond on its sleeve.' Evie watched Mrs Potter as she unpicked a black diamond-shaped piece of cloth from her coat and quickly stitched it onto Evie's. 'Now, with your black hat and gloves, you will look respectable.' She snatched a look at the big kitchen clock on the dresser. 'Best get his nibs' tea on or he'll play hell. Come on, you lot, clear your plates and up to the attic.' The attic, which rambled across the bedrooms, was the children's playroom when the weather was too inclement to go outside. The two older lads would go out to play, no matter what the state of the weather.

With Bencher's blessing, Ginny came to stay at the shop to look after James until Evie returned. Evie had felt nervous about asking Bencher. He stared at her before replying, and her heart flipped. 'Aye, that's fine with me, lass. I've got used to having folks around.' He sat back in his chair and lit his pipe, a twinkle in his eyes. 'I'm not so grumpy now, so folk tells me.'

Relief flooded her body, knowing that they would take care of James.

Early the next morning, she kissed her sleeping son and left the shop to catch the bus to town. There she caught a train to Inversea and hoped for a lift to Island House. Sitting on the train, she thought of her father, of her memories of him when she was a child, and of the special times they'd spent together. She had loved the walks around the lake, where he identified birds for her, like a woodpecker she had seen hard at work on a tree, and they watched the ducks swim in and out of the bulrushes with their young. At night time they would sit and listen to the owls hooting. Once, she had been mesmerised by a spectacular barn owl, its white plume illuminated by the moon as it flew majestically low over the fields adjoining the lake, hunting for mice to feed its young.

She sat up with a jolt as the train reached the destination. Carrying her overnight suitcase, Evie pulled her hat down over her face, not wanting to see anyone she knew, and went to look for a taxi. She was in luck. Settling back on the worn leather seat, she wondered what kind of reception she would receive at Island House.

CHAPTER TWENTY-EIGHT

May 1946

Evie stood gazing up at the front of Island House for a few moments, feeling the stillness in the air. The front door stood closed and forbidding, so she followed the path leading to the kitchen door. Pausing, she peeped through a window to see Mabel in the kitchen and tapped lightly on the door before entering. She wasn't ready to see her mother yet.

Mabel looked up from where she was making sand-wiches, and gasped, 'Miss Evie, I'm so pleased to see you!'

Within seconds, Evie felt the warm arms of this dear woman encircle her body, drawing her close. Her emotions burst like a dam, and she sobbed uncontrollable tears.

After some time, she entangled herself from Mabel's arms and, hiccupping, said, 'I want to see Daddy. Where is he resting?'

'He's in the drawing room.' She held up her hand to stop Evie, saying, 'First sit down and I'll make a pot of tea.'

'But . . .'

'No buts, young lady. Do you want your dad to see you like that?'

Despite her sadness, Evie saw the irony of this state-ment. She wanted to see her father and to tell him how much she loved him, not dribble her tears all over him. Sipping the hot, sweet tea, gradually her emotions calmed. Then, as an afterthought, she blurted, 'My mother . . . how is she?'

'She's resting. She has taken the death of Mr Sinclair badly. Doctor came and gave her a sedative to calm her down.' She paused, and then continued. 'She's not herself at all.'

Evie felt as if Mabel was going to say something else. Instead, she picked up the tray and placed the dirty crockery on the draining board. Evie rose to her feet, saying, 'I'll see my father now.'

She quietly made her way to the drawing room. Before opening the door, she took a deep breath, trying to steady her racing heartbeat. With her trembling hand grasped tight on the doorknob, she slowly opened the door. The darkness, due to the tradition of closing the curtains, startled her at first. Then, peering closer, she saw a small lamp, which cast a faint glow of light at the head of the coffin. She moved closer until she could see her father's body, clothed in a dark suit with a blue shirt and tie. She stood, letting her eyes come to rest on his beloved face. He looked so peaceful, as if he were asleep. The worry and pain on his face were gone. Fleetingly, her eyelashes fluttered, and she swallowed hard before she spoke to her beloved father. 'I've missed you, Daddy. I wanted to bring my son, your grandson, to see you. You would have loved him. He's a fine baby boy.' Then she whispered the words, 'Who now will never know his grandfather.' Softly, her tears fell. She stood by his side, talking about her childhood memories of happy times spent with him. She stayed until she heard movement above and the sound of her mother's voice. 'Goodbye, my darling daddy, until we meet again.' She kissed his cold cheek.

Outside in the corridor, Evie stood, taking deep breaths in readiness to see her mother.

* * *

The undertaker came at 2 p.m. to take Gerald Sinclair for his last journey. Evie, with her mother and a cousin of her father's and his wife, followed behind in a black limousine. Florence sat ridged and stared straight ahead. She had only spoken a few words to Evie. She was in shock, Evie thought, and she wanted to take hold of her mother's hand to feel some kind of contact, but Florence's hands remained clasped tightly together on her lap.

The small church was full of friends who had come to pay their respects to Gerald Sinclair. He had been respected and well liked in the community. Afterwards, most mourners came back to Island House. Evie noticed her mother acting as the host and talking to everyone, as if she was at one of her committee functions, knowing it was her way of coping. Evie helped Mabel with the refreshments and made sure everyone had plenty to drink and eat.

At last, everyone departed, and Florence retired to her room without speaking to Evie.

Evie said to Mabel, 'I'll do the tidying up, you get off. And thank you, Mabel.' She gave the older woman a hug. 'I couldn't have managed without you.'

Evie began collecting dirty crockery and glasses left lying around the house. In the kitchen, her hands deep in soap-suds, she washed everything up and tidied them away. Then she sat alone at the kitchen table in the silent house. She closed her eyes to conjure up her beloved son's face, desperately wanting to feel his small body in her arms. She wished she had a cigarette. Earlier, she had gone up to her mother's room and quietly opened the door to see her in her night attire, fast asleep.

Standing up, she looked through the kitchen window out across the lake. The last of the daylight streaked across the water, giving it an ethereal look. On impulse, she snatched her coat off the hook. In the tiny lobby hung her father's old waterproof coat and, instinctively, she put her hand into a pocket and felt a packet of cigarettes and a box of matches. 'Thanks, Daddy,' she whispered. 'You left them there for me.'

She stood at the edge of the lake and opened the packet of full-strength Senior Service. Lighting one, she drew on it and exhaled. This reminded her of every time she had finished a nightly duty as an Ack-Ack gunner girl. They would pass round their cigarettes, thankful each night that there had been no casualties. Thankfully, the war had ended, and with it came a new set of responsibilities. She had no regrets about having her son, her greatest joy in life, even though, deep down, if she was honest with herself, she wished him to have a father. But who was his father? Matt would have been a great dad if he'd survived the war. Then she thought of Richard. He could well be James's father, but he had vanished from her life. There was probably a girl waiting for him back home. She walked further along the edge of the lake, and by now the daylight had disappeared and twilight flitted about. She lit another cigarette, its glow shining as darkness fell and she turned to retrace her steps back to the house.

The next morning, she was up early and prepared a breakfast tray of tea and toast for her mother. Carrying it upstairs, she knocked lightly on Florence's bedroom door. Going into the room, shrouded in darkness, Evie set the tray on the bedside table and drew back the curtains to let in the sunlight. Florence stirred, and it appalled Evie to see how drawn her mother's face was without the rouge, powder and lipstick she'd worn yesterday. Her eyes held a vacant expression, as if she did not know who Evie was.

'How are you feeling, Mother?' Evie asked.

The empty look on Florence's face cleared. 'Tired,' she answered in a low voice.

Evie poured the tea and handed the cup to her mother, saying, 'You'll feel better when you've had breakfast and up and dressed.'

'Don't want to get up,' Florence said, her voice like that of a petulant child.

Evie did not answer, but waited until her mother had finished her breakfast. Then she said, 'I'll run you a bath.'

When she came back into her mother's room, Florence was still in bed. 'Come on, Mother,' she said, drawing back the beautiful satin eiderdown. 'I'll help you.'

Once in the bath, Evie noticed how frail her mother's body was, and she felt reluctant to leave her, but she knew she needed to return home for James. He was her chief priority.

Now dressed and in the kitchen, the warmest room, Florence sat staring into space. Suddenly she stood up, saying, 'I must go to Gerald. He needs me.'

Evie felt a wave of sadness wash over her, and her heartbeat quickened. She went to gather her mother into her arms, but Florence cried out, 'Don't touch me.' Evie froze like a statue.

The outside door opened and Mabel entered. Evie broke into tears and sat down at the table, resting her head on her arms, sobbing. She felt a soft hand stroke her hair and Mabel whispered, 'You let it all out, love.' Then louder, 'Mrs Sinclair, I'll take you through to the sitting room. You have your knitting to finish.'

After a while, Evie rose and swilled her face in cold water at the kitchen sink. She was patting it dry when Mabel returned. She looked at the older woman, saying, 'I will have to catch my train soon and return to my baby son, and I have to work.' Then she gave a deep sigh, saying, 'But I'm worried about Mother. Her health is deteriorating.'

'Aye, she's got worse since your dad died. I'll come as often as I can. If I leave the housework, I can spend more time with her and prepare nourishing meals.'

Evie said, 'I'll speak to the solicitor, ask him to arrange for Mother to have care. And I'll try to come again.'

The journey back seemed to take forever. She wanted to feel her darling son in her arms. Arriving, only Bencher was there. 'Where are James and Ginny?'

He looked up from where he was inspecting a set of dominos, and, seeing her anxious face, replied, 'They've only gone to shop. Won't be long.'

Relieved, Evie was about to go to meet them when the doorbell jangled and Ginny entered with the pram. On seeing his mammy, James held out his arms to her, and she lifted him from the pram and held him close, feeling the warmth of his small body against hers. He giggled, his tiny fingers pulling at a loose strand of her hair, and she kissed his chubby cheeks. Evie turned to Ginny after the moment with her son.

'He's a little terror.' She laughed as Evie's face dropped. 'No, he's been as good as gold. Ain't you, little fellow.' She tickled him under the chin, and he laughed. 'Best get back to Mam. She'll have loads of jobs for me.'

'Thank you, Ginny. Treat yourself.' She slipped a ten-shilling note into the girl's hand.

'Cor, thanks, missus. I'll look after him anytime.'

When James was fed, bathed and tucked up in his cot, she gazed upon her adorable son, and waited until he slept before going downstairs. Ginny had brought two meat pies, and peas were in the warming oven. Bencher produced a bottle of beer for himself and a sherry for Evie. They ate in companionable silence and, after the meal, he lit his pipe and said, 'How was it then?'

Evie poured out her grief and her worry about her mother's health. He listened, not interrupting. When she had finished, he poured her another sherry, saying, 'You need it, lass. I am sorry about your mother, but it's a pity she didn't take care of you when you needed her the most. Then you would have been there to help.'

Evie had never thought of that, but it was true. She vowed that if her son did anything wrong in the community or by law, she would not turn him away, but would do everything in her power to help him.

That night in bed, she lay listening to James's gentle breathing, and thought she was lucky to have her son. Her thoughts didn't turn to her mother, but to the other young unmarried mothers in the home. Mothers forced to give up their babies for adoption to conform to the prejudiced views of others. The sad face of Mary came to mind. If only there was a workable solution. With that thought, she drifted to sleep.

CHAPTER TWENTY-NINE

June 1946

A week later, Evie received a letter from her father's solicitor. Busy ironing a pile of laundry, she slipped the envelope into her apron pocket to read when she had finished. Then James woke up from his nap.

'He's crabby,' Bencher said, pushing his spectacles up on to his receding hairline and rubbing his eyes.

Lifting James from his pram, she replied, 'He's teething.'

'Huh, teeth. They're a bother coming and a bother going. Why we have to have them, God only knows.'

Evie gave James his morning milk, and when finished, he rammed his little fist into his mouth and gnawed on it. Gently, she wiped away his dribbles of saliva.

'He needs a dummy,' said a woman's voice.

Evie turned round to see Mrs Potter with her husband's suit across her arm. 'A dummy,' Evie repeated, not sure what that was.

'Aye, corner shop sells them. Mine have always had a dummy. Else we'd get no sleep. It comforts the baby.'

After the chores were done and a quick sandwich for dinner, Evie settled James in his pram to go shopping. She bought a dummy from the chemist and then went to see what the butcher's had to offer. Though she muddled along with preparing and cooking food, she found it tedious because it was still being rationed. Standing in the butcher's queue, she listened to other women grumbling.

'Bairn looks contented,' a woman commented, standing next to her.

Evie's eyes sparkled as she looked down at her son, a picture of contentment as he slept, sucking on his comforter.

She ended up with a piece of scrag-end of mutton and suet. Simmering it on the stove with carrots, an onion and an Oxo cube, she made suet dumplings to bake in the side oven. They had some savoury dumplings and the rest with home-made jam. Though she was not sure of the fruit in the jam, it still tasted all right, Evie thought, as she watched Bencher lick his lips.

She fed and bathed James, tucking him up in his cot. Her heart glowed with love for her son as she watched him smile up at her, and then his eyelids drooped and he slumbered. She stayed for a few minutes, drinking in the wonder of him, knowing he was her reason for living.

Downstairs, Bencher dozed in his chair. Sitting down, Evie picked up her sewing; she was mending an apron and putting a fancy frill around its tatty hem. Suddenly she remembered the letter and she jumped up, startling Bencher, who stretched and yawned. Dashing to the laundry basket, with relief, she retrieved the envelope from the apron pocket, her heart pounding. What if she had put the apron and letter in the copper of hot water? It did not bear thinking about.

On seeing her flustered face, Bencher poured her a glass of sherry. 'You look as though you need it, lass.' He returned to his chair and lit his pipe, but he did not turn the wireless on, as was his custom.

Evie smoothed out the crumpled envelope and opened it. Scanning the headed notepaper from the solicitor, she let out a sigh.

'Not bad news?' Bencher asked.

'No, a surprise. My father has left me some money in his will.'

'That's good news.'

Evie read on and then said, 'My mother's health is on the decline and the solicitor has arranged, as I instructed him, for her to have daily care, and possibly night care as well.' She stared at the letter, rereading it, and then she said, 'I will have to see her. Would you be agreeable if I went on Sunday and stayed over to Monday?'

'Aye, you do, lass. I reckon I'll survive.' He busied himself picking up a newspaper. He had an inkling, but would keep it to himself for now.

Ginny agreed to stay and look after James. 'I enjoy being here,' she said. 'It's like a holiday from Mam and the rest of them, and Bencher likes my cooking. And I love James to bits.' She tickled him under his chin and he laughed. 'He'll be talking soon, won't you?' James obliged by making rasping and gurgling noises. 'He knows what I said.'

Evie felt a surge of relief, knowing James would be in safe hands, though she hated leaving him.

When Evie arrived at Island House, the rain had been falling steadily. A mist hovered over the lake, and the trees and bushes were leaden with rain, making the leaves droop. In the kitchen, it comforted her to see Mabel baking.

On seeing Evie, Mabel's face lit up, and she dusted down her hands on her apron and held out her arms. 'I'm right glad to see you.'

'How is Mother?' Evie asked, after the lovely welcome hug.

'She's no bother. It's the other one. Right bossy boots.'

'Who?'

Just then, the door leading from the hall burst open and in strode a well-built woman in a nurse's uniform, her grey hair pushed beneath her cap. 'Idle chatter, I see,' she said in a brisk voice.

Evie turned, standing tall. She faced the woman and said, 'I am Evie Sinclair, Mrs Sinclair's daughter. And you are?'

At once, the woman's manner changed. 'So pleased to meet you, Miss Sinclair. I am Nurse Chatsworth, your mother's carer.'

'How is my mother today?'

'She is resting. The medication the doctor prescribed makes her sleepy. Her appetite has improved since I have been here.' She gave a knowing glance in Mabel's direction, as if to suggest Mabel's cooking was inferior.

'Thank you, Nurse Chatsworth. I think we can leave the cooking in the capable hands of Mabel. I would like a talk with you. Shall we?' Evie opened the door wide for the nurse to pass through.

They went into the sitting room and Evie showed the nurse to a chair, saying, 'Tell me about yourself.'

The nurse's face reddened slightly, and Evie guessed no one had asked her that question.

'I worked in a military hospital down south and came back north to nurse my mother until she died.'

'I am sorry to hear that.'

The nurse sighed. 'She was a difficult patient, but I did my duty.'

Evie let Nurse Chatsworth carrying on talking. She only half listened, looking out of the window at the misty lake beyond, and thinking of the carefree days of her youth when she would cross the lake on her little boat.

'How long are you staying for, Miss Sinclair?'

Evie brought herself back to the present, replying, 'Until tomorrow.'

The nurse looked surprised, saying, 'A brief stay.'

'Yes.' Evie rose. 'I will see my mother now.' The nurse made to follow her, but Evie turned and smiled, saying, 'I'm sure you have other duties to attend to.'

As Evie entered the room, Florence called out, 'Gerald, is that you?'

Evie drew back the curtains to let in some natural light and then went to her mother's bedside. Taking hold of her mother's thin hand, she gently stroked it. 'No, Mother, it's me, Evie.'

'Oh.' Florence looked puzzled.

'Dear Daddy has gone,' Evie said, her eyes welling with tears.

'Where's Donald? I want to see him.' Florence's voice rose to a screech.

'He's sleeping,' Evie replied, saying the first words that popped into her head. Her mother had never mentioned Donald to her before. Over the years she had caught snatches of conversation between her parents, which, as a young girl, had made little sense to her. Later, piecing the dialogue together, she'd learned Donald was her brother, who had died of meningitis when he was eighteen months of age. She, Evie, was an unsuitable substitute, a daughter Florence did not want.

Florence murmured something and relaxed back on her pillow.

'Would you like to go to the sitting room? Mabel's baking scones.' Evie went to call the nurse to attend to Florence.

Downstairs in the kitchen, Evie mentioned to Mabel, 'Mother talked about Donald. She thinks he is still alive.'

'Aye, she does.'

Evie paused, then said, 'What if I bring James to see her? What do you think?' She valued Mabel's opinion because the last thing she wanted to do was to upset her mother. Mabel began buttering the scones and did not speak. Evie's heart sank.

Then Mabel broke the silence. 'It's a grand idea. After all, James is her grandson.' She smiled broadly at Evie.

Evie let out the breath and felt relief run through her.

Upstairs in the attic, she went to fetch the box of photographs taken before the war. It had been Gerald's hobby then, and now long forgotten. She also found another box full of paraphernalia and, rummaging through, came across a plain paper album and box of little corner stickers she could use to affix a photograph to the paper.

She settled Florence in the sitting room and, after they'd eaten their scones, set out the oldest photographs on the coffee table. At first, Florence just stared into the distance. Then Evie watched as her mother's eyes flittered over the images until she reached out her hand and touched one. The sepia wedding photograph of Florence and Gerald, taken in a studio. Her mother's dress was long and flowing, with an equally long veil, and she held a large bouquet of roses. Evie could only guess at the colour of the roses — a dark shade, red? On impulse, she asked her mother, 'What colour were your flowers?'

For a few moments, Florence frowned, and then her face lit up like a child's, and her voice, a soft whisper, replied, 'Red for true love.'

While her mother became lost in her thoughts, Evie brought out more photos, her breath catching as she looked at one of her father alongside her mother, who held a baby in her arms. Her mother's face was full of adoring love. Instinctively, she knew this baby was Donald. The brother she had never known. The photo of her with her parents was official. One of duty. Her father had always had this picture, silver framed, on his desk. A sadness overcame her and tears wet her lashes. How she missed her dear father. And he had never seen his grandson. She laid down Donald's picture for her mother to see and watched as her eyes lit up.

Florence fingered the photo, then kissed it, and after a couple of minutes she held it to her bosom and, looking around, said, 'Where is Donald?'

Evie bit on her lip and said gently, 'He's sleeping.'

They spent a good hour poring over old photos until Florence's attention waned and she look tired. As if by magic, the nurse appeared, saying, 'Time for the patient's medication.'

The next day, on her way home to James, Evie felt sad for her mother's decline, but thankful she had the nurse to care for her needs.

The first thing Evie did when arriving home was to scoop her son up in her arms, kissing him. He cooed and dribbled over her blouse, but she did not care.

The next month, James was very fractious, another tooth coming through. He cried and held out his chubby arms to her. She spent all her spare time nursing him, and taking him out in his pram during the day as Bencher became irritable and short-tempered. 'Can't you do anything with that bloody crying brat?'

Evie abandoned her next planned visit with James to see her mother. Instead, they spent lovely summer days at East Park. The movement of the pram soothed James, and he loved to see the ducks on the pond and feed them with stale crusts of bread. There were plenty of distractions for him. Evie sat on a park bench and angled the pram so James could watch the children playing on the swings and slide.

A letter arrived for her that morning from Gloria, and while James's attention was engaged, she withdrew it from her handbag to read. Gloria wasn't much of a letter writer, so it was a welcome surprise to hear about her life in London. She sang mostly in clubs and bars, waiting until her big break of singing in a musical came along.

> *A group of us went to sing at a convalescent home for wounded forces and guess who I saw there. The pilot who Matt was pals with, Richard. He has a shoulder injury, and was recovering after an operation. I told him that you have a son. I hope you don't mind, but I mentioned you weren't married. Then he asked me for your address, but I told him I didn't have it with me. If I bump into him again, could I give him your address?*

Evie watched the children on the swing, their laughter and antics entertaining James, her thoughts far away. As the picture of Richard's face flashed before her, she felt a quickening of her heartbeat. Could he be the father of her son? Had she the right to deny him access to James?

That night, as she lay in bed, this thought kept her awake.

CHAPTER THIRTY

July 1946

Evie alighted from the taxi outside Island House with James in one arm and her overnight bag in the other. She was relieved to see Mabel in the kitchen as she passed the window.

Mabel had seen her and rushed to open the door, her arms outstretched to take James into them. Thankfully, he did not cry, as he was used to different people. 'My, my, he's a bonny lad,' Mabel enthused, as she held him in her arms.

Soon, James was sitting on a rug, sucking the teat of his bottle of orange juice and taking in his new surroundings while Evie enjoyed a refreshing cup of tea. 'How is Mother today?'

Mabel pulled a face and said, 'Irma Grese said she's resting. Your mam is spending too much time in bed.'

Mabel always called the nurse Irma Grese, though never to her face. Evie had heard of the cruel German prison guard in the women's concentration camps. And her name became the butt of many jokes.

'I will ask the nurse to dress Mother so she can see James.'

Surprise registered on the nurse's face to see Evie.

'Dress Mrs Sinclair, please, her grandson is here to see her. I'm here for the weekend, so you may take the afternoon off, if you wish.'

Settling her mother in the sitting room, Evie carried James, now smelling sweetly after a nappy change, into the room. Her mother stared at her grandson, then she broke into a smile and held out her arms, crying, 'Donald!'

James, though used to people, did not respond to this strange name. He clasped his chubby arms around his mother's neck and hid his face against her shoulder. Evie sat on the chair opposite Florence and said to her, 'Mother, this is my son James, your grandson.'

Florence said in a confused voice, 'It's Donald, my son.'

'No, this is James, my son.' Evie rose to her feet and went to her mother's side. She kissed the top of James's head and whispered to him, 'This is your granny. Say hello.'

James lifted his head to look at the strange woman, and then, at his mother's encouraging smile, gave a cautious wave.

The weekend proved to be a success, and Evie hoped that her mother would soon acknowledge James as her grandson rather than her dead son, Donald.

The money her father had left her gave Evie the freedom to travel more often to Island House. She only took James when she could stay overnight, usually on a weekend. During a weekday, it was a quick visit because she still worked at the shop and ran the household for Bencher. He did not complain outright, but muttered under his breath.

'She thinks I'm a charity case,' Evie heard him saying to a customer who often came in for a chat.

She felt guilty when she heard this. Bencher relied on her to cook his meals and do his laundry, besides other jobs. Now she didn't have time to queue at the greengrocer's or butcher's, so the meals she prepared were poor. On a rare visit to see Masie, she discussed her problems.

'I feel as though I'm cut in half. I know Mother was never fair to me by not wanting me home with James, but since Dad died she's become mellow and clingy.' Putting her cup on its saucer, Evie looked at Masie.

Masie eyed her back but did not speak straight away. Instead, she made a pretence of fussing with crumbs from the plate of scones. Then she spoke. 'You are in a quandary. You must decide whether to stay and work at the shop or leave to live with your mother.'

A cry came from the passage where James was sleeping in his pram. 'I'll fetch him,' said Masie. 'You prepare his milk and rusk.'

Once fed and changed, Evie watched Masie bouncing James on her knee. Her thoughts raced, then she spoke. 'I don't want to let Bencher down. He's been good to me.'

'Aye, he has, but you have also saved him.'

'Saved him! What do you mean?'

'I didn't like to tell you before, but his daughter, who lived with him, committed suicide.'

Evie felt the colour drain from her face. 'I never knew. I thought she died on service. Poor man.' Sitting back in her chair, she suddenly shot up again. 'But if I leave, how will he manage?'

'Ginny takes care of things when you are away.'

'I am uncertain if she would want it as a permanent position.'

'Ask her. She has her mother and family living nearby, if she needs support.'

Later, as Evie pushed the pram along Holderness Road, she had much to think about. She tried to find the right words to tell Bencher of her decision. On an impulse, she brought a fish fry from the fishmonger's to make a fish pie, one of Bencher's favourite meals. There were only four women in the queue. She gave James a rattle to play with and to bite on if his gums ached.

'Hello, love.' It was Mrs Potter in front of her in the shop.

Evie smiled in acknowledgement and said, 'How are you?'

'Fed up. Short of bloody money. I'll be glad when our Ginny can work and bring in some pennies.'

'Ginny, is she old enough for work?'

'Aye, next month.'

'Next!' called the fishmonger.

As soon as Mrs Potter was served, she hurried away, and Evie could not ask her about Ginny.

All that week, Evie busied herself, giving every room in the building a thorough clean and cooking nourishing meals from the old recipe book. She improvised some ingredients that were not available, baking a rhubarb pie using rhubarb supplied by an accordion player as part payment of monies borrowed against his accordion, which he played in pubs on a weekend.

Bencher bit into his pie, smacked his lips and devoured every morsel. After draining his tin mug of black tea and placing it on the table, he said to Evie, 'Now, young lady, tell me what you're up to.'

His question caught her off guard. 'Nothing,' she mumbled. She did not want to hurt his feelings when he had been her last hope of keeping her son. How could she tell him she was going to live at Island House?

As if he had read her mind, he questioned, 'You are leaving?'

She bit on her lip, gave a deep sigh, looked at him, and replied, 'My relationship with my mother has always been mostly distant, and she refused me a home with my son. Now in poor health, her illness is becoming progressively worse, and strange as it may seem, she needs me. I'm torn. Don't you see? You took me in when I needed help the most.' A lump came into her throat and she fought back tears. Her voice trembling, she continued. 'You were my salvation.' She put a hand across her mouth, but the sobs escaped and the tears ran down her cheeks. Though her vision was blurred, she was conscious of Bencher rising to his feet and moving away. She wondered if he would tell her to pack her bags and leave.

Instead, he said, 'Drink this.'

He thrust a glass into her hand, and her nostrils twitched as she smelled the whisky. Raising the glass to her lips, she let the rich, smooth liquid run down her throat, helping to ease her anguish. Warmth flooded her body and she felt in better control of her emotions. She looked up to see Bencher watching her.

He drew on his pipe and said, 'I knew you wouldn't stay long.' She looked at him curiously. 'Aye, you're far too intelligent to stay working in a pawnshop. It is me that's grateful for you living here when I needed company the most.' He leaned back in his chair, puffed on his pipe, and stared into the glowing fire-grate.

Evie wondered if he was referring to the sad death of his daughter, but she could not ask him.

Suddenly, she thought of Matt, her lost love, and then her dear father, and friends who'd died in battle while defending the country. She thought of the Ack-Ack gunner girls, who she had been proud to serve with and now missed their camaraderie. Lily was sailing off to America soon with the other GI brides to live a completely new life. Then she remembered the letter from Gloria that she had not replied to. Gloria had mentioned seeing Richard, and that he had asked where Evie was living. Maybe it would do no harm to give him her Island House address. Maybe he had a sweetheart waiting for him back home. She wallowed in self-pity, but was saved by the cries of James, her darling son.

The Wednesday of the following week, Evie went alone on a quick visit to see her mother and to seek Mabel's advice. When she arrived, the doctor was there to see Florence, whose health was deteriorating fast. Evie gasped on seeing how fragile her mother had become even since last week. She held her hand, so tiny in Evie's own. Then the nurse fussed to attend to Florence.

'Can you give her stronger medication?' Evie asked the doctor, as they left her mother's room and walked towards the front door.

'She is on the maximum dose,' he replied in a non-committal voice.

From the doorway, she watched him climb into his old Wolseley Hornet car, polished to perfection, and drive away.

Slowly she made her way to the back of the house, and as she entered the kitchen, the smell of Mabel's comfort food scones filled it with their delicious aroma. Evie felt like crying, but self-pity wasn't the answer. The two women sat in silence, and when they had eaten their scones and were drinking a second cup of tea, Evie spoke. 'I am coming home for good on Saturday and bringing James with me.'

Before she could add anything further, Mabel said, 'I can do extra hours. If you are willing, one of my daughters can cover the evenings. If that suits, Evie?'

Her answer was to jump up and hug Mabel. 'That's such a relief.'

Evie caught the bus back to Bencher's in Hull, her mind racing. She needed to know if Ginny would work for Bencher — if Bencher agreed, and Mrs Potter thought it was a suitable job for her daughter. When that was settled in her mind, she wondered how she would get James's pram and his cot to Island House. She didn't think the train was practical. She mentioned this to Bencher when he asked what was worrying her.

'Leave it with me. I know a man who owes me a favour.'

Next, she went round to Mrs Potter's, pushing James in his pram. This was to divert the other children's attention from Ginny and Mrs Potter. Once in the yard, the children crowded round the pram to entertain James. Evie watched from the kitchen window and, satisfied all was well, turned back to Ginny and her mother with her proposal.

By Friday, everything was falling into place.

Evie took a last walk around Bencher's house and shop, and sadness gripped her heart. 'I have been happy here,' she whispered.

'And I've been lucky to have you.'

Evie jumped at the sound of Bencher's voice behind her. Tears sprang into her eyes. 'Thank you.' And she hugged him, smelling his comforting whiff of tobacco and whisky.

Masie came round on the Saturday morning to help pack Evie and James's belongings into the van arranged by

Bencher to transport them to Island House. Masie offered to accompany Evie and James and to stay over until Sunday.

On the train, Evie watched Masie bouncing a gleeful James on her knee. She rested her head on the back of the seat, listening to the train's rhythm. I am going home. I am going home . . .

CHAPTER THIRTY-ONE

September–November 1946

'Thank you, Masie, for helping to settle us in.' Evie and Masie were having a quiet walk round the lake, while James had a nap under the guidance of Mabel.

Masie gazed wistfully across the lake as ducks skimmed and dived, and in the trees, wood pigeons cooed. 'It's been a pleasure. It's so beautiful and peaceful here. No honking of lorry horns and arguments in neighbours' houses, or men rolling home drunk and noisy.'

Evie looked at her friend and said, 'Wouldn't you miss working with the mothers and babies?'

Masie looked towards the house and answered, 'Yes. If only mothers and babies could live here, and the babies were not forcibly given up for adoption, but could stay with their mothers until their futures were secure.'

Evie slipped her arm through her friend's and said, 'A wonderful dream. If only.'

Back at the house, Mabel had prepared a snack of egg sandwiches, fruit scones and a bottle of her homemade lemonade for Masie to eat on the train.

Goodbyes said, Evie waved Masie off as she was driven away in the local taxi. She had promised to visit again when her shift at the home allowed.

James struggled in Evie's arms, wanting to be put down, so she sat him on the grass. Supporting him by holding his chubby arms, she walked him forward and each step he took made him gurgle with glee.

A wind suddenly whipped up, and the sun hid behind a cloud. 'Come on, my boy. We will go to see Grandma.' She lifted him up, and he cried. She kissed the top of his head, his downy hair soft, and her heart filled with tenderness and love for her son.

Florence was up and dressed, sitting in a comfortable chair with a tartan rug across her knees. Her face lit up when she saw James. Evie said to the nurse, 'Mabel has made you a cup of tea. I'll stay with Mother.' After Florence had kissed her grandson, Evie put him down on the rug and he crawled about, exploring. Both women watched in adoration as James circled the rug at record speed, and then, without warning, clung onto the legs of an upright chair, pulled himself up and did a jig, chanting jumbled-up words.

Florence gave a spontaneous laugh, something she hadn't done in a long time. Then she said, 'Yes, you are a clever boy.'

At the sound of his grandma's voice, James looked round, lost his balance and fell on his bum, but in seconds he was on the move, crawling at speed to Florence's chair. Then he hauled himself up and grabbed hold of her blanket, leaning into her legs and gabbling his baby talk. Evie watched in amazement. It was as if her mother understood what James was saying because she spoke back to him. Evie wished she had a camera to capture this moment forever.

Every day thereafter, the bond between James and his grandmother grew. Morning and afternoon, Evie would take James to his grandma's room. Evie had also managed, through the doctor, to secure a loaned wheelchair. When summer drifted into autumn, there appeared a hue of red, yellow and russet among the trees and bushes, making a rich tapestry of colour. On these golden days, Evie pushed her mother in the wheelchair, with James sitting safely on her lap as they circled the lake, stopping to look at the wildlife: the willow warblers were back, and James, who had only ever encountered the ducks in the park, appeared fascinated by them. Evie lifted the camera hanging on a strap around her neck and, having ensured that the wheelchair was safe, stepped back to snap a photograph of grandma and grandson enthralled in their birdwatching.

Evie had gained a second-hand camera, or rather Masie had, from Bencher's pawnshop. Masie brought it on one of her frequent visits, and a local amateur photographer, married to Mabel's daughter, developed the films. Evie made an album for Florence, and each day she would turn the pages and smile at the pictures. The album helped her mind to connect with what she loved. She would also look at her and Gerald's wedding day photo, and the one with baby Donald. Evie also sent photos of James to Lily and Gloria. She would love to meet up with her friends, though with Lily down in Kent and Gloria in London, it wasn't possible. She wanted to see Lily before she sailed to America, which could be soon, and Gloria too, to find out how her singing career was progressing.

On evenings when the house was quiet, while James slept soundly and her mother was settled for the night, Evie would perch on the window seat in her room. She sat in darkness, looking across the lake, and tonight the moon cast a path of lovely silvery light on the water. She thought about her days on the Ack-Ack gun sites, and of all the girls and men she'd served with, loving the camaraderie and their spirit. It had been a special time of her life, though she wouldn't wish for another war. Matt was forever her first love, and she wondered what her life would have been if he hadn't been killed on a flying mission. She dreamed of them being married, with their son James, enjoying their lives together. Stretching, she moved her stiff legs, and the face of Richard came to her, as if to say, I am still alive. If James was his son, would he feel trapped into a marriage of convenience. Would it work?

James whimpered in his sleep and she tiptoed across the room to gaze down on his serene face, his arms above his head in a relaxed position. Her heart overflowed with love for him. He was her reason for existing. And she must be content with that.

On 5 November, Bonfire Night, she collected dry twigs and the remains of an old tumbled-down shed, which she assembled on the gravel patch at the back of the house. Masie came especially, arriving on Tuesday morning and planning to go back the next day. 'Matron eventually granted me extra time off, if I would work longer shifts for the rest of the week.'

Evie glanced across the kitchen table at her friend. They were busy dipping apples on sticks into the dish of hot toffee which Mabel had made, placing them on a tray to cool and set. 'Are you very busy?' she asked.

Masie carefully twirled the apple until it was fully coated with toffee, before meeting Evie's eyes. 'Yes, full, and we have extra beds squeezed into all the dormitories.'

'Good heavens, so many young girls.'

'Aye, and we have three older women, too. The men they were hoping to marry were already married.'

Evie pondered how to reply without sounding patronising, when Mabel came bustling into the kitchen. 'Nurse has a headache with all the activity going on,' she said.

'I'll see her,' Evie offered. As she made her way to her mother's room, an idea occurred to her. Florence sat in her comfortable chair, enjoying the cup of tea and ginger cake Mabel had brought her. Florence smiled at her daughter. 'Hello, Mother,' she said, and glanced round, but the nurse was not in sight. Evie found her in her room with the curtains closed and looking ill.

'Can I help?'

Not opening her eyes, the nurse replied, 'It's a migraine.'

'I'm sorry. You must rest.'

Masie agreed to see to Florence's needs. 'You are a god-send,' Evie said with relief. And in the afternoon, she also looked after James, who was becoming quite adept at enter-taining his grandma. Evie stood for a few moments watching her son crawl across the floor at speed and pull himself up to stand by Florence's chair. To their delight, he performed an energetic jig, making them all laugh. She felt so proud of her son's antics, which gave joy to them all, especially to her mother. It was a delight to hear her tinkling laughter. Evie wanted to scoop him up in her arms and hug him. Later, she promised herself, as she slipped out of the room.

In the kitchen, she helped Mabel, whose daughter was coming with her family for the bonfire night. Evie had placed an invitation in the post office window welcoming families with young children, though anyone young at heart was welcome.

'There is a bonfire on the village green. I don't think anyone will go to yours,' sniffed the woman on the post office counter. Evie smiled, but didn't comment. She knew that people in the village disapproved of her having a child. Later, it might affect James as he grew up and went to the village school, but she would not worry about that now.

Mabel's daughter's husband sent a sack of potatoes to roast in the bonfire. And their neighbours were coming with their three children. Mabel had made lemonade for the youngsters and sloe gin for the ladies. 'The men can bring their own beer,' she remarked, as she set a batch of scones to cool on a wire tray. Then she popped some jam tarts in the oven. Evie twirled and shaped her cheese straws ready for cooking, then she boiled the eggs in readiness to make sandwiches.

At lunch time they'd had vegetable broth and hot bread cakes, so for tea it would have to be spam sandwiches and a pot of tea. Taking a breather, she popped up to her mother's room, where Florence was taking a nap. Evie felt excited, like a young child. As she carried James downstairs to his pram, where she could monitor him as he slept, she wondered about her mother's childhood. Her faint knowledge of her grandparents was that they were very strict, only allowing children to speak when spoken to.

In the kitchen, Evie asked Masie, 'How are you at fireworks?' Masie shrugged. Evie continued, 'When the old shed was demolished, I found a metal box with fireworks stored inside. I'm not sure if they work or if they're too damp. Come and have a look.' They left Mabel to listen out for James.

Wrapped up in their coats and scarves, the two women went outside. The November day had a bright blue sky, and a watery sun shone. Evie shivered as a chill breeze blew off the lake. Behind a stack of old bricks, under the shelter of a tarpaulin, rested the box of fireworks. She remembered her training with the Ack-Ack guns and was cautious as she levered up the lid. The two women stared at them. Evie pulled a pair of gloves from her pocket and put them on. Gently, she picked up a rocket, examining it for traces of spillage and dampness. Masie stood back as if the rocket was about to launch.

After some minutes, Evie had carefully checked the dozen assorted fireworks and was certain they were usable. Her primary concern was James and the other children, so she would ask the men to take charge. Carefully repacking the fireworks and placing the box under the tarpaulin, they went back indoors.

Later, James's face held a look of excitement as he flung his arms upwards as the bonfire was lit, his pram rocking and bouncing, loving his new-found freedom of movement. At first she sat him on Florence's lap, but James proved too active to sit still, and Florence was not strong enough to hold him. He shouted with glee as the flames danced and the wood sparked. Florence, next to him in her wheelchair, attended by the nurse who seemed to have made a quick recovery, was laughing along with her grandson and mimicking his actions. Like a child herself. Of late, her mother's illness had reduced her to childish ways. Strange, Evie thought, that as her son's life progressed, her mother's life regressed. And yet, her mother seemed happy.

'Fireworks ready,' called out Stan, Mabel's son-in-law. 'Stand well back.' Everyone obeyed. The jumping-jacks brought squeals of delight from the children and, true to its name, the firecracker performed to perfection. Then the Catherine wheels pinned to tree trunks spun. It all reminded Evie of the halcyon days before the war, when she was young and carefree. The rockets were last, flaring upwards into the sky to a chorus of cheers.

'I'm starving,' she heard a child say.

Someone cheered as Mabel and Masie appeared with a tray of hot jacket potatoes and sizzling sausages, and toffee apples for later.

Nurse whispered in Evie's ear, 'Mrs Sinclair is tired and I think it's best if she retires for the night.'

Evie looked across at her mother and agreed. Lifting James from his pram, she took him to kiss his grandma good night. He wrapped his chubby arms around his grandma's neck and planted a wet, excited kiss on her cheek.

Florence surprised Evie by saying in a clear voice. 'Night, night, my darling James.'

CHAPTER THIRTY-TWO

November 1946

After everyone had gone home and the grounds tidied up, Evie and Masie went indoors. Mabel had left a jug of cocoa warming on the stove. 'I'm whacked,' said Masie, flinging herself down on a chair. 'And I've an early train in the morning.'

Evie gave her friend a hug, saying, 'Thank you for your help and your friendship.'

'Get away with you,' Masie laughed. 'It feels like a holiday when I come here. Though I can't remember what holidays were like.'

Masie's life would have been very different if her husband hadn't been killed.

After turning off the kitchen lights, Evie went to James's room. She stood by her son's cot, her heart brimming with love for him, though a sadness crept over her: he would grow up without a father. Suddenly James kicked out his legs, pushing back his blankets, gave a brief murmur and then was quiet. She tucked him up and watched him again until certain he was settled.

Quietly, she left the room and went along to her mother's room. By Florence's bedside sat the nurse, reading a book. On seeing Evie, she closed it and rose to her feet. 'Mrs Sinclair has had her medication and is sleeping well. She talked a lot about James, and you as a child. I'll retire now, but call me if you need me.'

'Thank you, Nurse. I'll sit with Mother for a while.' She sat in the vacated chair and noticed the lovely, serene expression on her mother's face. Perhaps she was dreaming of happy times.

Suddenly Florence opened her eyes and looked up at Evie. 'Hello dear. How was school? Daddy will be here soon. He has a surprise for us.' She smiled and drifted back to seep again.

She's dreaming, Evie thought, as she straightened the counterpane and stood up, watching her mother for a few minutes, still with the serene smile on her face. Then, overcome with tiredness, she kissed her mother gently on the cheek and tiptoed from the room.

She undressed in her room and fell asleep in seconds.

From a distance, she heard someone calling her name. I'm dreaming, she thought, and turned over. Then someone was shaking her. She thought she was back on the guns with a raid imminent. In a flash, she jumped from her bed to be confronted by Masie.

'It's your mother. Nurse can't wake her.'

Not stopping to put on her dressing gown, Evie ran bare-footed to her mother's room.

There, the white-faced nurse stood by Florence's bedside, checking her pulse. On seeing Evie, she said, 'I have telephoned for the doctor.'

She heard a screech of tyres on the gravel drive and the front door opening. The sound of hurrying footsteps up the stairs echoed through the house and the doctor entered the room.

Evie felt her head spin as she watched him examine her mother, listening with his stethoscope to her mother's lungs. Silence filled the room. Evie held her breath.

Finally, the doctor straightened up and faced Evie. 'I am sorry, Miss Sinclair, but you mother has passed away in her sleep.'

'Oh,' Evie gasped, putting a hand over her mouth and letting the tears run unheeded down her cheeks. Moving in a trance, she stood by her mother's bedside and took hold of Florence's cold hand. Through her tears, she saw Florence's pale face, still with that serene look on it.

Mabel's daughter, Brenda, came and took James to stay with her and her children for the day. Masie told the Mother and Baby Home that she would be away for a while. Evie wasn't sure what reason she gave, only that she was glad of her and Mabel's support. Nurse cleaned Florence's room and took care of the dirty linen, and the doctor informed the undertaker to come and take Florence's body to the chapel of rest.

Evie needed to clear her head. 'I need fresh air,' she mumbled, hurrying from the kitchen, grabbing her coat and pulling on boots. Outside, she breathed in the air, still with a hint of wood smoke from last night's bonfire. She turned in the direction of the path to walk around the lake. Her feet seemed to move by their own will, taking her forward. She found it hard to comprehend that her mother had died. At the bonfire last night, Florence had seemed so alive, enjoying herself and laughing and talking to people with James by her side in his pram. She thought of Florence's last words and the mention of her father. Had Gerald come for his wife? Her legs suddenly felt weak, and she slumped down on an old fallen tree trunk. She stared down at the beetles foraging in the dried grasses. Then she lifted her head to gaze across the lake towards the house. This was her family home, except for when she'd served as an Ack-Ack gunner girl, and when she had been banished for having James out of wedlock. However, in the time she'd spent with her mother since, Florence had never once mentioned the subject. Evie's one regret was that her father had never had a chance to see James, his grandson.

Evie wondered how her and James's lives would change. The only income she had was the small allowance her father had left her. With the death of her mother, would the house have to be sold? She and James could be homeless. A chilly wind blew, shaking the last of the leaves from the trees. She shivered and thrust her hands deep in the pockets of her coat and strode on. When she had completed the circular walk, which helped to clear her head, she focused first on laying her mother to rest. Afterwards? She shrugged.

Taking off her outdoor clothes, Evie went into the kitchen and felt its welcoming warmth. The comforting smell of Mabel's freshly baked scones and a pot of tea tantalised her nostrils. Masie, at the sink washing up the baking utensils, turned and smiled at her, and so did Mabel, as she placed a plate of hot buttered scones on the table. Nurse came in with a pile of bedding in her arms and stood uncertainly. Mabel took charge. 'Leave them in the laundry room and then come and join us for refreshments.'

The four women sat round the kitchen table, reminiscing about Florence and how cheerful she had been in her last weeks. 'Young James seemed to bring her much happiness,' the nurse remarked.

They talked about the flowers she loved and her taste in music. The undertaker telephoned to say he would call tomorrow afternoon. Later that day, the vicar visited. Evie spent time on the formal arrangements for Florence's funeral. She also wrote to both Lily and Gloria about the funeral, but because of the distance Lily would have to travel, and Gloria's commitment to her singing, she did not expect them to attend. She had only seen them once since James's birth, though they had asked her to visit them. As she posted the letters, she felt guilty for not having made the effort to see them. She also longed to see her son, and walked on to Brenda's house to bring him home. As she arrived, she heard James laughing and chuckling with delight. In the playroom, he sat in the middle of the floor with Brenda's two children, playing with a set of wooden bricks. Evie watched as they built the bricks high, before they pulled away the bottom brick and the rest came tumbling down. The children exploded into fits of laughter.

'Again, again,' James cried out, and then he saw his mother and pulled himself up on to his feet and toddled over to her.

'Hello, my darling boy,' Evie murmured, falling to her knees. She kissed his soft, downy hair. He put his arms around her neck and gave her a sloppy kiss on her face. The other children began building up the bricks, and James squealed with delight and toddled back to the game. Bereft, she watched him, absorbed in the game once again. He was no longer a baby, but a boy with his own mind.

'They grow up fast,' said Brenda from the doorway. 'I've made a cuppa.'

Later that night, as Evie bathed James, she could see how sturdy his body had become, and felt the strength in his limbs as he kicked about as she balanced him on her knee, securing his nappy. He was testing himself. She thought he wouldn't sleep tonight with all the day's excitement, but he surprised her. Evie laid him in his cot and covered him with his blankets, expecting him to kick them off, kissed him on the cheek and watched. Within seconds, he slumbered. Her heart overflowed with love as she watched him, listening to his steady breathing.

Ten days after her death it was Florence's funeral. The weather was cold, and a winter wind blew from the north. Evie followed her mother's coffin down the aisle of the church, pleased that so many people had turned out to say a last farewell to her mother. The hymn, 'All Things Bright and Beautiful', was one of Florence's favourites and it rang out clearly. The vicar gave a glowing eulogy of Florence's dedication to the church and the wider community, especially during the war. Evie listened to his words of praise, but his voice sounded as if it was speaking from a great distance.

After the service, Evie followed the coffin from the church, glancing at the mourners. As she did so, her heart missed a beat, for there were her dear friends, Lily and Gloria.

They laid Florence to rest next to Gerald, in the quiet churchyard of Saint Lawrence. Evie closed her eyes as they lowered the coffin into the ground. She didn't relish this part of the service, the moment a loved one disappeared into a hole to be covered by earth.

They held the wake in the parish hall, which was convenient for most of the mourners, rather than at Island House. Evie spoke to people, mostly women, who had known Florence through the various committees she'd served on before becoming ill. 'A perfect organiser, Mrs Sinclair was.' 'You could always rely on Florence Sinclair.' Evie nodded and expressed her gratitude for their kind words about her mother. Suddenly, two women blocked her way. They stood on either side of her, placed their hands on her elbows, and steered her towards the small, empty vestibule.

Evie curbed a smile. It was like being on jankers when she'd served with the Ack-Ack unit. Letting go of her, Lily and Gloria both hugged her. Tears stung Evie's eyes as she whispered, 'You both came.'

'Of course, we did. To pay our respects to your mother and to give you our support,' said Lily.

Gloria smiled, saying, 'Our visit is long overdue.'

They hugged again and sat down, squashing together on the narrow settle.

Lily produced a packet of Lucky Strike cigarettes from her handbag and a flash lighter, and they all lit up.

Evie inhaled deeply, then let out a plume of smoke, saying, 'I haven't smoked since James was born, except when my father died.'

'Why not?' asked Lily, inhaling casually.

'I didn't think it was good for his health.' She didn't add that she couldn't afford to buy cigarettes. They chatted about their days on the gun sites. 'A million miles away,' Evie said. Then she told them how James was growing up fast. 'He's a little boy now,' she said with pride.

The door opened and Masie popped her head round. On seeing the other two women, she said, 'Sorry to interrupt, but the vicar's looking for you.'

Evie rose to her feet. 'Thanks, Masie, I'm coming.' In the doorway, she turned and said to her friends, 'Come to the house later, or do you have to dash away?'

'Actually,' said Lily, a mischievous twinkle in her eyes, 'we were hoping you could put us up for a couple of nights.'

Evie's eyes lit up as she said, 'I can squash you in. You are both the tonic I need.'

CHAPTER THIRTY-THREE

November 1946

Evie, with her friends, went to pick up James from Brenda's house. Darkness had fallen by the time they approached Island House, which stood silent and forlorn. 'It's a house meant for lots of children,' Masie remarked, as they went through the front door and she switched on the hall light. Lily and Gloria followed her in.

The house felt cold and Evie hugged James's warm, sleeping body close to her. 'We'll go into the kitchen. It should be warm.'

Masie took charge and put the kettle on the stove to boil, while Evie laid her sleeping son down in his pram. Then she peeped in the warming oven and, true to her word, Mabel had left a liver casserole full of chunky vegetables and a bread and butter pudding.

'Smells good,' said Gloria, peeping over Evie's shoulder. 'I miss Yorkshire cooking.'

'What's London food like?' asked Evie.

'Not bad,' Gloria replied, not quite meeting her eye. Evie looked again at Gloria and couldn't help but notice her friend looked thinner than she remembered her. She wondered how much she could afford on her wages as a singer.

They all ate their fill, and when James woke up, Evie mashed his food for him. She sat him on her knee and fed him mechanically, because the three pairs of eyes watching him fascinated James. Afterwards, he enjoyed sitting on their knees, loving the attention.

'He'll grow up to break a few girls' hearts,' Lily remarked, as Masie bounced him on her lap. 'Does he take after his daddy?'

Masie stilled James, and Evie felt the blood rush to her head and her vision blurred. No one spoke.

Then Masie scraped back her chair, saying, 'I'll give James his bath.' She hurried from the room with a startled James in her arms.

Lily jumped to her feet, exclaiming to Evie, 'God, I'm sorry. I didn't think. I should have known it was painful to mention Matt.'

Shaking, but trying to act natural, Evie said, 'Just give me one of your cigarettes and we'll forget about it.' As she lit up and took a long drag, she caught Gloria's eye. And, in that instance, Gloria knew what she, Evie, felt in her heart. She didn't know who James's father was.

Gloria didn't mention it. Instead, she pulled from her overnight bag a small bottle of whisky. 'A perk of the job,' she enthused.

Evie rose to fetch the glasses from the cupboard. They drank and smoked, laughed and reminisced about their days as Ack-Ack gunner girls: the crazy nights out, singing in the local pubs, the corporal who'd bellowed at them like a sergeant major on parade, omitting the tragedies and the disasters.

Masie returned to the kitchen and spoke in a cheerful voice. 'James is now shiny clean and in his cot, waiting for his mammy to say goodnight.'

'Drink, Masie?' asked Gloria, pouring her out a tot.

'Aye, just the one, and then I'm off to my bed. I've to catch the early train in the morning.'

In the quiet of James's room, Evie stood looking at her lovely son. He smiled at her and then his eyelids fluttered and sleep overcame him, and her heart overflowed with love for him. One day, he would ask about his father. She stood for a long time, unable to move away, for if she did, tears would spill from her eyes.

Suddenly conscious of the sound of light footsteps coming towards the room, she half turned, expecting to see Masie. Instead, Lily and Gloria stood framed in the doorway.

They moved forward, gently taking hold of her arms, and Lily said simply, 'We've run you a bath.'

She went with them, feeling in a trance, letting them peel off her funeral clothes and gently lower her into the lavender and chamomile scented warm water. As her body became immersed in the water, she felt the layer of tightness clogging her skin and mind melting away.

While Lily sat on the stool, Gloria perched on the side of the bath and she sang. A soft lullaby, the words unfamiliar to Evie, but it sounded like pure liquid gold. She hadn't realised that Gloria's voice was so beautiful. When they had sung together in concerts during their war, they had usually imitated The Andrews Sisters, which was always good fun. She relaxed back in the bath, listening to her friend's soothing voice until the water became cold.

'Come on, Evie, time to get out.' Lily's voice broke into her reverie.

Enveloped in a huge bathrobe, which must have been her father's, Evie sat cross-legged on the carpet of the bedroom that Lily and Gloria were sharing, drinking cocoa. She yawned, feeling drowsy. Finishing the last mouthful of her drink, she scrambled to her feet. 'I've not slept much since Mother passed away, but now I feel as though I could sleep on a telephone wire.'

She hugged them both, saying, 'Thanks for being here for me.'

That night, Evie slept soundly. When she stirred awake, she heard James laughing somewhere in the house, and then a light tap on her door. 'Come in,' she called, levering herself up in the bed.

Masie brought in a cup of tea. 'I'm off now to catch my train. When I have the time off, I'll come again.'

Evie scrambled from her bed, took the cup from Masie and placed it on her bedside table, then gave her a big hug. 'You've been a tower of strength to me. Thank you, Masie.'

Looking embarrassed, Masie replied, 'That's what friends are for.' Moving towards the door, she said. 'The girls are entertaining James and he's loving all the attention.'

Evie drank her tea and, glancing out of the window at the grey November sky, she dressed in a warm jumper and an old tweed skirt.

Walking into the kitchen, she saw James sitting on Gloria's knee, while Lily fed him a bowl of porridge. She used the spoon as an aircraft making a dive, and James's mouth the target, which opened automatically to take in the food.

After breakfast, dressed in their outdoor clothes and with James firmly strapped in his pram, they went for a walk into the small town. Lily and Gloria took turns to push the pram. 'I wonder how many children I will have,' Lily sang out.

Evie noticed Gloria didn't mention children, and she wondered if she was walking out with a young man. Then she thought about her own life. Would she ever walk out with a young man again?

A few people stopped to offer their condolences on the passing of Florence, and Evie thanked them for their kindness. Though as she expected, some people were quick to shun her, an unmarried mother who didn't fit their morals. And there was the added problem that she, Evie, a loose woman, might entice their husbands to abandon their principles. Evie noticed some of them were young women she had gone to school with. James laughed with glee as Gloria blew him a raspberry. Evie smiled. Her son was her life and she would always love and protect him.

Back at Island House, Evie lit the fire in the sitting room and drew the curtains against the wintry grey sky. They toasted bread when the fire was ablaze and spread butter and homemade plum jam on to it, and a boiled egg for James. Evie watched as Gloria cut off the top of the egg and showed him how to dip toasted soldiers into it. After a few attempts, he mastered the action.

Later, they sang nursery rhymes with actions for James until he got too excited. 'Bath time,' Evie announced, scooping him up from the floor into her arms.

'As a treat for us,' Lily asked, 'can Gloria and I bathe your lovely son?'

Evie smiled, replying, 'Of course.'

She tidied the sitting room, taking the used crockery to the kitchen to wash. Leaving the door open, she could hear the gleeful laughter from James and her two friends.

Checking on the contents of the pantry, she found a small dusty bottle hidden at the back of a shelf. Squinting to see the faded label, she read out loud, 'Sloe Gin.' She dusted off the bottle, eased out the cork and sniffed. It seemed all right, but to be safe, she poured a tiny drop into a glass and dipped her finger into it and tasted. 'Perfect.'

In the sitting room, she placed the tray holding the sloe gin and three small glasses on the table next to the reading lamp. Tossing a log on the fire, she crossed the room and drew the curtains, shutting out the dark night. Surveying the cosy room, a sense of something she could not quite grasp flittered across her mind. She tried to recall that fragile image, but it was elusive.

'Penny for them.' Lily came into the room.

Evie shook herself and said, 'This is a cosy room. I'll say goodnight to James.' She hurried from the room.

Gloria smiled at her, saying, 'He's all yours. Night, night, sweetheart.' She blew James a kiss as she exited the room.

Evie lowered the bar of the cot so she could hug her son and kiss his soft, downy hair, which she noticed was growing a shade darker. She watched his lovely face and his eyes close as he went to sleep and her heart contracted with overwhelming love for her son, for whom she would be both mother and father. She wished her own father were alive. He would be a wonderful role model for James. Sadly, it was not to be. Slipping the cot bar back into position, she tiptoed from the room, leaving the door ajar.

Downstairs, she joined Gloria and Lily in the sitting room. They continued to reminisce about their days spent together as Ack-Ack gunner girls, but, as they did so, Evie thought about how soon her friends would return to their lives and sadness filled her.

'Are you going to pour us a drink, or is it for show?' Lily said, grinning cheekily, pointing to the bottle and the glasses on the tray.

Jumping to her feet, Evie exclaimed, 'Sorry!' She gave them each a generous measure of the sloe gin. And Lily opened a packet of Lucky Strike and handed them round.

Drinking the sloe gin, Evie felt its warmth running through her body, taking away the tight, wound-up tension she hadn't realised she was carrying. She relaxed back in her chair by the fireside, smoking her cigarette, enjoying the friendly banter with her friends.

Gloria told them about the famous entertainers and singers she had met in London. 'Anne Shelton and Vera Lynn are two of my favourites.' When Lily asked her what they were like, Gloria went strangely quiet. Evie wondered whether it was out of modesty, or if Gloria was perhaps putting on a show of her own with her friends. Evie hoped she would achieve her dream of being a popular singer soon.

Lily enthused about the friendly GI wives who worked on the station, and their current agonising wait for details of their sailing date to be announced. All the wives were wondering if they would like life in New York. Evie hoped Lily would.

Midnight struck on the hall clock, and Evie yawned and rose to her feet. 'Time for bed for me. James is an early riser.' Her friends made to rise too, but she interrupted them. 'Stay up as long as you like.'

'No, I've had enough,' yawned Lily.

'And it's bed for me too,' said Gloria. 'We have to catch the mid-morning train.'

Early the next morning, Evie had James up and dressed, and he sat in his highchair. She had found it up in the attic, and guessed it must have been hers when a baby. She'd given it a good wash-down, but it needed painting. When Lily and Gloria came into the kitchen, both looking bleary-eyed, she looked at them both and said, 'I've made a pot of strong coffee.' It was the last of what Lily had brought with her.

The taxi arrived to take them to the station. Evie handed them a packet of cheese sandwiches each. 'You should be able to buy a hot drink when you change trains.'

'Thanks, love, we will be fine. You just concentrate on looking after yourself and James,' said Gloria. At the mention of his name, James banged a spoon on his wooden tray for attention. Gloria kissed him on the cheek and he babbled with glee.

'Write to me girls, won't you? And Lily, let me know your sailing date,' Evie said, wishing her friends were not leaving.

'Are you coming to wave me off?'

Tears sprang into Evie's eyes. 'I wish I could,' she said, a tremor in her voice.

Gloria hugged her and said, laughingly, 'I'll invite you to my West End show and you can stay in my penthouse.' They all laughed.

With James in her arms, Evie said goodbye to her friends and went into the silent, empty house. James, after all the excitement and attention he'd received, fell asleep. Gently, she laid him in his pram in the hall, where she could hear him if he cried.

It felt strange when she walked through the house. Never in her life had she known it to feel so empty. Her parents were both laid to rest in the churchyard, and Mabel was taking a well-earned break and spending time with her family. No committee members of her mother's had reason to call. She stared out at the bleak landscape, the sky laden with dark clouds; even the lake looked uninviting. She turned away.

Walking slowly to the kitchen, she wondered what the future held for her and James.

CHAPTER THIRTY-FOUR

Early December 1946

Evie felt overjoyed and stunned at the same time. She hadn't expected it. She collected James from the solicitor's secretary's office, thanked her for taking care of him, then wheeled the pram outside on to the main street. James was sitting up and taking notice of his surroundings and the people passing by, while his mother walked in a daze. Suddenly he shrieked with excitement, gurgling out, 'Mammy!' Then she focused on him and realised why he was so happy.

Flakes of snow fluttered down and James was trying to catch them. She smiled with delight at her son's first encounter with snow. As they hurried homewards, she saw a young woman she'd seen earlier huddled in a doorway, clutching a baby in her arms. She looked in distress and the infant was crying.

Evie stopped, noticing she was a girl of about sixteen, and asked, 'Are you all right?'

Her tearstained face looked pleadingly to Evie, and she cried out, 'Me dad chucked us out and I don't know where to go.'

Evie made a quick decision. 'Come home with me for now. Your baby needs feeding.'

'Thank you, missus,' the girl mumbled.

As they hurried along, Evie learned the girl's name was Betsy Miller, and her baby's name was Emily, who was only four weeks old.

Once in the kitchen's warmth and their outdoor clothes were off, Evie settled James in his highchair with a drink and biscuit. With the kettle boiling on the stove, she asked Betsy, 'ave you a feed for your baby?'

From a string bag fastened around her body, Betsy drew out a bottle of prepared feed. 'It'll need warming. Me mam gave it to me.' She hung her head and began crying.

Quickly taking the bottle from her, Evie stood it in a jug and added hot water from the kettle. The baby began to wail and James, sitting quietly, looked on in surprise at this moving bundle. Guiding Betsy to a chair, she gave the bottle of feed to her, watching as Emily latched on to the teat and sucked. After her feed and a nappy change, an old one of James's, Emily slept peacefully on a chair tucked in with cushions.

Evie set a cup of tea and a cheese sandwich in front of Betsy. 'Eat up and then tell me what has happened.'

The girl finished her food, licked her lips and flicked her hands down her skirt to brush away crumbs. Then, unable to stall any longer, she lifted her head and stared across the table at Evie, who had just placed James on a rug with a pile of wooden building bricks. Evie smiled encouragingly at Betsy, saying, 'Whatever you tell me is in confidence.' Betsy looked unsure of those words. Gently Evie said, 'I won't repeat to anyone without your permission.'

The girl gave a vast sigh of relief and spoke in a soft voice. 'It was all right until they demobbed me dad from the army. Mam said she didn't mind, but Dad said I was a disgrace and brought shame on the family's good name.' She choked back a sob and looked down at the checked tablecloth.

Evie glanced at James as he chuckled with merriment as the bricks came tumbling down, then gave her attention back to Betsy who had recovered herself.

'Me and Freddie, he's my sweetheart, we were saving up to get married. Mam minded Emily while I worked at the corner shop. And Freddie has a job at Nelson's garage, training to be a motor mechanic.'

Evie nodded. Her heart ached with sympathy for this young couple's plight. It only takes a moment of passion to change your life, as she knew from her own experience.

'I will give you a bed for the night and we will talk in the morning.' She picked up James and balanced him on her hip, waiting as Betsy gathered Emily into her arms. 'Follow me.' She showed them to a small bedroom at the end of the corridor, furnished with a bed and a tallboy. She pulled out the empty top drawer, saying, 'This will do as a cot for now. I will fetch clean bedding.'

Tears filled Betsy's eyes as she whispered, 'If you hadn't come along, I don't know what I'd have done.' She opened the string bag and pulled out clothes, damp to the touch.

Evie also brought a nightgown for Betsy. 'It's rather big, but it will be warm for you. And here's a clean nappy for baby. I'll take your clothes downstairs and air them for you.'

Betsy settled, and Evie readied James for his bath and bed. 'A quick bath tonight, my lovely one,' she said, lifting her dripping son from the water and wrapping him in a fluffy white towel. After his bedtime bottle of milk, and in his cot, she watched over him until he slept.

Downstairs, she tidied the kitchen and sat down, placing her hands on her head, wanting to stop her thoughts from whirling. She needed to straighten them and herself out. Today had been a bizarre day, certainly not how she had imagined it when she woke up this morning. She hadn't been sure what to expect from the solicitor. The will had been signed by her father and her mother as well. It had come as a total surprise.

Her father had left Island House to Evie. And there were other assets. Gerald Sinclair had invested his money wisely. 'Dear Dad,' she whispered. 'You thought of me.'

In her room, as she prepared for bed, she sat at her dressing table, brushing her hair, which had grown so long.

231

She studied her reflection in the mirror, a smile playing on her lips. 'So, Miss Sinclair, you are the new owner of Island House, and you are quite a wealthy woman.'

In bed, she lay thinking. Her and James's financial future was now secure. But what of their emotional future?

From down the corridor, she heard a baby whimper and the soft comforting words of a young mother's voice.

Evie sat up, startling herself, then relaxed back on to the pillow. An idea formed in her head. Would it be workable?

It was well past midnight before she finally slumbered, only to wake up at six-thirty in the morning. She looked at her son's cot, and he still slept. Quietly slipping from her bed and picking up her dressing gown from the chair, she made her way downstairs to the kitchen. Raking the warm embers in the fire-grate, she threw on kindling, and when alight, scooped coal from the scuttle, wafting newspaper to coax the flames higher. Satisfied, she filled the kettle with water and set it to boil on the stove.

She made a pot of tea and poured a cup, taking two of Mabel's shortbread biscuits from the tin. She settled down on a fireside chair, staring into the dancing flames.

Was her idea possible? Before discussing it with her solicitor, would it be better to have a firm plan? She tossed the idea back and forth until it started to develop in her mind. However, she needed to talk it over with someone who would understand before approaching her solicitor. Masie? Yes. She would write to her immediately. If she caught the early morning post collection, they would deliver the letter to Masie by the afternoon.

She hurried to her father's study and found writing material and stamps. She wrote in haste and went upstairs to dress quickly. James was still asleep. She went along to Betsy's room. She was awake and dressed. Her eyes filled with tears when she saw Evie.

'I'll get my things together,' she said.

'No, stay. I'm going to post this letter and I'll be back in a few minutes. James is asleep, so listen out for him. There's tea in the pot in the kitchen. We will talk later.'

Hurrying downstairs, she pulled on her boots, coat and scarf and dashed down the lane, the letter clutched firmly in her hand.

Later, James had his breakfast and played on the kitchen rug, and Betsy put Emily to sleep in James's pram. With a fresh pot of tea made, the two mothers sat down to talk.

Evie meant to be businesslike as she talked to Betsy about her own background, but as she began talking about having James in the Mother and Baby Home, a sadness overwhelmed her, pulling at her heart and her very being. She hadn't realised that she still carried the scars. 'I was told that James would be adopted.'

'Adopted!' shrieked Betsy, pushing back her chair and scrambling to her feet.

James looked up, startled, and cried, 'Mamma,' holding out his arms. Evie bent down to scoop him up and held him close.

'Sit down,' she said to Betsy. 'James is with me. I had to fight to keep him. It wasn't easy, but I have never regretted it.'

Betsy, now seated, said, 'But you have a home.'

Evie smiled. 'Like you, my parents threw me out. It was only when my mother became ill that I returned to care for her, otherwise I would still live-in and work at the pawnshop.'

'I can't imagine you doing that,' Betsy said shyly.

'At all costs, I would not give up my son. Now to business. I have a plan which I am going to discuss with a friend. It might take a while, but you are welcome to stay.'

'But I have only a few shillings. How can I pay my way?' Betsy stared, wide-eyed.

'Mabel will return next week, and she runs the house. However, I will need to see my solicitor and other people. If you take care of James for me, that will go towards your keep.'

'Why are you being kind to me, when my own family is not?'

Evie pondered for a few moments but knew her answer. 'I feel passionate about what I want to achieve. To give hope of a future life to unwed mothers and their babies.' James struggled in her arms, wanting to be put back on the rug to play.

The next day in the morning post, a letter arrived from Masie. She wrote she would come the day after, before the snow settled and travelling became difficult. Relief flooded through Evie as she read her friend's reply:

> *I like the idea of your plan, though I guess it will need a lot of work. Talk when I come.*
> *Your friend, Masie.*

As Evie drew back her bedroom curtains the next morning, she gasped with wonderment, seeing the beautiful landscape of snow covering everything. Even the tree branches sparkled with laden snow. She breathed in the pure freshness, which reminded her of her childhood, when her father had pulled her on the sledge and schoolfriends came to have a snowball fight. Later, they would build an igloo by rolling a snowball until it was huge, and they would stack them, making walls of snow, though she couldn't remember if they had a roof on the igloo.

Dashing away thoughts of her childhood, she hoped that the weather would not delay Masie coming.

Later, Evie dressed James in a warm red all-in-one suit, with attached mittens and wellington boots. 'You look like a miniature Father Christmas,' she told him, kissing the tip of his pert nose. Evie donned her coat, scarf, gloves and boots, and ventured out into the garden to the sheltered area near to the house, where the snow wasn't too deep. Clasping James's hands, she walked him in front of her, letting him kick at the snow. He squealed with delight, and she enjoyed the look of fascination on his face. After half an hour, they went indoors because she didn't want him to catch a chill.

Betsy greeted them in the kitchen with a cup of cocoa. James had his own beaker with a special lid so he could suck the liquid slowly.

Evie checked the pantry for what food Mabel had in stock, so they could make a hot meal for Masie. 'I shall need your ration book,' she said to Betsy.

'Do you really mean I can stay here?' asked an anxious Betsy, not sure of her good luck.

'Yes, I'm sure.' After a rummage along the shelves, Evie found a tin of stewing steak and ingredients to make a meat pie, a tin of peas, and on the stone floor of the pantry a sack of potatoes. She prepared the pastry for the pies. 'What can we have for pudding?' she asked Betsy.

Betsy called from the pantry, 'There's custard powder, dried egg powder, milk and a jar of homemade marmalade. I can make a bread and butter pudding.'

Evie looked out of the window again. 'Still no sign of Masie.' Glancing up to the laden sky, she prayed her friend was safe and had not met with a mishap.

Just as she was despairing, Evie heard a heavy truck coming up the drive. Flinging open the door, letting the hall light cast a path across the snow, she saw Masie being helped down from the truck by the coalman, who was delivering their weekly ration of coal.

She welcomed Masie into the house, taking hold of her case. She paid for the coal, but the man refused a cup of tea as he still had more to deliver.

James cried out with glee as he recognised Masie, and Betsy hung back with Emily in her arms. Masie sniffed, saying, 'What's that delicious smell? I am starving.'

Finally, when everyone had settled, and they were sitting around the table enjoying the meal and chattering, Masie suddenly said, 'I've given my notice at the Mother and Baby Home to help you run your venture, Evie.' There was a brief silence.

Then Evie cried with delight and surprise. 'You believe in what I will do?' Her heart was beating fast with relief.

'Yes, I do,' said Masie, with jubilation.

CHAPTER THIRTY-FIVE

December 1946

The weather thwarted Evie's plans. 'It's like living in the North Pole,' Masie declared, as they stood at the window watching the blizzard obliterating the landscape. Evie felt despondent. She strained her eyes to see if she could distinguish where the edge of the lake was, but couldn't. She turned to see James climbing up on to a dining chair to watch the snowflakes as they flittered by the window.

'It looks magical,' enthused a bright-eyed Betsy, as she cradled a sleepy Emily in her arms.

They all had different views on the weather, but they knew that it interfered with the process of welcoming unwed mothers and their babies into the house. 'I thought the authorities would be the ones to be difficult, not the weather.'

Masie spoke in her most practical voice. 'Evie, can you take me on a tour of the house and the rooms you intend to use?'

'I'll look after James,' Betsy volunteered.

They started with the bedrooms. 'Our bedrooms,' Evie said. Then she opened the door of what was once her parents' room. 'It's a large room, and two could share if needed.' She wrote details as they went along. Further along the corridor were two more bedrooms. 'We only have one bathroom,' Evie pondered. 'Though we can manage for now. I will engage a plumber to install washbasins in each room.'

'Where does this door lead?' Masie asked, tugging at a door which refused to open.

'Let me see,' Evie said, examining the door. 'Ah, I remember, you must reline the catch with the inner bolt. It will need replacing.' Opening the door, they went up the steep wooden stairs, both coughing as the disturbed dust motes flew about.

The two attic rooms were full of odd pieces of furniture, a couple of old trunks, boxes of contents unknown, broken toys, a wooden cot. 'Phew, this needs a good sort out. We'll leave the attic rooms for now.'

As they made their way downstairs, the delicious smell of fried, chipped potatoes cooking in goose fat came from the kitchen. 'Gosh, that smell makes me hungry,' said Evie, pushing open the door to see James seated in his highchair, dipping his chips into the yolk of a fried egg. Betsy was at the stove, lifting out another batch of chips. Evie thought how lucky she was to find Betsy. 'You are an angel!' she cried. Seated around the table, they enjoyed a tasty meal of eggs and chips with bread and butter.

While the weather still raged with blizzards, it cut them off unless the farmer came over on his snow-plough with supplies. A rota developed. They took it in turns to cook, wash and look after the children, and cleaned each of the unused rooms, repairing and utilising items from the attic rooms. The downstairs rooms were mainly in good condition. The kitchen became the hub of the house, where they met every morning to discuss the day's happenings, and where they had their meals. In the daytime, the sitting room was used for babies to rest, and the dining room became a playroom for the children. Opening a door to a small room, Evie surveyed it, saying, 'We could use this for the girls who have visitors and need privacy.' Masie nodded in agreement. Opening the door of her father's study, Evie's heart lurched on seeing his empty chair. In her mind's eye, she could see him sat at his desk, writing letters to various authorities during the war. Silently, she closed the door.

As Christmas Day drew near, Evie wondered how best to celebrate it. The farmer, out with his snow-plough, called with a goose. Evie thanked him and gave him her grocery order, making a mental note to buy him a bottle of his favourite tipple when the snow cleared. Then, turning to Masie, she uttered in dismay, 'I don't know how to cook a goose.'

'Give it here,' Masie said, taking it out of Evie's hands.

Checking the contents of the larder, Betsy called out, 'There are plenty of potatoes, and the flour bin is half full, and just one pack of lard. The milk-man is bringing carrots and onions when he delivers the milk.' Because of the exceptionally bad weather, he only delivered twice a week.

Mabel's son-in-law called, pulling a sledge and wearing snow shoes, delivering a box of Mabel's baking and a wireless because their old one needed repairing. 'Cup of tea?' Evie asked him.

'No, got more deliveries to make. Mabel's a slave driver.' They both laughed, and Evie made another mental note, adding to a long list of people who had helped them.

Betsy fiddled with the wireless, finding popular and traditional Christmas songs sung by an American singer. 'His voice is like velvet,' mused Evie, as she came into the kitchen. 'James is having his nap, so Masie and I will sort out the attic. And we might just find treasure.' They all giggled.

'I'll check on the children,' Betsy said, turning off the wireless.

Up in the attic there was no electricity, so Evie flashed her torch around. They rummaged in boxes, looking for Christmas decorations and any broken toys to mend.

Finally, they came down carrying a box each.

Kneeling on the kitchen floor, Evie opened her box to find a brand-new wooden train set in its unopened packag-ing. Her heart missed a beat, and she sat back on her heels. Her parents must have bought it for Donald, the brother she had never known. How sad. She looked up to see James sitting in his highchair, waiting for his tea. He must have sensed her gaze because he looked down at her and said, 'Mamma,' waving his spoon at her.

Overwhelmed with unconditional love for her son, tears pricked her eyes.

On Christmas Eve, the children fast asleep, Masie was preparing the goose to cook in the morning while Betsy peeled the potatoes. 'What do you think?' Evie asked. From old wire coat hangers, she had made a double hoop of mistletoe, decorated it with coloured paper and hung old-fashioned Christmas baubles from it.

'Where are you hanging it?' Masie asked, wiping her hands. 'It looks heavy.'

'It's not too heavy. The kitchen or the sitting room? What do you think?'

'The sitting room,' Betsy chimed in.

They all trooped to the sitting room. 'Where?' asked Evie, looking up at the ceiling. 'The chandelier fitting looks too fragile.'

'What about hanging it from the curtain pole?' said Masie, pointing to the window.

'I'll get the steps,' said Betsy, scooting off to the laundry room.

Evie climbed the steps and the two women carefully lifted it up to her to hang by its hook from the heavy curtain rail.

Their Christmas Day was cosy and intimate. James woke up early, sensing the excitement. Evie lay in bed, watching him play with the patched teddy bear she had found in one of the boxes brought down from the attic. She had cleaned it, and patched its torn arm. 'Patchy Bear is its name,' she told him.

Gleefully, he chanted, 'Patchy, Patchy.'

Evie laughed at her son, her ray of sunshine. She stretched and yawned. Time to get up.

Dressed and downstairs in the kitchen, with James playing safely on a rug in the corner with his wooden bricks and

Patchy, Evie set to work. She added more wood to the stove and then set the kettle to boil. Collecting a big pan, she filled it with part water and part milk, then added oatmeal to make porridge for breakfast, stirring it from time to time. Just as she made the pot of tea, Masie entered the kitchen.

'That's welcome,' said Masie, 'I function better after a morning cuppa.'

Evie poured out two cups and sat at the table opposite Masie. 'Strange, the house seems so different from when I was growing up here. As if it has taken on a whole new life.'

Masie looked quizzically at her friend and answered, 'Children make all the difference. If my Bert hadn't been killed, we would have had lots of children.'

'Oh, Masie.' Evie stretched out her hand across the table to grasp hold of Masie's hand. She didn't voice her thoughts about how war caused so much devastation in people's lives. And what for? One man's greed for power.

Betsy bustled in, carrying Emily in her arms, and the mood lightened.

They held Christmas lunch in the kitchen, the warmest room. Evie was in charge of the table setting. She smiled to herself, wondering, as she spread out one of her mother's best white damask tablecloths, what Florence would have thought. In the centre of the table, she placed a garland of pine cones, decorated with faded touches of gold paint, and a tall white candle, surrounded by sprays of cotoneaster with its scarlet berries, cut fresh from the bush near to the back door. For each place setting, she slotted a napkin through silver holders, which she had cleaned along with the silver cutlery, her mother's best.

Betsy turned to admire Evie's handiwork. 'Oh,' she gasped. 'It looks so posh. We never had owt like this at home.' At the mention of home, her eyes filled with tears.

Evie hugged her, saying, 'Betsy, this is your home for as long as you need it.'

Masie admired it too, and James, not wanting to be left out, clamoured to be lifted to see.

Her task done, Evie fed and changed Emily. 'She's coming on a treat,' she exclaimed to Betsy. 'And gaining weight by the feel of her.'

Betsy held out her arms for her daughter and crooned to her, loving her before settling her to sleep in the pram.

Evie lit the fire in the sitting room so it would be warm after lunch when they would open their gifts. She placed the fire-guard protectively around the fireplace, and watched the baubles on the mistletoe decoration glinting in the firelight. For a moment, Evie felt transported back to when she was a little girl. She missed her parents. And then a picture of Richard's face flashed before her and she wondered how he was spending his Christmas Day. She then went to her room to change into a red dress with a white Peter-Pan collar, brushed her hair and added her pearl necklace, which she was told had belonged to her father's mother.

Back in the kitchen, a delicious aroma greeted her. The goose, the crisp roast potatoes and the colourful vegetables were ready. Masie was stirring a pan of rich-smelling gravy.

'Gosh! I'm starving,' Evie uttered. At the sound of her voice, James pulled himself to his feet and began a little jig. Evie reached for him and fastened him into his highchair, wiped his hands and tied on his bib.

Masie and Betsy went to change into their best dresses, and Evie sang along with the Christmas carols playing on the wireless, with James happily singing his own version.

Later, after they had eaten their fill of the scrumptious Christmas meal, washed and tidied away the dishes, Evie, Masie, Betsy, James and baby Emily went along to the sitting room.

'This is cosy,' Masie remarked, looking appreciatively around the room. 'Look,' she said to James, gesturing to the mistletoe. He held out his arms, trying to capture the baubles as they twinkled like stars.

'Pretty, pretty,' he said, waving his arms with glee.

Evie set him down on the rug, saying, 'Now it's time to open our presents.' The first one was for Emily. Between them, Evie and Masie had knitted a pink pram set.

241

Betsy's eyes filled with tears. 'It's beautiful,' she whispered.

'You can take Emily out for walks in the pram when the weather improves. By then James will need a smaller pram, a Tansad.'

Next came a present for James. They all watched as he tore off the old brown wrapping paper, but when he came to the box, Evie stepped in. Carefully, she undid it, opening the lid to reveal a bright red and green train set. James's eyes were wide with wonderment. Carefully, Evie lifted out the trains and placed them before James. He looked at the trains, not sure what to do with them. Then he looked up to Evie and, gently, she held one of his chubby hands to touch the engine, which he then picked up to show to Patchy. Afterwards, with the board laid out on the rug, James trundled the engine and carriages, lying flat on his tummy, mesmerised by his own actions.

For Betsy, Evie had altered and fashioned an old blue paisley dress of hers, adding a belt and trimming the collar with white lace. Again, Betsy's eyes filled with tears. 'Put it on,' Evie said. And off she ran.

Evie gave Masie her gift, a pair of multi-coloured woollen mittens. 'They will see me coming,' she laughed.

Masie gave Evie a tube of pink lipstick. 'Oh!' gasped Evie. 'I can't remember the last time I wore lipstick.'

'Time you did.'

Just then, Betsy entered the room and gave a twirl in her dress, her eyes shining like diamonds. 'Look at your mammy, isn't she glamorous,' said Masie, holding Emily up to see, who gurgled with delight.

Betsy went to the kitchen and returned carrying a tray of gingerbread. On some of them she had written their names with a concoction of icing. Evie fetched glasses and the bottle of sherry sent by Mabel. She poured out a generous measure for each, and orange juice in his special beaker for James, while Emily lay on a blanket on the floor, kicking her legs.

While the children enjoyed themselves, the adults sang Christmas carols. Tired out by all the excitement, the children were soon asleep in their cots. From the sideboard, Evie pulled out a companion set of board games. Draughts, which Evie used to play with her father, Snakes and Ladders, Tiddlywinks and Monopoly, but by ten o'clock, they were exhausted, and their beds called.

As Evie lay snug and warm, listening to James's gentle breathing, she felt so happy and blessed. This was a Christmas Day she would remember, for it felt so special.

CHAPTER THIRTY-SIX

January 1947

The snow cleared, though banks of it still hugged the sides of roads and lanes. In the kitchen, while washing up the dinner dishes, Evie was singing along to a popular Vera Lynn song on the wireless when she heard a faint knock on the back door. Opening the door, she saw a thin, weary-looking young woman clutching a bundle in one arm and a bag in the other. A hungry wail came from the bundle, and an angry little fist shot out. The young girl lurched forward, falling into Evie's arms.

Evie caught the woman and the baby. Steadying herself, she helped them into the kitchen. Taking the crying child from the girl, she guided her to a chair, which the girl slumped into.

Hearing the commotion, Masie came into the kitchen, and quickly taking in the scene, put the kettle to boil to make a pot of tea and a feed for the baby. She fed the baby, a little girl, who soon guzzled the milk, while Evie poured the tea and made toast. The girl sipped her tea and ate a slice of toast. Her head hung with red hair and she didn't meet anyone's eyes. With the baby's hunger now satisfied and nappy changed, Masie laid her down on the big fireside chair with cushions tucked around her to keep her safe.

'Feeling better?' Evie asked the young girl. She nodded, still not looking up. The distant cry of James called. He had been having an afternoon nap. Betsy was out walking with Emily in the pram. Evie glanced at Masie, saying, 'I'm going to check on James.'

Masie turned her attention to the girl. 'What's your name, love?' The girl mumbled incoherently. 'Sorry, I didn't catch that. Lift your head, dear. We will not send you away.' The girl lifted her head, showing her tear-stained face. Masie gasped. 'You're Camilla Bentley?'

'Yes,' she answered in a small voice.

'I thought you were going to be married.' Camilla gave her a defiant look, which Masie remembered from the home.

'He didn't want us,' she sniffed, wiping her face on the sleeve of her cardigan. 'I had nowhere to go.' Tears welled in her eyes.

'Come here, love.' Masie reached out her arms to hold the girl close, feeling her thin body rack with sobs.

Later, Evie and Masie were baking hot bread cakes and making a broth of the remains of the stew left over from dinner. 'I'll be glad when food is off rations,' Evie remarked. 'Though there seems no sign of the government doing so.'

'And we won the war,' added Masie.

'Poor Camilla,' Evie said, as she brought out a fresh batch of cakes from the oven. 'She always appeared so feisty and focused.'

'Aye, not every man wants children. Though what rattles me is that they don't take responsibility for their actions. It's always left to the woman to hold the baby,' Masie prattled, having seen this first-hand working in the home.

Evie didn't answer. She didn't know if Matt or Richard was James's father. Richard had never been in touch. Would he want a child? 'I'll pop upstairs to see how Camilla is,' she said instead.

Both mother and baby were sound asleep, the girl in the bed and the baby, temporarily, in a drawer by her bedside. Evie tiptoed from the room and went downstairs to the children's playroom, where Betsy was with Emily and James. James played happily with his train set, Patchy by his side. Betsy looked up from her sewing. Evie had given her a ream of cotton material, which had been in her mother's room, and Betsy was busy sewing dresses for Emily and a dirndl skirt for herself. 'You could do with a sewing machine.'

'I suppose,' said a contented Betsy.

'Tea in half an hour.'

In the kitchen, Evie said to Masie, 'We need more cots for babies, and prams, and single beds.' She pushed back her hair from her face, frowning.

'I know where the home got their beds and prams from. I could see if any are available,' said Masie, as she stirred the broth.

'Oh, that would be a great relief. What about delivering them?'

'I'll see Bencher and ask if his mate will bring them. Though you will have to pay him.'

'Yes, and I must send Bencher a gift. I miss the old rascal. I could make him a cake?' Masie raised an eyebrow. Evie's cakes had previously sunk in the middle. 'Well, savouries then,' she laughed.

Within the week, beds, cots and prams arrived, and everyone mucked in to clean and polish them.

Camilla settled in with her baby girl of eleven months, Josephine, who was now thriving, and so was Camilla, who had put on weight and seemed happy.

Evie and Masie were alone one evening while everyone else was sleeping. 'We need a plan,' said Evie. 'We can't keep muddling along. What if more girls and their babies turn up?' She paused, then added, 'What if the locals object? Her at the post office is always off-hand with her snide comments. We don't want the girls to feel threatened. They've had enough negative remarks already in their lives. We need the women's committee on our side. They might be looking for alternative good causes.'

'It is worth a try, but I'll leave you to deal with them,' replied Masie, adding, 'I can check what employment is on offer for the girls.'

'I'm relieved that Mabel is returning to work, preparing and cooking meals at midday, though the girls will do their own laundry,' Evie said, pushing a strand of hair from her face as she folded a pile of freshly washed and ironed bed linen.

One morning, later in the week, Evie left the solicitor's office, feeling reassured that the money her father had invested was in a healthy state. Now, she could face the obnoxious bald-headed bank manager who tried to belittle her. Wrapped up in her thoughts, she bumped into a woman passing by. 'So sorry,' she said, then saw who it was. As quick as a swooping gull, she said, 'Mrs Dawson, please may I have a moment of your time?'

The woman, of middle-age, tall with a well-corseted figure, stared at Evie. And then recognition flashed across her face. 'You are the late Mrs Sinclair's daughter?'

'Yes, I would like to speak to you when you are free.' People hustled by on the pavement.

'Here is not the place,' said Mrs Dawson. 'You may call at two p.m. this afternoon. You know where I live?'

'Yes, thank you.' Evie hurried back to Island House. She needed to make notes.

After telling Masie of her encounter with Mrs Dawson, Evie sat at her father's desk with a notepad in front of her. She heard the gong for dinner. The gong was Mabel's prize bargain, bought from a jumble sale, which summoned them to dinner wherever they were.

'I've got my timetable to work to,' Mabel said, a twinkle in her blue eyes.

After kissing James goodbye, safe in the hands of Masie, Evie hurried off to meet Mrs Dawson.

She lived at the far end of the Esplanade, in an impressive Edwardian house overlooking the green, away from visitors who walked along the seafront. The sea defences had all been removed from the beach and Evie noticed a few winter visitors. Suddenly an idea popped into her already overfull mind.

She rang the doorbell, and Mrs Dawson opened the door and ushered her in. Evie had expected a maid to welcome her.

'We'll go into the kitchen where it's warmer,' said Mrs Dawson. Evie followed her down a dark corridor to a small kitchen, painted in brown and cream.

When both were settled at the kitchen table, with a cup of tea and biscuits, Mrs Dawson asked in a booming voice, as if she was addressing a room full of people, 'Miss Sinclair, how can I help?'

Evie reached for the notepad from her handbag, coughed, and cleared her throat. She outlined her plan to give unmarried mothers a chance to have a better life, and the need for them to be accepted into the community. 'People are unfair to judge unmarried mothers and their babies, while men appear blameless.' And then she thought of Matt, a casualty of war, and added, 'Though not all men.' She looked across the table at Mrs Dawson, who remained silent, and wondered what she was thinking.

Finally, she spoke. 'A difficult problem, but I thrive on a challenge,' she boomed. 'I will call a committee meeting and let you know the outcome. Though some ladies are not in favour of your establishment. They believe you are encouraging immoral behaviour.'

Evie replied firmly, 'Perhaps if they had the support of the men, they wouldn't be in this position. The young women at Island House wish to make a better life for themselves and their children. Our ethos is to give them our full support and reassurance in helping them to achieve their endeavour.' She stood up, her head held high, and said, 'Thank you for seeing me. Good afternoon.'

Outside, Evie felt her whole body trembling. As she made her way back home, she hoped she had done the right thing by involving Mrs Dawson and the committee. She wanted to gain support for the mothers who could work in the community.

When they were alone in the sitting room, she discussed this with Masie. 'Stop worrying and wait and see what happens,' Masie said. She went over to the sideboard and held up the sherry bottle from Christmas. 'Ah, good. Just enough for two tots.' She poured sherry into glasses and handed one to Evie. 'A toast to the future of our home for unmarried mothers.'

Two days later, Mrs Dawson called with good news. 'My committee has agreed to help you.'

Evie discussed her plans in more depth with Masie as they sat at the kitchen table, unravelling the wool from old jumpers to remake into garments for growing children. 'Looking towards the Easter holidays, families, especially from Hull, want to escape its devastations. With dads now home, families want fun in their lives.'

'Oh, aye. What kind of fun?' Masie raised her eyebrows.

Laughing, Evie answered, 'Family fun. I noticed they have cleared the beach of all the objects of war defence. Families can relax there now, and the children can once again build sandcastles.' She thought back wistfully to her days spent with her father as a young girl, combing the beach for her coloured pebble collection. 'I am sure they will want refreshments. What do you think?'

Masie pretended to ponder and then smiled at her friend. 'Sounds as though you've hit on a great idea. How are you going to put it into practice?'

'There are bound to be planning regulations. This is where the ladies' committee will be helpful with how to negotiate permission.'

'Do you mean to open a café?'

'I think at first a wooden hut, situated either on the sands or the promenade. Then, if it is successful, we can open a café. Easter Sunday is early, on the sixth of April.' Evie rose from the table, saying, 'I must write it all down so I don't forget when I contact Mrs Dawson.' She paused in the doorway, her face serious. 'What if we invite Mrs Dawson here? Do you think it will create a good impression?'

'I am sure it will.'

With a spring in her step, Evie went to her father's study to jot down notes of her ideas.

CHAPTER THIRTY-SEVEN

January–March 1947

Early the next morning, before she'd had time to contact Mrs Dawson, a knock came on the back door. Evie opened the door to a young woman cradling a baby, along with an older woman. She ushered them into the kitchen, where she had just made a pot of tea.

Masie entered the kitchen and recognised the young woman. 'You are from the Mother and Baby Home?'

'Yes,' answered the girl in a weak voice, lowering her head.

Masie asked the older woman, who she knew was the girl's mother, 'I thought Joan was going home to you?'

The woman, Mrs Harper, shifted uncomfortably. 'She was, but my lads are home from war.' She sniffed. 'We haven't room at home for a young baby as well. Besides, her young man wants to marry her, so he's saving up. But what with the housing shortage, it's difficult for them.'

Evie poured out cups of tea for all. They held discussions around the table, then welcomed Joan and her baby son, Malcolm.

Somehow, word of what Evie offered at Island House spread. Two more young women came with their babies.

Nancy had had a baby to another man, no longer on the scene, and her husband refused to accept it.

Then Doreen arrived. She'd got herself entangled with a married man. At first, she cut a pathetic figure with her big dark eyes. 'I don't want to lose my baby. He's all I've got in the world,' she cried.

If possible, they encouraged the mothers to seek employment while Evie and Masie looked after their children. Having employment gave them contact with the outside world and helped them to decide their future. Evie and Masie held weekly meetings for the women to attend and air their views about whether being at Island House benefited them.

Most wanted the best for their child, except Doreen. She would sneak out at night to further her ambition of prostitution. She gained a reputation for being a loose woman and bragged about it to the other girls.

'We must resolve the situation,' Evie said to Masie. 'But how?'

'I wonder why she wants to keep her son, for she seems to have no interest in him. I think we must have a frank talk with her.'

In conversation with Doreen, it turned out that the father of the child paid her an allowance. 'So that is your reason for keeping the child?'

'Yes,' she answered, with a toss of her black, wavy hair. 'Why else would I be saddled with a bairn?'

'But what about your son's future? Have you thought of it?' Masie asked.

Evie opened her notebook and picked up her pen and said, I think we need to talk to your son's father in confidence. If you give us his name and address, we will contact him.'

'Bleeding hell, no. His wife will have a fit.'

Later, Mabel mentioned to them the gossip she'd heard when at the butcher's. 'Doreen's exploits are gossiped about in the town, and some people have the idea that all the mothers living here are immoral.'

Both Evie and Masie listened in silence. Then Evie spoke. 'I had a niggling feeling this might happen. It's becoming clear she can't stay here. It reflects on the other mothers, and it is damaging to what we set out to achieve — to provide a safe environment for mothers and their babies.'

'I can enquire discreetly about the father of the child.'

'Sounds a way forward,' remarked Evie, knowing she trusted Mabel.

Evie instructed Doreen not to go out at night and leave her child alone. For a week, things seemed settled, until the night her son woke up, crying. Before he disturbed the entire household, Evie jumped from her bed and flung on her dressing gown as she hurried to the room where the baby was crying. His mother was missing.

'You poor little mite,' she said, lifting the baby from his cot to cradle him in her arms, feeling his sopping wet nappy. She sat down to change him, and once she'd given him a feed, he settled. She watched over him in his cot, the steady rise and fall of his tiny body. 'You deserve a loving family home, someone to care for you.' His life with Doreen as his mother would be one of neglect. What sort of future would he have? Doreen would never alter her ways, because she was happy with her life.

Doreen was missing for two days. 'As bold as brass,' Masie commented to Evie. 'She just trotted in as though she'd been for a walk.'

Mabel arrived, a bit out of breath. 'Sorry I'm late, but I've got news.'

They waited, watching her take off her hat and coat and hang them on the door-hook. Evie felt her insides contract with impatience and bit on her lip.

Mabel flopped down on the chair. 'It's him who has the public house off Main Street, Bert Black. They say his wife is a right old battle-axe. She makes him do the cleaning up on a night time while she goes to bed. That's when the shenanigans happen.'

Evie smiled to herself at Mabel's choice of words, then said, 'I need to speak to this man. When is the best time to go?'

'Morning, while he's stocking shelves before opening. It's best to go round the back door.'

The three women sat at the table to discuss their plans and decided. Evie said, 'I'll go to see Mr Black on Thursday and see what he has to say about his son. And, depending on the outcome, we must think how to involve Doreen.'

On Wednesday night, Evie slept fitfully, thinking about the baby boy whose future, wasn't secure. On Thursday morning, she looked in shop windows until Mrs Black left the pub on her way to the hairdresser's. Shivering against the morning chill, she drew her coat tighter and pulled down the brim of her felt hat to hide her face. After a quick, furtive look around, she opened the yard door of the pub and slipped inside. There was no sign of Mr Black. She stood in the yard and pondered whether to knock on the door.

A voice boomed, 'What do you want?'

Startled, she turned to see a burly man in shirtsleeves with brown braces holding up his rough trousers and a flat cap on his head. A cigarette dangled from the corner of his mouth. 'Mr Black?'

'Who are you?'

'I'm Evie Sinclair and I run Island House to help mothers and their babies.'

'What's that got to do with me?'

'I believe we have your son and his mother, Doreen Whitehead, staying with us.'

His ruddy face blanched white, then he recovered himself. 'I ain't giving her any more money.'

'Money isn't the problem, but your son's future is. Doreen is not concerned about his welfare, only about the money she receives from you.'

Some of his colour returned, and he said gruffly, 'Come indoors.'

She followed him to his cubby-hole office, where he picked up a bottle from a shelf and took a long swig from it. She took a deep breath. 'My colleagues and I believe you have three options for your son's welfare and future. First, to be adopted into a family; second, to be fostered by a family, which means you pay for his upkeep; third, for you and your wife to have him live with you.' She watched his face blanch white again.

'Bloody hell! No!' He took another swig from the bottle.

She waited a few moments, and asked him, 'Would you like to be involved in your son's future? If he were to be fostered?'

'No. The wife will want to know about the money. She is already suspicious and making my life hell.'

'So, adoption is the best way forward for your son.' He nodded his agreement. 'I will discuss it with Doreen, though she might demand money from you.'

Reluctantly, he nodded and growled, 'Wish I'd never got snared with her.'

Slowly, Evie walked back to Island House, mulling over in her mind the outcome of the conversation with Bert Black. She needed to speak to Doreen.

They sat in the privacy of the sitting room. 'Doreen, you can't continue living here. If you want to carry on with prostitution, that's your business. However, it does not fit with our ethos of helping mothers and babies to a better life and future.'

At first, Doreen fumed and stormed about the house, banging doors until her anger abated. Then she returned to the sitting room.

'You didn't really expect to stay here indefinitely?' Evie asked the now subdued girl.

She shrugged and replied, 'I never thought that far.' She gave an enormous sigh. 'I can't look after a young nipper. I don't want to be a mother and have a string of bairns, like my mother. She never had time for us and was always hitting the bottle.'

'Would you consent to having your son adopted?'

Doreen replied without hesitation, 'Yes, missus.'

* * *

'I couldn't help feeling sorry for Doreen. She didn't have a happy childhood,' Evie related to Masie and Mabel. 'I think Mr Black will give her a one-off sum of money. She says she wants to go up the coast to either Bridlington or Scarborough.'

'When she goes, I'll make her a parcel of food,' Mabel said.

'I'll give her a washbag and a few essentials,' offered Masie.

'I'll buy her a train ticket,' agreed Evie. 'It's the least I can do.'

They arranged matters with the adoption authorities with the help of Mrs Dawson and her ladies. Doreen signed the documents. She wasn't at all miserable, but happy to be parting with her baby. 'Sad,' Evie murmured, as they watched Doreen climb into a taxi, eager to be on her way.

Her baby stayed with them for another month before, on a bright March day, his adopted parents came to collect their son. They were a couple in their mid-thirties, unable to have children of their own.

'We both come from big families,' the woman said joyously. 'And now we are having a baby of our own. He won't be lonely.'

Evie, Masie and Mabel watched the happy couple leave with their son.

Evie lay in bed, listening to the gentle breathing of James, and thought of the little boy who now had two parents. She turned to gaze upon her adored son's face, and whispered to him, 'If only I knew who your daddy is. Matt or Richard?'

CHAPTER THIRTY-EIGHT

March 1947

Their plan to open a hut which served refreshments near the seafront was on hold. Apparently, the council was still clearing up after the war and housing was their chief priority.

When Mrs Dawson relayed this to Evie, she felt despondent. 'However,' Mrs Dawson continued, 'I have a favour to ask of you.' Silence echoed down the telephone line, and Evie thought someone had cut them off. Then she heard another voice, someone talking to Mrs Dawson.

Evie moved restlessly and stood up from the desk to stare out of the window. She saw James in his pram, with Masie pushing him along, both laughing, and the sight pulled at her heart strings as she wished she was out there with her son. As she waited for the conversation on the other end of the telephone line to finish, Evie wondered if what she was doing, taking in young women with their children to prepare them for a better life, was foolhardy?

'Sorry for the interruption, my dear,' Mrs Dawson's voice boomed in Evie's ear. 'As I was saying, a favour to ask of you. We were planning to reintroduce our May Day Fair, but unfortunately, the church hall is experiencing structural damage and it is not safe. At Island House you have extensive grounds and we could erect tents.' She paused for effect. 'And you and the young women could provide the refreshments. This would be a splendid opportunity for you all to be part of the community.'

Evie sat down again. She hadn't been expecting that. Taking a deep breath, she answered, 'Yes, it is an ideal chance. I will discuss it with my colleague and contact you as soon as possible.'

Pulling on her coat, Evie ran outside to catch up with Masie. She was out of breath when she reached her.

'Where's the fire?' Masie asked, putting out her hand to steady Evie, while James stretched out his arms to his mother.

Walking back to the house, Evie pushed the pram and blew raspberries at James, making him laugh. Once in the kitchen's warmth, and James had settled on a rug with a drink of milk and a biscuit, the two women sat at the table with cups of tea. Then Evie relayed to Masie Mrs Dawson's bad news about a hut on the sand, and her good news about the May Day Fair.

'What do you think?' She realised she was sitting on the edge of her chair.

Masie poured out two more cups of tea before speaking. 'It's a marvellous idea. The villagers will see that our girls are not wanton women, but young mothers doing their best for their children.'

Evie laughed. 'Masie, I am so pleased that we are both on the same wavelength, as my dear dad used to say.' She wondered what her parents would think about mothers and their children living at Island House?

The news that the fair was going to be held in the grounds of Island House excited everyone. The committee also mentioned trips on the lake by rowing boat. Evie surveyed her old boat, which the weather had damaged and needed repairing.

'We could do with a handyman,' Masie remarked, as she and Evie walked back to the house. 'There are plenty of jobs in the house and grounds to keep someone occupied.'

Evie glanced up at the roof, where some of the ridge tiles were missing. 'I guess so. I have given little thought to the maintenance of the property.' She dismissed it from her mind. The May Day Fair was taking up all her time, and she needed to see her son, who was fast growing up. She watched him as he played outside in the safe fenced area close to the house and next to the vegetable patch. Although the lake was a distance away from the house, she had had the fence installed.

Masie took a day off once a month to visit her family in Hull. Occasionally, Evie went to visit Bencher with James. Bencher was always pleased to see them, making a fuss over James. 'My, he's growing into a fine boy. Like his dad?' Bencher looked at Evie. Never had he mentioned James's father, but soon James would ask, or even say the word, 'Daddy'.

Just then, the shop doorbell tinkled and the awkward-ness passed.

Later, going back to Island House on the train, and with James asleep on her lap, Evie wished with all her heart that she could tell James who his father was. She couldn't say he had a choice of two: Matt or Richard. As her son slept, she studied his features, looking for traces of his father, but he just seemed to look like her. But then, he might change. Her head ached with thinking and she longed to close her eyes and obliterate the problem. But it would always be there. The other young mothers talked openly about their young men, though Camilla didn't anymore. She was hoping her parents would accept her and her child. Camilla wrote to them every week, but their letters to her were sporadic.

Evie didn't have an address for Richard and no way to reach him. He knew she had a son, for Gloria had told him. Would he look for her? He may be married by now and have no interest in her. She didn't want to upset his life by trying to trace him. Her only option was to tell James that his father had died fighting.

She stepped down from the train. James was awake, and he loved to see the engine, especially when the smoke billowed out. He lifted his arms, trying to catch the smoke.

At Island House, her attention was firmly on the forth-coming May Day Fair, and everyone in the house was excited. They now had five young women and their babies staying. 'Just the right number,' Evie confided to Masie, as they sat down to discuss their part in the fair.

'It's a bank holiday, so all the girls can help,' Masie added.

Three of the girls had jobs: Joan worked the early morning shift at the newsagent's, having afternoons free. Audrey worked afternoons at the hardware shop. Doris, shy at meeting the public, cleaned for the local doctor, whose wife was on the ladies' committee. Betsy loved baking and had improved under the watchful eye of Mabel, and now worked at the bakery. Camilla, who had never worked before, had wanted to try sewing, so Evie had bought a second-hand Singer sewing machine. She sorted out her late mother's clothes for Camilla to unpick seams and use the material to fashion garments for the young women. Evie encouraged the women to save the money they earned in their own bank accounts, except for an amount of pocket money so they could buy treats or go to the cinema.

'It's important that the girls have some kind of social life,' Evie mused. 'I hated living at the home when we were forbidden to go out.'

'Punishment!' said Masie. 'The people who ran the home had that philosophy. Wayward girls, like you, who had committed an immoral act must suffer the consequences.'

Evie could laugh now, but not then. She wanted the girls at Island House to have a future. She heard the laughter of children. Rising, she said to Masie, 'Come on, let's have fun. It's bath time.'

A few weeks later, Masie called from the study, 'Evie, Mrs Dawson's on the telephone.'

Evie was helping Mabel wash the dishes after dinner, so quickly dried her hands and hurried to the study. Picking up the telephone receiver, she said politely, 'Good afternoon, Mrs Dawson.' Listening, she focused her attention.

'What was all that about?' asked Masie, as she looked up from the accounts book.

'On Saturday, men are coming to erect the tents. She asked if we could possibly give them refreshments.'

'Let's hope the weather remains fine,' Masie said.

On Saturday morning, Evie glanced up at the glorious cerulean sky from her bedroom window. Holding James in her arms, she said, 'Look at the clouds drifting by.' He reached out his hand as if to catch them, like he did with the smoke from the train. After an early breakfast, they went outside. She held her son's hand as he toddled along. She loved this quiet time with James. As much as she enjoyed everyone's company, this time with her son was precious.

They walked down towards the lake and spied water hens darting in and out among the bulrushes. This fascinated James, and she had to hold tight to his hand to stop him from running off to follow the birds. His shouts of glee echoed across the lake. A man and his dog walking on the far side waved. Evie scooped James up in her arms and they both waved back. As she turned, she saw a truck coming round the house from the front. It stopped and four men jumped from it and glanced around. Mrs Dawson had sent them the plan for the fair site, with details of where the tents were to be erected.

'Hello,' she called, and James mimicked her. 'Cheeky,' she said, kissing his cheek. As she neared, she saw they were young men. They stood surveying the site, and one man passed a packet of cigarettes around. James looked on in awe as one flicked a lighter, as it was something he hadn't seen before, being too young to remember Bencher smoking. As she drew nearer, James wriggled in her arms and she gently set him down. Before she could grasp his hand, he toddled off. He moved at such speed, it amazed her, and then it happened. He toppled forward on to the path and cried.

'Whoa, little fellow,' the tall, fair-haired man said, as he crouched down and raised James up into his arms. Mesmerised, James stopped crying to gaze into the man's face and touch his ear.

'I'm sorry,' Evie began. Then stopped. Her heartbeat suddenly erratic, her legs weak. She uttered one word. 'Richard.'

The other men were unloading the gear so the three of them were alone.

'Evie.' He stared at her, his silver-grey eyes searching her face. And then, remembering he was holding James, he said, as he gazed at the boy's face, 'He has Matt's eyes.'

'Oh,' Evie uttered, the colour draining from her face. She covered her hands over her mouth, her body shaking. Then she broke into uncontrollable tears, her body reeling.

Unexpectedly, she felt the strength of Richard's powerful arm as he gathered her close to the warmth of his chest, feeling his heartbeat, which matched hers. He supported her in his embrace while James played with her hair, oblivious to the significance of the moment.

CHAPTER THIRTY-NINE

Late April 1947

Evie heard Masie's voice, and it sounded far away. 'I have a treat for you, James.' She blew raspberries, and he laughed, wriggling away from Richard's hold.

'Evie,' Richard whispered, 'shall I take you indoors or shall we stroll down by the lake?'

She sniffled, slowly lifting her head and looking into his face, then she nodded towards the lake. Uncurling her body from his warmth, they walked side by side, not touching.

At the edge of the lake, they stood for a few moments. Then Evie led the way to the path, to its familiar haven. They walked in silence. Only the call of birds pierced the air, and the scent of new mown grass captured by the gentle breeze twitched her nostrils. She could see the men working on the tents from the far side. On seeing them, her brain suddenly came back into gear. The shock of hearing Richard say those words had now become reality.

She looked at him and said, 'I was never sure who James's father was, until now.'

He stared at her, taking hold of her arms and looking into her eyes. 'You thought I might be James's father?' he uttered.

She held his gaze and heaved a sigh. 'It was always a possibility.'

'Why didn't you let me know?'

'I didn't know how to contact you.'

'I saw Gloria in London. If only she had given me your address, I would have come.' Then he paused, his eyes holding a faraway look. Quietly, he said, 'Matt was my friend, and I always felt guilty about the night we spent together.'

'Matt's death devastated me and we both needed comfort. If it's any consolation, I had pangs of guilt too. How to tell James who his father was has been my greatest concern. Now I know.'

'So now you can. Time I did some work.'

They walked back in silence. Evie wondered if Richard was relieved that he wasn't James's father and that he could walk away with no sense of responsibility. She glanced sideward at him. Why was he here at Island House? Purely to erect the tents? She wanted to ask him, but now wasn't the right time.

They parted without a word. He joined the men, and she went to see James.

She found her son with Masie in the children's playroom. Standing on the threshold, she gazed at James, who was lying on his tummy, playing with his train set. He was totally unaware of the turmoil in his mother's heart. Evie was glad she finally knew who James's daddy was. Had she hoped it was Richard? Why? Because then he would have married her. Or would he? Her head spun.

Just then, Betsy came along the corridor with Emily, and Evie stepped aside, letting her pass. Masie rose to her feet and said to Betsy, 'Will you keep an eye on James, please?' Then she steered Evie away towards the quiet of the sitting room.

Masie sat Evie down on the comfy sofa, then went to the sideboard to find any remnants of Mabel's homemade sloe gin. 'Ah,' she said, as hidden beneath a pile of napkins was a bottle. She poured a generous measure into a glass and placed it into Evie's hand, saying, 'Drink this, love.'

Evie obeyed. Taking a gulp, she felt its soothing warmth slipping down her throat into her body. The next gulp shot up to her head, taking away the dull thudding lodged there. She thought she could smell tobacco, and wished for a cigarette, but didn't want to take up the habit again. Masie grabbed the empty glass and put a cigarette in her hand.

Surprised, Evie took a long draw and exhaled, letting some of the tension flow from her body. 'So,' said Masie, 'this is the Richard you mentioned. Is he the father of James?'

Evie took another long draw and exhaled again, watching the smoke plume drift upwards. Then she answered, 'No. Matt is James's father. He has Matt's eyes. Richard confirmed that.' Her voice was flat and toneless.

'At least you know. And now you can have James christened.' Pausing, she said slowly, 'You could ask Richard to be his godfather.'

Evie looked up and gazed at Masie, saying, 'Do you believe he will want to be?'

'In my humble opinion,' she stated, 'yes, he will.' She stood up. 'Right, feeling you can cope now?'

Evie roused herself and jumped to her feet. 'Yes, we have plenty to do to help make this May Day Fair a success. And this is a positive move to introduce our girls and their children to the community.'

In the kitchen, Evie and Masie made a pile of assorted sandwiches for the men erecting the tents, and a big pot of tea and juice, though she guessed the men would have preferred beer. The mothers and children joined them with their picnic, sitting in the area where the children played safely.

The atmosphere was light-hearted and everyone chatted. Evie watched James toddle towards the men, and to Richard, holding out his arms to be lifted, which Richard did. Realising she was still holding her breath, she let it out. James was touching Richard's ears again, and over the top of the boy's head, Richard looked at Evie and smiled. She didn't know how it happened, but she was on her feet and then standing in front of them both, blurting out, 'Richard, will you be James's godfather?'

He gazed at her in astonishment, speechless at first. And then he spoke. 'Evie, it would honour me to be James's godfather.' His eyes locked with hers. All around them, the chatter seemed to recede, and it was as if the three of them were completely alone in their own little nest.

The voice of a man called out, 'Time we were off!'

Panic in her voice, Evie asked Richard, 'Where are you staying?'

'At the inn, far end of town. I'm here until the fair is over.' He held James aloft in the air, making him shout out with glee for more.

After the men had gone, Mrs Dawson and members of the ladies' committee arrived to inspect the tents, and Evie accompanied them. Mrs Dawson, efficient with her clipboard, a relic of her war years, announced, 'This is the tent for people to show their produce.' She pointed to the trestle tables. 'Vegetables on this side and cakes on the other side. Come, ladies.' And she marched off to the next tent. Here, they had laid a small dance floor, and a platform for the band. There were folding wooden tables, with chairs arranged around, and a corner set up for refreshments with only one table.

Evie voiced her thoughts. 'You will require two tables for all the refreshments we are supplying.'

'Very well,' Mrs Dawson said, adding a note to her list. In the next tent, they only looked in briefly. 'Um. Men's beer tent.'

Evie offered the ladies a cup of tea. 'Sorry, no cakes, they are all for the fair.'

They sat in the sitting room, and Evie was relieved to see the glass she had used earlier was gone. She opened a sash window to let in the fresh air and take away any traces of tobacco.

Masie came in with a list of all the cakes, buns, savouries and sandwiches they were providing. And as Mrs Dawson perused the list, Evie heard two of the ladies talking in loud whispers.

'I wonder what Florence Sinclair would have made of all these unmarried mothers in her house.'

'She would turn in her grave,' said the other one.

Evie bit back an angry retort. There would always be someone who would disapprove. And her focus wasn't on them, but on the young women and their children making better lives for themselves. So far, except for Doreen, the women had all shown the desire for a better future. She looked across at the photograph of her father on the wall. And she could have sworn he winked at her.

'What do you think, Miss Sinclair?'

Evie mentally shook herself and gave her attention to the matter in hand.

After the ladies had departed, Evie followed the delicious smell to the kitchen, where everyone who wasn't working or looking after the children was busy baking and preparing. Her heart felt full of joy when she gazed round at their cheerful faces.

Later, when the children were all in bed, and everyone was doing their own thing, Evie slipped outside and lit a cigarette from the packet Masie had produced earlier. She sat on the bench, looking across the lake, watching as the daylight faded and the ethereal in-between time cast its shadows to let the night slip in. An enchanted time, she recalled from her childhood. The moon glinted on the ripples on the lake and, if she half closed her eyes, she saw fairies dancing there.

Was she fantasising about Richard? She knew deep down she felt a stirring for him, but was it because she wanted a father for her son? Or a husband for herself? She couldn't differentiate between the two.

Then a jolt shook her. He could be married!

The next day, she debated long and hard with herself. What reason could she give for going to see Richard? None.

Suddenly, Masie's voice broke into her reverie. 'Are you coming or going?'

Evie looked up to see her hand resting on the pantry doorknob. What was she going for? Her mind whirled.

'Time for a cuppa,' Masie declared. 'Sit down, Evie.'

The tea poured, the two friends sat across the table from each other. 'Now, Evie, tell me what is bothering you?' Masie asked, though she could guess the answer.

And then it all came spilling out. 'Richard told me where he is staying, and I thought of going to see him, but . . .' She paused and took a drink of her tea. 'What if he's married?'

'The only way you will find out is to see him and ask.'

'You make it sound so simple.'

'It is. And it will save you hours of agony. I'll look after James while you go and see Richard.'

'But what if . . . ?'

Masie jumped to her feet, scraping back her chair. 'For heaven's sake, just go.'

Evie changed into a white cotton summer dress, patterned with yellow daisies, and set off to see Richard. She thought longingly of her old boat. Rowing across the lake would have eased the tension within her. Then she reprimanded herself for feeling like a schoolgirl with her first crush.

The inn Richard was staying at came into sight at the far end of the town, a quiet area away from the centre, and on the road to Hull. She must have passed it many times when she had rowed across the lake, but had taken no notice of it. In the days of coach and horses, this inn provided rest for the weary travellers and their horses. During the war, her father had sometimes held his meetings here, and it was a regular hive of activity. Now, as she glanced at The Old Sun Inn, nothing or nobody stirred. She inhaled, then slowly let out her breath, pushing the door open. After the brightness outside, it took her a few moments to adjust to the gloom. There were a few men drinking at the bar, but she couldn't see Richard.

'Can I help you, miss?' the barman asked her.

She edged forward and said, 'I'm looking for Richard Marsden.'

'Oh, aye, and what would your business be?'

Evie stepped backward and was about to respond when a voice said, 'That's all right, Joe.' And Richard stepped into view. He smiled at Evie and said, 'We will sit outside.' She waited until he collected two glasses of shandy.

Outside in the evening light, they sat side by side on a bench with a barrel for a table. He lit two cigarettes and gave one to Evie and their eyes met. Her heartbeat quickened, for in his pearl-grey eyes she saw a longing. But she had to know if he was married or had a sweetheart. No sooner had she had the thought, than the words came tumbling out. 'Are you married or have a sweetheart, Richard?' She inhaled on the cigarette and then blew out a plume of smoke.

Gently, he took hold of her hand and she felt the electricity flow between them. He leaned his face closer to hers and spoke, his warm breath fanning across her face. 'No, Evie, I don't have a wife or a sweetheart. Does that set your mind at ease?'

She nodded, at a loss for words, for she hadn't thought this through. What would the next step be?

Then Richard continued speaking. 'I've always felt guilty of the night we spent together after Matt died. Though when Gloria told me you had a son, I wondered, I hoped, he could be mine. But when I saw him for the first time, with Matt's deep brown eyes, I knew he wasn't.' She squeezed his hand gently, knowing the emotions he was experiencing. Then he surprised her with his next words. 'From the first time I set eyes on you, Evie, I felt an attraction towards you, but you were Matt's girl.'

'Is it a coincidence that you came here to Island House, or did you know where I lived?'

He gave a sheepish grin. 'I heard you were living in Hull and tracked you down to a pawnshop, and this old guy gave me your address.'

'Bencher. He is a great man. He gave me a home and a job so I could keep James. Otherwise, the authorities at the home would have had him adopted.'

'Good heavens, Evie. I didn't know that anyone could force you to have your baby adopted. That is so cruel, bloody hell! You fought in the war to keep people safe, and that is how they repay you?' His eyes flashed with anger.

Evie shrugged and shuddered at the thought. 'That is the reason why I have turned Island House into a home for mothers who want to keep their babies.'

Richard lit another cigarette, offering Evie one. She shook her head. 'Can we walk?'

They both rose, and headed away from the centre of town along an overgrown path. The air smelled fresh and tangy; the breeze blowing off the sea ruffled her hair. Gulls up above wheeled and dived, giving a sense of pure freedom. As they walked, she felt the tension leave her body. And then Richard slipped his hand in hers. A natural connection. She turned and smiled at him.

CHAPTER FORTY

April–May 1947

After their walk along the cliffs, her head was full of everything she and Richard had talked about. Evie returned to Island House and Masie greeted her after putting James to bed. Mabel, Betsy and Camilla were in the kitchen, busy baking. 'You look happier. Come along to the sitting room where it's quiet. I'll fetch a tea tray.'

Evie sat on a chair and closed her eyes. It wasn't that she was tired. She wanted to relive the walk with Richard and what they had spoken about. She knew Matt would always be her first love, and the daddy of James, but she and her son needed Richard in their lives. This thought surprised her. Had she hidden it away? Hopeful, but never sure. Until now.

Masie came bustling in with the tea tray and, when settled, she asked, 'Can you tell me?'

'Tell you what?' Evie answered, a smile playing on her lips, her eyes twinkling mischievously. Then she relented, putting Masie out of her misery. Setting her cup on the saucer, Evie continued. 'We cleared the air after we talked about our feelings for each other. I love him, Masie, and he loves me. Matt will always be my first love, and James's father.

Nothing can ever change that. When he's older, Richard and I will explain to him why he has two daddies.'

'Oh, love. I am so happy for you both,' Masie said, fumbling for her handkerchief in her apron pocket. She dabbed her eyes and, eager for more news, asked, 'When will you marry?'

'Not sure when. We have much to sort out. Richard has his own construction business and will be based in Hull. He's renovating and rebuilding war-damaged houses, so he will be busy. After the fair is over, I want to arrange James's christening. Richard will be one godfather, and I will ask Bencher to be a godfather too.'

'And who is the godmother?' asked Masie, rising to her feet.

Evie smiled and answered, 'It's a lovely friend of mine.'

'One of them you were in the war with?'

She thought of her wartime friends, who had both moved on to pastures new, Lily in America and Gloria involved with her singing career. She turned to Masie, saying, 'You, my dear friend, and it will delight me if you accept.'

Masie's answer was to fling her arms around Evie and give her a loving hug.

Richard stopped by every day, sometimes to talk with Evie or, if she was busy, he would take James for a walk or watch him play with the other children. Once he stayed for James's bath time. Listening to the shouts of glee, Evie smiled as she stood in the doorway, watching Richard with James, her heart overflowing with joy. Then James saw his mammy, his eyes wide with happiness. He flashed his gorgeous brown eyes at her. Matt's eyes. She should have known. Perhaps she had.

* * *

A beautiful blue sky shone on the early morning of the May Day Fair. Evie stood at the bedroom window, holding James. He stretched out his little chubby arms to catch the tiny puffs of cotton-wool clouds. She quickly dressed in her old skirt and blouse, planning to change into a dress later for the fair. James wriggled as she dressed him in a blue and white romper suit, made by Camilla, who was proving a dab-hand at dress-making. She hadn't mentioned the father of Josephine for some time. Evie encouraged her to maintain contact with her parents, even though it was only the odd letter, as far as she knew.

She entered the kitchen with James in her arms, and he with Patchy tight in his. Camilla was already there, stirring a big pan of fragrant porridge, while Josephine sat in a highchair, banging a spoon on the tray. The back door opened and a happy Mabel entered. Soon, everyone filled the kitchen, the children quiet as they ate, and the grown-ups chattering, excitement filling their voices as they discussed today's main event. A baby show, for the bonniest baby.

Evie sat back in her chair, absorbing the scene. Never in her wildest dreams could she have imagined feeling such happiness for these young women and their children. They had time to think about what they wanted from life at Island House. Evie choked back a sob of emotion. While there was a need, she would continue helping mothers and babies to seek a better future for themselves.

'Shall we make a start?' Masie's voice cut into Evie's thoughts.

'Yes, I'll check on the tables,' she said, picking up a pile of oilcloths.

Outside, a hazy morning mist drifted away across the lake, and a pair of swans gracefully landed. These were the first ones she'd seen since before the war. She longed to take a leisurely stroll round the lake, to breathe in its freshness, but instead she turned towards the tents.

She stood and adjusted her eyes to the inside of the refreshment tent. She was pleased to see the two tables for the food. She spread a large oilcloth over each one, which also covered the front, so that they could stack extra crockery beneath one table, along with a bucket of fresh water for cleaning. Beneath the other table would be supplies of fresh food. Sandwiches covered by clean, damp tea towels, buns and cakes in tins, and bottles full of juice to dilute with fresh water. She must remember to bring the jugs. The only thing she wasn't happy with was the tea urn. It would have to be brought hot from the kitchen. She spread cloths on the small wooden tables, checking there were four chairs to each table, though people could move them around if needed. She looked towards the raised platform where the band would play, and guessed they would be here soon to assemble their equipment.

As she turned back, a shadowy figure appeared in the doorway, and thinking it must be Mrs Dawson, Evie moved forward, then stopped, surprised. 'Richard!' She'd known he was coming, but hadn't expected him so early.

'Evie.' His action was swift, and he held her in an embrace, his lips seeking hers.

She smelled the morning dew on his clothes, felt his trembling body pressed close to hers. His kiss was gentle at first, then breathtaking, with pent-up emotions swimming to the surface.

'Oh, God, Evie, I want you so much,' he whispered. 'I think of you every moment.' He leaned away from her, looking deep into her eyes, her soul. 'Is that wrong of me?'

Her thoughts of the last few days, and the hours they had spent together, never alone, ran through her mind. She noticed the longing in his eyes. She knew she felt the same. 'No, it's not wrong, but . . .' How could she word it? She held his hands to steady herself, as if she were freefalling. Taking a deep breath, she said, 'I don't want to be an unmarried mother again.'

He stepped back, stunned, and gasped. 'Evie, I would never let that happen.'

'How?'

He looked her full in the face, his lovely silver-grey eyes so tender, and said, 'Evie Sinclair, will you marry me?'

She stared wide-eyed at him, not quite believing what she had heard. Did he really mean it? Then he put a finger under her chin, his eyes on her lips, waiting for her reply. Her voice a whisper, she said, 'Yes, I will marry you, Richard Marsden.'

'Whoopee!' He lifted Evie up and swung her round until they both collapsed into each other's arms. Their lips met with a long, passionate kiss. Their bodies hugged, shaping as one as the buzz of electricity, a current of love, sparked between them.

'Good morning. Can I interrupt?' The authoritarian voice of Mrs Dawson echoed in the tent.

Richard spoke. 'Miss Sinclair has just done me the honour of accepting my proposal of marriage. You are the first to know.'

'Oh!' Surprise oozing from her, and her composure regained, she offered, 'Congratulations!'

Needing to escape before Mrs Dawson could ask questions, Evie said, 'I must return to the kitchen.' Holding hands, she and Richard emerged from the shadow of the tent into the glorious sunlight.

CHAPTER FORTY-ONE

May–June 1947

Evie returned to the kitchen and her day became so busy that she didn't have time to tell anyone of her engagement to Richard.

Masie's brother, his wife and children came for the day. They were astonished that she looked so happy. Masie confided in Evie as they snatched a few moments together. 'They thought I was making a terrible mistake leaving a secure job at the home to live and work here. Best move I ever made.'

'And I couldn't manage without you.'

Evie and Masie manned the refreshment tent, which left the younger mothers and their children free to enjoy the fair. Betsy had taken James along with her and Emily to enjoy all the fun. The refreshments were in danger of running out because it was such a great success. When Evie ran to the kitchen, she saw that Mabel had made a fresh batch of scones. 'Don't you overdo it,' said Evie to a hot-looking Mabel.

'I'm loving it. The women on the committee want to have my recipe for scones. Would you believe?'

Evie smiled at the older woman, saying, 'Yes, indeed.' Collecting the tray of scones, she balanced it carefully, for it was heavy.

A voice behind her said, 'I'll take that.' Strong hands relieved her of the tray.

'Richard!' she exclaimed. 'I thought you were manning the dart-board stall?'

'I'm having a break and thought you might too.'

Inside the tent, the band was now playing. People were coming in to listen to the medley of popular songs. Evie recognised 'Sentimental Journey'. 'Mammy, mammy,' James called, on seeing his mother. He ran to her, and she caught him up in her arms, and he snuggled his face into her shoulder.

She kissed the top of his head and whispered to him, 'My sweet darling boy.' And then he wriggled. Looking up, he spied Richard.

Betsy and Camilla were there with their children, too. 'Guess what,' Betsy said. 'Camilla's little Josephine has won the bonny baby competition.'

'How wonderful,' Evie enthused, glancing at the pram where Josephine lay sound asleep.

'Me and Camilla will look after the refreshments. You and Masie take a break,' offered Betsy.

James held out his little arms to Richard, who took him and hoisted him on to his shoulders, and the three of them set off. Masie went in search of her brother and his family.

They strolled around the fair. Surprise filled Evie at how many local people acknowledged them. Some stopped to admire James, and said, 'What a splendid home and grounds you have. A topping place to hold the fair.' She felt overwhelmed with jubilation. And Mrs Dawson, so impressed by the congratulations she had received, asked Evie, 'Would you consider allowing the fair to take place next year in the grounds of Island House?'

Later, the children were all in bed and sleeping soundly while the young mothers were in the sitting room. Evie heard the music from the wireless and their excited chatter as they talked about the day. Masie, taking a well-earned break, had gone home with her brother. Mabel, tired but happy, was at her daughter's home. Evie went outside to catch a breath of evening air, and marvelled that only a few hours ago the grounds had buzzed with people. She sat down on the bench, watching the swans cross sedately to the far side of the lake. She wished she had a cigarette to relax with. Instead, she closed her eyes.

On the gentle breeze, she thought she could smell tobacco smoke. A fanciful thought, she mused. There was the sound of a twig snapping and she sat up with a jerk. Opening her eyes, she saw the glow of a cigarette near the shadow of a bush. 'Hello,' she called.

Then, from the shadow, he stepped forward. 'Richard! I wasn't expecting you.'

'Evie.' He stamped on the cigarette butt and opened his arms.

She felt the racing rhythm of his heartbeat matching hers as she slipped into his embrace. He smelled fresh and masculine, his face smooth as she traced her fingers over its contours until she touched his lips. Inviting lips, so tender as she kissed him. Holding hands, they strolled down to the edge of the lake and sat on the old fallen tree stump. He put an arm around her and she leaned her head on his shoulder. They sat in contented silence for a few minutes until Richard spoke.

Talking hold of her hand, he pressed it to his heart, saying, 'Evie, how soon can we be married?'

Now, she wanted to say, but that wasn't practical. She gazed into his pearl-grey eyes and saw his longing mirror her own.

'As soon as we can arrange it.'

They clung to each other, their lips sealing the promise.

Still holding hands, they stood up, and she looked across the lake, seeing the gentle ripples as moorhens swam in the reeds. Her heartbeat steadied, for she was no longer afraid of what the future held. There was just one more thing she had to do. And she hoped Richard would.

* * *

The reading of their wedding banns took place at the nearby village church, because the church in the town was undergoing foundation repairs. Evie felt blessed because she wanted a small wedding.

Island House filled with excitement when the mothers and their children heard about the wedding. 'And you are all invited, children as well,' Evie told the startled young women.

'Do you mean we can go as guests to your wedding?' Betsy blurted.

Evie laughed and replied, 'I want you all at my wedding.'

'I've never been to a wedding before,' Camilla said wistfully, her eyes brimming with tears.

Evie gave her a hug and knew that she still dreamed of marrying Josephine's father.

Then the young women began discussing what to wear and trooped off to inspect the contents of their wardrobe.

Evie sat in the kitchen with James on her knee, having a cuddle, clutching Patchy. She gently ran her fingers through his hair, thinking he would need a haircut.

'The wedding breakfast?' asked Mabel. 'My daughter and I will cater for it, if you agree?'

'Yes, thank you, Mabel.' She put James down on the rug to hug her.

Later, when Masie arrived back from visiting her family and the house was quiet, she and Evie were in the sitting room when Evie said, 'I've a favour to ask you, Masie.'

Masie turned from the fire where she had placed a log. It crackled and sparked as it caught alight. She looked enquiringly at her friend, and offered, 'Oh, aye?'

'Would you do me the honour of being my Matron of Honour?'

The clock ticked, the log crackled more.

'Evie, yes, I will.'

Evie jumped to her feet and retrieved the bottle of sherry, which she'd won at the fair, from the sideboard.

Now all the arrangements were made, the house seemed to enjoy the excitement building within its walls. 'The last wedding here was my parents' and before that, my grand-parents',' Evie told Richard a few days later, as they strolled hand-in-hand around the lake. They saw each other most nights, and had been to the cinema a few times, though she could never remember much about the films afterwards.

'What about your brother?' She knew his parents were dead, and his other brother, a soldier, had not survived the war. Unless she prompted him, he never talked about his family.

He stopped walking and kicked a stone into the lake, its splash filling the silence. He looked at her. 'I've asked my brother Ken to be my best man.'

That night, in bed, she thought of the special visit they needed to take after their wedding. Her heart raced at the thought and filled her with troubling feelings.

Evie and Richard's wedding took place on a glorious day in June. Led by Betsy, the young mothers placed posies of fragrant flowers at each end of the pews. Evie carried a bouquet of pink roses. She stood on the threshold of the church, her arm tucked safely in Bencher's. He smiled with pride, looking years younger in his dark suit and white shirt with a silk tie. As she walked down the aisle to Mendelssohn's 'Wedding March', her dress of white gossamer lace floated around her. She heard a child say, 'She's a fairy princess.'

Then she arrived at Richard's side. So handsome in his suit of silver grey, almost matching his eyes, and she felt the strength of his hand in hers. She passed her bouquet to Masie, who looked elegant in her long blue dress.

'Dearly beloved, we gather here today . . .'

Afterwards, Evie tried to recall the service, but couldn't. But she remembered her dear friend, Gloria, singing the beautiful love song 'Love Letters'.

The children, who had been so well behaved, now called out in joyful voices as they ran down the aisle after the bridal party. James flung himself into Evie's open arms and she hugged him. Then he wriggled, wanting to play with the other children.

Richard engaged a photographer to take pictures of everyone, and an extra set for the mothers and children. The mothers would come to mount these pictures on a blackboard and easel, where they would spend hours looking at them, the children pointing themselves out with glee, as if it were magic.

Later, at the reception at Island House, Evie spoke to Gloria. Hugging her friend, she said, 'I am so delighted you came.'

'I wasn't sure I could make it. You look lovely, Evie, glowing with happiness.'

'Thank you for singing such a beautiful song. I wish Lily could have been here,' Evie said wistfully. 'I hope she is happy living so far away.'

'I miss her, too. One of the best days of my life when I met you and Lily on the train, on our way to join the ATS.'

Someone handed them both a glass of wine. 'Cheers to that,' they said, and both raised their glasses.

'At the first opportunity, Richard and I will travel to London to see you.'

Smiling, Gloria replied, 'I'll look forward to that.' She lit a cigarette and Evie noticed the trembling of her hands.

Gloria boarded her train and returned to London, so there wasn't time to talk anymore.

After bath time, the children went to bed, tired out, to sleep sweet dreams. The grown-ups in the sitting room were having a party. Bencher played a penny-whistle, and they all sang, though not always in tune, which caused much hilarity. Then, with the rug rolled back, they danced to the American boogie. Evie didn't know where everyone got their energy from.

'I need a rest,' Bencher stated. Richard gave him a tot of whisky, and Bencher sat down and lit his pipe.

Someone tuned in the wireless, and a band was playing. Evie sat down next to Richard and watched the young mothers twirling around and dancing steps with such vigour. They looked so happy and relaxed that it gladdened her heart. Ken partnered Masie and both seemed to enjoy each other's company.

'Time we were going,' Mabel said, as her daughter collected their coats. 'Thank you, Evie. It has been a very special day.'

Evie threw her arms about Mabel, hugging her. She felt tears prick her eyes.

Masie made the sleeping arrangements. She moved James into her bedroom, so the bridal couple could have privacy, and she made the downstairs study into a bedroom for Bencher. Evie wanted her dear friend to stay over.

Then, at last, Evie and Richard were alone in their bedroom. With their clothes discarded, she felt shy for a few moments, and then Richard took her in his arms and kissed her. Her body swayed slightly, then she relaxed and her nerves vanished. The touch of his powerful arms as he gathered her up and laid her gently on the bed sent currents of electricity through her body. She looked up into his adoring eyes and held out her arms to him, welcoming the desire of his body heat on hers as their limbs entwined together.

CHAPTER FORTY-TWO

Late Summer 1947

Evie posted the letter and a week later she received a reply. She held the envelope in her hands, her heart racing, wondering what the response would be. She popped it into her apron pocket to read later when she was on her own.

She and Maisie were busy turning out and cleaning the room occupied by Joan Harper and her son Malcolm. They had moved up to Bridlington, where she was helping her aunt to run a guest house and safeguarding her future, securing work and a home for her and her son. Joan had saved ten pounds in her bank book and Evie added another ten pounds.

'I feel a sense of pride at our achievement,' Evie said to Masie, as they stripped the sheets and blankets off the bed, ready for washing.

Masie paused, as she reflected, 'This is what you set out to accomplish.'

'Yes, but . . .' Evie opened the sash window, taking deep breaths of the fresh morning air.

'But what?' asked Masie.

Evie came to sit on the edge of the bed, speaking the thoughts she'd harboured away. 'It seemed madness at first, and doubts flooded my mind about Island House being the best place to bring these unmarried mothers and their babies, given the prejudices people held against them. We've had a few scary situations, but the girls, on the whole, are decent and want a better future. And my finances depended on my dear father's investments which, with the help of the solicitor, I have kept afloat.' She paused, looking down at her hands folded on her lap. Then she added, glancing at her friend, 'What do you think, truly?'

'Oh, Evie!' Masie cried, coming to sit next to her. 'I have every confidence in what you set out to do. Otherwise, I would never have worked for you. You underestimate yourself.' She hugged her friend. 'Come on. The washing needs to be done.'

That evening, Betsy and Camilla had gone to the cinema. The children were all in bed and the other mothers were in the old dining room, now their sitting room, listening to music on the wireless. Masie enjoyed listening to a play on her own wireless in her bedroom-cum-sitting room. Evie and Richard had the privacy of the sitting room. Everyone shared a midday meal together in the kitchen.

Richard's work took him into Hull, mainly dealing with the rebuilding and repairing of houses damaged during the war, and the erection of prefabs. These temporary homes were used to ease the housing shortage. He came home, had a wash and changed his clothes, while Evie bathed James, and then Richard read him a story. Evie prepared their evening meal, though sometimes Mabel left a casserole in the side warming oven. Tonight, Evie had bought fresh fish, which she'd been lucky to purchase as she was at the fishmonger's when it was delivered. Haddock, chipped potatoes and peas fresh from the garden. The table was set and the plates warming. She made a pot of tea when Richard entered the kitchen.

He came over and kissed her tenderly on the lips. 'Hello, Mrs Marsden,' he whispered. He held her close, and she never tired of the feel of his body next to hers, breathing in the smell of his freshness. Then he stepped away, saying, 'I'm starving.' He sniffed the air. 'It smells good.'

She laughed. 'You are always hungry.' She loved the banter between them, which came so naturally.

After the meal, they washed and dried the dishes, leaving the kitchen tidy and retired to their sitting room. Evie had lit the fire earlier, so the room looked cosy as the firelight sent a glow around the room. Now the sun set earlier and the daylight faded, she had taken to using an oil lamp on an evening, adding to the ambience. They sat together on the two-seater sofa, a wedding gift from Bencher. Not new, but in a good condition, and Evie wondered who had sat on it before, whether they had been as happy as she and her husband were. Husband. She had never thought it possible after Matt's death.

She slipped her hand into her dirndl skirt pocket and withdrew the unopened letter. 'This came today.' She held it up for Richard to see.

'You've not read it?'

'No.' Her hands shook as she held it.

Gently, he took it from her and opened the envelope, withdrawing the single sheet of paper. 'We will read it together.' She moved closer to him, feeling his strength. When they had read it, he said, 'We will go this weekend.' She nodded in response, her eyes filling with tears.

For the rest of the week, Evie immersed herself in her work, knowing this journey they were about to take was important. She told Mabel and Masie, and the girls, 'We are going on a belated honeymoon.'

'You can leave James with us,' said Masie. 'He will be safe.'

'Thank you, but no. James is coming with us.'

As she left the kitchen, she heard Mabel say, 'There's something up with yon, lass.'

Evie dashed outside to where James and the other children were playing, whipped him up into her arms and held him tight, only setting him down when he squealed.

* * *

They set off early on Friday morning, taking a bus into Hull and then boarding a train to their destination. An excited James bounced on Evie's knee as they sat in a compartment. She pointed to the cows in the field as the train sped on. Then he clambered over to sit on Richard's lap and promptly fell asleep.

Richard felt for Evie's hand and gently squeezed it. 'When we arrive, we will go straight to the hotel I've booked and freshen up.' She laid her head on his shoulder, wanting to connect to him. This darling man who'd come into her life, and into James's life. She wasn't sure she could go through it without his support.

They arrived in the village of Grassington, and James squealed in delight. A shepherd with his dog was driving a flock of sheep through the cobblestone square. Richard held James's hand tight, while Evie sat on a wooden seat, watching with amusement. This was the first time that James had come face to face with the animals; in the past, only seeing them from a distance. She wondered if he would want to work on a farm when he grew up.

Their small hotel was on the other side of the square, and after a freshen up, they went for a stroll down by the River Wharfe, both holding James's hands as he swung between them as they walked. Over the bridge, they scrambled down the bank to look for fish. They walked on, stopping to talk to a man ambling along with his dog. Evie thought about how idyllic the countryside was here, lush with plenty of overhanging trees, and becoming more rugged as they walked further on. It was quite different from home. Home. Her haven of safety. She wished she was there now.

Richard took hold of her hand and said, 'Are you all right?'

She gave a weak smile and said, 'To be honest, I am dreading it.' She looked to where James was chasing a butterfly up the bank, then sat down on a boulder.

Richard sat beside her and slipped his arm around her shoulder, drawing her close to him.

Quietly, he said, 'Once it is told and out in the open, you will feel much better. This is something they never dreamed of.'

'Yes, but won't they wonder why I didn't tell them before?' She looked pleadingly into his eyes.

'Oh, Evie, my darling.' He gathered her into his arms and kissed her gently on the lips. 'Think about it. Where were you when James was born?'

'In the home,' she whispered.

'And afterwards?'

'I worked for Bencher and lived in. Then father died and then mother became ill and died, and . . .' Tears welled up in her eyes.

'Time passes too quickly. The time is right now,' he soothed.

Just then, James cried out as he tumbled over. Richard went to scoop him up, and hoisted him on to his shoulders, the tumble forgotten.

Later, they enjoyed a meal of fresh trout and vegetables, and treacle sponge and custard. With James tucked up in bed and slumbering soundly, Evie and Richard sat in the tranquil hotel garden and enjoyed a quiet drink. She thought about what they had talked about earlier, and realised that until Richard came into her life and they married, she hadn't been a whole person. She could always sort out other people's problems, but never her own. She reached for Richard's hand, feeling his strength transfer into her body and her heart. How she loved this man so dearly.

The next morning, after breakfast, Evie and Richard, both holding James's hands, set off for the farm. The sky was a hazy blue with a few clouds drifting by, and it promised to be a lovely summer's day. On the way, they said good morning to a few locals, but they didn't stop to chat. James pulled away from them, spying a kitten hiding in a bush, and ran to look. Evie reached for Richard's hand. He smiled at her, warming her troubled heart.

'You will be fine,' he said, pulling her close to hug her.

She gave a deep sigh. 'Yes, I know. I have to do this for Matt.'

Richard hoisted James on to his shoulders again, and they continued on their way as the path sloped up to the farm.

Entering the farmyard, a dog barked and the kitchen door opened and Matt's mother stood there, framed in the doorway. Evie's heart lurched. Mrs Goodwin gave her a welcoming smile. Then she saw James, perched on Richard's shoulders, and her smile disappeared. She ushered them into the kitchen and promptly left them. Puzzled, they sat down, not speaking. James sat on her knee and snuggled close. Over the top of his head, she looked at Richard and he shrugged.

The clock on the dresser ticked and the minutes passed, but no one moved.

Then Mrs Goodwin returned carrying an album and placed it on the table. Opening it, she turned a few pages until she found what she was looking for. Without a word, she slid it across the table to Evie.

Evie looked at the photo of Matt when he was James's age, and she was looking at a mirror image of her son. James was the double of Matt, his father. The words whirled around in her head. Then she looked up at Mrs Goodwin and whispered, 'Yes, James is Matt's son.'

Mrs Goodwin sank on to a chair, buried her head in her hands and sobbed.

Evie could not stop her tears from flowing as well.

Quietly, Richard gathered a startled James up into his arms and left the kitchen. Outside, he breathed in the warm air. James wriggled as the chickens came into view. He set him down and watched attentively as the boy stretched out his arms to them and followed them round the farmyard.

Deep in thought and wondering what was going on inside, Richard didn't see the man approaching. 'How do. Yon lad seems a natural,' Mr Goodwin said.

Richard blurted, 'Yon lad is your grandson, James.'

'Aye, thought I saw a likeness.' He pushed back his cap and scratched at his grey hair.

Richard saw tears well in the older man's eyes. Both men stood watching James, who was unaware of the surrounding drama.

Inside the farmhouse, Evie told Mrs Goodwin how much she had loved Matt and how, when he died, she had been unaware of her pregnancy. Discharged from the ATS and having nowhere else to go, she went into a mother and baby home.

'What about your parents?'

Evie pondered, and said, 'My parents were ill. After James's birth, I lived in and worked for Bencher, who ran a pawnshop. His kindness helped me through a difficult time. When my parents died, they left the house for me. I now run a home for young unmarried mothers.'

'You could have come to us,' Mrs Goodwin said, reproachfully.

Evie shrugged, replying, 'I was juggling life, which was so full of uncertainty, and I didn't always think clearly.'

The older woman rose. 'I'll make a cup of tea.'

Evie glanced out of the window to where Richard and Mr Goodwin stood, both with serious faces. James was their grandson, that was all they needed to know. Not about the dilemma of James's parentage.

The men and James came into the kitchen for tea and scones, while James drank milk and ate biscuits, happily playing with a box of toys. From her bag, Evie withdrew the silver-framed photograph of James, taken at the wedding, and presented it to his grandparents. They spent the whole day at the farm. Evie watched James toddle off with his grandmother to feed the hens. And his grandad showed him the litter of newborn pups. Everyone made a fuss of James, but soon it was time for goodbyes.

Mrs Goodwin smiled through her tears as she whispered, 'My Matthew lives on in his son, James. I cannot thank you enough for bringing him to see us. Come as often as you can so we can see the little fellow grow up.'

'Aye, do that. We want to see him often,' said Mr Goodwin, putting a comforting arm around his wife.

James, looking bewildered, reached up into his mother's arms. Evie held him close, kissing his soft cheek. Her heart full, she whispered back, 'I promise. We will come often.'

She felt Richard's arm around her waist as he spoke. 'We will never forget Matt. He was my best friend and I promise to always look after his son for him.'

It was a sad farewell, but they knew they would return.

They arrived back at Island House. 'I'm glad to be home,' Evie murmured to Richard, who carried a tired James indoors. After Evie fed her son and Richard bathed him, he was soon fast asleep in his cot, with an old teddy bear of Matt's clutched in his hands. Masie watched over him.

Evie and Richard strolled hand-in-hand around the lake. She breathed in the balmy night air, feeling so happy. Reaching the far side of the lake, they stopped walking, and Richard drew her into his arms. She felt the rhythm of his heartbeat and she reached up to him. Richard, her husband, her mainstay, who she loved dearly, was by her side. His lips found hers, a kiss so tender and full of promise and hope for their future together.

THE END

ACKNOWLEDGEMENTS

The idea to write about the Ack-Ack gunner girls came quite by chance, when historian Dennis Chapman mentioned he would be conducting tours of a locally preserved Anti-Aircraft battery site and that women helped to man the guns. The tour proved fascinating, and Dennis was generous in recommending books and internet sites for my research. One book was *Sisters in Arms*, written by Vee Robinson, who served as an Ack-Ack gunner girl, which was interesting.

I am grateful to Joy Sharpe for sharing her personal story of her stay in a Mother and Baby home for unmarried mothers. Joy had a happy ending. She kept her baby and eventually married her sweetheart.

Many thanks to my agent, Kate Nash, and to Beth for their sterling support, and indeed to all the Kate Nash Agency team.

And last, but not least, my lovely readers, for your continuing support. Thank you.

THE JOFFE BOOKS STORY

We began in 2014 when Jasper agreed to publish his mum's much-rejected romance novel and it became a bestseller.

Since then we've grown into the largest independent publisher in the UK. We're extremely proud to publish some of the very best writers in the world, including Joy Ellis, Faith Martin, Caro Ramsay, Helen Forrester, Simon Brett and Robert Goddard. Everyone at Joffe Books loves reading and we never forget that it all begins with the magic of an author telling a story.

We are proud to publish talented first-time authors, as well as established writers whose books we love introducing to a new generation of readers.

We won Trade Publisher of the Year at the Independent Publishing Awards in 2023. We have been shortlisted for Independent Publisher of the Year at the British Book Awards for the last four years, and were shortlisted for the Diversity and Inclusivity Award at the 2022 Independent Publishing Awards. In 2023 we were shortlisted for Publisher of the Year at the RNA Industry Awards.

We built this company with your help, and we love to hear from you, so please email us about absolutely anything bookish at: feedback@joffebooks.com.

If you want to receive free books every Friday and hear about all our new releases, join our mailing list: www.joffebooks.com/contact

And when you tell your friends about us, just remember: it's pronounced Joffe as in coffee or toffee!

Milton Keynes UK
Ingram Content Group UK Ltd.
UKHW031033150224
437886UK00004B/115

9 781835 262627